THE BOSS WHO STOLE HER HEART

BY
JENNIFER TAYLOR

MILLS &
BOON

Published in Great Britain 2017
By Mills & Boon, an imprint of HarperCollins*Publishers*
1 London Bridge Street, London, SE1 9GF

© 2017 Jennifer Taylor

ISBN: 978-0-263-92643-9

Our policy is to use papers that are natural, renewable and recyclable
products and made from wood grown in sustainable forests. The logging
and manufacturing processes conform to the legal environmental
regulations of the country of origin.

Printed and bound in Spain
by CPI, Barcelona

Dear Reader,

When I had the idea for this book I didn't realise how much I was going to enjoy writing it—or that it would lead to a whole trilogy set in The Larches GP practice in the Yorkshire Dales!

As soon as Ellie and Daniel appeared on the page they had me hooked. Then, as I built the story around their budding romance, other characters started to clamour to have their stories told as well. It was a real snowball effect, and I hope you get as much pleasure from reading the series as I am having writing it.

Both Ellie and Daniel have a lot of baggage when they meet, and they certainly aren't looking for love. However, they soon discover that it isn't always possible to do the sensible thing. Whilst they both know it isn't the right time for them to have a relationship, they simply can't help themselves—even though they're sure it can't last.

Helping them realise that they can find a way around their problems was totally engaging. I agonised over the decisions they made, felt for them when they thought they had to part, and rejoiced when they realised they simply couldn't live without each other. Some characters are simply meant to be together. Like Ellie and Daniel!

Love,

Jennifer

For Leo and the team at Cancer Care, a huge thank you.
You really are the best!

Books by Jennifer Taylor

Mills & Boon Medical Romance

Saving His Little Miracle
One More Night with Her Desert Prince...
Best Friend to Perfect Bride
Miracle Under the Mistletoe
The Greek Doctor's Secret Son
Reawakened by the Surgeon's Touch

Visit the Author Profile page
at millsandboon.co.uk for more titles.

**Praise for
Jennifer Taylor**

'A superbly written tale of hope, redemption and
forgiveness, *The Son that Changed His Life* is a
first-class contemporary romance that plumbs deep into
the heart of the human spirit and touches the soul.'
—*CataRomance*

CHAPTER ONE

SHE COULD HAVE been beautiful with that fine clear skin and those huge grey eyes. However, the severely cropped black hair and strictly functional clothing did nothing to enhance her appearance. As he took stock of the woman seated in front of his desk, Daniel Saunders found himself wondering why Eleanor Munroe had failed to make the most of her considerable assets. Was she *deliberately* trying to disguise her femininity for some reason, playing down the fact that she was a highly attractive woman?

'Right then, Dr Munroe, we may as well get straight down to business.'

Daniel dismissed that strangely unsettling thought as he picked up her CV. He skimmed through it once more, although he already knew the facts by heart. Dr Eleanor Munroe was thirty-five years old, with a birthday coming up the following month. She had read medicine at Cambridge and graduated with a First Class Honours degree. After completing her rotations at St Linus's Hospital in London, she had opted to go into general practice and had trained at a busy practice in Kent and subsequently been hired by them too. She had supplied references from the head of the practice and had added a codicil to the bottom of her CV that gave Daniel permission to phone and speak to her referee directly.

Although it was unusual to do that so early in the proceedings, Daniel had taken up the offer and he had to admit that he'd been impressed by what he had heard. According to her former employer, Dr Munroe was above reproach and any practice who hired her would be extremely fortunate to secure her services. It appeared that Eleanor Munroe ticked all the boxes on paper, at least, but he still needed to be sure that they could work together.

'A most impressive CV, Dr Munroe,' he said, glancing up. 'Backed up by the conversation I had with your former colleague. He was highly complimentary and even mentioned that you were in the running for a senior partnership. It makes me wonder why you decided to leave your last post when you were so successful there.'

'I left for personal reasons, Dr Saunders.'

Her voice was cool, distant even, so Daniel had no idea why the hairs on the back of his neck sprang to attention. He glanced at her CV again, needing a moment to collect himself. He hadn't felt this aware of a woman in a very long time, not since Camille, his wife, had died, in fact. That it should happen now, and with seemingly so little reason, surprised him. He cleared his throat.

'I see. So what attracted you to the post here at The Larches? You do understand that it's only temporary? Beth—Dr Andrews, that is—is planning to return once her maternity leave is over. Barring any unforeseen changes to her plans, she will be back at work next September.'

'I understand that. It was perfectly clear from your advertisement.' Eleanor Munroe pinned him with a chilly stare. 'I wouldn't have wasted your time or mine by applying for the post if I wasn't happy with the terms.'

'Quite so.' Daniel summoned a smile although he couldn't help feeling uncomfortable at the frosty rebuke. She certainly wasn't a pushover, he decided, storing that titbit away for future reference.

'Right, now we've established that, let me tell you about the practice,' he continued briskly, needing to take control of the proceedings once more. He wasn't normally indecisive when it came to his work—he was always single-minded and focused. However, Dr Munroe seemed to possess the ability to unsettle him and he wanted to get back on track. 'The Larches, whilst being a rural practice, is extremely busy, mainly because we cover such a wide area of the Yorkshire Dales. As you will know from our advertisement, as well as the main surgery here in Beesdale we run a branch surgery at Hemsthwaite. Between the two sites we have roughly four and a half thousand patients on our books. So if you thought it would be easier working here than in your previous post then I'm afraid you were mistaken.'

'I didn't apply for the job because I thought it would be the easy option,' Eleanor Munroe said brusquely. 'On the contrary, I am looking forward to being kept busy should I decide to accept the position.'

Daniel could feel his eyebrows rise and struggled to control them but Dr Munroe's confidence was more than a little startling. There had been no trace of doubt in her voice that she would be hired, no hint at all that she saw this interview as anything more than a formality. Eleanor Munroe obviously knew her own worth. And what was more, she intended to make sure that everyone else was aware of it too!

* * *

Ellie could feel perspiration trickling down her back. That had come out completely wrong! She knew it wasn't a given that she would be hired for the job. Despite first-class references and glowing endorsements, there were other factors to consider, the main one being that Dr Saunders needed to be sure they could work together. That seemingly arrogant statement would hardly have endeared her to him, would it? If she could have taken back the words she would have done so, but there was nothing she could do now except brazen it out.

Ellie sat up straighter, curbing the urge to run her hand over her newly short hair. She had never worn her hair so short before but she had decided to make a lot of changes to her life and changing her appearance had been first on her agenda. Once she had sorted out her new hairstyle, she had bagged up all the pretty, feminine dresses, the jewel bright tops, the high-heeled shoes, and given them to a charity shop. Her wardrobe now consisted of serviceable tailored trousers and shirts—neat, tidy, professional. Now that she was concentrating on what *she* wanted, she didn't need any more frippery.

'Well, there's no doubt that anyone who works here will be kept extremely busy,' Daniel Saunders said evenly, although Ellie could tell that her comment had been added to the minus column on her score sheet.

She bit back a groan, not wanting him to guess how mortified she felt. She wanted this job—no, not wanted it, *needed* it. If she moved to Yorkshire it would be the first step towards rebuilding her life. Maybe the future wasn't going to turn out the way she had thought it would but she intended to have a good life and on her terms too. Even though she'd been betrayed in the worst possible way, she was going to use what had happened to her advantage. She had always been a rather cautious person, preferring to stick to what she knew, but not any more. No, she intended to travel and see something of the world while she furthered her career. Maybe what had happened had been a blow but she would get over it. She was determined about that!

Ellie was so lost in her thoughts that it was a moment before she realised Dr Saunders had asked her a question. 'I'm sorry,' she said, feeling the embarrassed colour run up her neck. She hated to be caught unawares. She thrived on order and preferred to be prepared at all times. However, there was something about the man seated opposite that unsettled her.

'I asked if moving up here would create any problems for you, Dr Munroe.' Daniel Saunders shrugged, drawing Ellie's unwilling attention to the width of his shoulders. He was casually dressed in navy chinos and a light blue shirt with the sleeves rolled up to his elbows and, despite herself, Ellie couldn't help noticing how the blue of his shirt brought out the midnight blue of his eyes and highlighted the steel-grey streaks at his temples before she forced her mind away from such nonsense.

'Problems?' she repeated uncertainly. 'In which way, Dr Saunders?'

'You may need to consider someone else's views. It's a long way from Kent to Yorkshire and a lot of people might not be happy about relocating so far away.'

'I don't need to consider anyone else, I assure you.' Ellie sat up straighter, annoyed that he should have asked her a question like that. Maybe she should have let it go but, after what had happened recently, it stung. She glared at him. 'So if you're trying to find out if I have a husband or a partner who might object then I consider it a blatant infringement of my rights. I think you will find that no prospective employer has the right to discriminate against a female employee on such grounds.'

'I'm sure that's correct, Dr Munroe. However, to set your mind at rest, it's a question I would ask any potential employee. Male *or* female.'

His tone was as hard as flint and Ellie realised with a sinking heart that she had completely blotted her copybook now. No way was he going to offer her the job after this. Pushing back her chair, she stood up, wanting to bring the interview to a conclusion before she did something unforgivable. She hadn't cried, not even when she had found her fiancé in bed with one of their colleagues that day. She had held onto her composure throughout it all, right through the apologies and the ever more elaborate excuses. She hadn't even lost it when Michael had tried to blame *her* for his behaviour yet, for some reason, at that moment she could have stood there and wept.

'I apologise. I should never have said that. It was completely out of order. Thank you for seeing me, Dr Saunders. I hope you find someone suitable to fill the post.' Ellie swung round and headed towards the door. She knew it was directly behind her but she couldn't seem to see where she was going. She blundered into a filing cabinet and winced when the metal dug painfully into her hip. What was wrong with her? Why couldn't she find her way out?

'Here. Come and sit down.'

A large and surprisingly comforting hand closed around her arm as she found herself being led back to the chair. Ellie dropped down onto the seat because she really didn't have a choice. Tears were streaming down her face now, blinding her to everything else; she could only sit there while Daniel Saunders went to the sink and filled a glass with cold water.

'Drink this.' He crouched down beside her, so close that she could smell the clean fragrance of shampoo that clung to his hair. Holding the glass to her lips, he urged her to take a sip. A few drops of water trickled down her chin but before she could find a tissue, he wiped them away with his fingertips. 'Better?'

Ellie nodded, not trusting herself to speak. At any other time she would have been mortified by her loss of control but, oddly, she felt nothing. Daniel Saunders straightened up and put the glass on the desk then regarded her with eyes that held only compassion. He obviously wasn't the type to pass judgement, she thought, and found the idea strangely comforting.

'I apologise if I upset you, Eleanor. It wasn't my intention.'

His deep voice rolled softly over her name, affording it a surprisingly pleasing inflection. She had never really liked her name, had always thought it was too formal and old-fashioned. However, it sounded different when he said it, softer, gentler, far more appealing. She bit her lip, aware that she was allowing herself to be sidetracked. What did it matter how he said her name? The only thing that mattered was that she had made a fool of herself.

Pushing back the chair, she stood up, wanting to get away as quickly as possible. Maybe she had been pinning her hopes on getting this job but there would be other jobs in other parts of the country or abroad. Maybe she had promised her parents that she would stay in the UK until she had thought things through properly, but if she moved overseas, to Australia or New Zealand for instance, there would be no risk of her having to see Michael ever again…

'Right, it's time I gave you the conducted tour. We were lucky enough to secure funding to improve the facilities here so you may be surprised by what we offer our patients.' Daniel Saunders stepped around her and opened the door. His eyebrows rose when Ellie failed to move. 'Whenever you're ready, Eleanor.'

'Oh! But I thought…' Ellie tailed off, unsure what was happening. Why on earth was he offering to show her around when there was no chance of her being offered the job?

'You thought that you'd blown it?' Daniel Saunders laughed softly. 'On the contrary, Eleanor, it seems to me that you're exactly the sort of person I want working here.'

'I am? But why? I mean, I made a complete and utter mess of my interview, didn't I? And if that wasn't enough, I compounded my mistakes by breaking down and crying.' She shook her head. 'If I were in your shoes, Dr Saunders, I wouldn't hire me for all the tea in China!'

'It's Daniel. If we're going to be working together then I can't see any point in us standing on ceremony.' His blue eyes were filled with certainty when they met hers and Ellie felt a surge of warmth flow through her and start to melt the ice that had enveloped her these past terrible months. It was all she could do to concentrate as he continued in the same quietly assured tone.

'As for hiring you, from where I'm standing you seem like the ideal choice. I don't want someone working here who can't relate to our patients, someone who fails to understand that the problems life throws at them can and do impact on their health. I also don't want someone who's afraid to show her feelings either. So will you take the job, Eleanor? Please?'

CHAPTER TWO

'BASICALLY, WHAT I'D like you to do, Beth, is help her settle in. Every practice has its own way of doing things and I think it would help if Eleanor was shown the ropes rather than simply being thrown in at the deep end.'

Daniel leant back in his chair, wondering if his partner had any idea how important it was to him that Eleanor wasn't put under any pressure. Even though he couldn't understand why he felt this way, he knew that he wanted to make the move to The Larches as stress-free as possible for her. Maybe she had appeared supremely confident at the start of her interview but it had soon become clear that it wasn't the case. There was a vulnerability about Eleanor Munroe that had aroused all his protective instincts.

'Of course.' Beth Andrews smiled at him. 'It will be a big change for her, working here. Just basics, like the fact that we're almost an hour's drive from the nearest hospital, will be a challenge for her. We're far more hands-on when it comes to our patients than a lot of practices.'

'Exactly.' Daniel breathed a little easier when Beth gave no sign that she considered his request strange. Maybe it wasn't either, he mused. After all, if Eleanor was unable to do the job she had been hired for then it would impact on him. The last thing he wanted was to have to put in more hours at the surgery when Nathan was in his final year at sixth form college.

When Camille had died four years ago, his son had gone completely off the rails. He had dropped out of school and fallen in with a bad crowd too. Daniel had been afraid that Nathan would never get his act together but, after a lot of heartache, he'd come through. However, if Nathan was to achieve the grades he needed for university, he had to stay focused, and to do that *he* needed to be there to support him. Little wonder that he had been so worried about his new locum, was it? The thought reassured him, helped to settle his mind. If he was honest he had felt more than a little concerned that Eleanor Munroe had occupied his thoughts so much lately. He had lost count of the times she had popped into his head and it was good to know why it had been happening.

'Thanks, Beth.' Daniel smiled as he pushed back his chair and stood up. 'I really appreciate it.'

'No problem.'

Beth grimaced as she levered herself up off the chair. She was eight months pregnant and Daniel guessed that she was finding it difficult to get around. He remembered how tired Camille had been when she had been expecting Nathan and she had stopped work well before this stage. However, as a soon-to-be single mother, Beth didn't have the luxury of leaving work early. She had opted instead to continue working and take the bulk of her maternity leave after her baby was born. Nevertheless, Daniel made a note to ask Marie, their head receptionist, to redirect as many of Beth's patients as possible to him. He didn't want Beth pushing herself too hard during her final week, neither did he want Eleanor being placed under too much pressure. It would be better if he took up the slack for now.

Once again Daniel found himself worrying how his new employee would fare. Oh, there was no doubt about her ability—her CV was proof of that. However, would she be able to deal with whatever had led her to leave her previous post? he found himself wondering as he made his way to Reception. Although he knew nothing about Eleanor on a personal level, instinct told him she had suffered some kind of major blow and recently too. Had she been let down in love, perhaps? Treated badly by some man?

Daniel was surprised by how angry the idea made him feel. Bearing in mind that he had met her only the once, and that it hadn't been the most auspicious of meetings either, it shouldn't have had this effect on him. Nonetheless, the thought of some guy hurting her made him feel extremely angry and it was completely out of character for him to react that way. His expression must have been unusually grim as he stopped at the reception desk because Marie looked at him in surprise.

'What's wrong?' she demanded. In her forties, with two grown-up sons, Marie had worked at The Larches ever since Daniel had taken over the practice and didn't believe in standing on ceremony. 'Has something upset you? Because I have to say that you could turn the milk sour with a face like that!'

'Sorry.' Daniel dredged up a smile. Admitting that he was upset at the thought of their new locum being unlucky in love would have caused no end of questions, most of which he couldn't have answered even if he'd wanted to. He swiftly changed the subject because he really and truly didn't want to start searching for explanations at that moment. 'I know it's short notice, but can you redirect as many of Beth's patients as possible to me? I don't want her tiring herself out by doing too much in her last week.'

'Of course. But what about the new doctor? What's her name again? I wrote it down somewhere…'

'Eleanor Munroe,' Daniel said promptly, and felt a little thrill course through him as her name rippled off his tongue. He glanced at the clock above the desk, needing a moment to collect himself. The last thing he wanted was Marie suspecting how he felt. 'She should be here any minute…'

'Good morning.'

Daniel swung round when he recognised Eleanor's voice. In a fast sweep his eyes ran over her from the severely styled hair to the sensible shoes on her narrow feet and he felt his nerves start to tingle. What was it about this woman that affected him so much? he wondered dizzily. As an eligible widower, he'd had his share of women pursuing him over the past four years. However, he had never taken them up on their invitations to lunch and dinner, or whatever else had been on offer. The fact was that he hadn't been interested in them.

Not once had he felt that spark, that flicker of desire ignite inside him, yet as he looked at Eleanor, he felt it now. And in a big way too. Why it was happening was a mystery but he couldn't lie to himself, couldn't pretend that he didn't feel it. He was attracted to her and it couldn't have come at a worst time either. If she had been let down, as he suspected, the last thing she needed was to embark on another relationship, especially with him. He didn't have time for a relationship. He needed to focus on Nathan: his son's future *had* to take priority over everything else.

Daniel took a deep breath, clamping down on the

surge of disappointment that rose inside him. There was no question about what he was going to do. He was going to ignore all these crazy feelings and be there for Nathan.

Ellie could feel her tension mounting as Daniel continued to stare at her without uttering a word. Was he having second thoughts? she wondered anxiously. Regretting whatever impulse had led him to offer her this job?

She bit her lip, unsure what she was going to do if that proved to be the case. She had given up the lease on the flat in Kent, sold all her furniture, and got rid of everything that reminded her of Michael. One of the main attractions about this job was the fact that it came with accommodation. There was a furnished flat above the surgery, which had seemed like a godsend. However, if she lost the job then it was going to be extremely difficult to start all over again. She had been living off her savings for the past months but they certainly wouldn't stretch to cover the costs of renting a flat and furnishing it. The prospect of not only having to find herself another job but somewhere to live as well was daunting to say the least.

Ellie breathed in deeply when she felt her eyes prickle with tears. Since her interview, she had found herself breaking down all too often. It was as though Daniel's kindness that day had opened the floodgates and all the hurt she had held at bay kept flooding out. However, there was no way that she intended to break down again in front of him. He might think she was playing the sympathy card and that was the last thing she wanted.

'Hi, Eleanor. Nice to meet you. I'm Marie, the head

receptionist and general factotum around here.' The middle-aged woman behind the desk leant over and offered Ellie her hand.

'Good to meet you too,' Ellie replied automatically, shaking hands. She glanced at Daniel, wishing he would say something. If he was having second thoughts, it would be better if he said so rather than standing there, looking at her…

'Sorry.' Daniel suddenly roused himself. He smiled apologetically as he offered her his hand. 'I was woolgathering. Welcome to The Larches, Eleanor. It's good to have you on board.'

Ellie felt relief wash over her as she reached for his hand. She had completely misread the situation, it appeared. Daniel wasn't thinking of rescinding his offer after all. His hand closed around hers and a frisson ran through her when she felt the strength of his fingers envelop hers. For some reason she couldn't explain, it felt right to have him hold her hand, right and wonderfully reassuring. Even though she knew nothing about him, she felt safe with him. Safe and cherished.

'It's good to be here,' she murmured, quickly withdrawing her hand. She dredged up a smile, needing to rid her head of such nonsense. Daniel Saunders was her employer, no more and no less than that. He wasn't going to have any impact on her life outside work.

'So where would you like to start? I imagine you'd like to see the flat first.' Daniel's voice held no trace of anything yet Ellie felt herself flush when he addressed her. It was so unlike her to react that way that she found herself stammering.

'I…ahem… Whatever suits you best, Dr Saunders.'

'It's Daniel,' he reminded her, his blue eyes holding hers fast for a moment before he turned away. 'Maybe we can leave the flat till later then. I've had a word with Beth and she's going to show you the ropes so you can get an idea of how we do things around here.'

'I'm sure that won't be necessary,' Ellie said swiftly, wanting to put an end to the pleasantries. The sooner she got down to work, the more comfortable she would feel. It was the newness of it all that was unsettling her, of course, not Daniel per se. It was a relief to have found an explanation and she hurried on. 'I've been a GP for some time now and I'm completely up to speed when it comes to all the paperwork and everything else that comes with the job.'

'I'm sure you are. However, every practice has its own way of doing things and The Larches is no different, so I'd appreciate it if you would indulge me on this point.' He smiled thinly, making Ellie wish that she hadn't said anything. The last thing she wanted was him thinking that she was someone who made a fuss.

'Of course. I… I just didn't want to waste Dr Andrews's time,' she explained lamely. 'I'm sure she must be very busy.'

'She is.' Daniel placed his hand under her elbow as he led her away from the desk.

Ellie drew in a quick breath, trying to stem the nervous fluttering of her heart, but it refused to quieten down. It was as though Daniel's touch had set off a chain reaction, ripples of awareness flowing from where his fingers lightly gripped her arm and spreading throughout her entire body. It was hard not to show how alarmed she felt when he stopped and looked at her.

'However, between you and me, Eleanor, I'm trying to cut down the amount of work Beth is doing. She's eight months pregnant and this is her last week in work before she goes on maternity leave, so I don't want her overdoing things and making herself ill. If she's show-ing you the ropes, at least I know that she isn't rushing around all over the place.'

'Oh, right. I see.' Beth carefully withdrew her arm, stifling a wholly ridiculous feeling of disappointment. Of course Daniel was more concerned about his long-time colleague than he was about her!

'I knew you'd understand.' Daniel treated her to a strangely intimate smile before he led the way along the corridor. He stopped at one of the doors, tapping lightly on the beechwood panels before opening it. 'Beth, I've got Eleanor with me. If you can show her how we do things, as we discussed, that would be great.' He ges-tured for Ellie to step forward, winking at her as she passed him. Ellie felt a rush of warmth engulf her. It was as though they were two conspirators sharing a se-cret and she had to admit that she rather liked the idea. She was smiling when she stepped into the room and the pretty, fair-haired woman seated behind the desk smiled back.

'Hi, Eleanor. It's good to meet you. Come on in and make yourself comfortable.' She chuckled, her hazel eyes filled with mischief as she glanced at Daniel. 'This is going to be your room next week, so it will give you a chance to try it out for size. Anything you don't like tell the boss. I'm sure he'll do *everything* possible to sort it out!'

'Don't go putting ideas into Eleanor's head,' Daniel retorted. 'She'll be giving me a list of things she wants before I know it.' He rolled his eyes. 'Like that singer who demanded a basket of kittens to play with in her dressing room before she would go on stage and per-form!'

'Oh, you don't need to worry about finding me any

kittens,' Ellie said, completely deadpan. She waited a beat then grinned at him. 'I much prefer puppies!'

Everyone laughed, Eleanor included, and it was such a shock that she found it hard to believe what was happening. She couldn't remember the last time she had laughed, couldn't recall when she had felt so light-hearted. Ever since that dreadful day when she had found Michael and Stacey together, her world had been filled with darkness, but all of a sudden it felt as though the gloom had lifted and it was all thanks to Daniel. Even if they were destined to be no more than colleagues, Ellie knew that she would be grateful to him for ever for that.

The morning flew past. Ellie was surprised by how differently things were done at The Larches. Although there were all the usual forms to fill in, the surgery offered a range of services to its patients that hadn't been available on-site where she had worked before. She mentioned it to Beth when they stopped to drink the coffee Marie had made for them.

'It's all down to our location,' Beth explained, blowing on the hot liquid to cool it. 'It takes almost an hour to reach the nearest hospital on a good day and far longer than that if the weather's bad. A lot of patients both here at The Larches and at Hemsthwaite can't undertake that kind of a journey. That's why Daniel fought so hard to secure funding to provide more facilities on site.'

'So what else do you offer?' Ellie asked as Beth paused to sip her coffee. 'You said that several consultants from the hospital hold clinics here—did you mention something about a dentist as well?'

'Yes. That's right. We have an arrangement with a dental practice—they see patients here once a week.

The same goes for the optician—patients can make an appointment to see him here on a Wednesday,' Beth explained and grimaced. 'Dratted Braxton Hicks contractions. They woke me up this morning. I was not pleased either as it was the first time I hadn't had to get up through the night to go to the loo.'

'What a nuisance,' Ellie said sympathetically. 'Daniel said that you only have a few weeks before your baby is due.'

'Hmm, three, although first babies are notoriously late.' Beth wriggled around, trying to get comfortable, and Ellie frowned.

'Are you sure they're Braxton Hicks? You do seem to be in a lot of discomfort.'

'Oh, I'm sure it will pass,' Beth said, levering herself up off the chair. She let out a gasp as water suddenly gushed out from between her legs.

'I doubt it!' Ellie exclaimed, jumping to her feet. Putting her arm around Beth's waist, she helped her to the couch and got her settled. 'It looks as though it's the real thing so let's get you out of those wet undies and have a look. If your waters have broken then it won't be long before your baby's on its way too.'

'I can't believe this!' Beth exclaimed, wriggling out of her sodden underwear. 'I should have another three weeks before the baby arrives.'

'It's easy to get confused about the dates,' Ellie said soothingly, lifting Beth's skirt so she could examine her.

'But I'm not confused. I know exactly when I got pregnant. It was the night before Callum went away. It couldn't have happened any other time because we hadn't spoken let alone made love for almost a year before that!'

'Oh.' Ellie wasn't sure what to say, and Beth sighed.

'Callum and I split up last year. We'd been trying for a baby for the best part of three years—ever since we got married, in fact—but it just didn't happen.' Her voice echoed with pain and Ellie's heart went out to her.

'It must have been difficult for you,' she said quietly.

'It was. We tried fertility treatment but it didn't work, and in the end the constant pressure of hoping that this time we'd get lucky proved too much.' Beth bit her lip. 'Callum told me that he couldn't handle it any more and that he wanted a divorce.'

'I'm so sorry,' Ellie said sincerely. 'It must have been awful for you both, although surely it made a difference when you found out you were pregnant?'

'I was thrilled, thrilled and shocked that it should have happened right out of the blue like that. As for Callum, well, I've no idea how he feels, although I can guess.' She laughed harshly. 'I wrote to tell him I was pregnant, you see, but he's never bothered to reply. I think that says it all, doesn't it? No, this baby's my responsibility and no one else's.'

She broke off as another contraction began. Ellie frowned, wondering how she would have reacted in similar circumstances. She sighed because the likelihood of her having found herself in the same position was zero. Michael had been fanatical about making sure she didn't get pregnant. At the time, Ellie had thought it was because he had wanted to do the right thing, make sure they were married before they embarked on parenthood. Now she wasn't so certain any more. Had Michael been desperate to avoid her getting pregnant so that it wouldn't impact on him?

It was something Ellie knew she needed to think about but not right now. Now she needed to focus on Beth and the baby. She waited until the contraction had passed then examined Beth again. 'You're already about six centimetres dilated so your baby's definitely going to make his appearance very soon.'

'Oh, no!' Tears filled Beth's eyes. 'It's too early! I couldn't bear it if something went wrong now. I've waited so long for this child.'

'Nothing is going to go wrong,' Ellie assured her, mentally crossing her fingers that she wasn't tempting fate. Delivering Beth's baby wouldn't have posed a problem if they'd been in a fully equipped maternity unit. However, after what she had learned about the nearest hospital being an hour's drive away, she couldn't help feeling anxious. She summoned a smile, determined not to let Beth know that she was worried. 'Now can you tell me what arrangements you've made for the birth? I take it that you're booked into the maternity unit with it being your first child.'

'That's right.' Beth made an obvious effort to calm herself. 'I wanted to have the baby at home but Polly talked me out of it. She said it would be safer if I had it in the hospital seeing as I'm a first-time mum and that bit older too.'

'And who's Polly?' Ellie asked, needing to be clear about the details.

'She's the local midwife—Polly Davies,' Beth explained. 'I've been seeing her for my antenatal checkups. In fact, I saw her only last Friday.'

'And what did she say?' Ellie asked.

'Oh, that everything was fine—blood pressure, baby's heartbeat, et cetera.' Beth frowned. 'She did say that the baby seemed to be quite low down, now I think about it.'

'Probably getting ready to make his exit,' Ellie said, laughing.

'Probably. The little rip!'

Beth laughed as well and Ellie was relieved to see that she appeared far less anxious. Good. The last thing she wanted was for Beth to be uptight if they had to deliver the baby here. The thought helped her focus on what needed to be done and she squeezed Beth's hand. 'I'll go and phone the hospital and let them know what's happening. I'll also get hold of Polly. With a bit of luck, she'll be able to lend a hand here. I'll be as quick as I can. OK?'

Beth nodded, her face screwing up as another contraction began. Ellie hurried from the room and made straight to Reception, knowing that Marie would have all the phone numbers. She was dealing with a patient and Ellie waited until she had finished. Lowering her voice so it wouldn't carry across the waiting room, she quickly explained what was going on.

'Really!' Marie's mouth dropped open. 'But she's another three weeks to go. Are you sure it isn't a false alarm?'

'Quite sure,' Ellie said firmly. 'This baby is definitely on its way and there's nothing we can do to stop it. Can you phone the hospital and let them know? We'll need an ambulance, although I doubt if it will get here before the big event.'

'Of course.' Marie picked up the phone, although she still appeared slightly stunned.

'Oh, and can you get hold of Polly too? Apparently, she's been responsible for Beth's antenatal care. It would be a huge help if she could give me a hand.'

'I'll phone her first,' Marie promised. 'She lives in town so she can be here in no time.'

'That's great. Thanks.' Ellie started to turn away then paused. 'Daniel needs to know what's going on. Which is his room again?'

'First door on the right,' Marie explained, then turned her attention to the phone. 'Polly, it's Marie. You won't believe what's happened…'

Ellie left the receptionist to make the calls and hurried back to Beth, pausing en route to tap on Daniel's door. She popped her head into the room when he bade her to enter. 'I'm sorry to disturb you,' she said, smiling apologetically at the young woman holding a fractious toddler on her knee. 'But can I have a quick word?'

'Of course.' Daniel excused himself and stepped out into the corridor. He frowned. 'There's nothing wrong, I hope. I thought Beth was showing you around.'

'She was but we've hit a snag.' Ellie felt decidedly awkward about interrupting him during a consultation but there was really nothing else she could have done in the circumstances.

'A *snag*?' he echoed in a voice that hinted at displeasure. 'What are you talking about?'

Ellie's mouth compressed, not enjoying the fact that he obviously thought she was being a nuisance. She prided herself on her self-sufficiency and it stung to realise that he thought she was the type of person who needed constant support.

'Beth's baby is coming,' she explained coldly. She raised her hand when he went to speak. 'No, there's no doubt about her being in labour. Marie is arranging for an ambulance and phoning Polly to see if she can come and help. I thought you should know, although I apologise for disturbing you.'

With that she turned away, making herself walk steadily along the corridor even though in truth she felt like running off and hiding. She bit her lip when she felt the far too ready tears spring to her eyes. Maybe it hurt to have Daniel speak to her so sharply but she could live with it. After all, he was her boss, nothing more. It didn't matter how he spoke to her so long as he wasn't rude.

It all sounded so sensible in theory but as she opened the door, Ellie realised that it did matter, that it mattered a great deal. For some reason she wanted Daniel to speak to her with warmth and make her feel that she was valued. How pathetic was that!

CHAPTER THREE

DANIEL COULD HAVE bitten off his tongue for speaking so sharply to Eleanor. If it weren't for the fact that he had a patient waiting, he would have gone after her and apologised. Taking a deep breath, he went back into the room and sat down.

'I apologise for the interruption, Mrs Walsh,' he said to the woman seated in the chair. 'You were about to explain how you hurt your arm.'

'I… I tripped, Dr Saunders. Over…ahem…one of Alice's toys.'

The young woman ran a trembling hand over her daughter's wispy blonde hair. Although both mother and child were neatly dressed in expensive outfits, there was something not quite right about their appearance. The little girl's hair looked as if it hadn't been brushed and yet Madeleine Walsh had taken the time to apply a heavy layer of make-up. Daniel leant across the desk, using the excuse of reaching for Mrs Walsh's file while he examined her face more closely. Was that a bruise he could see on her cheek? And another on her neck?

'I see,' he said, sitting back in his seat. He smiled at her, although he had a bad feeling about this. It wasn't the first time that Madeleine Walsh had come to see him after a supposed fall; this was her third visit in the last six months. Although he hadn't noticed any sign of bruising then, it could be because he hadn't been looking for it. He needed to get to the bottom of this situation and soon. 'Did you hurt yourself anywhere else apart from your arm? Your face looks bruised to me—did you bang it?'

'Oh…erm…yes, I must have done.' The woman put her hand to her cheek and Daniel could see the fear in her eyes. 'I'm ever so clumsy,' she muttered. 'Always tripping up and banging into things.'

'Easily done,' Daniel said evenly. 'As long as you're sure that it was an accident. Anything you tell me won't go any further, Mrs Walsh, I assure you.'

'Of course it was an accident!' the woman declared, flushing. 'I tripped over one of Alice's toys—one of her dolls, actually—and fell down the stairs. I… I must have put out my hand to save myself and that's how I hurt my arm.'

'Let me take a look.' Daniel got up and came around the desk. Crouching down, he went to examine her arm, stopping when little Alice shrank away from him. 'It's all right, poppet,' he said softly. 'I just want to look at Mummy's arm so I can make it better.'

'She's not good with strangers,' Madeleine Walsh said hurriedly, cuddling the trembling child to her.

'Does she attend the nursery school?' Daniel asked levelly, although the bad feeling he had was growing worse by the second. Alice was four years old and in his experience most children her age had got over their shyness and were happy to socialise with people outside the family unit.

'No. I decided not to send her.' Madeleine Walsh bit her lip then rushed on. 'She's very shy and it didn't seem right to send her to a place where I know she'll be unhappy.'

'She'll have to go to school next year, though, won't she?' Daniel pointed out, gently examining the woman's arm. The wrist was swollen and heavily discoloured. It was obviously painful because Mrs Walsh gasped when he touched it. 'Sorry. I can tell how painful it is, although I can't say if it's broken or badly sprained. Can you move your fingers?'

'Yes.' Madeleine grimaced as she wriggled her fingers the tiniest bit. 'It's really painful, though.'

'It will be.' Daniel sat down again. 'I'm afraid it really needs X-raying to establish if it's broken or not. Is there anyone who can drive you to the hospital, your husband perhaps?'

'No, Nigel's in court this morning and I don't want to bother him,' Madeleine Walsh said quickly. 'Can't you put a bandage on it, Dr Saunders? I'm sure it's not broken and just needs some support while it heals. I wouldn't have bothered you if I could have done it myself.'

'I really think it needs to be X-rayed,' Daniel insisted. 'If it is broken then the last thing you want is for it to set badly and end up with a deformed wrist. If you don't want to contact your husband then I can arrange for someone to drive you to the hospital. We have a team of volunteers who very kindly ferry people there and back in situations like this.'

'Oh, I don't know… I've no idea what Nigel would say about that.' She looked so stricken that Daniel almost wished he hadn't suggested it. However, it was vital that she have her wrist X-rayed to avoid any future problems.

'I'm sure he will take the sensible view and be pleased that you got it attended to. I'll phone Mrs Goodison and see if she's free. She used to be a teacher at the junior school and she's very nice,' he added encouragingly as he reached for the phone.

'But what about Alice?' Madeleine Walsh protested. 'There's no one to look after her and I can't leave her.'

'You can take Alice with you. I know for a fact that Mrs Goodison has a child seat in her car—she has grandchildren, you see. She'll be more than happy to look after Alice while you have the X-ray done too.'

Daniel made the call, not wanting to give Madeleine Walsh any more opportunities to wriggle out of the hospital visit. Fortunately, Barbara Goodison immediately agreed to run Mrs Walsh to the hospital and bring her back again afterwards. Once he had explained to Madeleine that she would be collected from home, he saw her out. He intended to follow up the case and find out if he was right to suspect that the woman was being abused by her husband. He didn't know Nigel Walsh personally as the man had never been to the surgery since the family had moved to Beesdale just over a year ago. However, from what he had heard Walsh was very high up in legal circles.

Daniel sighed as he went to ask Marie if she would wait a few minutes before sending in his next patient. Sadly, social standing had no bearing on that type of behaviour. It crossed all boundaries. Had Eleanor been a victim of abuse? It was obvious that something awful must have happened to her, something so bad that she had left her job and relocated to a different part of the country. His hands clenched. The thought of Eleanor suffering such treatment was more than he could bear.

'You're doing great,' Ellie said encouragingly as Beth breathed her way through another contraction. She checked her watch, frowning when she realised how close together the contractions were coming. It was obvious that the baby was going to be born very soon and she couldn't help feeling anxious. It was several years since she had delivered a baby during her rotations and it had been in the safety of a modern maternity unit with a couple of experienced midwives standing by. The thought of delivering Beth's baby by herself was decidedly scary. According to Marie, Polly was on her way back from one of the local farms and would get there as soon as she could; however, it seemed to be taking her an awfully long time. Ellie looked round when the door opened, hoping it would be her, but her hopes were dashed when Daniel came into the room. Even though she could do with some support, she wasn't sure if she was glad to see him after their run-in earlier.

'How are we doing in here?' he asked as he came over to the couch. He smiled at Beth. 'Not quite how you planned it, I imagine.'

Beth laughed then grimaced as another contraction began. Daniel turned to Ellie, his mouth still curved into a smile, and she felt some of her unease dissipate. Surely he wouldn't smile at her like that if he was still annoyed with her?

'I'm sorry about before. I didn't mean to snap at you. Suffice to say that I was worried about the patient who was with me, not that it's any excuse.'

'It's all right,' Ellie said quickly, not wanting him to suspect how thankful she felt. She hated being in the wrong and had always done so ever since she was a child. Oh, she knew what lay behind it—she had worked that out a long time ago. Learning that she was adopted had made her aware of how different she was from Gemma, their parents' natural daughter. Gemma hadn't needed to be on her best behaviour all the time to earn their love; she hadn't needed to be kind or considerate because their parents would always adore her. Gemma, with her golden curls and laughing blue eyes, was the child they had longed for whereas Eleanor, with her straight black hair and solemn demeanour, had been the cuckoo in the nest.

Ellie pushed the thought to the back of her mind. She wasn't a child any more and she didn't need anyone's adoration to prove her worth. 'The contractions are coming roughly two minutes apart now. Do you know how long it will be before Polly gets here? Marie said she was on her way back from Outhwaite Farm.'

'Oh!' Daniel grimaced. 'It's the farm that's probably furthest away from here. It'll take Polly a good thirty minutes to get back, I expect, but I'll go and check where she is.' He strode to the door then paused to glance back. 'I meant what I said, Eleanor. I didn't mean to snap at you.'

He didn't wait for her to answer and Ellie was glad. She turned to Beth after he left, forcing down the bubble of happiness that had risen up inside her. She didn't need Daniel's approbation any more than she needed to be adored, she told herself sternly, but to very little effect.

She sighed. It had taken her a long time to develop a sense of her own worth. Growing up, she had always felt second-best compared to Gemma. Although her parents had been unfailingly kind and supportive, they had found it impossible to hide their delight in their natural daughter. Gemma had been so pretty and precocious and everyone had adored her—or so it had seemed to Ellie. Ellie had faded into the background after Gemma was born when Ellie was eight years old. It was only when she went to university that she had come into her own—made her own circle of friends, had her first boyfriend. She had slowly gained confidence and, once she had qualified and started practising, she had forgotten about the disappointments of her childhood. When she had started dating Michael Ross, another of the doctors at the practice where she'd worked, and had become engaged to him, her life had felt complete. And then she had let herself into his flat that morning and found him in bed with Stacey Roberts, one of the practice nurses, and her world had fallen apart...

'Ooh!'

Beth's groan brought Ellie back to the present. Bending down, she checked what progress they were making, her heart racing when she discovered that the baby's head was crowning. 'You're almost there,' she told Beth, trying to inject a note of confidence into her voice. 'Baby's head is crowning so it won't be long now.'

'The sooner the better,' Beth muttered through gritted teeth. Her face screwed up as another contraction began and Ellie quickly gathered together everything she would need once the baby was born. Fortunately, they had birthing kits in the supply cupboard so she put on a pair of gloves and placed everything close to hand—scissors to cut the cord, a soft cloth to dry the infant, some narrow tubing to clear its airway if it was necessary. The head was emerging now and she slid her hand beneath it, gently supporting its weight as first one shoulder and then the other followed.

'One more push should do it,' she told Beth, thanking her stars that Beth was so clued up about what to do. 'Here we go!'

The baby slithered out, screaming lustily, which was more than Ellie could have hoped for. It was a little girl, slightly on the small side, but absolutely perfect in every respect. Ellie wiped the mucus off the little one's face, smiling as she wrapped her in a towel and handed her to Beth. 'Congratulations. You have a beautiful little daughter.'

'A girl!' Beth exclaimed as she took her first look at her daughter. 'I was convinced I was having a boy!'

'Not disappointed, are you?' Ellie teased her.

'No way! She's gorgeous.' Beth dropped a kiss on her baby's head.

Ellie turned away when she felt her eyes fill with tears. She had always dreamed of having a child of her own. Maybe it had become even more important because she and the baby would have been related by blood and that would have been even more special. Now the dreams she'd harboured had been bagged up and disposed of along with all that unwanted clothing. She wouldn't have a child now because the last thing she planned to do was to fall in love again and risk being let down a second time. It hurt to know how much she would miss because of what had happened.

'Well, it looks as though you've managed fine without me!'

Ellie swung round when the door opened to admit a tall, red-haired woman. Taking a quick breath, she hurriedly composed her features into a welcoming smile. Maybe her life wasn't going to turn out how she had hoped it would but she would make the best of it. 'I take it that you're Polly,' she said, holding out her hand. 'I'm Eleanor Munroe, the new locum.'

'Polly Davies.' Polly shook hands then went over to Beth, smiling as she looked at the baby. 'What a little poppet! And not a bad size too considering you had another three weeks to go.'

'She's gorgeous, isn't she?' Beth murmured, stroking the baby's wrinkled little cheek.

'Oh, so it's a girl?' Polly laughed, her pretty face lighting up with amusement. 'That's ten pounds you owe me.' She looked round, deliberately drawing Ellie into the conversation. 'Beth was convinced she was having a boy but I was equally sure it would be a girl so we had a bet on it. Looks as though I'm the winner!'

'We're both winners,' Beth corrected her, laughing.

Ellie laughed as well but she couldn't pretend that her heart wasn't heavy at the thought of never having children of her own. It was hard to rid herself of the thought as she helped Polly deliver the afterbirth then get Beth and the baby ready for the transfer to hospital. Although Beth was reluctant to go, Polly managed to persuade her that it would be in her and the baby's best interests. By the time Daniel led in the paramedics, everything was ready.

'Let me know if they keep you in, Beth,' he said, planting a kiss on his partner's cheek. 'We'll set up a rota—that way you won't be inundated by everyone wanting to visit at the same time.'

'That would be great.' Beth's voice caught as she looked at the baby nestled in her arms. 'It'll be nice for this little one to have all her aunties and uncles there for her, even if her father isn't interested.'

Ellie stepped aside as the paramedics wheeled Beth and the baby out to the ambulance. Polly was following on by car and she left as well. Daniel sighed as he watched them go.

'I can't believe that Callum doesn't want anything to do with his own child, but he's never even bothered to contact Beth since she wrote to tell him she was pregnant.'

'So she said,' Ellie said quietly. 'It must be very difficult for her.'

'It must. It's hard enough bringing up a child on your own when it's the result of circumstances beyond your control, but it must be much worse when it's because the other parent doesn't want to be involved.'

There was real regret in Daniel's voice and Ellie found herself wondering if he was speaking from experience. She knew nothing about his personal life, whether he was married and had a family or what. However, before she could attempt to find out, he made an obvious effort to collect himself.

'Anyway, leaving all that aside, I wanted to thank you, Eleanor. Talk about being thrown in at the deep end!' He laughed ruefully. 'And here was I, trying not to put too much pressure on you!'

CHAPTER FOUR

DANIEL COULD HAVE bitten off his tongue when he saw Eleanor's face tighten. That she hadn't appreciated the comment was obvious and he couldn't blame her. No one liked to be made to feel that they weren't up to doing the job they had been hired for. He desperately wanted to explain but how could he when it would mean admitting that he had been worried about her, that he cared?

'Right. Better get back to work or the patients will think we've gone on strike. Any problems, buzz me.'

He swung round, not giving her a chance to say anything as he headed back to his room. Maybe he was taking the coward's way out but the thought of confessing how much she had been in his thoughts lately was out of the question. Maybe she did have issues that still affected her but he doubted if she would appreciate his concern. From what he had learned, Eleanor preferred to keep her own counsel and he would be well advised to remember that whenever he was tempted to interfere.

The morning flew past as it always did. They held open surgery each morning and they were always very busy. Although patients could make an appointment to be seen during the afternoon, Daniel had found that they preferred this system. Being a mainly rural community, it allowed more leeway for the farmers and their families. Livestock came first and people appreciated being able to visit the surgery when work allowed, rather than be tied to a set time and date. It was almost one by the time his last patient left so he tidied up and made his way to Reception. Marie had been joined by Lucy Burrows, who was doing her pre-registration training in their on-site pharmacy. It was obvious that Marie had brought her up to speed about the morning's events.

'I can't believe that Beth has had her baby here!' Lucy declared when she saw Daniel.

'I know. It came as a bit of a shock, not least of all to Beth,' Daniel replied, laughing. Lucy had been born and raised in Beesdale and had returned to the town after she had completed her degree. With a Master of Pharmacy degree to her credit, she could have moved anywhere in the country, but she loved the Dales and wanted to remain here.

'I wonder what she's going to call her,' Lucy continued, happily. 'Beth was convinced she was having a boy so she'll have to think of some girls' names, I imagine.'

'She will,' Daniel agreed, although he was only half listening. His ears had caught the sound of footsteps and he knew without needing to check that they belonged to Eleanor. How or why he was able to recognise them with such certainty, he had no idea, but he knew he was right and his heart seemed to beat a shade faster all of a sudden. It was an effort not to show how alarmed he felt as he turned to her. 'All done?'

He'd been aiming for lightness, for nonchalance, for…for *heaven knew what*, but he hadn't achieved it. No way! He inwardly winced when he realised how stilted he sounded. What made it worse was that out of the corner of his eye he saw Lucy and Marie exchange a look, confirmation, if he'd needed it, that he had messed up. All he could do was hope that Eleanor didn't know him well enough to realise how strangely he was behaving.

'Yes. Thank you.'

Daniel felt a jolt of shock hit him when he realised that Eleanor sounded the same as he did. Uptight. Stilted. *Aware*. His blood heated, gathering several degrees as it rushed through his veins. Eleanor was aware of him? Not just the normal sort of recognition of one human being for another but completely and totally aware of *him*? As a person? As a man? If his mind hadn't been already boggled it would have been so then. Daniel could barely get his head round the idea and definitely couldn't chase it away. It was a relief when Lucy unwittingly stepped into the breach.

'Hi, Eleanor, I'm Lucy Burrows. I'm doing my pre-reg training in the pharmacy. I also do a turn on the desk if we're pushed.'

'Nice to meet you, Lucy.' Daniel heard Eleanor take a quick breath and didn't know whether he felt relieved or sorry when he heard how normal she sounded. 'Actually, most people call me Ellie. I always think it sounds less, well, formal.'

Ellie. Daniel tried it out for size, oh, not out loud—he wasn't that far gone! It rolled around his tongue pleasantly enough yet for some reason it didn't feel quite right. He shot a glance at the woman standing beside him and felt his nerve endings start to fire out signals. Ellie was a pretty name, slightly more modern, a little more accessible, but it wasn't right for her: it didn't fit. He preferred Eleanor, preferred the sound of it, the feel of it, the sense of completeness. With Eleanor one got the whole woman. Whereas Ellie was just a fraction of the whole, the bits she wanted folk to see, not the bits she kept hidden. The bits, he realised, that *he* desperately wanted to get to know.

Ellie forced herself to respond as Lucy asked her how she had enjoyed her first morning at The Larches but it was an effort to concentrate. She had no idea what was going on in Daniel's mind but she could almost see the thought bubbles forming above his head. That he was thinking about her was a given and it was unsettling to say the least. It was a relief when the phone rang.

'I expect you're keen to see the flat. I've got the keys here so I'll take you up there now.' Daniel offered her a small bunch of keys that he'd taken from his pocket as they moved away from the desk.

'Thank you.' Ellie took them off him, trying to ignore how warm they felt from being tucked against his body. 'There's no need for you to come, though,' she said hurriedly, not sure she appreciated that idea. 'I'm sure you must have more important things to do. I can sort myself out.'

'It isn't a problem. Anyway, there are a couple of things I need to show you—how to work the boiler and where to find the stopcock, things like that.' He didn't give her time to protest any more as he led the way from the surgery, taking the path round to the rear of the building. 'The flat is completely self-contained,' he continued over his shoulder. 'Camille and I lived there when I took over the practice. We only moved out because of Nathan.' He laughed. 'We needed more space to fit in all his paraphernalia!'

'Oh. I see.' Ellie felt her heart sink. Although she knew it was silly, learning that Daniel was married and had a family was disappointing. She pushed that ridiculous thought to the back of her mind, determined that it wasn't going to set down roots. 'It must have been handy living on site, so to speak.'

'Yes and no.' Daniel paused so she could catch up with him. 'It was great not having to drive miles each day to get to work but the downside was that I was always on call. Folk knew exactly where to find me, day and night.'

'Mmm. I can see how that could be a problem,' Ellie agreed, frowning.

'You don't need to worry about that,' he said quickly. He put his hand on her arm and laughed. 'We've managed to train our patients now. They phone the out-of-hours number rather than hammer on the front door these days.'

He patted her arm then moved away but it was a moment before Ellie followed him. She could feel her arm tingling from where his hand had rested on it and had to resist the urge to rub it. Daniel had reached a flight of steps leading to the upper floor of the building and he paused again to wait for her.

Ellie forced her feet to move in his direction but inside she could hear alarm bells ringing. She was already far too aware of Daniel, more aware of him, in fact, than she had been of anyone before, including Michael. Her attraction to her ex had developed over time; it definitely hadn't been instantaneous as this had been. Was it the fact that she had suffered such a huge blow? she wondered. That being betrayed had left her vulnerable so that she had latched onto the first attractive man who had shown her any kindness?

Ellie wanted to believe it with a fervour that bordered on frenzy. Quite frankly, *any* explanation was better than thinking that this attraction she felt could develop into something more!

* * *

'And this is the main bedroom. The bed's new and so is the carpet. I decided to change them when I had the flat redecorated. The old ones were well past their use-by date.'

Daniel stepped back so that Eleanor could go ahead of him but she merely glanced into the room. Her eyes swept over the soft *café-au-lait*-coloured carpet and matching curtains and he found it impossible to decide if she liked what she saw or not. It had been the same with every room—a swift glance, a brief nod, and that had been it. Even though he knew it was ridiculous to feel even the tiniest bit miffed, he couldn't help it.

'So what do you think?' he said, trying to mask his disappointment. She wasn't to know how much effort he had expended getting the place ready for her. She had no idea that he had devoted a whole weekend just to choosing the colour for the walls or that buying new curtains had been such a nightmare—widths and lengths, patterned or plain—it had been like tiptoeing through a minefield! However, all the effort he'd expended wouldn't be worth a brass farthing if she didn't like it.

'I don't know what to say.'

She sank down onto the sofa and stared around the bright and airy living room. He'd chosen sheer curtains for in here—well, he hadn't actually chosen them but had gone with what the sales assistant had advised— and he had been particularly pleased with the result. The view from the window was spectacular, the greens and mauves of the surrounding hills shown to advantage without heavy curtains to detract from it. But had he made an error of judgement? Would Eleanor have preferred something more substantial, more private?

'Look, I understand if you want to change things,' he said quickly. 'Don't think you have to live with what I've chosen…'

'I love it. The walls, the curtains. Everything.' She looked up and he could see tears shimmering in her eyes. 'I never expected this, Daniel. Thank you so much. It's perfect.'

'I'm glad you like it.' Daniel felt a lump come to his throat and had to swallow hard. He dredged up a rather rusty laugh. 'I had a horrible feeling that you loathed the place when you didn't say anything.'

'I was just overwhelmed.' She dashed away her tears and smiled self-consciously. 'Sorry. I was expecting something fairly basic, you see, not this. This…well, this looks like a proper home.'

'Good. It's going to be your home for the next year, so I'm pleased you feel that way.' He took a deep breath, clamping down on the urge to tell her that it was her home for as long as she wanted it to be. Eleanor was here to cover Beth's maternity leave and once that was over she would leave. Better to get that clear in his head from the outset.

'Right then. Do you need any help?' he said, determined to get a grip on his thoughts. 'Those steps can be a real bind if you've got anything heavy to fetch up here, so I'll give you a hand.'

'Thank you but there's no need.' She stood up and he couldn't help noticing that her face had closed up again. 'I got rid of most of my things before I left Kent so there's nothing really heavy—just clothes and bedding mainly.'

'I see.' Daniel frowned, wondering why she had got rid of all her belongings. He longed to ask but some tiny shred of caution held him back. He had teetered on the very edge of that invisible line between colleagues but he hadn't crossed it. Yet. Once he did so there would be no going back and that wouldn't be wise. He had to concentrate on Nathan. He couldn't afford to involve himself in Eleanor's affairs. At the end of the day, his son came first.

Daniel's heart was heavy as he walked to the door. Maybe he was doing the right thing, but there was no denying that it felt as though he was abandoning Eleanor and the idea hurt him probably far more than it would have hurt her if she knew how he felt. Eleanor had no problem keeping to her side of that line.

'I'll leave you to it then. I've half a dozen home visits this afternoon so if you need anything, ask Marie.' He forced himself to smile, although it was an effort to appear upbeat. 'She's the fount of all knowledge and any problems, she can usually solve them.'

'I'll remember that.' Eleanor's voice was cool, proof, if he'd needed it, that she didn't feel anywhere near as confused as he did.

Daniel sketched her a wave and left. He went back to the surgery and collected the list of calls that Marie had left for him. His first call was to one of the outlying farms so he got into his car and headed out of town. It was a good twenty minutes' drive there and that should give him time to get his thoughts together. Quite frankly, he couldn't understand why he was behaving this way. It wasn't as though he was desperate to have a relationship again, desperate to have sex. He hadn't slept with anyone since Camille had died, hadn't wanted to despite the fact that he'd had many opportunities. It was as though that side of him had died along with his wife and he had never imagined he would feel desire again.

Was that what he felt for Eleanor? Did he want to sleep with her? Yes, he did. However, deep down he knew that sex wasn't at the heart of this attraction he felt, that there was more to it than that, although he wasn't going to make the mistake of working out what that 'more' was. It was too risky when he needed to stay focused on Nathan.

Daniel's expression was grim as he turned in through the farm gates. Meeting Eleanor couldn't have come at a worse time.

Ellie couldn't help feeling a deep sense of satisfaction as she switched off her computer. The day had gone much better than she had hoped. The patients she'd seen had been friendly and welcoming, genuinely grateful for her help. The other members of the team had also been highly supportive, going out of their way to make her feel at home. She knew she had made the right decision by applying for this job. It would help her get over what had happened, help her forget her disappointment and heartache. She just needed to concentrate on her work and everything would be fine.

'All finished?'

Ellie felt her heart lurch when the door opened and Daniel appeared. She hadn't seen him since he had shown her round the flat and she had forgotten the impact he had on her. Now, as she took stock of his rangy figure, she could feel that flicker of awareness shoot through her once more. Was it just his looks that caused her to react this way? Or was it more than that, the air of kindness, of caring, of compassion he exuded?

She had been attracted to Michael initially because of his looks, although, if she was honest, it had taken a while to find anything attractive about his personality. Michael had very strong views on most matters and Ellie had had to reconcile herself to the fact that they didn't see eye to eye on a lot of subjects. Had that been a mistake? she wondered suddenly. Should she have compromised her views to accommodate his simply because she had been afraid of losing him?

'Eleanor?'

The concern in Daniel's voice brought her back to the present and Ellie jumped. 'Sorry, I was miles away. Yes, I'm all finished.'

'Good. I was hoping we'd be able to finish on time with it being your first day.' Daniel gave her a quick smile and she felt her heart flutter once more and fought to control it. This was ridiculous! She wasn't some infatuated teenager but a mature woman, a woman who knew what was what too.

'Well, it seems to have worked out that way,' she said lightly, standing up. She took her bag out of her drawer then glanced around, checking that the cupboard was locked and the tap wasn't running—all the itty-bitty jobs that she did automatically and yet for some reason seemed to have taken on a far greater importance with Daniel watching her…

'Humph!' She didn't realise that she had actually snorted in disgust at her behaviour until she saw his brows rise. Colour flooded her cheeks and she hurried to the door, praying that he couldn't read minds along with his other talents. Wanting to make a good impression on him was pathetic!

Ellie hurried along the corridor as though the hounds of hell were snapping at her heels. Marie looked up and grinned when she saw her approaching.

'Looks as though someone's eager to leave. It's not been *that* bad a day, has it?'

'No, of course not.' Ellie dredged up a smile but she was very aware that Daniel was standing right behind her. 'I just didn't want to hold you up. I'm not sure of the routine yet,' she added lamely.

'Oh, no fear of that.' Marie laughed. 'We're like a well-oiled machine. Aren't we, Daniel?'

'You could say that.'

His voice rumbled in Ellie's ear and she couldn't help herself: she shivered. It was as though the sound of his voice had seeped through every pore in her skin. She looked round and felt her breath catch when she found herself staring into his deep blue eyes. She could see her own reflection in them, tiny images of herself imprinted on the midnight-blue, and the shiver turned into a shudder. She had the craziest feeling that he was absorbing her very essence, drinking it in, making her part of him. And the scariest thing of all was that she wanted it to happen.

CHAPTER FIVE

A WEEK PASSED, then another, and life at The Larches settled back into its normal routine. Or, at least, on the surface it did. Daniel, however, was very aware of the difference it made having Eleanor there. Oh, it wasn't her work—he was more than happy with that. No, it was this feeling he had, this constant awareness of her being in the room next to his, and it was highly unsettling. He managed not to think about it when he was with a patient but as soon as they left, he found himself listening for any sign of her presence—a cough, the scrape of chair legs on the floor—*any* little thing at all.

In an effort to rid himself of such nonsense, he decided to do a stint at the Hemsthwaite surgery, using the excuse that it would benefit the staff as well as the patients if they all got to know one another better. Sandra Nelson, who worked there part time, was delighted at the thought of a change of scene. However, Bernard Hargreaves, the full-time member of staff, made it clear that he wasn't interested. Daniel suspected that Bernard was planning to retire shortly and didn't push him. It wouldn't benefit anyone if the older man was reluctant to take up the offer.

He spent a busy morning. With it being Monday, a lot of people had waited over the weekend before seek-

ing medical attention. Daniel dealt with the usual sore
throats and chesty coughs then saw a young man who
had been brought into the surgery by his mother. Steven
Applethwaite was seventeen years of age and attended
the same college as Nathan. A tall, gangly young man
with sandy hair, he looked pale and listless as he sat
slumped in front of the desk.

'I had the devil of a job getting him here this morning, Dr Saunders, but he can't carry on the way he's
been doing, that's for sure.' Mrs Applethwaite settled
herself on the adjoining chair. A comfortably plump
woman in her forties, she exuded an air of confidence.
Daniel knew that the Applethwaites were a large farm-
ing family and guessed that Diane Applethwaite was
used to taking charge.

'What exactly has been happening?' he asked, ad-
dressing the question to Steven.

'He's always tired no matter how much sleep he has,'
Diane answered immediately. 'He stayed in bed most of
the weekend but I still couldn't get him up this morning
in time for college. It's as though he's got no energy.'

'Is that right, Steven?' Daniel asked neutrally. He
held up his hand when Diane went to speak. 'If you
wouldn't mind, Mrs Applethwaite, it would be better
if Steven told me how he feels.'

Steven looked uncomfortable at being put on the
spot. 'I just feel tired all the time, like Mum said,' he
mumbled.

'Anything else?' Daniel prompted. 'Have you had a
temperature or a sore throat, perhaps?'

'No.' Steven hesitated then rushed on. 'I feel thirsty
all the time, though—I'm always drinking water and
juice.'

'I see.' Daniel nodded. Getting up, he went to the

cupboard and took out a sample jar. 'I'd like to check your urine, Steven. The bathroom's along the corridor to your left so can you go and pee in this for me and bring it back?'

Steven blushed right red as he took the jar. He was at an age when being asked to do such things caused him acute embarrassment. Diane Applethwaite looked Daniel straight in the eyes after her son disappeared.

'You think he's got diabetes, don't you, Dr Saunders?'

'I think it's a possibility, although I can't be sure until I've tested his urine,' Daniel explained carefully, not wanting to alarm the woman maybe unnecessarily.

'I should have realised it myself,' Diane said, shaking her head. 'Our Cathy—that's my sister—she's had diabetes since she was a girl. I remember her drinking pints of water before they found out what was wrong with her, but I never put two and two together.'

'It's easy to overlook things when you're busy. And, let's be honest, teenaged boys aren't exactly forthcoming when it comes to any issues they have,' he added ruefully. 'I know from bitter experience how hard it is to get them to talk.'

'You're right there. I've got five lads and they're all very tight-lipped when it comes to anything personal,' Diane agreed. She sighed. 'Very different from the girls, they are.'

Steven came back just then and handed the specimen to Daniel. Daniel took it over to the worktop to test it. He nodded when the chemically coated strip showed an extremely high level of glucose. 'It's as I suspected, Steven. Your glucose level is far higher than it should be.' He came back and sat down. 'I'll need to do a blood test as well, but it appears that you may have diabetes mellitus.'

'That's what Auntie Cathy has, isn't it?' Steven said, turning to his mother. He went pale when she nodded. 'Does it mean I'll have to have injections like Auntie Cathy does?'

'Most probably,' Daniel confirmed, knowing what a shock it must be for the boy. He could imagine Nathan's reaction and tried to make the situation sound as positive as possible. 'However, if you do have to inject yourself with insulin you'll be shown what to do. After a while, it will just become part of your daily routine.'

'It's not routine, though, is it?' Steven said angrily, his eyes filling with tears. 'None of my friends have to inject themselves!'

'Perhaps they don't but they may have other health issues you know nothing about,' Daniel replied soothingly. However, his words had little effect as Steven leapt to his feet and rushed out of the room.

'I'm sorry, Doctor,' Diane said, getting up. 'He's always been a bit...well, sensitive. But that doesn't excuse his rudeness.'

'He's bound to be upset, Mrs Applethwaite. It's a lot to take in so please don't worry about it. The main thing now is to ensure he gets the appropriate treatment. I'd like him to do a fasting blood test, i.e. he's not to eat anything after his evening meal until blood is taken the following morning. It can be done here and if it confirms my suspicions then I'll refer him to the hospital.'

'I'll make sure he has it done,' Diane said staunchly.

'Good. Jessica will give you a leaflet explaining the procedure,' he told her, referring to one of the two practice nurses who covered both surgeries. 'She can also

take the sample, although you can have it done at Beesdale if you'd prefer the phlebotomist to do it.'

'Here'd be better. It's a busy time at the moment—
the sheep need bringing down from the hills before
the weather turns and I'll be needed to lend a hand.'
Diane sighed. 'Will Steven have to attend the hospital
every week?'

'No. He will be seen by a specialist initially who
will decide on a course of treatment for him. After
that, he can be monitored here at the surgery. There's
a monthly diabetes clinic, which the hospital staff run,
so you won't need to be driving back and forth to town
all the time.'

'Oh, that's a relief!' Diane exclaimed. 'Not that I'd
have let Steven miss an appointment if he had needed
to attend the hospital. But it will make life easier if he
can be seen here.'

Daniel saw Diane out then buzzed in his next patient.
The rest of the morning flew past and before he knew
it, it was time for lunch. He exchanged the usual pleasantries with Bernard Hargreaves but he didn't linger.
He was eager to get back to Beesdale to check what had
been happening in his absence. He sighed as he got into
his car. Why bother lying? Why not admit that he was
eager to get back to see Eleanor?

It had been a busy morning but Ellie had enjoyed it.
The range of problems she had dealt with had been
very different from what she had encountered in her
previous post. She knew that she was gaining valuable experience by working at The Larches, and that it
would stand her in good stead when the time came to
move on. Although she wouldn't be leaving for several
months, she must never forget that she wasn't here on a

permanent basis. It was a strangely depressing thought
and she pushed it to the back of her mind as she left her
consulting room. Sandra Nelson was just leaving Daniel's room and she greeted Ellie cheerfully.

'Been nice and busy, hasn't it?'

'It has.' Ellie returned her smile. She had taken an
immediate liking to the older woman when they had met
that morning. Sandra had a friendly and down-to-earth
manner that had instantly put Ellie at her ease. 'So, have
you enjoyed working here for a change?'

'I have, especially as I've had someone to talk to.'
Sandra smiled conspiratorially. 'Bernard isn't one for
chatting, let's just say. He prefers to get the job done
and go home. I wouldn't be surprised if he handed in
his notice soon. I get the impression he's looking forward to calling it a day and retiring.'

'Really?' Ellie frowned, wondering if it might be the
opening she needed. If a post became vacant maybe
Daniel would consider hiring her on a permanent basis,
although she wasn't sure if it would be a good idea.
Although she could learn a lot from working at The
Larches, she was already far more aware of him than
she should be. Would it really be wise to place herself in
the position of seeing him day after day? She had sworn
after she and Michael had parted that she wouldn't make
the mistake of getting involved in a relationship again
and she intended to stick to it.

'Would you consider applying for the post if Bernard does decide to leave?' Sandra asked, unconsciously
latching onto Ellie's train of thought.

'I'm not sure,' Ellie replied. She shrugged when Sandra looked at her in surprise. 'I took this job knowing
it was only temporary. I'm not sure if it's what I want
to do long term, though.'

'Well, only you can decide that, although you could do a lot worse than work here. Isn't that right, Daniel?'

Ellie looked up in surprise, feeling her heart lurch when she saw Daniel standing by the reception desk. She hadn't seen him since the previous Friday and she found herself taking stock all over again. It was a chilly day, a brisk October wind giving a hint of what was to come, and he had dressed accordingly in a thick quilted coat that added bulk to his rangy figure. With his dark hair ruffled by the wind and his blue eyes sparkling, he was an arresting sight and Ellie couldn't stop staring at him. It was only when she realised that he had asked her a question that she dragged her thoughts together.

'Sorry. What was that?' she said hurriedly, willing the betraying colour not to flood her cheeks. She didn't want him thinking that he had an effect on her, even if it was true.

'I was just asking if you planned to stay in this part of the country,' he repeated.

'I… I'm not sure what my plans are yet,' Ellie said hastily. 'I may decide to move abroad. There are plenty of exciting opportunities for general practitioners in Australia and New Zealand.'

'There are indeed.' Daniel gave her a quick smile then turned to speak to Lucy Burrows, who was manning the desk that lunchtime.

Ellie headed for the door, not wanting anyone to suspect how hurt she felt. Oh, she knew it was stupid; after all, why should Daniel try to persuade her to stay in England? She was only here to cover Beth's maternity leave so why should he care where she went after that? And yet in some fragile corner of her heart she knew that it did matter, that it mattered a lot, and it worried her. She mustn't make the mistake of becoming dependent on Daniel, on thinking that his opinion counted. She had been down that road before with Michael and look how that had ended. The thought lent wings to her feet. Ellie had already left the building before Sandra caught up with her.

'Are you all right, love?' the older woman asked in concern. 'You dashed off as though the hounds of hell were after you!'

'Sorry.' Ellie drummed up a laugh, inwardly wincing when she realised how false it sounded. She rushed on, not wanting Sandra to guess how confused she felt. Maybe Daniel did have a strange effect on her but she wasn't prepared to alter her plans for him or any man. 'I skipped breakfast this morning and I'm absolutely ravenous. I can't wait to get something to eat!'

'I know the feeling!' Sandra laughed as well, accepting the excuse at face value. 'I'm on one of my never-ending diets and I'm always hungry. I even dream about food—how pathetic is that?'

'Poor you,' Ellie sympathised, although she couldn't help feeling guilty about the small white lie.

'Hmm, not what my hubby says when I wake him up, muttering about how many calories are in this or that delicious concoction.' Sandra grinned. 'Anyway, enough of my problems. I wanted to invite you to our autumn barbecue. We have one every year around this time as a kind of swansong before everyone hunkers down for the winter. We're having it on the nineteenth this year, if you're free.'

'My birthday,' Ellie told her.

'Really? What a coincidence! So can you come or do you already have plans, with it being your birthday?'

'No, I've nothing planned,' Ellie admitted, refusing to think about the previous year and how she had celebrated with Michael. There was no point harking back to the days when it had felt as though she'd had the world at her feet.

'Great! Tim and I will look forward to seeing you then.' Sandra turned to leave then paused. 'If you want to bring anyone it's fine. The more the merrier, we always say.'

'Thank you,' Ellie replied, not wanting to admit that she had no one to bring. She went up to the flat after Sandra left and opened a can of soup and poured it into a bowl. Popping it into the microwave to heat up, she went to the window, wondering when she would stop measuring time by the things she had done with Michael. Was she still in love with him, even after the way he had treated her?

Closing her eyes, she tried to conjure up his face, something she had never had any difficulty doing before, but for some reason it didn't work this time. She could picture each feature separately—hazel eyes, light brown hair, a rather thin-lipped mouth—but they wouldn't coalesce into a whole no matter how she tried... Another face suddenly started to form and Ellie's breath caught. There was no need to force these features to take their rightful place. One minute there was nothing in her head except that jumble and the next there was Daniel. Whole. Complete. Unmistakable.

Ellie's eyes few open but the image stayed with her, etched into her mind so clearly that it seemed to belong there. Was it a sign? But a sign of what? That she was far too aware of him? She already knew that, didn't she? It was what she did with the knowledge that mattered now. If she was to avoid any more heartache then she had to stop what was happening and not allow it to progress any further.

If she could.

Daniel couldn't get the conversation he'd had with Eleanor out of his mind. *She was planning to move abroad after her contract here ended?* He knew that it shouldn't have mattered a jot what she chose to do, but it did. The thought of her moving thousands of miles away was like a heavy weight, pressing down on him. He longed to talk to her about her plans, even ask her to stay on at The Larches, but it wasn't up to him to interfere. He mustn't forget that he was simply her employer and nothing else.

The afternoon turned out to be as busy as the morning, so they ended up running over time. Daniel offered to lock up so that Marie and the rest of the staff could get off home. Nathan played basketball on Monday evenings so he didn't need to rush home for once. He set the alarm then realised that Beth's keys to the surgery were hanging in the cupboard. Eleanor would need them to unlock the surgery. Daniel lifted them out, wondering if he should give them to her now or leave it until the morning. However, it would be typical if some kind of emergency happened and neither he nor Marie were available to open up. He would give them to Eleanor now and be done with it.

The wind was icy as he made his way round to the rear of the building. Although it was only the beginning of October, the weather was gearing itself up for winter. Winters in the Dales could be extremely harsh and definitely weren't to everyone's taste. Was that why Eleanor was thinking of moving overseas, so she could enjoy year-round sunshine? It would have been easy to accept that was the explanation, yet Daniel suspected that her reason for wanting to move abroad was linked to what had happened in the past. He frowned as he climbed the steps to the front door. Whatever it was, it must have been a particularly traumatic experience. Eleanor opened the door almost immediately when he rang the bell and Daniel could tell that she was surprised to see him.

'I'm sorry to bother you,' he said, clamping down on the thought as he held up the bunch of keys. When all was said and done, what business was it of his what she did? Nevertheless, he had to admit that he hated to think that she might move abroad for the wrong reasons. 'But I need to give you the surgery keys and explain how the alarm works. It would be absolutely typical if something happened and you needed to open up and didn't have any keys!'

'Oh. Right. You'd better come in then.' She led him into the living room, waving him towards a chair. 'I was just about to have a glass of wine,' she said, making an obvious effort to appear hospitable. 'Will you join me?'

'Better not.' Daniel shrugged. 'I've got to pick Nathan up in an hour's time. He's playing basketball,' he added, more for something to say than because he thought she would be interested. He was very aware that he was intruding on her free time. 'He plays for his college team and really enjoys it.'

'Nathan's your son?' She poured herself a glass of wine and sat down. 'How old is he?'

'Nineteen.'

'And he's still at college?' she queried, lifting the glass to her lips.

'Yes. He dropped out of school just before his GCSEs and missed over a year, so he's had to catch up,' Daniel explained, his eyes drawn to where her mouth touched the glass. She took a sip of wine then lowered the glass but his gaze remained locked on her mouth. There was the faintest sheen of moisture on her lips now and he felt his senses reel. Would her lips taste of wine? Would their sweetness be all the more potent if he kissed her?

'Was he ill?'

'Sorry?' Daniel forced his eyes away from her mouth, but he could feel the blood racing through his veins. The thought of kissing her and savouring the wine-sweet temptation of her lips was irresistible. When was the last time he had felt this kind of craving? he wondered, dizzily. When had the thought—the mere *thought*—of a kiss made his blood race and his body throb? He couldn't answer either question simply because he couldn't remember feeling this aroused in his entire life.

'Your son—did he drop out of school because he was ill?' Eleanor repeated, setting down the glass with a tiny clatter that made him jump.

'No.' Daniel took a deep breath as bile rose to his throat, the bitter taste of guilt and betrayal. How could he have imagined that what he had felt just now had been more potent than what he had felt for Camille? It was hard to hide his dismay as he continued. 'His mother died and it sent Nathan off the rails for a while. Thankfully, he got himself together in the end but it was a struggle. That's why he's my number one priority and always will be. I owe it to Camille to make sure our son has a happy and fulfilling life.'

CHAPTER SIX

ELLIE DIDN'T KNOW what to say. She had deliberately avoided delving into Daniel's personal life. It had seemed the sensible thing to do, to maintain her distance. However, finding out that his wife had died was a shock, even more so when she could tell by his expression that he was still grieving. Picking up the glass, she took another sip of wine while she searched for something to say but everything seemed trite. How did you offer comfort for such a huge loss?

'I'm sorry,' she finally managed.

Daniel inclined his head. 'Thank you.'

'I had no idea about your son. Or your wife.' All of a sudden Ellie felt that she should apologise for inadvertently upsetting him. 'I would never have asked you about Nathan if I'd known…' She tailed off, afraid of compounding her errors.

'It's fine. Really.'

He smiled but there was a bleakness in his eyes that told her it *did* matter, it mattered a lot. Ellie bit her lip but the words wouldn't come. Not the right ones, anyway, the ones that might make him feel better.

'It's OK, Eleanor. Honestly.' Leaning forward, he touched her hand. 'It's four years since Camille died.

I'm past the stage of bursting into tears if her name is mentioned.'

'It must be hard, though,' Ellie said quietly.

'It is. But you learn to accept what's happened after a time, and that helps.' He gave her fingers a gentle squeeze then let her go. 'Having Nathan has helped as well. I've had to focus on him, especially in the beginning. It hit him extremely hard.'

'He's all right now, though?' she queried. Funnily enough, she realised that she wanted to know everything now, every little detail that she hadn't wanted to hear before, although she wasn't sure why.

'Oh, yes. He's got his act together and is planning to go to university next year if he gets the grades. And that is something I never thought would happen a couple of years ago.'

'Good. I'm glad everything has worked out,' she said truthfully.

'Thank you. But how about you? Are you over whatever caused you to move up here?'

'How did you know?' she began, then stopped when she realised how revealing it was.

'That something bad had happened to you?' He sighed. 'Most people don't abandon a promising career and move hundreds of miles away from everything they know unless they're trying to escape from a very painful situation, Eleanor. It doesn't take a genius to work it out, does it?'

'I suppose not,' she conceded.

'So, do you want to talk about it?' He smiled at her, his eyes filled with warmth. 'I'm a good listener, I promise you.'

'There's not a lot to talk about.' She shrugged, not sure if she wanted to disclose all the unsavoury details.

Would it help or would it make her feel even worse if Daniel knew how she had been humiliated? It was hard to decide yet in the end the words came tumbling out, almost as though she needed to rid herself of them. 'It's an all too familiar story, I'm afraid. I was engaged to be married until I discovered that my fiancé was sleeping with someone else.'

'It must have been a shock even if you aren't the first woman it's happened to,' Daniel said gently.

'It was, although I should have realised that something was going on.' She gave a bitter laugh. 'The signs were all there. I just failed to read them properly!'

Daniel frowned. 'What do you mean?'

'That Michael—my ex—had been behaving strangely for months, cancelling dates or claiming that he was meeting friends for a drink. I just accepted what he said without questioning it, more fool me!'

'It's easy to be wise after the event,' he said quietly. 'But you were engaged so it was only natural that you believed him.'

'That's what my parents said.' Ellie sighed. 'I felt such a fool, though, especially when Gemma said that it had been clear to everyone that Michael had been leading me on.'

'Not the kindest thing to have said,' Daniel observed, frowning. 'Who's Gemma?'

'My sister. Or, to be absolutely correct, my adopted sister, although that isn't right either as I'm the one who was adopted.' Ellie realised that she wasn't making much sense but talking about what had happened wasn't easy. She took a deep breath, forcing herself to speak calmly and rationally. Daniel didn't need her gibbering on like an emotional wreck.

'I was adopted as a baby, you see. Apparently, my

parents had given up any hope of having a child of their own so they decided to adopt. Then, eight years later, Mum discovered she was pregnant and along came Gemma.'

'I see. And how did you two get on? Were you close?'

'Not really. We were very different even as children. I was rather shy and introverted, whereas Gemma was far more outgoing. Oh, my parents did their best not to show any favouritism but they couldn't help it. Gemma was the child they had longed for and they adored her.'

'Did you resent it, that they appeared to love her more than you?' Daniel said softly.

'I'm not sure resent is the right word,' Ellie said, slowly. Funnily enough, she had never tried to work out how she felt about the family dynamics before. 'I suppose I just accepted that was how things were. My parents loved me, and I knew it, but they loved Gemma more. The only thing I can remember thinking was that I had to be better behaved than Gemma.'

'You felt that you had to earn their love?' Daniel observed, and she frowned.

'I suppose so.' She looked up and felt her heart lurch when she saw the way he was looking at her with such concern. Daniel cared about what she was telling him. He cared about *her*. The thought unlocked the last of her reservations. 'Gemma and I didn't see very much of each other once I went to university—she had her life and I had mine. I introduced Michael to her when I took him home to meet my family and they seemed to get along well enough. I had no idea she had reservations about him.'

'Where did you meet him?'

'At work. He was a junior partner, the same as me.' She shrugged. 'To be honest, I didn't take to him at first.

He had very strong views and could be, well, rather bombastic at times. Then the head of the practice invited us both to dinner one night and things progressed from there.'

She paused, needing a moment before she told Daniel the rest. 'Anyway, we started seeing one another and eventually became engaged. Michael used to joke that it would be good for his career as the senior partners were very keen on folk being married rather than merely living together. They thought it lent stability to the practice.'

'Hmm. I see,' Daniel said dryly, and she sighed.

'You're wondering if that was the reason he was so keen to get engaged, aren't you?' She didn't wait for him to answer. 'I've wondered that myself so I don't blame you, although it's not very flattering to think that there was an ulterior motive behind it all.'

'What happened to cause you to break up?' he asked quietly.

'I found him in bed with one of the practice nurses. It was a Saturday morning. Michael had told me that he was going out for a drink with a couple of friends from university on the Friday night so I decided to surprise him—take him some coffee in case he had overindulged and generally minister to him. I had a key to his flat so I let myself in and headed upstairs.' Ellie felt tears start to stream down her face as she recalled the moment when her life had fallen apart. 'They were in his bedroom. The door was open and as I went up the stairs, I could see him and Stacey in bed. It didn't take a genius to work out that they'd spent the night together!'

Daniel acted instinctively. Standing up, he went over to her and drew her up into his arms. He couldn't begin to describe how horrified he felt by what he had heard.

That anyone could treat her that way was beyond his comprehension. All he could do was try to comfort her any way he could. Tilting her face, he wiped away her tears with his fingers, murmuring to her under his breath.

'It's all right. I know it must hurt like crazy right now, but it will get easier, believe me.'

'Will it?' She looked at him and his heart ached when he saw the plea in her dove-grey eyes. She was desperate for reassurance and somehow he had to find a way to convince her that she would get past this low point in her life.

'Yes. No matter how painful it is at the moment, it will get better.' A single tear dripped off her lashes and he wiped it away with his fingertips. Her skin felt so soft, as soft and as smooth as satin, and a jolt of awareness flashed through him. He knew that he was stepping into dangerous territory, yet it was impossible to relinquish his hold on her when she needed to be held so much. 'You just need time, Eleanor, that's all. Time to put it all behind you. Then, when you meet someone else, it will no longer matter.'

She was shaking her head before he had finished speaking. 'I don't want to meet anyone else. I've no intention of putting myself in the same position again.'

'You'll change your mind,' he demurred. 'Once you've had a chance to put this into perspective, it will be a very different story.'

'I doubt it!' Her eyes blazed up at him. 'I know exactly what I intend to do with my life and it doesn't involve being at the beck and call of any man. From now on I intend to answer to one person only: me!'

She stepped back, effectively breaking his hold on her. Daniel felt a wave of sadness wash over him. Eleanor was turning her back on love. She planned to live her life on her own, never marry and probably never have a family either. He couldn't bear to imagine her leading such a lonely existence.

'Eleanor,' he began, then stopped when his phone rang. Taking it out of his pocket, he felt his stomach sink when he discovered it was Nathan calling. Basketball practice wasn't due to finish for another half-hour and he couldn't help worrying what was wrong. 'Is everything all right?' he demanded, turning away while he answered the call. He felt his anxiety subside as Nathan explained why he was phoning. 'OK, I'll be there as soon as I can.'

He ended the call and turned to Eleanor. 'That was Nathan. They've finished early because the lights in the gym have fused. I'll have to go and fetch him.'

'Of course.'

She led the way from the room and Daniel could tell that she was making an effort to collect herself. That she regretted her outburst was obvious and he sighed. Eleanor had grown used to hiding her feelings while she had been growing up but he wasn't convinced it was a good thing. Sometimes it did more harm than good to bottle things up, although he doubted if she would appreciate him telling her that. He was trying to rid himself of the thought of how lonely she was going to be if she carried out her plan when she turned to him.

'What about the keys?'

'Oh. Yes, of course.' Daniel took them out of his pocket, silently berating himself for forgetting the reason why he had come. He'd got so caught up in Eleanor's affairs that it had slipped his mind. 'It's quite straightforward,' he said hurriedly. 'The Yale key unlocks the front door and the other one is for the back.

The alarm cupboard is behind the reception desk and the code is 7826. You just need to key it in and that'll stop the alarm going off.'

Daniel busied himself with practicalities, relieved to have something else to focus on. He'd had his doubts about her moving abroad and, after what she had told him, he was less convinced than ever that it was a good idea. However, it wasn't his place to tell her that. At the end of the day, it wasn't as though he could offer her an alternative, not just a job but a life that wouldn't mean her being on her own. He must never forget that Nathan came first.

The thought was strangely disquieting and he hurried on. 'Would you like me to write it down for you?'

'There's no need,' she said quietly. '7826—I'll remember it.'

'Excellent!' Daniel winced when heard the falsely hearty note in his voice but there was nothing he could do about it. Eleanor had opened the door and it was clear that she expected him to leave now that he had done what he had come for.

Zipping up his coat, he went to step past her, pausing when she said quietly, 'Drive carefully. The wind's really strong tonight.'

'I will.' He wasn't sure what prompted him to do what he did next. Maybe it was her unexpected show of concern but he bent and kissed her on the cheek. His lips lingered for the briefest of moments before he drew back, but he could feel the impact of what he had done spreading throughout his entire body. 'Goodnight, Eleanor,' he said, his voice sounding so strained that it was like hearing a stranger's voice, but in a way that was what he was, a stranger to himself, a person he no longer recognised.

'Goodnight.'

Her voice drifted after him as he ran down the steps. It seemed to follow him as he made his way round to the car park. Daniel got into his car then sat staring through the windscreen. After Camille had died, he had felt numb. The long months they had spent fighting the cancer that had eventually claimed her had left him drained. There had been nothing left inside him, not even anger at the fact that he had lost the woman he had loved. The only emotion he'd felt had been the need to protect Nathan. Oh, he had cared about his patients and had wanted to do his best for them, but, personally, he had felt nothing. Wanted nothing. Needed nothing. But not any longer.

Daniel drove out of the car park, forcing himself to concentrate as he drove along the narrow winding roads. He couldn't afford to let his mind wander, mustn't allow himself to think about what *he* wanted now. In a few months' time Eleanor would leave Beesdale, leave *him*, and go heaven knew where. That was all he needed to know.

Ellie was already in her room when Daniel arrived at the surgery the following morning. She had spent a restless night, going over what had happened, but she still wasn't sure why he had kissed her. Had it been a token gesture, like those meaningless kisses everyone exchanged on meeting or parting nowadays? Or had it been an attempt to comfort her after what she had told him? She could make a case for either and yet Daniel didn't strike her as a man who went in for kissing women in an ad hoc fashion. On the contrary, he was the kind of man who only kissed a woman when he meant it.

A frisson ran through her and she jumped up. Going over to the cupboard, she checked the shelves to make sure that she had everything she needed. She mustn't make the mistake of thinking that Daniel had kissed her because he had wanted to kiss *her*. As she knew to her cost, men were experts at disguising the truth!

'Good morning. Looks as though it's going to be another busy day. We already have a queue out there.'

Ellie swung round when she heard Daniel's voice. He was standing in the doorway and there was something about the way he was looking at her, a kind of wariness to his expression that made her heart surge. Had he been thinking about that kiss as well? Thinking about it and remembering how it had felt? For if she had spent time trying to work out why it had happened, she had spent an equal amount of time recalling how his lips had felt when they had touched her cheek…

A shudder ran through her and she gripped hold of the shelf when she felt her legs start to tremble. The memory of how warm his lips had felt as they had brushed her cheek had imprinted itself into her mind and it would take a long time before she rid herself of the memory. 'Ahem…yes. It looks like it,' she murmured, struggling to get a grip.

'Well, I'd better make a start. I don't want to create a backlog so early in the day.'

He gave her a quick smile then left and she heard his footsteps echoing along the corridor. Ellie went and sat down at her desk, refusing to let herself think any more about that kiss or its whys and wherefores. It had happened. Period. Pressing the button, she summoned her first patient, determined to put the incident behind her. However, in her heart she knew it wouldn't be possible to do that. That kiss had changed things, changed her, even though she wasn't sure how.

Her first patient was Nigel Walsh. A good-looking man in his forties, he cut an imposing figure, somewhat belied by the anxiety on his face as he sat down. 'So what can I do for you today, Mr Walsh?' Ellie asked, smiling at him. It was surprising how nervous even the most confident of people could become when they needed to consult a doctor and she wanted to put him at his ease.

'I've not come about me.' Nigel Walsh leant forward, looking even more strained. 'It's my wife, Madeleine. I'm extremely worried about her and that's why I've come to see you.'

'I'm afraid I can't discuss another patient with you, not even if it's your wife,' Ellie explained gently.

'What if I tell you that I'm afraid she's going to really harm herself?' Nigel Walsh ran his hand through his perfectly groomed hair. 'I'm at my wits' end, Doctor. I have no idea what to do or how to help her.'

Ellie frowned. This definitely wasn't what she had expected to hear. 'Why do you think she may harm herself?'

'Because her behaviour is getting worse. At first it was just cutting herself, but in the last few months it's been spiralling out of control. She threw herself down the stairs last week and then, yesterday, I found her in the kitchen, holding her arm over the gas ring…' He broke off and gulped. 'I don't think I can take much more. And then there's Alice. What's it doing to her to see her mother doing all these things to herself?'

'Does your wife have a history of self-harm?' Eleanor asked, feeling in a real quandary. Patient confidentiality meant that she shouldn't discuss Mrs Walsh's behaviour even with her husband; however, if what he said was true, it appeared the woman urgently needed help.

'Oh, yes. According to her parents it started when she was a teenager but she had counselling and she was all right after that. Then, after we had Alice, it started up again, just little things at first—cuts and bruises—clumsiness, Madeleine claimed. However, it's gone way beyond that now and I've no idea what to do for the best.'

'Have you tried to get her to see someone?' Ellie asked.

'Of course I have!' Walsh sounded angry now. 'I made an appointment for her to see a psychotherapist but she refused to go. That's why I've come today, to see if you can talk some sense into her.'

'I can certainly ask her to come in and see me,' Ellie said carefully. 'But if what you say is true, she really needs specialist help.'

'Of course it's true!' the man exploded. 'Why would I make up something like this? Oh, I get it. You think I've been abusing her and that's why she keeps turning up with all those injuries.' He leapt to his feet. 'Well, I am not a wife-beater, Doctor. Far from it!'

He stormed out of the room before Ellie could stop him. Jumping up, she ran after him but he had already left. She went back to her room, wondering what she should do. She couldn't leave it like this, not when there was the risk of Mrs Walsh doing herself serious harm. No, she would have to speak to Daniel and see what he thought was the best course of action. Her heart lurched at the thought of them working together to resolve this issue. Even though she knew it was foolish, she couldn't deny that the idea appealed…

Ellie sighed as she pressed the buzzer to summon her next patient. She had to stop thinking like that. Maybe she did like Daniel but it wouldn't progress beyond liking. She had made her plans for the future and love and all the rest of it didn't feature in them.

CHAPTER SEVEN

ELLIE WAS SURPRISED to find Daniel in the office when she went to file some requests for hospital appointments. It was gone six and the rest of the staff had left. He glanced round and she couldn't help noticing how tired he looked.

'I didn't know you were still here.'

'Snap.' She shrugged when he looked blankly at her, regretting her flippancy. She had decided that the best way to handle this situation was by maintaining a strictly professional demeanour whenever she was with him and remarks like that wouldn't help. Last night she had overstepped the boundaries by telling him about Michael and she needed to redress the balance. 'Actually, I'm glad you're still here,' she said more formally. 'I wanted to speak to you about something that happened this morning.'

'Oh, and what was that?' he asked, turning to face her. Ellie felt her heart give another of those unsettling little lurches as she suddenly found herself the subject of his attention. It was an effort to concentrate on what she wanted to say.

'I had a man come to see me this morning, not about himself but about his wife. Apparently, she's been self-harming and her behaviour is spiralling out of control.'

'Really?' Daniel frowned. 'I take it that she's a patient here?'

'Yes. Madeleine Walsh—do you know her?'

'I do. In fact, she came in only last week because she'd hurt her arm falling down the stairs. Turned out that it was just badly sprained but it could easily have been broken.' His expression darkened. 'I take it her husband is claiming that she did it to herself?'

'Yes. That's right. Why? Do you think he was lying?' Ellie asked, in surprise.

'I think it's possible. Walsh wouldn't be the first to lay the blame for his actions on his victim. It's an old trick, I hate to tell you.'

Ellie bridled when she heard what sounded very much like condescension in his voice. That Daniel believed she was too gullible to recognise the excuses some people used to cover up their behaviour stung. Michael had displayed the same high-handed attitude towards her at times, but she was nobody's fool and it was time Daniel understood that.

'I am well aware of that,' she said curtly. 'However, I don't believe that was what Mr Walsh was trying to do. He's genuinely worried about his wife, in my opinion, and I feel that I should take his concerns seriously. It's not just Mrs Walsh I need to think about, after all. They have a young child and I intend to ensure that she isn't put at risk. However, I apologise for involving you. I'll sort this out myself.'

Ellie spun round, refusing to stand there and beg Daniel to believe her. He would accept that she was right or he wouldn't, but it was up to him. No matter what he thought, she intended to do something about this situation.

'Wait!'

She stopped reluctantly when Daniel called her back, hating the fact that she felt so upset. Why should it matter if he thought she was wrong? It didn't make sense, or not the kind of sense she was willing to accept. Admitting that she cared what he thought about her was too dangerous; it hinted at a closeness she didn't want to foster. She'd had her chance at the happy-ever-after and it had failed. Miserably. She'd be a fool to dip her toes into that particular water again!

Daniel could have bitten off his tongue. It was obvious that he had upset Eleanor and that was the last thing he wanted to do. Nevertheless, he knew it would be wrong to let her carry on believing Walsh's claims when the man was undoubtedly playing her for a fool. The thought cranked up his anger another notch so that his tone was gruffer than it otherwise might have been.

'Why do you believe that Walsh was telling you the truth?' he said brusquely.

'It's obvious that you've made up your mind about him so I can't see any point in discussing it,' she shot back.

'Maybe not, but indulge me.' He stared at her, watching the angry colour flood her cheeks. Despite the fact that she gave off that aura of coolness, there was passion bubbling beneath the surface. The thought sent a flash of heat through him and he cleared his throat, afraid that he would give himself away. Knowing that Eleanor felt such passion was strangely erotic.

'I've never met Walsh so I'm basing my opinion on what Madeleine Walsh told me,' he said flatly, determined to get a grip on his emotions. He held up his hand when she went to interrupt. 'Just hear me out, will you? She seemed frightened when I suggested contacting her husband so he could drive her to hospital to have her wrist X-rayed. She was also deliberately vague at first about how she came to fall down the stairs. Then, when I pressed her, she went into all kinds of detail about how it had happened.'

'All classic signs of someone suffering abuse.' Eleanor sighed. 'There were a couple of cases where I worked before, a man and a woman who were being abused by their partners. It was hard to get them to admit what was happening so I could set things in motion and try to help them.'

'Exactly,' Daniel agreed, regretting his earlier comments more than ever. It appeared that Eleanor had experience of this type of situation so maybe he should listen to what she was saying and not jump to conclusions.

The thought that he was guilty of that hit him hard, especially coming on top of the guilt he already felt about what had happened the night before. Maybe that kiss had been no more than a token but it had aroused a lot of emotions inside him, guilt being the biggest one of all. How could he have kissed Eleanor like that? How could he have forgotten, even for a moment, about Camille? She had never even entered his head and he knew that the fact he had forgotten about her would continue to upset him.

'The situation is very similar with people who self-harm, though, isn't it? They go to great lengths to hide what they're doing too.' Eleanor's voice roused him and he nodded, relieved to think about something else.

'Yes, that's true. They're ashamed of their actions, even though they feel compelled to continue hurting themselves.'

'Then can't you see that Madeleine Walsh could fall

into that category…that she's self-harming rather than being abused?'

'I'll admit you could be right, although I'm still not convinced. Apparently, Nigel Walsh is a solicitor, a very good one from all accounts too. He must be adept at presenting his case,' Daniel observed, flatly, reluctant to concede that she was right. Maybe he was holding out as a kind of defence mechanism, refuting Eleanor's claims because he didn't want to side with her. He sighed, knowing he was wrong to allow his personal feelings to skew his judgement this way.

'Look, Eleanor—' he began, then stopped when the phone suddenly rang.

Lifting it off its rest, he listened intently to what the caller was saying. 'Right. I'll meet you there…' He stopped and listened again then glanced at Eleanor. 'I'll sort something out. Leave it with me.'

'Has something happened?'

Daniel turned when Eleanor spoke, doing his best to find a level. Maybe that kiss had knocked him for six but he had to put it into perspective. It had been just one moment out of his life, one tiny episode that would soon be forgotten if he didn't keep thinking about it. He had to let it go and not keep on poking at it like an aching tooth.

'There's been an incident,' he said, deliberately confining his thoughts to the present.

'An incident?' Ellie repeated, confused by the swift change of subject. One minute they had been discussing the Walshes and the next—this.

'Yes. A party of teenagers doing their Duke of Edinburgh Award left the hostel where they're staying just before eight this morning and they haven't been seen since.' Daniel sounded worried, as well he might, Ellie realised, glancing at her watch. Twelve hours was a long time for the youngsters to be out on the hills. She had no difficulty focusing on what he was saying as he continued.

'The staff who've accompanied them have checked the route they should have taken and they're nowhere to be found. We can only conclude that they've got themselves lost, which is why the mountain rescue team has been called in. I'm part of the team so I'll be going along but we need another doctor. Is there any chance that you'd come along, Eleanor?'

Daniel watched as one of the rescue team spread an Ordnance Survey map across the bonnet of the vehicle and weighted it down with stones. The wind was howling across the hills now, heralding the arrival of the storm that had been forecast that night. Quite frankly, the teenagers couldn't have chosen a worse time to have gone missing. He glanced at Eleanor and could tell that she was thinking the same as him. For some reason the thought sent a little thrill of pleasure coursing through him.

'Right, guys, gather round.' Joe Thorne, leader of the local cave and mountain rescue team, called them to order. Daniel hurriedly cleared his head of any more such foolish ideas as Joe pointed to a red line that had been marked on the map. He needed to focus rather than allow his mind to run off at tangents.

'That's the route the kids were supposed to take,' Joe explained. 'We know they followed it for several miles as one of their teachers found a water bottle belonging to the group. However, it appears that they wandered off course, probably around here.'

Daniel frowned when Joe pointed to the Witch's

Cauldron, so-called because the deep depression in the land was shaped like a gigantic bowl. Although the view from the surrounding cliffs might be spectacular, it was also one of the most dangerous places around. Rock falls were rife and many a walker had been caught out when the ground had given way beneath him.

'It's not going to be easy to get there let alone find them in this storm but we can't wait until the morning,' Joe continued. 'Although the teachers are adamant that the group are properly kitted out, I doubt if any of the kids has experience of being outside in weather like this. We need to find them and find them fast.'

There was a murmur of agreement from the team. Daniel knew they were all aware how quickly hypothermia could set in under these conditions. He turned to Eleanor, wanting to make sure that she understood the dangers too. 'Hypothermia is going to be our biggest problem, for us as well as for those kids. Your body temperature can drop before you're aware of it.'

'I understand.' Eleanor pulled the collar of the waterproof jacket around her neck. She didn't possess any waterproofs so Daniel had called at his house and collected an old set of Nathan's. The trousers were far too long for her but she had rolled them up and used string to tie them around her ankles. A pair of Nathan's outgrown walking boots, worn with several pairs of socks, had solved the problem of her footwear too. Daniel was as sure as he could be that she was suitably protected against the elements but he still intended to keep a watch over her. The last thing he wanted was her coming to any harm.

The thought made his stomach churn and he turned away, not wanting her to suspect how worried he felt. Not for the first time that night he found himself curs-

ing Bernard Hargreaves for refusing to come along. He
didn't believe the other man's claim that he wasn't feeling well. Bernard had been doing the bare minimum for
months now and Daniel knew that he would have to do
something about it. He had let it slide because he'd had
too much else to think about, what with Nathan and his
exams, and Beth going on maternity leave. Nevertheless, there was no way that the situation could continue
indefinitely. No way he would let it!

Once again, Daniel was surprised by the strength
of his reaction. He hadn't realised how flat he had felt
for the last few years. His concern for Nathan had used
up every scrap of energy he'd possessed and there had
been nothing left for anything else. Now, all of a sudden, he felt different, more alive, more in touch with
his feelings. It was as though he had surfaced from
some dark place and stepped back into the light. Was
it a good thing? He wasn't sure. In that dark place he'd
not had to think about himself, about his needs and his
desires; he'd only had to exist.

It was an unsettling thought so it was a relief when
Joe started to divide the group into teams. They could
cover more ground if they split up, although Daniel
wasn't happy at the idea of Eleanor being sent off with
someone else. She had no experience of this kind of terrain and he would never forgive himself if she got hurt
when he was responsible for her being there. He drew
Joe aside, wanting to make the position clear.

'I'm not happy about Eleanor wandering around in
this storm,' he said bluntly, not wasting any time. The
sooner they found the missing teenagers the better and
there was no point beating around the bush. 'I'd prefer
it if she stayed here at base.'

'I understand your concerns but surely the whole

point of her coming along was to act as back-up if more than one of the group is injured,' Joe pointed out. 'OK, we're all trained in first aid, but with Alan in hospital we don't have the medical know-how to deal with any serious injuries.'

Daniel knew he was right. Alan Hunter, a former paramedic and mainstay of the team, had suffered a heart attack a couple of weeks earlier and they hadn't found a replacement for him yet. It was the reason why Daniel had asked Eleanor to come along after Bernard had refused, and he could hardly go back on his decision. He sighed. 'All right, but can you keep an eye on her? She's no experience and I don't want her coming to any harm.'

'Don't you worry—she'll be perfectly safe. We're going to stick to the main path so it shouldn't be too difficult for her to keep up.'

Joe didn't say anything else but Daniel saw the look the other man gave him and felt himself colour. He turned away, refusing to speculate about what Joe was thinking. He would be equally concerned about anyone who had so little experience, he assured himself as he swung his backpack over his shoulder. However, even to his ears the claim had a hollow ring. He was concerned because it was Eleanor and, like it or not, she was special.

Eleanor trudged on, bracing herself against the wind. The storm was raging around them now, the rain forming horizontal sheets as it pelted across the hillside. She had never been out in weather like this before and she found it exhilarating to test herself against the elements. If she could survive this, she could survive anything!

'All right?'

She looked round when Joe Thorne came alongside her. 'Yes, although this wind is something else. I've never been out in a gale like this before.'

'Welcome to the Dales,' Joe replied, tongue very firmly tucked in his cheek. 'The weather here takes some getting used to but you're doing great.' He laughed. 'At least I don't need to worry about falling foul of the doc now. I got the impression he'd have my guts for garters if anything happened to you!'

He moved away, leaving Ellie to digest what he had said. Daniel had been worried about her—really? The thought sent a rush of warmth through her even though she knew how stupid it was. They trudged on for another mile or so. Ellie's legs were starting to ache now, unused to having to carry her over such rough terrain. When Joe called a halt she sank down onto a rock and rubbed her aching calves, determined that she was going to keep up with the others. The last thing she wanted was to be a burden to them, she thought, then glanced round when she heard what sounded like a shout coming from behind her. The rest of the team were gathered around Joe, checking the map, and didn't appear to have heard anything, and she frowned. Had she imagined it?

Ellie sat quite still, listening. The wind was howling now and it was difficult to hear anything above the noise it was making. She had just decided that it had been her imagination when she heard it again. Jumping up, she ran over to Joe. 'I heard a shout!' She pointed towards the rock she'd been sitting on. 'It seemed to come from over there.'

'Right, let's take a look.' Joe led the way, the others fanning out on either side of him. Ellie wasn't as quick as they were but she did her best to keep up. She gasped when she spotted a figure lying on the ground. Hurrying forward, she dropped to her knees beside the girl. She was soaking wet and shivering violently. It was obvious that she was in the first stages of hypothermia and Ellie knew that she urgently needed to warm her up.

'My name's Ellie and I'm a doctor,' she told her. 'What's your name?'

'Hannah.' The girl could hardly speak because her teeth were chattering.

'Right, Hannah, can you tell me if you've hurt yourself?'

'My ankle—I think I've broken it,' Hannah managed.

Ellie took a look at her right ankle while one of the team shone a torch onto it. She sighed when she saw how swollen it was. 'Hmm, it looks very painful. I won't try to remove your boot. We'll leave that until we get you to hospital as it will be less painful to do it there. Is there anything else—cuts, bruises, anything at all?'

'No, just my ankle. That's why I couldn't go back to find the others.' Hannah bit her lip as tears started to pour down her cheeks. 'I should never have gone off and left them then this wouldn't have happened!'

'Let's worry about that later,' Ellie said firmly. 'We need to get you warm at the moment.' Unzipping the girl's sodden jacket, she slid it off. Hannah was wearing a T-shirt underneath and it too was soaking wet.

'Get that off her as well, Doc,' Joe instructed, taking a thermal top from his backpack. He helped Ellie get it on the girl then added a fleece jacket over the top with a foil blanket over that. Within a remarkably short time, Hannah was being strapped to a stretcher. Ellie also helped to fit an inflatable splint around the girl's ankle to prevent it being jolted on the way to the rescue vehicle. Taking out his radio, Joe contacted the rest of the team to let them know what was happening and they set off.

Ellie could feel her legs trembling as she struggled to keep her footing on the rain-slick path. How the men carrying the stretcher managed to remain upright was beyond her. By the time they reached the vehicles she was exhausted but she had to find the reserves to keep going somehow. Until Hannah had been handed over to the team at the hospital, she was her responsibility. It took the best part of an hour to reach the hospital. Ellie kept a close watch on Hannah, knowing that she wasn't out of danger yet. Hypothermia could still set in and that was the last thing they wanted. It was a relief to finally hand her over to the A and E staff, who rushed her off to Resus. At least, the girl would receive the care she needed now.

'They've found the rest of the kids.' Joe came back into the waiting area after having gone outside to answer his phone. He grinned at Ellie and the others. 'They were sheltering in a cave close to the Witch's Cauldron. They're cold and wet but otherwise unharmed.'

'Thank heaven for that!' Ellie exclaimed. 'Have they said what happened?'

'Apparently, Hannah and another girl had an argument over one of the boys. It seems he's been playing the field and, when Hannah found out, she went storming off. When she didn't come back, the others tried to find her and got themselves lost.' Joe rolled his eyes. 'The course of true love has a lot to answer for!'

Everyone laughed, including Ellie, although she couldn't help thinking how true the comment was. Love could ruin a person's life, as she knew to her cost. It made her see that any thoughts she may have been harbouring about trying again in the future had been madness. Why expose herself to the risk of heartache all over again?

'Oh, by the way, Ellie, I told the doc that we'd drop you off at home. There didn't seem any point in him driving over here to collect you,' Joe told her as they left the hospital. 'I hope that was OK?'

'Of course.' Ellie dredged up a smile, not wanting Joe to suspect that she felt the tiniest bit disappointed. She took a quick breath, knowing how stupid it was. She had just decided that she was going to stick to her decision to focus on her career so what was the point of wishing she could have spent more time with Daniel? 'Thanks, Joe. I appreciate it.'

'No problem,' Joe said cheerfully, unlocking the car. They all piled in, squeezing into whatever space they could find. Ellie found herself tucked into a gap between the various piles of equipment. It wasn't the most comfortable of position but it was better than waiting around for Daniel, she assured herself. Just for a moment the image of his handsome face floated before her eyes before she blanked it out. She knew what she had to do and she wasn't going to change her mind. For anyone.

CHAPTER EIGHT

THE DAY OF Sandra and Tim's barbecue dawned bright and clear. After the recent rain, it was a relief to enjoy some dry weather for once. Everyone from the surgery had been invited and were looking forward to it. Sandra and Tim were excellent hosts and their barbecues were renowned as fun occasions. Daniel, however, had mixed feelings about the evening. Whilst it would be good to socialise with his friends and colleagues, he was wary of doing or saying the wrong thing around Eleanor.

There had been a marked chill about the way she had treated him since the night they had gone looking for the missing teenagers. Although she was unfailingly polite, she had made it clear that she preferred to keep her distance. He had no idea what he had done but it was obvious that he had upset her. The thought of spending the evening tiptoeing around her wasn't appealing, especially when he knew that if it had been anyone else he would have asked them what the matter was. However, for some reason he was wary of doing that with Eleanor. And his own ambivalence unsettled him even more.

Although it was a busy day, they finished on time for once. Daniel had offered to lock up so that Marie and the rest of the staff could rush off home to get changed.

He set the alarm then headed to his car. Nathan had been invited as well as he was friendly with Sandra and Tim's son, Jack. It wasn't often that Daniel got the chance to spend an evening with his son; between his college work and various sporting activities, Nathan was usually busy of an evening.

At any other time, Daniel knew that he would be looking forward to them having some time together, but Eleanor's attitude had cast a pall over the evening even though he knew it was ridiculous to let it affect him. So she didn't want to be friends with him—so what? As long as she did her job what did it matter? And yet deep down he knew that it did matter, that it mattered a great deal. He wanted to be her friend, to have her confide in him and turn to him for help, even though he couldn't understand why.

The party was in full swing by the time he and Nathan arrived. Sandra came to greet them, shaking her head. 'At last! I thought you two had got lost.'

'Sorry. My fault. I ended up sorting out some bills that I've been meaning to pay,' Daniel explained, aware that it was only partially true. Fair enough, he had ended up writing out some cheques but it had been more a delaying tactic than a necessity. His eyes skimmed over the people gathered in the garden and his heart sank when he spotted Eleanor. He had delayed leaving home because he had been reluctant to find himself on the receiving end of any more chilly treatment. How pathetic was that!

'There's Jack,' Nathan announced as Sandra excused herself to greet some more late arrivals. 'See you later, Dad.'

Daniel watched as his son headed over to where a group of youngsters had gathered. The sound of their laughter carried across to him and he sighed. Nathan seemed happy enough and now it was his turn to join the fray. Maybe he was persona non grata in Eleanor's eyes but he could hardly stand here on his own like Billy-no-mates, could he? Steeling himself, he headed over to the group from the surgery.

'Good evening, everyone,' he said, forcing himself to smile as he looked around. Marie was there with her husband, Ken, and Polly was with her fiancé, Martin. Lucy was there as well, although she was on her own as her boyfriend, James, a firefighter, was working that night. His gaze moved from one smiling face to another before it came to rest on Eleanor and he felt his heart sink even further when she nodded coolly at him. What on earth had he done to upset her?

Ellie felt her stomach churn. She had been dreading this moment when she would be forced to speak to Daniel, so much so that she had been tempted to phone Sandra and make some excuse as to why she couldn't go. However, the thought of spending the evening on her own had been an even worse prospect.

She had done her best to ignore the fact that it was her birthday, even going so far as to leave the card and present her parents had sent her unopened. She didn't need any reminders about how different this birthday was going to be compared to the last, but the downside was that she would have to socialise with Daniel and she wasn't sure if it was wise.

Oh, it had been easy enough in work; any conversations had been strictly confined to their patients. However, an occasion like this was very different. She would have to make the usual small talk and that was what worried her. The more she got to know Daniel, the more she grew to like him.

The conversation flowed on. Polly and Martin were getting married the following Easter and Lucy asked them about their plans. Marie chipped in, reminiscing about her own wedding many years earlier. Eleanor was happy to let them talk and merely listen. Although Daniel added the odd comment, he was almost as quiet as her, she noticed. She glanced at him and felt her heart leap when she met his eyes and saw the question they held. Was he wondering why she was behaving so distantly? She sensed it was true but there was no way she could explain that it was what she needed to do rather than run the risk of becoming involved with him. After all, Daniel hadn't given any sign that he was interested in her. On the contrary, he had made it clear that he was still very much in love with his late wife.

It was a depressing thought. Ellie was still trying to deal with it when Tim called for silence. 'Right, folks, I have it on good authority…' he paused and looked meaningfully at his wife before continuing '…that someone here tonight is celebrating a birthday. So I would like you all to join me in drinking a toast to Ellie. Happy birthday, love!'

Ellie flushed when everyone raised their glasses. She had forgotten that she had told Sandra it was her birthday that day and hadn't been prepared for this. Now she found her mind swooping back to the previous year before she could stop it. Michael had showered her with presents: roses and champagne at breakfast; lunch at a Michelin-starred restaurant; an evening at the Opera. Tears prickled her eyes as it struck her how very different this year was.

'Well, you certainly kept that quiet!' Marie declared, sounding put out. 'You never said a word about it being your birthday!'

'I didn't think it was worth making a fuss,' Ellie murmured, feeling guilty.

'Hmm, you still should have said something.' Stepping forward, she kissed Ellie on the cheek then wagged a finger at her. 'We'll let you off this time, so long as you bring in some cakes tomorrow. Deal?'

'Deal,' Ellie agreed, laughing. Ken kissed her as well, quickly followed by Polly and Martin, and then Lucy.

'Happy birthday, Eleanor.' Daniel stepped forward, hesitating only briefly before he bent and kissed her on the cheek. 'May the coming year bring you everything you want,' he said softly so that only she could hear.

He stepped back but it was several seconds before Ellie moved. She put her hand to her cheek, feeling her skin tingling where Daniel's lips had touched it. None of the other people's kisses had left its mark on her but Daniel's had. Why? What was so special about his kiss?

It was a relief when Tim announced the barbecue was ready. Ellie followed the others as people started to queue up. Daniel was ahead of her and her eyes lingered on the strong line of his back. He was a very attractive man so was that the reason she had reacted differently to his kiss? She could see the sense in that yet she had difficulty believing it. She had met other attractive men but not responded to them this way, had she? Why, even with Michael she hadn't felt the awareness she felt whenever she was around Daniel.

Although Michael was very good looking, she had never been overwhelmed by desire for him. In fact, she knew that Michael had grown impatient when she had refused to sleep with him at first, but she had been unwilling to compromise her views. After a couple of less than satisfying relationships, she had decided that sex needed commitment for it to mean anything. Admittedly, she had never found it that fulfilling when she and Michael had finally made love after they'd got engaged, but she had told herself it would get better with time. Now, all of a sudden, she found herself wondering if she'd been wrong, if it wasn't commitment that made a difference but the person. If she slept with Daniel, for instance, wouldn't it feel wonderful? The thought shocked her so much that she found it impossible to focus on what was happening. When Daniel turned and handed her a plate, she stared blankly at it.

'Are you all right, Eleanor?'

His deep voice rumbled softly, stirring her already heightened senses, and Ellie shivered. What would Daniel think if he knew what thoughts were going on inside her head? Would he be shocked or merely accept them as any experienced adult would do? Had she been naïve to believe that sex could only be enjoyed within certain boundaries? Wrong to assume that it needed commitment to make it feel right? She took a deep breath, trying to contain a rush of fear as the next question flowed into her head: Was it time she found out?

Daniel had no idea what was going on but the expression on Eleanor's face worried him. Taking the plate out of her unresisting hand, he placed it back on the pile then led her from the queue. Fortunately, the others were too interested in their supper to notice what was happening as he steered her across the garden to the old wooden gazebo. 'Sit down.' He eased her down onto the seat and sat beside her. Sandra had placed tea-lights in jam jars around the garden and they gave out just enough light to see by. Bending forward, he stared into Eleanor's face. 'Are you feeling all right? You seem a bit, well…out of it.'

'I'm fine.' Her voice was so low that he had trouble hearing her.

'Are you sure?' Maybe it was wrong to press her but all of a sudden he needed to know what he had done to upset her. 'You've not seemed yourself for a while, I have to say.'

'Haven't I?' she murmured, avoiding his eyes.

Daniel's breath caught when he realised that she understood exactly what he meant. So it wasn't his imagination, she *had* been keeping him at arm's length, although he was no closer to knowing why. 'No. You've been very distant since the night we went looking for those teenagers,' he said quietly. 'Did I do something to upset you?'

'Of course not.' She gave a little shrug. 'I just think it's better if I focus on my job. That's all.'

'Better? In which way?' he prompted, wanting to understand what she was saying.

'Better than getting involved,' she said flatly. 'I'm only going to be here for a few months and after that I'll go somewhere else. I don't want any…complications, quite frankly.'

Daniel wasn't sure what to say. Oh, he could appreciate her logic—he didn't need any complications in his life at the moment either. He had enough on his plate. However, the thought of her cutting herself off this way was more than he could bear.

'I don't see how it would complicate matters if we were friends, Eleanor.'

'Maybe not.' She shrugged. 'However, I'd prefer it if we stick to being colleagues.'

'Doesn't that seem a little harsh?' he suggested, his heart aching at the thought of how lonely she was going to be if she continued behaving that way. 'Everyone needs friends, people they can rely on in a crisis.'

'I don't.' She stared back at him, her face set. 'I just want to be left alone to get on with my job.'

'Oh, Eleanor!' Daniel wasn't sure why it hurt so much to hear her say that but the thought of the joyless existence it would lead to was more than he could stand. Reaching out, he grasped her by the shoulders, 'I know you've been badly hurt. And I know that today of all days—your birthday—it must make it even harder, but cutting yourself off isn't the way. You have your whole life ahead of you and you need more than work to fill it!'

Pulling her to him, he hugged her, wanting to show her what she would miss. Turning her back on love was bad enough but rejecting any offers of friendship as well was just too much and he needed to make her understand that. Her body felt so tense as he held her to him, resisting his attempts to convince her, and he groaned in frustration. He had to make her see what a terrible mistake she was making!

Whether it was that thought that spurred him on, but all of a sudden Daniel found himself bending towards her. He hadn't meant it to go any further than a hug yet the moment his mouth touched hers, he was lost. Her lips were cool from the night air, cool and as unresponsive as the rest of her, and his heart ached all the harder. It was as though she had packed up all her emotions and thrown them away. The thought of how hurt she must have been to have done that brought a lump to his throat. If he could do just one thing then he wished with all his heart that he could set her free.

'I think I saw your father heading towards the gazebo, Nathan.' Sandra's voice carried clearly on the night air. Daniel jumped as he was brought back to the present with a rush. He just had time to let Eleanor go before Nathan appeared.

'Oh, sorry—I didn't mean to interrupt,' Nathan said when he saw Eleanor.

'You didn't. Eleanor and I were just discussing a few things,' Daniel said, grateful for the fact that the dim lighting hid his discomfort. He didn't dare to imagine what his son would have thought if he had found him *kissing* Eleanor. It would have seemed like the ultimate betrayal of his mother and Daniel couldn't bear to think about the effect it might have had on him. The last thing he wanted was for Nathan's world to be turned upside down at this stage.

'You two haven't met yet, have you?' he said, hurrying on. 'Eleanor this is my son, Nathan. Eleanor is covering Beth's maternity leave,' he explained for Nathan's benefit.

'Hi, there. Good to meet you.' Nathan smiled and Daniel was relieved. Obviously, Nathan didn't suspect that anything had been going on.

'You too,' she murmured politely.

Daniel felt the tiny hairs on the back of his neck stand to attention when he heard the quaver in her voice. Was she shocked by what had happened? he wondered. And yet it wasn't shock he could hear in her voice but something else, an emotion that eluded him… It was an effort to drag his thoughts together when he realised that Nathan was saying something. 'Sorry, what was that?'

'Jack and the rest of the guys are going into town,' Nathan repeated. 'There's a band playing at the Fox and Goose so we thought we'd check it out. Jack says I can stay here tonight so you don't need to wait for us to get back.'

'Fine. Just be careful what you're doing,' Daniel said,

trying to clamp down on a familiar rush of alarm. Nathan had come a long way since the days when he had got himself into trouble, he reminded himself, and *he* had to trust him.

'Will do.' Nathan sketched them a wave then headed back to his friends. A couple of minutes later they departed.

Eleanor suddenly stood up. 'I think I'll go and sample the barbecue,' she said, avoiding his eyes.

'Good idea.'

Daniel stood up as well, at a loss to know what to do. Should he apologise for kissing her or should he ignore what had happened? The kiss had caught him unawares because he hadn't planned on it happening... Had he?

Heat fizzed along his veins as he realised with mind-boggling honesty that he had thought about kissing Eleanor more than once in the past few weeks. Oh, he hadn't planned it, per se. There had been no set time or date when it would happen, but the idea had started to set down roots. Kissing her on the cheek when he had visited her at the flat and then again tonight when he had wished her happy birthday had been mere forerunners to the main event. If Nathan hadn't appeared then he would have carried on kissing her until he had received a response, until her lips had softened, warmed, kissed him back. That was what he'd wanted, of course. He'd wanted her to respond, wanted to break down her defences and admit that she was wrong to cut herself off from everyone. Especially him.

The thought hit him with the force of a physical blow. Daniel sank back down onto the bench. There had been nothing altruistic about that kiss—it had been wholly selfish. He had kissed her because he had wanted Eleanor to respond to *him*. But what good would it do to encourage her to rely on him? What could he offer her when he had Nathan to think about? He took a deep breath but the facts had to be faced. He could end up hurting her and that was the last thing he must do.

CHAPTER NINE

ELEANOR COULDN'T SHAKE off the memory of what had happened. Oh, she tried, she tried everything she could think of, but the taste and feel of Daniel's mouth had imprinted itself into her consciousness. Finally, at four a.m. she got up and made herself a cup of tea, hoping that the age-old panacea would help her put it into perspective. It had been a kiss, a very brief one too, not something to get worked up about. And yet there was no way she could pretend that it hadn't had an effect on her, no way at all that she could simply brush it aside. Daniel had kissed her and if they hadn't been interrupted then she would have responded.

Carrying the steaming mug into the sitting room, she curled up on the sofa. That was the real nub of the problem, of course—the fact that despite everything she would have responded. She could lie to herself and pretend it wouldn't have happened but what was the point? Surprise may have held her immobile at first but she knew that she would have kissed him back and with passion too. She'd felt her desire suddenly awaken and it shocked her that she should have felt so strongly about Daniel's kiss when she had felt so little whenever Michael had kissed her. She'd thought she had loved

Michael but had she? Really? Or had it been more a case of loving the *idea* of having someone special in her life?

Questions rampaged around inside her head and she closed her eyes as she tried to deal with them. Had Michael sensed that something hadn't been right with their relationship? Heaven knew, the sex hadn't been that wonderful for him as well as her, so had she been guilty of short changing him, of driving him into Stacey's arms through her own shortcomings? She didn't want to believe it but she couldn't deny it either. She had never really enjoyed sex, never experienced an overwhelming desire for intimacy. She had gone through the motions but, deep down, it had left her cold. But not tonight. Not when Daniel had kissed her. For the first time ever she had felt emotionally engaged and it scared her.

Ellie opened her eyes. She hadn't switched on any lights and, through the window, she could see the moonlight gleaming off the surrounding hills. The scene was devoid of colour, like a photographic negative. It was a bit like how she had always felt, flat and colourless, but was it how she wanted to feel for the rest of her life? Was Daniel right to insist that she should want more, that she *needed* more? Was she really content to continue living this half-existence, always feeling as though she had been relegated to the sidelines rather than being centre stage?

Her head ached as the questions pounded inside it. Ellie knew that she needed to think long and hard before she reached a decision. She needed to be absolutely sure she was doing the right thing before she made any more changes to her life. After all, she had a lot to lose. The thought of suffering another humiliation was more than she could bear but that's what she would risk if she stepped off the sidelines. Was it really worth it? She wished she knew.

A week passed, the days zipping past at a rate of knots. The weather had changed again, becoming bitterly cold. Ellie dealt with a number of patients suffering from chest infections. Some were long-term problems, borne with a kind of weary stoicism that she came to admire. The people of the Dales were not the sort to make a fuss. Ninety-year-old Arnold Brimsdale was her final patient on the Friday morning. He came marching into the room, wheezing heavily as he sat down on the chair. A wiry old man with a full head of iron-grey hair, he fixed her with a piercing stare.

'Morning, Doctor. I've not had the pleasure of meeting you before. Marie says that you're filling in for Dr Andrews while she's off looking after her young 'un.'

'That's right.' Ellie reached across the desk and shook the old man's hand. 'Nice to meet you, Mr Brimsdale. What can I do to help today?'

'Oh, it's me chest again. This cold snap's playing havoc with me breathing.'

'I see from your notes that you have chronic bronchitis,' Ellie observed.

'Aye, that's right.' Arnold Brimsdale sighed. 'Like so many lads of my generation, I took to smoking in a big way. We had no idea the damage it could cause, you see. Folk didn't in them days. Anyway, add that to the fact that I used to work in one of the borrow pits—digging out sand and aggregates—and my lungs took a fair hammering. There was no such thing as health and safety in them days. You just got on with the job.'

'How long did you work in the pit?' Ellie asked curiously, thinking what a hard life it must have been.

'Twenty-odd years, till me dad died and I decided I'd had enough.' He shrugged. 'You didn't get a choice back then. Your dad decided where you'd work and that was it. But once he'd gone I left the pit and got a job on a farm. Best thing I ever done. All that fresh air to breathe instead of muck—' He broke off and smiled. 'Anyways, I shan't bore you with all that, Doctor. Suffice to say that it felt as though I'd died and gone to heaven. The pity is that the years I'd spent in the pit had left their mark, although I'm better off than a lot of folk. Not so many of me pals has got to be ninety.'

'I'm sure they haven't,' Ellie agreed, admiring the old man's positive take on life. Maybe he had suffered some major setbacks but he had come through them in the end. Perhaps she could do the same?

Ellie pushed that thought to the back of her mind as she listened to Arnold's chest. It soon became apparent that he had quite a severe chest infection, something he was prone to because of his bronchitis. She filled in a script for antibiotics and emailed it to the pharmacy so that it would be ready for him to collect before he left. He used an inhaler but she could see from his notes that he had renewed his prescription the previous month so that was covered. She saw him out, holding the door open for him. There was no doubt that he was a gutsy old man and the thought that she needed to adopt a more positive approach to life reared up again.

She sighed as she went back to her desk to clear up. At some point soon she would have to make a decision about what she was going to do, either stick to her plan to focus strictly on her career or accept that she needed more than just work to fill her life, as Daniel believed.

It wasn't going to be easy. There were advantages to both, as well as drawbacks, but she needed to make the right decision. She couldn't bear to think that at some point she might come to regret her actions.

Daniel had steered clear of Eleanor since the night of the barbecue. The thought that he could end up hurting her, albeit unintentionally, had made him wary of spending time around her. It wasn't difficult to keep out of her way in work; they were both so busy that it was easy enough to avoid her. Outside working hours, too, his free time was limited. Although Nathan travelled to and from college by bus, if he stayed late to take part in some sort of activity, Daniel needed to collect him. During the episode when he had run amok, Nathan had got involved in joy-riding and he had been banned from driving until he reached the age of twenty. It meant that Daniel had to ferry him here and there, but he was glad to do it, especially at the moment. It meant that he could claim, quite legitimately, that he was far too busy for a social life.

The weekend dawned, dry but cold. A field trip had been arranged for the students in Nathan's year who were studying medieval history. They were off to York before travelling on the following day to Chester. Daniel had offered to drop off both Nathan and Jack at the college so he drove them there and left them outside the gates, waiting for the coach to arrive. It was still early and the town was just preparing for the day. Saturday was market day and the stall holders were setting up.

For some reason Daniel felt reluctant to go straight back home. There was nothing urgent that needed doing and the thought of going back to an empty house held little appeal. He decided to have a coffee then buy some local produce. One of the farms made some wonderful cheeses and he fancied some with a glass of wine that evening.

The coffee shop was just opening up and he was their first customer. He ordered a double espresso and a croissant then sat down near the window. There were a few more people about now, shoppers eager to get some early bargains. Daniel watched a harassed-looking young mum pushing a pram over the cobbles. She had a toddler with her and he was intent on running off. Daniel's heart lurched when the child suddenly made a bid for freedom and ran into the road, straight into the path of a van that was backing up. Daniel shot from his seat and raced out of the café but before he could reach the child, a woman ran into the road and scooped him up. He could only see the back of her as she carried him back to his distraught mother so it wasn't until she turned round that he realised it was Eleanor.

He went to meet her as she walked back across the street, taking note of the pallor of her skin. That she'd had a shock at the near-miss was obvious. Instinctively, he placed his hand under her elbow as she came to a halt beside him. 'Are you OK?' he said solicitously, bending toward her.

'Daniel!' she exclaimed, staring at him in confusion. 'What are you doing here?'

'I was in the café when I saw what was happening. Talk about a close shave…'

'I know.' She shuddered, her face turning even paler. 'I didn't think I'd get to him in time.'

'But you did.' He smiled at her. 'Let's hope his mum puts some reins on him. He might not be so lucky next time.'

'Don't!'

She still looked deeply shaken and, despite every reservation he had, Daniel couldn't leave it there. How could he simply walk away when she'd had a shock like that? Taking a firmer grip on her arm, he steered her toward the café. 'What you need is a dose of caffeine,' he said firmly, ignoring all the warning bells that were clanging away inside him. It was what he would do for anyone, he reasoned, make sure they took time to re-cover before they went on their way. However, deep down he knew that the fact it was Eleanor who needed his help made a world of difference.

'Oh, but, you must have things to do.' She bit her lip and he could tell that she was doing her best not to let him see just how shaken up she felt. 'I'm fine—really I am.'

'Then why are you trembling?' He sighed when she didn't say anything. 'It's just a coffee, Eleanor, nothing more than that. I understand how you feel, believe me.'

Ellie flushed, realising how ridiculously she was be-having. Daniel was right because it had been a shock when she'd seen the child run out into the road… An-other shudder passed through her. When Daniel opened the café door and ushered her inside, she didn't protest any more. He sat her down near the window then went to the counter. He came back a moment later, unwind-ing his scarf as he sat down.

'I've ordered you a flat white—I hope that's all right?'

'Yes, fine. Thank you.' Reaching up, she pulled off her knitted hat and placed it on the table. Normally, she never wore a hat but it was much colder here than it was down south, plus her hair was so short that she felt the chill more acutely. Running her fingers through the short black strands, she smoothed them into place as best she could.

'Here.' Reaching out, Daniel smoothed down a strand of hair that had escaped her attentions then smiled at her. 'That's better. All nice and tidy now.'

'I…erm…thank you,' Ellie muttered, feeling heat well up inside her. She hurriedly unzipped her coat and shrugged it off, hoping he would attribute her heightened colour to the layers of clothing she was wearing. No way did she want him to guess that it was his touch that had caused it.

'So what are you doing here, apart from rescuing escaping children?' he asked after the waitress had brought over their drinks.

'I thought I'd visit the market,' she explained. 'Marie said that it sells mainly local produce and I thought I'd sample what's on offer.'

'It's renowned throughout the Dales for its produce,' Daniel agreed. Picking up his cup, he took a sip of his coffee. Ellie bit her lip when she saw the sheen of moisture on his mouth as he lowered the cup. All of a sudden all she could think about was how his lips would taste if he kissed her. Would they be flavoured by the coffee, perhaps? Rich and fragrant from the aromatic beans? It was an effort to concentrate as he continued.

'The cheese stall is exceptionally good. They sell a wide range of cheeses made by local farmers and they'd give anything produced on the Continent a run for their money.' He laughed as he kissed his fingertips. 'One of their blue cheeses in particular is *magnifique*!'

Despite herself, Ellie found herself laughing. 'Obviously you're something of a connoisseur. You'll have to write down the name of it for me. My cheese buying has been confined to whatever the supermarket has in stock up till now.'

Daniel rolled his eyes. 'Your education has been

sorely lacking! We'll have to do something about it. How's your coffee? Not too strong, I hope?'

'No. It's fine,' Ellie assured him, although normally she would have chosen something less potent. When he picked up the plate and offered her the croissant, she shook her head. 'No. That's yours.'

'We'll share then.' Daniel tore the flaky pastry apart, placing his half on a paper napkin before setting the plate in front of her. 'Come along, eat up. Carbs are very good for shock.'

'Not so good for the figure,' Ellie countered ruefully, biting into the buttery rich pastry.

'Not something you need to worry about,' Daniel declared, taking an appreciative bite out of his half.

Ellie concentrated on the pastry, refusing to let the compliment affect her. Daniel thought she had a good figure—so what? However, no matter how hard she tried to dismiss the remark, it refused to go quietly. It settled into a tiny corner of her mind and stayed there. By the time they had finished their coffee, several more people had come into the café. Daniel smiled and nodded as everyone wished him good morning. He grimaced as he looked over at Ellie.

'The downside of being the local GP is that everyone knows you. There's no chance of being anonymous!'

'It's rather nice, though, isn't it?' Ellie said slowly. She shrugged when he looked at her in surprise. 'It must make you feel…well, a sort of *connection* to the people who live here.'

'That's true.' He glanced around the café then turned back to her. 'Being part of people's lives is a privilege, I always think. It also makes it easier when they have a problem. They already know me so there isn't that need to gain their trust—it's already there.'

'It's very different from where I worked before,' Ellie admitted. 'The population changed very rapidly as people moved in and out of the town. It was rare that we got to know our patients.'

'It makes it harder for the doctors as well as the patients, don't you think? People are reluctant to open up when they don't know you and it makes it all the more difficult to get to the root of their problems.'

'It does.' Ellie was surprised that he understood the drawbacks. 'I didn't think you'd understand that with working here.'

'I worked at an inner city practice before I moved here,' he explained. 'Even then, the population tended to fluctuate, and it must be much worse now when people travel about to find work.'

'Is that why you came to the Dales?' she asked curiously, even though she shouldn't ask questions like that. She shouldn't be delving into Daniel's life, getting to know more about him. Even if she did decide not to cut herself off as she had planned to do, she mustn't allow herself to grow attached to him.

'Partly. Camille grew up in a very rural area of France and she never really settled in the city. I thought it would be easier for her if we moved somewhere similar. As luck would have it, a job came up here and I applied for it. It turned out to be the right thing to do. Camille loved living here. We were very happy.'

CHAPTER TEN

DANIEL HEARD THE catch in his voice and fought to control it. If he was honest, he was stunned that he felt so emotional. He had long since passed the stage of breaking down whenever Camille was mentioned so what was going on? Why was it that Eleanor seemed to possess the power to unleash his emotions this way? He had no idea but he knew that if he didn't change the subject he would regret it. Pushing back his chair, he made a determined effort to get a grip.

'Right, time to show you the delights of the market before it gets too busy,' he said with false heartiness. 'It will be bedlam here in an hour's time—we won't be able to see what's on the stalls.'

'If you're sure?' she said quietly.

Daniel felt the back of his neck prickle. Had Eleanor realised he was upset? he wondered with a sinking heart. He shot a glance at her but she was bending over to pick up her bag and he couldn't see her face… He drove the thought from his mind, determined not to make matters worse by letting it run away with him. Of course she hadn't noticed. Why should she when she didn't really know him?

'Of course I'm sure. If you don't get a guided tour then the odds are that you'll miss something.' He drummed up a smile, trying to quash the equally unsettling thought that he wished she *was* interested enough to want to get to know him. 'Let's start at the cheese stall. I guarantee that you won't be able to resist.'

Eleanor laughed as she followed him out of the café. 'You aren't on commission by any chance? Free cheese whenever you bring them a new customer?'

'What a good idea!' he exclaimed, feeling easier now that the conversation had moved on. He would steer clear of anything personal in future, he told himself as he led the way across the road. Stick to topics that wouldn't cause problems for him as well as for her. He had come to terms with Camille's death and he didn't want to start thinking about the hole it had left in his life. He should be grateful for what he'd had and not start wishing that he could experience that kind of closeness again. That would be plain greedy. One love, one lifetime. That was enough for anyone.

Wasn't it?

Ellie did her best but it was impossible to shake off the feeling of sadness. She'd heard the catch in Daniel's voice and the thought that he was still suffering was hard to bear. He must have loved his wife very much to feel this way after so much time had elapsed. Once again, she found herself thinking about Michael. She had been so sure that it had been the real thing, the kind of love that lasted for ever. However, the more she thought about it, the more doubtful she became. Could she really imagine herself still feeling so unhappy in a few years' time? It was a relief to put the thought out of her mind as they reached the cheese stall. As Daniel had promised there was a huge range of cheeses on offer. He pointed to a creamy blue cheese in the middle of the display.

'That's my favourite. It's made on a farm just a couple of miles from here and it's delicious. A chunk of that, a glass of red wine, and you're in seventh heaven.'

'High praise indeed,' Ellie declared, smiling at the young woman behind the counter. 'Have you got Dr Saunders on commission? Because I have to say that he's a wonderful advocate for your produce.'

'Not yet, but it sounds like a good idea,' the woman replied, laughing. She cut a sliver of cheese off the round and passed it to Ellie. 'See what you think.'

Ellie popped the cheese into her mouth, savouring its rich and creamy flavour. 'Mmm, it's delicious.' She glanced at Daniel, determined to keep things on an even footing. There must be no more comparing her relationship with Michael to Daniel's relationship with his late wife. It was pointless and needlessly upsetting to know that she always came off worse. 'You definitely know your cheeses, Dr Saunders.'

'What can I say?' Daniel hammed it up for all he was worth, assuming an expression of modesty. 'It's just a natural inborn talent. I can't claim any credit for it.'

'Put like that then, no, you can't.' Ellie laughed as his face fell. 'It's your own fault. You shouldn't go fishing for compliments.'

'Hm. Probably not.' He smiled ruefully at the young woman behind the counter. 'That's me put in my place, isn't it? Anyway, I'll have some of the Outhwaite Farm Wensleydale as well as that blue. I shall cheer myself up by having a cheese fest!'

They made their way round the market, stopping at the various stalls. By the time they had done a full circuit, Ellie was weighted down with bags. She shook her head in dismay. 'I only came to have a look round so I'm not sure how I ended up with all this. I only hope I can eat it all.'

'Me too. I bought far more than I intended, especially as Nathan's away this weekend.' He shook his head. 'You're a bad influence, Eleanor. You're going to have to make amends.'

'How?' Ellie asked in surprise.

'By coming home and having lunch with me, that's how.' He laughed softly, causing a tiny frisson of awareness to ripple through her. 'That way at least some of this stuff won't go to waste. To my mind it's the least you can do for encouraging me to be so greedy!'

Daniel unlocked the front door, still not quite able to believe that Eleanor had agreed to have lunch with him. Even as he had issued the invitation, he had expected her to refuse, yet she hadn't. Had it been guilt at the thought of wasting the food that had spurred her on? Or because she wanted to spend more time with him?

He clamped down on that thought as he made his way inside. Eleanor was parking her car so he left the front door open and headed to the kitchen. Dumping the bags on the table, he turned to watch as she came down the hall. It was obvious that she was taking stock and all of a sudden he was conscious of how little he had done to the place recently. It was years since the house had been decorated and everywhere was starting to look decidedly shabby. He would have to do something about it, although it was odd that it should have taken Eleanor's visit to make him see the place through fresh eyes.

'It's a lovely house,' she said as she came into the kitchen. 'Very warm and welcoming.'

'Thank you. I've always liked it, although it needs a bit of a spruce up,' Daniel replied, pleased that she liked his home even if it wasn't looking its best.

'It's hard to fit everything in when you're working,' she said quietly, but he heard the undercurrent in her voice and knew that she was wondering if he had failed to make any changes because of Camille. Was she right? Had he held off redecorating because he'd wanted everything to remain as it had been in happier times?

He suspected it was true and it was uncomfortable to face up to how he had placed his life on hold. How many times had he counselled a bereaved patient about the importance of looking towards the future and yet he was guilty of ignoring his own advice. He knew that he would have to address the situation and soon. After all, there were going to be a lot of changes when Nathan went to university; he would be here on his own after that.

'Right, first things first—let's get that soup heated up,' he declared, not wanting to dwell on the thought of how lonely he was going to be. 'We can have it with some of that fresh bread and cheese we bought.'

'Let's use some of my cheese,' Eleanor suggested immediately. She grimaced as she slipped off her jacket and hung it on the peg behind the back door. 'I've bought far too much—I'll never manage to eat it all by myself.'

'Fine. There's plates on the dresser and cutlery in the drawer… Oh, and the cheese board's in that cupboard,' Daniel told her as he set about opening the carton of soup.

'Right.' Eleanor started to gather together what they needed, laying out plates and cutlery and even finding the butter dish in the fridge. 'Napkins?' she asked, glancing round, and he grimaced.

'Not sure where they are, to be honest. I do have some but, as I never entertain, I don't use them.'

'Not to worry. This will do.' She tore off a couple of sheets of kitchen roll and folded them neatly into triangles before setting them on the table.

Daniel laughed. 'I'm glad you aren't too fussy.'

'I'm more practical than fussy,' she said, smiling back. Her eyes met his and Daniel felt his heart give a little bounce, as though it had suddenly discovered it had a spring in it. He turned back to the soup, concentrating on stirring it so that it didn't catch on the bottom of the pan. It was just a smile, nothing to get het up about, and certainly nothing to make him think how much he would love her to smile at him again if he kissed her...

A blob of hot soup spat out of the pan and landed on his hand and he jumped but at least it helped to clear his head. By the time the soup was ready and the bread was sliced, he felt back on an even keel. Ladling the soup into a couple of earthenware bowls, he placed them on the table. 'Spiced carrot and coriander. I've not had it before so I hope it tastes good.'

'It's lovely,' Eleanor declared, taking an appreciative sip. She helped herself to a slice of onion bread and buttered it liberally. 'Hmm, this is delicious too.'

'Better than the supermarket's best white sliced?' Daniel asked, his tongue firmly in his cheek.

'*Yes*' She rolled her eyes. 'Not all of us have been lucky enough to be able to buy such fresh produce. Where I lived before it was the supermarket or nothing.'

'So you aren't sorry you moved here?'

'Not at all.' Ellie hesitated, not sure it was wise to

admit how glad she was that she had made the move. It wasn't just the food; her whole outlook on life seemed so much more positive since she had come to the Dales. However, the reason why it felt so much brighter stopped her elaborating. Telling Daniel that meeting him had been a major factor was out of the question.

'Good. It must have been a big decision and I'm glad you don't regret it.'

'I don't.' Eleanor busied herself with her lunch, not wanting to be drawn into saying too much. The problem was that Daniel was so easy to talk to that she found it hard to hold back as she normally would do. She had never been someone who wore her heart on her sleeve: just the opposite. Yet, when she was with Daniel it was as though she wanted to tell him everything—every tiny concern she had, every emotion she was feeling. She had never felt this way before and it was hard to understand how he had this effect on her. What was it about him that breached all her defences?

It was a relief when Daniel changed the subject by telling her about Nathan's trip. That he was extremely proud of his son was obvious and she found it incredibly moving. Although she knew that her parents were proud of what she had achieved, she had never felt that they gained such pleasure from her success as Daniel seemed to derive from Nathan's.

'You're very proud of him, aren't you?'

'Is it that obvious?' Daniel sighed. 'Sorry! I didn't mean to bore you to death by playing the doting parent.'

'You aren't boring me. I think it's great that you two have such a close relationship. Not many parents are as close to their children as you are.'

'It's probably because of what happened,' Daniel said quietly. 'Camille's illness was a testing time for us.

After she died, Nathan went completely off the rails. I honestly thought that he'd never get back on track, but in the end he came through. I'm incredibly proud of what he's achieved because it wasn't easy for him.'

'It mustn't have been easy for you either,' Ellie suggested, her heart aching at the thought of what he had been through. She glanced around the kitchen, taking note of the photographs pinned to the cork board above the fridge. There were several family photos, proof that Camille was still very much in his thoughts. 'Dealing with your grief as well as trying to help Nathan must have been very difficult.'

'It was a dark period, but we got through it.' He smiled, obviously wanting to dispel the sombre mood. 'Now it's time to look to the future, me as well as Nathan.'

'That sounds as though you're planning on making some changes,' Ellie observed.

'I am.' He glanced around the room and shrugged. 'I never realised until today that I've slipped into a bit of a rut. The house desperately needs redecorating and I shall have to do something about it, or even think about moving.'

'Really?' Ellie couldn't hide her surprise. 'It's a beautiful house, though. Maybe it does need updating but that's all, surely?'

'With Nathan about to move out I have to ask myself if I need all this space. We bought this house as our family home but when there's just me rattling around in it, it seems a waste. Moving somewhere smaller might be a good idea.'

'A fresh start,' she suggested, her heart surging at the thought that Daniel was making a positive move toward putting the past behind him.

'Yes.' He looked at her and her breath caught when she saw the expression in his eyes. 'I think it's time to move on, Eleanor. I don't want to live in the past any more. I want a future to look forward to.'

Eleanor didn't know what to say. Did he mean that he wanted her to feature in that future? Just for a moment her mind whirled as she pictured the life they could have. There was no doubt that she found Daniel very attractive. She also found him wonderfully easy to talk to, but was that enough? Surely it needed more than sexual attraction and compatibility to guarantee a life-long relationship? There had to be love as well, a deep abiding love that would withstand everything that life could throw at them. He'd had that with Camille but was it possible to find that kind of closeness with anyone else, or would the other person always be second-best?

Ellie felt a searing pain clutch her chest. She knew how that felt, how dispiriting it was to know that you weren't enough, not number one. Gemma had held the key position in their parents' hearts and Ellie had been aware of that when she had been growing up. That's why meeting Michael had been so wonderful; for the first time ever she had felt she was the most important person in someone's life, but it hadn't lasted. How could she risk that happening again? Why would she choose to put herself through that heartache a second time?

She took a deep breath. Maybe she was attracted to Daniel, as he was to her, but it wasn't enough. Not when he would never love her as he had loved his late wife.

Daniel could feel shock waves reverberating throughout his body. Where on earth had that idea sprung from? he wondered as he got up to make some coffee. One minute he'd been wondering if he should embark on a spot of decorating and the next he'd been thinking about selling up!

As he filled the cafetière he let the idea roam around his head, hoping to find an explanation and preferably one that didn't involve Eleanor. Letting himself think that they might have a future together was crazy. She was only just recovering from a painful experience with her ex and she was in no state to embark on another relationship. Even if she had been it certainly wasn't the right time for him! He knew all that, so all he could do was put it down to some sort of mental aberration, an overload of crazy ideas that had addled his brain.

He placed the coffee pot on the table then took some mugs off the dresser and found the milk and sugar. By the time that was done he had managed to calm himself down. 'Coffee?' he asked, resuming the role of host as it was a much safer option than exploring any more crazy ideas.

'Please.' Eleanor popped the last bit of bread into her mouth and sighed. 'That was delicious. Oh, I know folk go on and on about the meals they've had at all those fancy restaurants but you can't beat what we've just had.'

'I'm glad you enjoyed it. I don't feel so guilty now for egging you on to buy so much,' Daniel declared, rustling up a smile.

'It's my own fault,' she replied, laughing. 'One of the dangers of having eyes bigger than my belly, as mum used to warn me.'

'I can't imagine you needed warning,' he observed lightly. 'You're a perfect weight from what I can tell.'

'Thank you.' She coloured at the compliment. 'I

wasn't always, though. I was quite a podgy teenager and mum was worried in case I put on too much weight.'

'Really? Had it something to do with your home circumstances?'

'Yes.' She sighed. 'It wasn't a very happy period in my life and I consoled myself by eating. Fortunately, things improved once I went to university.'

'I'm glad,' he said softly, his heart aching at the thought of the struggle she'd had to find her rightful place in the family dynamics. It made him see just how devastating it must have been for her when she had found her fiancé in bed with another woman. Eleanor had been through the mill and he must never forget that.

They drank their coffee, keeping up a carefully casual conversation. Daniel sensed that she was reluctant to reveal anything more about her past and respected her decision even though he longed to learn all he could about her. When Eleanor announced that it was time she left, it was a relief. Even though he had enjoyed the time they had spent together, he needed to take a step back. He had just unhooked her coat from the back of the door when the telephone rang.

'I'll just get that. Won't be a moment,' he said, hurrying into the hall. Picking up the receiver, he listened while the caller identified herself, a wave of coldness enveloping him as she briskly explained that she was the sister in charge of the Accident and Emergency unit at York. The coach carrying Nathan and his fellow students had been involved in an accident: could Daniel come?

Daniel hung up, his hand shaking so that he had difficulty placing the receiver on its rest. He heard footsteps behind him and turned round, his heart hammering so hard that he thought he was going to pass out.

'What is it? What's happened?' Eleanor took hold of his arm and shook it. 'Daniel, tell me!'

'There's been an accident… Nathan's in hospital,' he managed at last.

'Which hospital?'

'York.'

'Right, we'll go straight there.'

'Oh, but you don't have to come,' he began, but she shook her head.

'There's no way that you can drive in that state. And no way that I'll let you. I'm coming with you, Daniel, whether you like it or not!'

CHAPTER ELEVEN

A and E was frantically busy. It turned out that the coach was just one of several vehicles that had been involved in the collision. Nobody seemed to know what had caused it, but that was less important than how Nathan was. He was currently undergoing a CT scan for a head injury and Ellie knew that Daniel was beside himself with worry.

'It shouldn't be long now until we hear something,' she said, trying to keep up his spirits, although she suspected it was a waste of time. Which parent wouldn't be scared stiff at the thought of their child being injured?

'It seems to be taking ages!' Daniel exploded, leaping up from his seat. They had been shown into the waiting room attached to Resus and he strode to the door and stared through the glass. 'He should have been back by now. Obviously, something's wrong…'

'Or maybe it's just taking that bit longer because of the number of casualties they're having to deal with,' Ellie countered.

'I suppose so,' he conceded, coming back and slumping down in the chair. He ran his hand over his face and she could see that it was trembling. Reaching out, she covered it with hers. She hated seeing him like this—

so afraid and filled with angst—but there was little she could do apart from be there and offer her support.

'Sorry. I know I'm behaving like a complete idiot, but I'm just so scared.' He turned his hand over and captured hers. 'I don't know how I'd cope if anything happened to him.'

'I understand. But the registrar said that the CT scan was more a precaution than anything else. He thinks Nathan has a concussion but that it isn't serious,' she reminded him gently.

'He did. But things can and do go wrong when it comes to head injuries…' He broke off and leapt to his feet when the sister appeared and beckoned to him. Ellie stood up as well, her own heart racing. She may be a doctor but it wasn't easy to take a balanced view when one knew the people involved.

'You can come through and see your son now, Dr Saunders. The CT scan was clear, you'll be happy to hear.'

'Thank heavens!' Daniel exclaimed. He went to follow the sister into Resus, pausing when Ellie stayed where she was. 'Aren't you going to come with me?'

'If you want me to,' she said uncertainly, not wanting to intrude.

'Of course I do!' He held the door for her, placing his hand under her elbow as they followed the sister to a screened-off area in the corner. Nathan was having his obs done by a young male nurse so they stood to one side and waited. Although there was a huge bruise on the side of his face, Nathan managed to smile at them.

'Hi, Dad… Eleanor. Sorry about this.'

'It's not your fault,' Daniel said gruffly. He went over to the bed once the nurse had finished and squeezed Nathan's hand. 'Or at least I don't think it was!'

'Thanks very much!' Nathan laughed then grimaced. He had a broken rib as well as the head injury, although that would heal in its own time, as Ellie knew, and shouldn't cause any major problems.

'So what happened? Do you know?' Daniel asked, sounding better now he knew that Nathan wasn't in any immediate danger.

'Apparently, a tanker overturned and a couple of cars ran into it. We ploughed into the back of the pile-up.'

'Was anyone badly injured from your group?' Daniel asked. 'What about Jack?'

'Not a scratch. He's waiting for Sandra and Tim to collect him. There were a couple of others with bumps and bruises, and one of the girls has a broken wrist, but that's it. We were very lucky.'

'How did you hit your head?' Eleanor asked, curiously.

Nathan sighed. 'I'd just got up to get a can of cola out of my bag when it happened and I went flying. If I'd been sitting down then I'd have been OK.'

'Typical, although it could have been worse.' Daniel squeezed the boy's shoulder. 'Thank heaven it wasn't is all I can say.'

'Me too.'

Ellie felt a lump come to her throat as father and son exchanged a look. There was no doubt that they knew exactly how much they meant to each other. It was hard to tamp down her emotions so she excused herself when the registrar came to speak to Daniel. At the end of the day, they weren't her family, even though she would have loved to be part of their lives. The thought shocked her so much that it was hard to dismiss it when Daniel came to find her a short time later.

'They're going to keep him in overnight. It's purely

a precaution—they're not anticipating any problems. But they'd prefer to cover all bases.'

'So what are you going to do?' Ellie asked, trying to get herself together. There was no chance of her becoming a permanent part of Daniel's family and it was pointless thinking that she could. His life was mapped out and, to put it bluntly, she didn't feature in his plans. 'Are you going to stay here or go home?'

'There's not much point in my staying. Nathan is being moved to a ward soon and he needs to rest.' He glanced at his watch and frowned. 'Is that really the time? I had no idea it was so late. No, I'll go home and come back tomorrow morning to pick him up.'

'Sounds like a good idea,' she agreed. She led the way to the car park, shivering as rain gusted across the open ground as they left the building. 'It's so cold, much colder than when we arrived.'

'Winter's on its way. It'll get colder than this in a few weeks' time.'

'What a cheering thought!' she exclaimed, and he laughed.

'Sorry!'

They got into the car and drove back to Beesdale. Ellie took her time, not wanting to risk them having an accident as well. The roads were slick with rain and with the wind blowing more rain against the windscreen it was difficult to see. It was a relief to pull up outside Daniel's house.

'Come in and have a cup of tea,' he instructed, forcing the door open as the wind tried to slam it shut. 'You've had nothing since lunchtime and you must need a drink.'

'I really should get off home,' she demurred, not sure it would be wise to prolong her stay. Far too many crazy thoughts had invaded her head today and she needed to be on her own while she got things straight again. She must never forget that she was only here for a limited period of time and after that she would move on.

'Please.' Bending, he looked at her through the half-open door and she couldn't fail to see the plea in his eyes. 'I could really do with some company, Eleanor. What happened today really shook me up.'

'In that case a cup of tea would be very welcome.'

Ellie got out of the car, unable to resist the appeal for support. From what she knew, Daniel didn't ask for help very often. Rain lashed at them as they ran up the path and he grimaced as he let them into the house.

'What a night! You're soaked. Go into the sitting room while I fetch you a towel.'

He ushered her inside, pausing only long enough to light the gas fire before he went to find the towel. Ellie took off her wet coat and draped it over the back of a chair then sat down next to the fireplace, holding her hands out to the blaze. He came back a few seconds later with a towel and handed it to her.

'Here you are. I'll pop the kettle on and be right back.'

Ellie started to rub her hair dry as he disappeared again. With it being so short, it didn't take very long. She could have done with combing it afterwards but she hadn't thought to put a comb in her bag when she had set out that morning. She did her best, using her fingers to smooth the short dark strands into some semblance of order. Daniel came back with a tray of tea as she was checking her appearance in the mirror and grinned at her.

'You've missed a bit.'

'Have I?' Turning her head, she attempted to find the wayward strands but couldn't spot them.

'Just here.' Daniel placed the tray on a table and came up behind her. Lifting his hand, he smoothed down the tufts of hair and Ellie stiffened when she felt his fingers sliding down her skull. She bit her lip as she waited for him to move away but he stayed right where he was. 'Your hair is beautiful, Eleanor, so soft and silky.'

His deep voice rippled through the silence, the words charged with so much emotion that she shivered. When his hand returned to her hair, she didn't move. Couldn't. It was as though his touch had cast a spell over her. When his fingers came to rest on the nape of her neck and began to stroke it too, she closed her eyes, letting the sensations pour through her. She could feel her skin tingling, feel the heat building wherever his fingers touched, and sighed. She knew that she should stop what was happening but it was beyond her. How could she call a halt when it felt so good to be touched this way, so right?

'Eleanor?'

There was a question in his voice when he said her name and even though he didn't say it out loud, she knew what he was asking. Her heart caught, panic and excitement bringing it to a halt. All she had to do was to say no and that would be the end of the matter, but for some reason it seemed like the hardest thing she had ever been asked to do. If she refused then she had a feeling that she would always regret it, always wonder what she had missed.

She turned to face him, watching the firelight playing over the strong planes of his face. When he bent towards her, she kept her eyes open, wanting to remember every second of what was happening. Whether it was the shock of Nathan's accident that was responsible for what was happening, she had no idea, but she needed to store away the memory of this moment. It would be something to look back on, something to cherish. His lips were so gentle as they settled over hers and yet beneath the tenderness there was a hunger that shook her. Daniel wasn't kissing her because he was seeking comfort. He was kissing her because he wanted her!

Daniel felt desire surge inside him and gasped. In the space of a heartbeat the kiss had gone from a need for closeness to something far more urgent. He drew Eleanor to him, shuddering when he felt her breasts pushing against his chest. It was a long time since he had been this close to a woman. Camille had been so ill that lovemaking had been out of the question. Now his senses seemed to be swamped by the feel and shape of the woman in his arms.

He drew her closer, marvelling at the fact that they fitted so perfectly. It was as though each curve and hollow had been created so that it would accommodate the shape of the other. Eleanor was quite tall, just a couple of inches shorter than him, and her head rested so comfortably in the crook of his shoulder, the perfect angle to allow him to deepen the kiss. His mouth plundered hers, tasting, testing, savouring the sweetness of her lips. When his tongue began to explore the delicate curve of her mouth, she moaned, the tiniest sound imaginable, but unmistakable all the same.

Daniel shuddered as a wave of desire swept over him. The fact that he was responsible for causing her this pleasure was a heady feeling and he did it again, letting the tip of his tongue trace the perfect curve of her upper lip and the tantalising fullness of her lower one. Her mouth was beautiful, so beautiful that he could have stood there and kissed her for ever and a day, but there were more delights to explore.

His hands slid down her body, skimming over the slender curves. He had never touched her this way before and yet there was a strange sense of familiarity, of rightness, that shook him. Had he unconsciously imagined doing this, pictured himself exploring her body and getting to know its shape and feel? He knew it was true and it was a revelation to realise that she had got under his skin to such an extent. He hadn't realised he was so vulnerable where Eleanor was concerned.

Fear suddenly rose to the surface of his mind as he wondered if he was making a mistake, but then she moved, just slightly, and his seeking hand came to rest on the side of her breast. Daniel felt a red-hot flame of desire shoot through him as his hand stilled for a moment before it moved on, sliding down from her breast to her waist then onto the softly rounded curve of her hip as he drew her closer and let her see the effect her nearness was having on him. Maybe he should have tried to hide what he was feeling but he didn't have the strength.

'Daniel...'

His name was little more than a rush of air as it escaped her lips, but it was nonetheless potent for that. Daniel felt a tremor pass through him. There was such hunger in the sound that he could almost taste it, such need that he was overwhelmed. This wasn't all down to him and *his* needs: Eleanor wanted him too. When he took her hand and led her to the door, she didn't hesitate, and his heart swelled with joy. Why should they pretend that this wasn't what they both wanted?

Light spilled into the room from the landing, just a pale glimmer, but it was enough. Eleanor stood at the end of the bed and waited as Daniel reached out to her. His hands were trembling as he drew the sweater over her head but she understood. He hadn't planned this; it had simply happened. It was little wonder he felt so shocked. She did too.

He dropped her sweater onto the floor then reached for the hem of the T-shirt she wore beneath. That too was quickly dispensed with. Eleanor watched as his eyes grazed over her breasts, barely concealed by the lacy bra she was wearing. When they rose to her face his pupils were dilated, filled with so many emotions that she couldn't have put a name to half of them and didn't try. She didn't need to wonder what he was feeling when she felt it too.

'You're beautiful. So very beautiful.'

The words stroked along her flesh like a caress and she shuddered. When he unfastened the snap on her jeans and started to slide them off her hips she closed her eyes. She didn't need to watch what he was doing now when she could feel it—feel his hands trembling, feel the touch of his fingers smoothing the fabric down her thighs. Bending, he cupped her foot in his hand and eased off first one leg of her jeans and then the other. All she had on now was her underwear and she waited, wondering when—not if—he would remove that as well, but instead he gathered her into his arms and held her close, held her so that she could feel exactly what her nearness was doing to him.

'I want you so much,' he whispered hoarsely. 'I want to hold you, touch you, be inside you, but are you sure it's what you want? It isn't too late if you want me to stop…'

'I don't.' Her voice was firm, her gaze steady as she opened her eyes and looked at him. She didn't want there to be any mistake about what she was saying, didn't intend for there to be room for recriminations later. Daniel wanted to make love to her and it was what she wanted too. Maybe there would be regrets at some point—who knew? But at this moment it was what she wanted. Needed. Desperately.

He closed his eyes, almost as though the moment was too intense to bear, and maybe it was. This was a big step for both of them and it would be foolish to pretend that it didn't mean anything. When he held out his hand, she took it and let him lead her to the bed. Kissing her softly on the mouth, he eased her down onto the quilt then straightened. Stripping off his sweater and jeans, he tossed them onto the floor and lay down beside her, drawing her into his arms so that she could feel the heat of his skin seeping into her flesh. His body was hard and firm, its shape and feel so new and so different; there was so much to discover.

Ellie let her fingertips graze over the well-developed pectoral muscles, feeling the crispness of hair and the smoothness of the skin beneath. Daniel's shoulders were broad and her fingers skated along his collar bones until they reached the tips then retraced their route, coming to rest above his heart. She could feel its beat beneath her palm, feel the blood surging, the power of his life-force, and realised that she had never felt this close to anyone before. Right here, at this moment, she could feel his heart pounding, and it was pounding for her.

Her hands moved on, grazing lightly over his rib cage, the firm flat muscles in his abdomen until she came to his hips. He was fully aroused and she took him into her hands, feeling the power, the proof of his need for her. She had never taken the lead when making love before and yet she didn't hesitate as she stroked and caressed him. This was different from anything she had experienced before. This was Daniel.

'Eleanor!' His voice rasped harshly as he cried out her name. Rolling her over onto her back, he kissed her with a passion that made her head swirl. Drawing back, he stared into her eyes and she could feel him trembling with the force of his feelings. 'I don't have anything,' he murmured. 'Nothing to keep you safe…'

'It's all right,' she said softly, moved almost beyond bearing that he should worry about protecting her at such a moment. 'I'm still on the Pill.'

He didn't say anything, simply kissed her with great tenderness as he entered her. Eleanor felt her body open to allow him in, felt it close around him and hold him there. There was no fumbling, no wondering what to do. It was instinctive, as though they had had been created for this very purpose. They climaxed together, shivering, shuddering, and utterly sated as they slid back down to earth. Daniel cupped her cheek in his hand and she could see the wonder in his eyes.

'I never thought…' he began then broke off as though he found it impossible to describe his feelings.

'No,' she agreed, her voice trembling from the aftermath of what had happened. 'Neither did I.'

He didn't say a word as he drew her to him and Ellie felt tears come to her eyes. He understood how she felt, how shocked she was, how moved, because he felt the same way. When he started to caress her again, she immersed herself in the magic they were creating. This time their lovemaking was slow and tender but just as intense. She had never experienced this kind of closeness and rapport. It was a world away from mere desire and touched on realms that scared her. She didn't want to fall in love with Daniel—she wouldn't take that risk. She couldn't bear to have her heart broken again, especially when she knew that it would be so much worse this time.

Ellie bit her lip as euphoria faded and was replaced by fear. If she allowed herself to love Daniel then there would be no holding back, no reservations, no safeguards. She would have to give him her heart and every tiny bit of her being. She would have nothing left if he rejected her.

CHAPTER TWELVE

DANIEL COULD FEEL the shock waves reverberating throughout his entire body. It felt as though he had undergone some kind of traumatic evolution, everything he knew and understood ripped apart and put back together in a different order. Making love to Eleanor had changed him from the man he had been. It was no wonder that he felt so disorientated.

When Eleanor pulled away, he let her go. He needed to get his thoughts together and he couldn't do that while he held her. He rolled to his feet, feeling sick as he wondered where they went from here. Maybe they had gone into this with their eyes open, but how must she be feeling? he thought as he dragged on his jeans. She was still struggling to come to terms with what had happened with her ex and now to be faced with this!

Guilt rushed through him as he picked up his sweater, guilt about how Eleanor was feeling as well as guilt about what he himself had done. He hadn't thought about Camille—she hadn't entered his mind once. However, there was no point pretending that he wasn't going to feel guilty about betraying her memory when he knew that he would.

'I'll make us a drink,' he said roughly, avoiding looking at Eleanor. Maybe she had been a willing participant but she hadn't thought through what they were doing any more than he had done.

Daniel took a deep breath and tried to damp down a surge of remorse. Blaming desire for his actions wasn't acceptable. He should have thought about what he was doing and not allowed himself to be influenced by his needs. The funny thing was that he had never been led by his emotions before, but it was different with Eleanor; he felt more and thought less.

'The bathroom's through there if you want a shower,' he said, trying not to dwell on that thought. 'I'll make us some coffee.'

'Thank you.'

Her voice was low, the uncertainties it held tugging at his heartstrings, but he forced himself to ignore them. After all, people slept together all the time and it didn't have to make a huge impact on their lives, did it? However, in his heart, he knew that dismissing what they had done wasn't going to be easy. Like it or not, it was going to have an effect.

His heart was heavy as he made his way downstairs and switched on the kettle. It was pitch-dark outside and all he could see through the kitchen window was his own reflection staring back at him. It was like looking at the face of a stranger. This morning he had known exactly who he was: Daniel Saunders, widower, father, doctor, a man who lived his life the best way he could. Now it felt as though he was someone completely different and he hadn't a clue who he was any more. It was as though all the certainties that had shaped his life had melted away and there was no framework any more. He could be whoever he wanted but the hard part was deciding who that was.

'I think I should go.'

Daniel swung round when Eleanor spoke. She was fully dressed and he experienced a rush of regret that he could no longer enjoy looking at her beautiful body but he squashed it. He needed to sort out his head and thoughts like that wouldn't help him do that. 'Are you sure you won't stay and have a cup of coffee?' he said politely.

'Thank you, but no.' She stood up straighter and he could tell that she was steeling herself to continue. 'About tonight, Daniel, I think it's best if we forget what happened.'

'Do you think that's possible?' he asked wryly, and she flushed.

'It won't be easy, but it's the sensible thing to do, unless, of course, you'd prefer me to leave the surgery.'

'No. That's the last thing I want,' he said quickly, his heart sinking at the thought. He took a deep breath, struggling to retain his composure. 'We're both adults, Eleanor, and we both understand that these things happen. Put it down to an emotional overload after what happened today, but there's no point us making a song and dance about it. Bluntly, I'd find it very difficult to replace you at this time of the year so I'd appreciate it if you would stay on.'

'I would prefer not to have to find another position right now too so it's fine with me.' She gave him a quick smile although Daniel was very aware how empty it was. 'I'll be happy to stay. Thank you.'

She didn't say anything else. Daniel followed her into the hall, aware that he had handled things badly. He didn't want her to think he was dismissing what had happened between them as meaningless but what else could he have done? The fact was that Eleanor had made it clear that she wouldn't welcome it if he told her just how much tonight had meant to him.

She fetched her coat from the sitting room and went to the door. 'I hope Nathan makes a speedy recovery,' she said, glancing back. 'If you need anything—'

'Thank you but you did more than enough today,' he interjected swiftly.

'I was glad to help.'

Her eyes met his for a moment before she turned round and opened the front door but it was long enough. Daniel's hands clenched when he saw the pain they held. That she regretted what had happened tonight was obvious. He longed to say something to make it easier for her but the words wouldn't come. He couldn't make any declarations or promises, could he? Maybe the boundaries within which he lived his life had altered, but some things were exactly the same. He was still Nathan's father and now, more than ever, he needed to put him first.

Ellie was dreading seeing Daniel when she went into work on Monday morning but, in the event, he wasn't there. It appeared that Nathan had been kept in hospital and Daniel had taken the day off to be with him. Marie sounded concerned as she relayed the news to her.

'Apparently, Nathan started complaining of a headache then lost consciousness. They did another scan and discovered a bleed on his brain and decided to operate. They phoned Daniel and he went rushing back to the hospital in the early hours of Sunday morning.'

'Good heavens!' Ellie exclaimed. 'Nathan seemed fine when I saw him. There was no indication that something like that would happen.'

'You were at the hospital!' Marie exclaimed in surprise.

'Yes.' Ellie could feel herself blushing as she recalled what had happened on Saturday night. She had spent the rest of the weekend vacillating between trying to forget it and remembering every single glorious second. She had never imagined that she and Daniel would end up in bed together. That had been a big enough shock; however, the fact that their lovemaking had been so wonderful made it even more alarming. She knew that she couldn't simply ignore what had happened. She was going to have to live with the memory... If she could.

'I...erm... I ran into Daniel at the market,' she said, opting for part of the truth. 'We got a bit carried away and ended up buying so much food that he invited me back to his for lunch so it wouldn't get wasted. I was there when the hospital phoned to say Nathan was in A and E and I drove Daniel over there.'

'I see.' Marie was obviously agog to hear more and Ellie swiftly moved on.

'As I said, Nathan seemed fine when we left so it's a shock to hear what's happened. But there again head injuries are notoriously difficult to spot.'

'I suppose so. What time did you and Daniel get back to Beesdale?' Marie asked, not to be deterred.

'Oh, not too late. Anyway, how is Nathan doing?' Ellie said quickly.

'All right, apparently. Daniel phoned me just after seven this morning to tell me what had happened and that he wouldn't be at work,' Marie explained, success-fully distracted. 'He'd already phoned Sandra and asked her to cover for him so she should be here shortly.' Marie grimaced. 'No doubt Bernard will have a face on him because he'll be on his own, but tough. It's about time he actually did some work!'

Ellie laughed as Marie rolled her eyes. Fortunately, their first patient arrived just then so she was able to make her escape. However, as she went into her room, she made herself take a deep breath. It was time to put what had happened out of her mind and focus on work, although she knew it would be only a temporary reprieve. It would be a long time before she forgot about making love with Daniel.

Daniel could feel tiredness dragging at him. He hadn't slept since he had arrived at the hospital in the early hours of Sunday morning. Even though he had been assured that the operation had been a complete success, he had stayed awake, watching over his son. Nathan had been moved to the Critical Care unit, an indication that his status had changed for the worse. Although Daniel knew that he was receiving the best possible care, he wouldn't relax until Nathan regained consciousness. He had been heavily sedated to give his brain a chance to heal and it could take some time before that happened. Meanwhile, Daniel intended to stay at his bedside. Sandra would cover for him and Eleanor would be there as well.

His heart jolted at the thought of what had gone on in the past forty-eight hours. First Nathan's accident and then him and Eleanor making love. Maybe the first event had been the catalyst for the second but deep down he knew it would have happened at some point. Ever since they had met, he had felt drawn to Eleanor. He'd only ever felt this way once before, when he had met Camille, but even then it had been different. He and Camille had been so young when they had met and fallen in love. They'd had their whole lives ahead of them and being in love had been wild and exciting. With Eleanor, however, the feeling was different, quieter, deeper, more intense in a way. Was he falling in love with her? He didn't know. All he knew was that he wanted to be with her and not just in bed either.

Thoughts tumbled around his head. They were intermingled with so many emotions, guilt being the main one. How could he fall in love with Eleanor when it would mean him letting go of Camille? He had sworn to love Camille until his dying day and he would have done so too if he'd had the chance. But would it be right to allow himself to love someone else? Or would it be a rejection of everything he and Camille had had together?

Then there was Nathan; how would *he* feel about his father loving another woman? The last thing Daniel wanted was to upset Nathan, especially now when his son had this to contend with. He had already let Nathan down by leaving him in the hospital on his own. Oh, maybe he couldn't have done anything to prevent what had happened but he should have been here, taking care of him, rather than satisfying his own needs. It was something he had no intention of doing again.

He took a deep breath. He and Eleanor could never have a relationship, no matter how much he might want to.

Ellie was kept extremely busy all morning long. The plus side was that she had no time to brood about what had happened. She had just ushered out her final patient when Marie buzzed to tell her that there was a Dr Margaret Hamilton on the phone, wanting to speak to Daniel, but would she take the call seeing as he wasn't there.

'Of course,' Ellie agreed immediately. She listened carefully as Dr Hamilton introduced herself. It appeared she was a psychotherapist and worked with both private patients as well as those referred to her through NHS channels.

'I am extremely concerned about a patient who is on your list. Her name is Madeleine Walsh—I don't know if you've been involved in her care, Dr Munroe?'

'In an indirect way, yes, I have, although she is Dr Saunders' patient.' Ellie quickly explained about Nigel Walsh's visit and heard the other woman sigh.

'Oh, there's no doubt that she's self-harming, or that it's spiralling out of control. I've only seen her the once but it was obvious that she urgently needs counselling. The problem is that she's failed to attend the last two appointments I set up for her.' Margaret Hamilton sounded worried. 'Letters and phone calls have been ignored too, which is why I was hoping that Dr Saunders could have a word with her. Madeleine knows him and he might just be able to make her see how important it is that she gets the help she needs.'

'I'm sure he would be happy to speak to her,' Ellie said slowly, hoping that she wasn't making too many assumptions. Daniel had had his doubts about the situation but now that Dr Hamilton was involved, surely it would allay his concerns? She hurried on. 'However, his son is in hospital at the moment, which is why he isn't in today, and I'm not sure when he will be back. I could have a word with Mrs Walsh if you think it would help, although, as I said, I don't know her personally. I'd hate to do more harm than good by jumping in,' she added.

'Hm. That's a valid point. People who self-harm are reluctant to admit to what they do at the best of times. Madeleine could respond adversely if you confront her and that's something I want to avoid.' Dr Hamilton paused, obviously weighing up their options. 'I think it would be best to wait until Dr Saunders returns.'

Ellie hung up after they had said goodbye. Although she wasn't happy about the delay, the last thing she wanted was to create more problems for the patient. She brought up Madeleine Walsh's file and made a note on it to the effect that Dr Hamilton had expressed concern then emailed a copy to Daniel so that he would see it when he returned. When that would be was open to question. It all depended on Nathan and how swiftly he recovered. Or didn't.

Ellie's heart contracted. Now that she had met Nathan she felt personally involved. He was Daniel's son, after all, and she couldn't bear to think that he might not recover from his injuries. Tears suddenly welled to her eyes. She couldn't bear to imagine how Daniel would cope if anything happened to the boy.

Nathan finally regained consciousness at lunchtime the following day. Daniel had been warned that he might have difficulty remembering what had happened and not expect too much. This type of head injury often resulted in memory loss and no one could predict if Nathan would be affected by it. Nathan's initial response seemed to confirm his worst fears.

'What's going on, Dad? What am I doing here?'

'You had a bit of a bump on Saturday when you were on that field trip,' Daniel explained carefully. 'You hit your head so they brought you to the hospital.'

'Really?' Nathan looked around in astonishment. 'I don't remember anything about it. What happened?'

'The coach you were on was involved in a pile-up,' Daniel replied, keeping it brief as the consultant had told him to do.

'Weird. The last thing I remember is talking to you and Eleanor at the barbecue—how odd is that?'

'It can happen sometimes when you've had a knock on the head,' Daniel replied lightly, although he had a bad feeling about this.

'S'pose.' Nathan frowned. 'Is Eleanor here? I have this funny feeling that I was talking to her.'

'You're right—she was here,' Daniel agreed, feeling slightly better now that Nathan was starting to piece things together.

'I thought so!' Nathan sounded relieved. 'So where's she gone then?'

'Oh…er…ahem… She went to fetch some coffee,' Daniel replied then wished he had thought of something else to say. Nathan obviously had no concept of time and was going to wonder what was going on when Eleanor failed to appear.

'Good idea. I could do with a cup. I'm parched!'

'No coffee for you, young man. You're getting water.' Daniel filled the plastic beaker and inserted a drinking straw through the spout. Nathan grinned when he passed it to him.

'It's been a while since I had a straw!'

Daniel chuckled, heartened by the fact that Nathan seemed to be taking things in his stride. The last thing he wanted was him getting stressed when it would make the situation even more difficult. 'I'll buy you a pack next time I go shopping.'

'Hmm, tempting, although I'm not sure it would do much for my street cred.' Nathan drank thirstily then sank back against the pillows with a sigh. 'I'm knackered. D'you mind if I have a sleep? Eleanor can keep you company when she gets back with the coffee, can't she?'

'Erm…yes.' Daniel waited until Nathan's eyes closed then left the room, feeling in a quandary. Nathan would think it very odd if Eleanor wasn't there when he woke up and he wasn't sure what to do. The consultant had been adamant about him keeping everything as normal as possible so as not to put any pressure on Nathan, so maybe he should phone Eleanor and ask if she would come to the hospital?

Daniel's heart lurched. Part of him was desperate to have her there with him while the other part was just as desperate for her to stay away. If he was brutally honest, he wasn't sure he could trust himself not to do something stupid when he saw her. Nathan's relapse had shocked him to the core and his emotions were all over the place. The last thing he wanted was a repeat of what had happened on Saturday night.

It was hard to know what to do but in the end the need to make things appear as normal as possible for Nathan's sake won through. He went outside to make the call, sheltering from the rain in the porch. When Eleanor answered he steeled himself to sound as impersonal as possible. This wasn't for his benefit, he told himself sternly. It was to help Nathan and he had to make that clear from the outset. He couldn't afford to let Eleanor know how much he wanted her there—it wouldn't be fair.

Eleanor had just let herself into the flat when her phone rang. Hunting it out of her pocket, she felt her breath catch when she realised it was Daniel calling. Just for a moment she considered rejecting the call before she thought better of it. Daniel wouldn't be calling unless it was urgent.

'Hello?'

'Look, I'm really sorry to phone you like this, Eleanor, but I have a problem.' Daniel's tone was brisk. 'Nathan has regained consciousness but he doesn't remember what happened leading up to the operation. I was warned this could happen and that under no circumstances must I try to jog his memory.'

'I can see how worrying it must be,' she agreed, her heart going out to him.

'It is. He thought it was still Friday, straight after the barbecue. He does recall talking to you, however, because he asked where you'd gone.' She heard him sigh. 'I don't know why but I told him you'd gone for some coffee. It was a really stupid thing to do as Nathan immediately latched onto it. I know it's a lot to ask but is there any chance that you would drive over here? I just want to make things as normal as possible for him.'

Ellie wasn't sure what to do. If it would help Nathan then of course she would drive to the hospital. However, was it really wise to get more deeply involved in Daniel's affairs when she should be trying to keep her distance? She hesitated and Daniel obviously misinterpreted her silence.

'Look, I'm sorry. I should never have phoned you, Eleanor. It was a really bad idea,' he began.

'I'll come straight over,' she said, cutting him off. She would never forgive herself if she refused to go and something happened to Nathan.

'Are you sure?' The relief in Daniel's voice was like balm and helped to calm her nerves.

'Quite sure. Where exactly are you?'

'Critical Care. I'll tell them to expect you so just give your name in at the desk when you arrive.'

'Right. I should be there within the hour,' Ellie told him, opening the front door.

'Thank you. I really appreciate this.'

Ellie didn't say anything as she cut the connection and headed out to her car. Maybe it wasn't the most sensible decision she'd ever made but she wouldn't go back on it now. She drove out of the surgery, forcing herself to concentrate on the road rather than the mistake she might be making. Daniel had asked her to help his son and she couldn't refuse. It was as simple as that.

CHAPTER THIRTEEN

ELEANOR ARRIVED AT the Critical Care unit just as Nathan was waking up from his nap. He grinned when he saw her coming into the room.

'Hi, Eleanor. Good to know the old man's had some company while I've been doing my sleeping beauty routine.'

'I'm not sure the beauty bit is correct,' she retorted, deliberately keeping her tone light. 'That's some bruise you've got on your head, young man!' She glanced at Daniel and felt her stomach sink when she saw his expression. That he had misgivings about her being there was obvious, even though it had been his idea to ask her to come. For some reason the thought annoyed her so that her voice had a definite edge when she addressed him. 'What do you think, Daniel?'

'I've seen worse,' he replied rather curtly.

'He certainly has.' Nathan laughed. 'Remember the time the shed roof gave way when I was trying to get my football? I ended up with a massive bruise on my head. Mum tore a strip off you for letting me climb up there to fetch it.'

'Mum hauled me over the coals, all right. She said *I* should have gone up and got it even though the roof would never have held my weight.' Daniel rolled his eyes. 'Apparently, that would have been a much better option in her view than you getting hurt.'

'I remember,' Nathan replied, grinning. 'You were seriously not impressed!'

Ellie turned away, trying not to think about what a happy family they had been. It simply highlighted how devastating it must have been for them when Camille had died. How could anyone hope to replace Camille let alone replicate the kind of closeness they'd had? It was hard to put that thought out of her mind, even though she knew how stupid it was to dwell on it. Daniel hadn't asked her to come here so she could step into his late wife's shoes. Nobody could fill Camille's role in either Daniel's or Nathan's eyes, and any woman who tried would only ever be second best. It was such a painful thought it was relief when the consultant arrived to examine Nathan and they were asked to leave. At least it provided a breathing space, time to get herself together. Daniel might have asked for her help for Nathan's sake but that was all.

They stepped out into the corridor while they waited for the consultant to finish. Daniel sighed as he stared at the closed door. 'The longer the amnesia lasts, the less likely it is that he'll recover that part of his memory.'

'I thought you said that he'd remembered us being at the barbecue and me being here on Saturday,' Ellie said quietly, her heart aching for what he must have been going through.

'Yes, although I'm not sure he has the time scale exactly right.' He ran his hand through his hair, his face grey with a mixture of fatigue and tension. 'And what if there are other gaps in his memory and we know nothing about them? They might only surface later on.'

'There's nothing to say that's going to happen, Daniel,' she pointed out firmly. 'Nathan could remember everything else perfectly well.'

'Or he might have forgotten something important, maybe something to do with his college work.' His tone was grim. 'He's worked so damned hard to get his act together. If something like that happens then heaven knows the effect it could have on him.'

'Don't go borrowing trouble, as my grandma used to say,' she instructed. 'It's all ifs, ands and buts at the moment. There are no facts to base your assumptions on, are there?'

'No,' he said slowly, then grimaced. 'Sorry. I'm getting several steps ahead of myself, aren't I?'

'Yes. But it's understandable.' She touched his hand then realised immediately what a mistake it was when she felt a rush of awareness hit her. All of a sudden she was transported back to Saturday night, to how his skin had felt when she had touched him, and how his body had throbbed for hers. Her hand fell to her side but she could tell from his expression that he knew what she was thinking, feeling, knew because he was thinking and feeling it too. The thought shook her. It hadn't ended on Saturday night. What had started then was still going on. The question now was what should she do about it? Assuming that she had a choice.

Daniel could feel the tension sizzling in the air. One minute he had been totally consumed by worry over Nathan and the next he was awash with feelings he didn't know how to handle. When the door opened and the consultant asked them if they would come in, it took him a moment to respond. However, one glimpse of Nathan's face soon cleared his head. His son looked scared to death.

'Did you know that I've got a gap in my memory?' Nathan demanded as soon as they stepped into the room.

'I suspected you had,' Daniel replied as evenly as he could. He glanced at the consultant, who nodded as though giving him permission to continue. 'What exactly do you remember?'

'I remember the barbecue and talking to you both there. And I have this vague impression of Eleanor being here at the hospital—' Nathan broke off and gulped. 'I don't remember anything after that—passing out, going down to Theatre—none of it. It's as though the days are all muddled up. I thought it was still Friday but the doctor says it's Tuesday. Is that right?'

'Yes.' Daniel tried to sound reassuring, although it wasn't easy when Nathan's obvious distress was affecting him. 'It's quite normal to forget things after a head injury. More often than not the missing bits come back later.'

'But what if they don't come back? And what if I've forgotten other things and don't *know* I've forgotten them?' Nathan was sounding increasingly alarmed, which was the last thing Daniel wanted.

'Then they may come back as well.' Eleanor stepped forward, bending so that she could look into the boy's eyes. 'It's early days, Nathan. You've just had surgery and, like any other part of your body, your brain needs time to recover. The best thing you can do is rest and try not to worry, although I can see how hard that must be.'

The advice had an instant soothing effect. Daniel was overcome with gratitude when he saw Nathan relax just a little. Somehow, Eleanor had managed to calm him down, succeeding where he himself had failed. By the time the consultant had added his endorsement to Eleanor's advice, Nathan was looking a lot better. When the sister informed them it was time they left so that Nathan could rest, Daniel felt calmer too. Maybe this wasn't going to turn out as badly as he had feared thanks to Eleanor. They left the Critical Care unit and made their way to the car park. Eleanor had parked next to him and Daniel stopped when they reached her car, aware that everything he was feeling must be clear to see on his face.

'Thank you for what you did back there. You managed to do what I couldn't and calmed him down. I don't know what would have happened if you hadn't been here tonight, Eleanor.'

'You'd have managed.' She smiled up at him, her eyes filled with a tenderness that touched his heart. That she cared not only about Nathan but about him as well was clear to see.

'Maybe,' he said huskily. 'But sometimes managing by yourself isn't enough. Sometimes you need someone to help you.'

He drew her into his arms, feeling the softness of her body nestled against his. It felt like a homecoming, that he had found the place he wanted to be as well the person he wanted to fill it. Holding Eleanor in his arms, he felt whole, as though he was no longer missing some vital part of him. It was a revelation to realise it and yet it was a quiet revelation; it didn't need a fanfare to herald its arrival when it filled him with such an intense feeling of happiness.

Tilting her chin, he kissed her, unable to hold back when every fibre of his being demanded an even greater closeness. He needed her so much! Needed her to fill his heart, his life, to give him peace. When she kissed him back, he could have shouted out for joy only his mouth was too busy to waste a single precious second when it could be better employed. The kiss ran on and on so that they were both trembling when they drew apart, both aware that they had reached a point of no return. They couldn't go back. They could only go forward. Whichever way it led.

'Will you come home with me?' Daniel didn't try to couch his needs in euphemisms—there was no point. They both knew what he was asking so why bother? Eleanor looked into his eyes and he knew what she was going to say before the words left her lips, and shuddered. She wasn't going to pretend either.

'Yes.'

They spent the night at the flat. It wasn't a conscious decision to stay there because they didn't discuss it; it just felt right. Here, at the newly decorated flat that held no reminders of the past, they were free to be themselves. When Daniel took her in his arms, Ellie knew that it was what she wanted more than anything. Maybe she didn't know what the future held in store, but at that moment *this* was what she needed, Daniel's arms around her, his heart beating in time with hers. They made love with an intensity and passion that moved them both to tears but they weren't embarrassed by their feelings, by the fact that they cared. Even if they didn't know what was going to happen, they needed this, needed each other.

They fell asleep still wrapped in each other's arms and woke the next morning way before the day had dawned, feeling both sated and content. Raising herself up on her elbow, Ellie brushed a kiss over Daniel's brow. 'That was the best night's sleep I've had in ages,' she told him, smiling into his eyes. 'You, Dr Saunders, have a magical touch.'

'Hmm. Good to know, although I suspect the magic only works for selected people.' He brushed her mouth with a kiss, kissed her again when she responded, and groaned. 'I could do this all day. I just wish I had the time but I need to go home and get changed. I want to get to the hospital early to see how Nathan's doing this morning.'

'Of course you do,' Ellie agreed, simply, because no way was she going to put pressure on him to stay with her. Nathan's health was his number one priority and everything came second to that, herself included. Just for a moment the old thoughts about being second best came rushing back before she drove them out of her mind. Daniel needed her help, he needed her support, and no matter what it cost her, she would give it to him.

They showered together, laughing and giggling like teenagers as they squeezed into the stall. When Daniel offered to soap her back, Ellie agreed because it was easier than trying to do it herself. However, it soon became apparent that his interest wasn't wholly focused on matters of hygiene. She shuddered when she felt his hands smoothing the lather over her buttocks. Everywhere he touched, her skin was tingling. When he turned her around and lathered her breasts, she closed her eyes, too awash with sensations to remonstrate with him. They made love again right there in the shower, the water raining down on them as they loved each other with a desperation that was in total contrast to the night before. However, it was equally stirring, equally moving in its own very special way. They wanted one another. Needed one another. And there was no escaping that fact.

Daniel left after downing a quick cup of coffee, leaving Ellie to get ready for work. She dressed with care, suddenly wishing that she had something prettier to wear than the sensible trousers and shirt. She sighed as she studied her reflection in the dressing table mirror, understanding only too well why she wanted to look attractive. She wanted this—whatever it was—to continue, but would it? Could it? Should it? Daniel hadn't made any promises. He hadn't made a commitment either. He had held her, loved her and shown that he'd needed her, but that was all.

Ellie bit her lip as she looked at herself in the mirror. She might be what he needed right now, at this moment, but there was no guarantee his feelings would last. She must never allow herself to forget that.

It was the strangest time of Daniel's entire life. As one week flowed into the next, he found himself adrift. Nathan had been moved to the neurosurgical unit and he spent as much time as possible there with him. Amazingly, Bernard Hargreaves had come up trumps for once, which meant he could take time off without feeling guilty. Work could wait. He needed to be there for Nathan, now more than ever.

Worryingly, it soon became clear that there were other gaps in Nathan's memory, little glitches that caused the boy immense concern. It was very frustrating: one day he would recall something that had happened and the next he'd realise that he had forgotten something else. All Daniel could do was try to reassure him but he was worried to death that it wouldn't be enough. If the pressure became too great and Nathan went off the rails again...

It was Ellie who kept him grounded, only Ellie who could calm him and make him see beyond the bad bits so he could hope for the good. She never put any pressure on him by telling him that he shouldn't worry as everything would be fine: they both knew it wasn't true. However, she was always there, a calming presence in the background, and Daniel knew that he wouldn't have coped without her. He needed her so much, even though he felt guilty about taking what she offered when he had so little to give in return. At the end of the day, Nathan still came first.

Two weeks after the accident, Nathan was allowed home. Physically, he was perfectly fit, but mentally he was a different person. Daniel watched him like a hawk but there were no signs that he was going to relapse into his old ways and he grew quietly hopeful that they would get through it eventually. It was a big decision to return to work but Daniel knew that he had to do so if only to show Nathan that life could return to normal. Nathan was going into college that morning to talk to his tutors so at least he had the comfort of knowing where he was.

Marie greeted him with delight when he walked through the surgery doors. 'Hello, stranger! It's a wonder I still recognise you,' she declared, leaning over the desk to hug him.

'I know. It seems ages since I was last here,' Daniel admitted, blanking out any thoughts about the nights he had spent at the flat above. The time he'd spent there was different, special. It had nothing to do with work.

'Good morning. It's good to have you back.'

His heart flip-flopped when he recognised Eleanor's voice. Although they hadn't managed to spend as much time together since Nathan had returned home, they had managed the odd occasion. Daniel was very conscious that Marie was watching them as he turned. Did Marie suspect that something was going on? he wondered, and then realised in surprise that he didn't care. What he and Eleanor had together had nothing to do with anyone else. It was their business, their pleasure. The thought unravelled the knot of tension inside him and he smiled.

'It's good to be back,' he said softly, his eyes meeting Eleanor's and holding them fast.

'That's nice to know.' Her smile was gentle and his heart managed to fit in another roll, like a seasoned circus tumbler warming up before a routine. Just looking at her made him feel better, Daniel realised, made him feel more positive, more alive than he had felt for years, all the years since Camille had died. What did it mean? Was he in love with her?

Questions raced around his head, but it would take longer for the answers to come. It wasn't the questions that scared him after all, it was the answers, the fact he knew that once they came there could be no going back. He would have to make a decision then, make choices.

'Right. I'd better show willing and make a start. I'll see you both later.' Daniel made his way to his room and sat down at his desk, his thoughts in turmoil. How could he choose between Nathan and Eleanor? Yet that was what he would have to do. His heart felt like lead as he picked up the framed photograph that stood on his desk. It showed Camille and Nathan standing on a beach with their arms around each other, laughing. It had been taken during a family holiday to Cornwall, the last holiday they'd had together, in fact. Camille had been diagnosed with ovarian cancer shortly after they had returned home and she had been too ill to go on any more holidays.

Now Daniel felt his eyes fill with tears as he looked at their smiling faces. He had honestly thought their happiness would last for ever but he'd been wrong. It had been snatched away from them and there was no going back to those days. Now he had a choice to make. He could put his own happiness, the happiness he knew he would find with Eleanor before everything else, including Nathan. Could he do it? Could he put himself first when it could have a detrimental effect on his son?

'Oh, I'm sorry. I didn't mean to interrupt you but I just wanted to make sure you saw the memo I left for you.'

Daniel started when Eleanor opened the door. There was no time to hide how emotional he was feeling and he saw her eyes darken. Placing the photo back on the desk, he stood up and went to the sink, needing a moment to gather his thoughts. 'What memo was that?' he asked, making a great production out of washing his hands.

'The one about Madeleine Walsh. A Dr Hamilton phoned while you were off. Apparently, Mrs Walsh has been referred to her privately for counselling. Dr Hamilton is convinced she is self-harming and she's worried because Mrs Walsh keeps missing her appointments. She wanted to know if you would mind having a word with Madeleine. Her phone number is on the memo if you want to call her back,' she added, starting to withdraw.

'I see. I'll phone her later.' Daniel made a determined effort to collect himself and dredged up a smile. 'It seems you were right about the situation, Eleanor, and I was wrong. I apologise for questioning your judgement.'

'It doesn't matter,' she said huskily. 'Being right isn't the be all and end all.'

She didn't say anything else before she left. Daniel frowned as he stared at the closed door. He had the feeling that there'd been more to that comment than first appeared. He sighed as he went and sat down again. What did it matter? He had more important things to worry about. He had to make up his mind what he intended to do and he had to do it soon. It wasn't fair to Eleanor to leave her in this state of limbo.

CHAPTER FOURTEEN

SOMEHOW ELLIE MANAGED to get through the day, even though she wasn't sure how. Seeing the sadness on Daniel's face as he had studied that photograph had proved once and for all how stupid she was to hope that he would ever come to love her. Nobody could replace Camille in his life, and anyone who tried would only ever be second-best.

The thought made her feel sick. Several times she found herself almost overwhelmed by nausea but struggled to control it. However, by the time the day ended, her head was throbbing and she felt genuinely ill. Marie took one look at her and grimaced.

You don't look too good to me—are you OK?'

'I've got a headache, that's all.' Ellie drummed up a smile but it was a poor effort.

'You need some paracetamol or something,' Marie declared. She looked over Ellie's shoulder. 'Ellie's got a headache, Daniel. Can you give her something for it?'

'Of course.'

Ellie didn't turn round. There was no need when she could hear the concern in his voice. Daniel might never love her but he cared about her and she knew he did too. Tears welled into her eyes because all of a sudden it was too much to bear. Daniel might care about her, but his heart still belonged to Camille and it always would. It was a moment of such utter despair that she couldn't contain her feelings and she saw the worry in his eyes as he bent over her.

'You should have said that you weren't feeling well!' He laid the back of his hand on her forehead. 'You feel rather hot to me. Do you have a temperature?'

'No. It's just a headache. I'm making a fuss over nothing. Sorry.'

The apology got swallowed up by a sob and the sob turned into another before she could stop it. When Marie rushed around the desk and led her to a chair, Ellie didn't protest. It was easier to let them think that she was ill rather than admit that her heart was aching, breaking, ripping itself apart. Daniel would never love her like he loved Camille. Deep down she had always known that but it hadn't stopped her falling in love with him, had it? The thought almost brought her to her knees. She had done what she had sworn she would never do and fallen in love with him!

'Here. Take these. They should take the edge off the pain.' Daniel's voice reflected his anxiety but Ellie knew that she mustn't make the mistake of reading more into it than that. She didn't say anything as she took the tablets, swallowing them down with some of the water that Marie fetched for her.

'It'll take about twenty minutes before they have any effect,' he said quietly. 'I'll help you upstairs so you can lie down and rest.'

'There's no need,' Ellie began, but he cut her off.

'Of course there is! It's all down to me that you're feeling this way, Eleanor—we both know that.'

Ellie flushed, hoping that Marie would attribute the comment to the extra work she had been doing during his absence. As far as she was aware, nobody knew about them and that was how she wanted it to remain. Licking her wounds in private when they parted would be preferable to doing so in public.

Marie fussed around, fetching her coat, finding her bag, and giving her advice. Ellie was touched when she offered to stay with her, even though she refused. She needed to be on her own to deal with this and it would make it all the harder if she had to pretend and hide how she was feeling. She had done that when she and Michael had split up. She hadn't wanted anyone to know how hurt she had been so she had played down her feelings. However, breaking up with Michael had been very different. Maybe her pride had been hurt but her heart had been intact. And it made it all the worse to realise it and understand that real heartbreak was a very different beast.

Ellie didn't say a word as Daniel led her out of the surgery and round to the flat. She had gone into this with her eyes open and it was her fault—hers alone—that she had believed she could handle it when it ended. When Daniel asked her for the key, she handed it over, too heartsick to refuse. This was the end for them and she knew it was, knew it had to be because she couldn't carry on, not now she knew for a fact that he would never love her like he had loved his late wife. No, it was better to let him go now rather than wait until later and suffer even more.

'I wish I could stay.' Daniel opened the door, his face reflecting the battle he was having, concern for her warring with his need to take care of Nathan. 'But I have to get back to Nathan, Eleanor. I'm so sorry.'

'Of course you do.' Ellie nodded then winced when her head throbbed even harder.

'You do understand, don't you?' He touched her cheek, his fingers brushing her skin, so lightly, so gently, so familiarly that she could have wept all over again. She remembered every touch, every caress; they were as familiar to her as the feel of her own skin.

'Yes. You go, Daniel. I'll be fine. Really.'

'You're sure? Promise that you'll ring me if you feel any worse.'

'I'll be fine,' she repeated, desperately wanting him to go so that she could grieve in peace. 'You go and check on Nathan then I can stop worrying about how he is too.'

'I will.' He dropped a kiss on her mouth, taking her words at face value, thankfully. 'I'll see you tomorrow, although you're not to come in if you still feel rotten. OK?'

'Uh-huh.' Ellie managed to smile, even managed to hold it until he had gone down the steps, but once he disappeared that was it. Sobs tore at her throat as she closed the door, dry racking sobs that seemed to come from somewhere deep inside her. She stumbled into the bathroom and was violently sick then leant against the basin, shuddering and shaking as she wondered where she would find the strength to keep going, but what choice did she have? She had to learn to live without Daniel because he would never be hers.

Ellie made her way to the bedroom and lay down on the bed, too exhausted to undress. The painkillers were starting to work and the headache was easing enough to let her think. She had to work out what she intended to do. She couldn't stay in Beesdale—that was obvious. No, she would have to find another job, preferably abroad because that would be easier than remaining in England and allowing herself to carry on hoping. She and Daniel were over. What they'd had was finished. The sooner she accepted that, the better.

She drifted off to sleep only to wake in the middle of the night with her heart racing. Somewhere during those bleak hours a thought had surfaced: she had felt sick and nauseous all day. She had also missed a period. Was it possible that she was pregnant?

It turned out that Daniel's fears about how Nathan might have fared at college had been groundless. Far from unsettling him, it appeared that the chat with his tutors had reassured him. He was in a buoyant mood when Daniel got home and cheerfully informed him that he intended to carry on with his studies and, if there were bits he had forgotten, well, he would just have to learn them again.

It was a huge relief, although Daniel knew it was too early to relax. Nathan could change his mind if he encountered a major setback so no way was everything cut and dried. However, it did help to relieve some of the tension he had been under for the past few weeks. Maybe the situation wasn't as dire as he'd thought it was. Maybe Nathan could cope with the idea of him having a relationship with another woman. After all, Nathan seemed to genuinely like Eleanor so perhaps it wouldn't be as stressful for him as Daniel had thought.

If he handled things slowly and gave Nathan time to come to terms with the idea, it could work. He desperately hoped so. Not only did he owe it to Eleanor not to string her along, he owed it to himself as well. It was about time that he enjoyed some personal happiness again. He went into work the following morning, feeling more upbeat than he had felt in a very long time. Marie was setting up for the day and she grimaced when she saw him coming in.

'Ellie just phoned to say that she still feels rotten so she's taking the day off. I offered to go up and make her some breakfast but she said she'd rather be on her own.' Marie lowered her voice when an early patient arrived for a fasting blood test. 'Apparently, she's got some sort of sickness and diarrhoea bug, the poor love.'

'Maybe I should pop up and check on her,' Daniel said in concern.

'I wouldn't. I got the impression that she'd prefer to be on her own. I can't say I blame her. I wouldn't want anyone watching me throwing up or worse!'

'All right,' Daniel conceded reluctantly, although he would have preferred to see for himself how Eleanor was. However, the last thing he wanted was to embarrass her.

He went to his room, aware that it wouldn't make any difference to how he felt to see her at her worst. He would wipe her brow, soothe her, care for her, and be happy to do so too. After Camille had died, the one abiding thought that had filled his mind was that he couldn't go through an experience like that again. But he could. And he would if Eleanor needed him. If that wasn't love, *true* love, then what the heck was it?

The thought settled into his mind, filled the gaps and the empty spaces not with fear, as he had expected, but with joy. He loved Eleanor. He loved her without reservations, without doubts or regrets. He and Camille had had their time and he would never forget it, always cherish it, but now it was time to look to the future. With Eleanor. If she would have him, please, God.

Ellie spent the day holed up in the flat. Although she genuinely felt sick, the rest was pure invention. She simply couldn't have gone into work and faced Daniel wondering if she was pregnant. She would have to buy a pregnancy testing kit and find out for definite, although she knew deep down it was true. The missing period, the sickness and nausea, the fact that her breasts felt heavy and swollen were all indications. Although she was on the Pill there had been a couple of occasions when she had taken it later than normal after she had spent the night at Daniel's house and it was that which had probably caused it to fail. Once she knew for certain that there was a baby on the way then she could make plans, although one thing was certain: she had no intention of getting rid of it. Although she doubted if Daniel would want this child, she wanted it. Desperately. Caring for their son or daughter would give her a purpose and make all the heartache worthwhile.

Ellie managed to slip out in the middle of the morning and drove to a supermarket on the outskirts of a neighbouring town where there was less chance of her being recognised. She bought a pregnancy testing kit and drove back. She took the kit into the bathroom and followed the instructions, unsurprised when two pink lines appeared in the tiny window. So she was pregnant and now she needed to formulate her plans so that when Daniel came to check on her this evening, she knew exactly what she intended to do.

The last thing she wanted was him becoming suspicious. Even if he didn't want this baby, she knew that he would want to do the right thing—offer to support her, maybe even suggest marriage. It would be so very tempting to agree and take what he offered and not worry about what he never could. However, Ellie knew that it would be unbearable to live her life knowing that he hadn't really wanted her, that he had simply done his duty. Better to be alone for the rest of her days than be second-best. When the knock on the door came shortly after six p.m. she forced herself to her feet. This was something she *had* to do. For her sake. For Daniel's sake. And, most important of all, for the sake of their child. She didn't want their child to grow up feeling that it wasn't truly wanted.

'How do you feel?' Daniel asked as soon as she let him in.

'Not too good,' she told him because it was true. She felt as though she could drop down dead on the floor, although it wasn't some horrible bug that was making her feel this way but a broken heart.

'I wanted to come up and see you before, but Marie said you wanted to be on your own.'

'I did. Chucking up and racing to the loo is not a good look,' she replied offhandedly. 'Not even in front of friends.'

'I thought we were more than friends, Eleanor,' he said quietly, his brows drawing together.

'Did you?' She shrugged. 'That's nice of you but let's not get carried away. We're friends—oh, and colleagues, of course, Daniel, or that's what we are in my eyes anyway.'

'I see. So these past few weeks, they've been what exactly? An expression of our *friendship*?'

His voice echoed with hurt, with disappointment and so many other emotions that Ellie almost gave in and begged his forgiveness. How could she lessen what they'd had, diminish it this way? It had been the most wonderful time she had ever experienced, the most magical, the most meaningful, but she couldn't tell him that when it could have devastating consequences for all of them. Daniel had to love her. He had to want her.

He had to *need* her for it to mean anything. Anything less wasn't enough.

'Probably. Oh, I know things got rather intense but, if we're honest, it was circumstances that made it that way, don't you think?'

She carried on when he didn't say anything, needing to fill the void before temptation proved too much and she told him the truth—how much she loved him, how much she wanted him, that she was willing to accept whatever crumbs he could give her rather than lose him. Maybe it would work for a while but it wouldn't work for ever, wouldn't be enough to know that she didn't own his heart as he owned hers. 'Nathan's accident was the trigger. We would never have got together if it hadn't happened, would we? It's better if we accept that and move on.'

'So that's what you want to do, is it?' he said harshly. 'Move on?'

'I think so.' She stared back at him, the tears falling in her heart where he couldn't see them. 'It was fun while it lasted but all good things have to come to an end. If we go back to what we were before—colleagues—then it will be simpler.'

'And what if I can't go back? What if I don't want to?' He stepped forward, his eyes blazing, although Ellie wasn't sure if it was anger or pain she could see in them. Probably a bit of both, she decided sickly. Daniel had every right to be angry. He had every right to feel hurt by what she was saying. He had held her, loved her, made her his, and he had earned the right to have an opinion. She just couldn't afford to listen to what that opinion was in case she weakened.

'Then I'm sorry but you'll leave me no choice other than to leave.' She stood up straighter, needing to look and sound convincing. 'I have no intention of staying somewhere where I feel uncomfortable. I'd rather look for another job than find myself in that position.'

'In that case I suggest you start looking immediately. Don't worry about working out your contract. I shall be happy to release you.'

He wrenched open the door, his face set, his body rigid. That he was furiously angry was bad enough but that he was deeply wounded as well was more than she could bear. Ellie half reached towards him but he ignored her as he ran down the steps. Ellie closed the door, listening to the sound of a car engine being revved to within an inch of its life. Daniel was furious with her and no wonder. He probably felt betrayed, cheapened, insulted, the whole damned lot, but he couldn't feel any worse than she did. She bit her lip to hold back another desperate sob. *His* heart wasn't broken but *hers* was.

CHAPTER FIFTEEN

DANIEL COULDN'T BELIEVE what had happened. No matter how many hours he spent each night thinking about it, he couldn't believe it. Eleanor didn't love him. She didn't want him. She had no intention of spending her life with him!

It was work that kept him going, work and his need to carry on for Nathan's sake. However, he knew that he would reach a point where he would have to let go, give in and grieve. He just needed to stave off the moment because he didn't want anyone to witness his devastation and especially not Eleanor. He couldn't bear to think that she might imagine he was playing the sympathy card. He might not have much left but he did have his pride!

The atmosphere in the surgery grew so tense that he knew people were speculating about what had happened between him and Eleanor. That they had their own theories didn't concern him, although he did worry about the effect it could have on team morale. He did his best to put a positive spin on things but he felt too raw to be positive, too wounded to sound hopeful.

As for Eleanor, the best he could say was that she was reserved. She was unfailingly polite with everyone, him included, but she held herself at one step removed.

There was no idle chit-chat, no gossip, just work. It made him long for the day she would tell him that she was leaving at the same time as he dreaded it. Could losing her physically really be any worse than her cutting him out of her life like this?

When the day arrived, it was pouring with rain. The River Bees had breached its banks and there was widespread flooding throughout the area. Daniel couldn't help thinking how fitting it was that she should have chosen this day to leave. Even the heavens were crying.

'I've found another post.' She came into his room without bothering to knock, proof of how eager she was to get this show on the road. 'A practice in Surrey is desperate for cover over Christmas and the New Year and I've agreed to do it.'

'I see. So you've decided to go for a short-term contract,' he said as calmly as he could, not that he cared how long the wretched contract lasted. She was leaving and that was all that mattered.

'Yes.' She shrugged as she pushed back her hair, which had grown longer since she had been at The Larches, and it suited her…

'Sorry. Say that again,' Daniel instructed as his mind drifted off. What did it matter how she looked? She didn't give a damn about him or his opinions, as she had made it abundantly clear.

'I've decided to apply for a job overseas eventually, Australia probably, although I haven't made the final decision yet so it could be New Zealand.' She met his eyes. 'It's something I've thought about before and now seems like a good time to do it.'

'If that's what you want,' he said neutrally, although the thought was making his heart race. If she went overseas he would never see her again and he wasn't sure if he could bear it.

'It is. Anyway, I'm leaving at the end of the week, if that's all right with you? I know it's short notice but you did say that you'd be willing to release me from my contract,' she reminded him briskly.

'I did and I shall.' Daniel stood up and offered her his hand because that was all he could offer her when she didn't want his heart. The thought made him feel all choked up but he hid it well. 'I wish you every success wherever you go, Eleanor. You've made a valuable contribution while you've been here and I appreciate it.'

'Thank you.' She started to leave, paused, half turned back, and then shrugged. 'Thank you too, Daniel. I've enjoyed working with you.'

Only enjoyed? he wanted to ask, but didn't because there was no point when it wouldn't change anything. He sat down after she left, feeling worse than he had felt in his entire life. He felt cold and empty and desperately alone. What made it all the worse was that he had allowed himself to hope, to dream, to *want* more than he would ever have. If he couldn't have Eleanor, he didn't want anyone else and he never would.

Eleanor just made it back to her room before the tears came. She let them pour down her face, needing the release from all the tension. She had done what she'd had to do and now there was no turning back, no second chances, no reason to hope that there might be a better solution, one that wasn't so painful.

She would get through this for the sake of her child, a little boy or girl who needed her to be strong. She would love and care for it, make sure he or she knew that it was wanted, cherished. She understood how it felt to feel that you weren't enough and her baby would never be allowed to feel lacking in any way. She would give this child all the love it needed, love it to eternity and beyond, love it enough for her *and* Daniel. No child would be better loved. She would make sure of that!

It was Friday afternoon and the day Eleanor was leaving when Daniel decided to visit Madeleine Walsh. It was a premeditated decision. If he visited Mrs Walsh, he could collect Nathan from college afterwards and then drive straight home. He wouldn't have to return to the surgery, wouldn't need to speak to Eleanor and wish her well before she left. He could get that over with at lunchtime and maybe it would help lessen the impact in some way.

He kept it brief, shook her hand, thanked her, and left. Marie was muttering something about them all meeting up for a drink that night but he pretended not to hear. He wasn't going to sit in the pub and celebrate, neither was he going to drown his sorrows with a pint of best bitter. He was going to handle Eleanor's departure with dignity even if it killed him!

He drove out of the surgery, taking the road to Hemsthwaite as the Walsh family lived that way. The rain was lashing down and the River Bees was overflowing, muddy brown water swirling over the banking and across the road. Potholes had formed where the tarmac had been washed away and Daniel slowed down as he tried to steer around them. He had almost reached the turning to Cherry Tree Lane when the road gave way, a huge chunk of it falling into the swirling river. Daniel had just seconds to react and he wasn't quick enough, probably because his mind wasn't focused when he was thinking about Eleanor and her imminent departure. He swerved to the right, praying the tyres would find something to grip onto, but more of the road collapsed. All of a sudden he felt himself floating, the car spinning round and round as though he was on some kind of crazy fairground ride, like those teacups that Nathan had loved as a child…

The car hit a tree and Daniel hit his head on the side window. Teacups and water and roads that were collapsing suddenly started to jumble themselves up together and he had no idea what was real any more. It was a relief when blankness descended on him and he could no longer see, think or feel. There was less pain that way, less heartache, maybe even a smidgeon of hope. Maybe there was a way to stop Eleanor leaving if it wasn't too late.

Eleanor was in her room, trying to come up with an excuse not to go to the pub that night, when Marie came rushing in to find her.

'There's been an accident!'

'An accident,' Ellie repeated blankly like some fifth-rate actor struggling to remember her lines.

'Yes! It's Daniel. The road's collapsed and his car's been swept into the river.'

It took a second, one precious second that Ellie knew she would relive over and over again, before she reacted. She shot to her feet, her heart racing in fear. 'Is he all right? They've got him out, haven't they?'

'Yes, but it was a close call. If Philip Applethwaite hadn't seen what happened… Well, it doesn't bear thinking about! Apparently, Phil and one of his lads—Steven, the youngest—waded in and managed to get a chain on the car while it was wedged up against a tree and they pulled it out with their tractor. A couple of seconds later, the tree disappeared.'

Ellie sank down onto the chair as her knees buckled. 'Where is he?' she whispered hoarsely.

'Daniel?' Marie gave her a funny look. 'They've rushed him off to Leeds. York's flooded and the ambulances are being diverted wherever they can squeeze them in.'

'I'll get straight over there.' Ellie stood up and gathered up her bag. She was halfway out of the door before Marie spoke.

'Wouldn't it be easier to phone and ask how he is?'

'I need to see him.'

'Ah. Right. I get the picture.' Marie smiled smugly. 'I *thought* something was going on. Seems I was right.'

Ellie had no idea what she meant and didn't wait around to ask. She had to get to the hospital and check that Daniel wasn't badly hurt. A sob caught in her throat but she didn't have time to cry when she needed to drive there. The journey seemed to pass in a trice, even though it took hours to negotiate the flooded roads and all the traffic. She parked outside on the road, not caring if the car would be towed away. Daniel needed her. That was more important than anything else.

A and E was frantically busy but she persisted until she found a young nurse who knew where Daniel was. She followed her along the corridor, around the corner, and there he was, lying on a trolley, eyes closed, a huge dressing covering the right side of his head. Ellie didn't know if she felt relieved or what. He was obviously injured but he was alive and, so help her, he was going to stay that way. No way was she going to let him go now, not after this, after being so scared, so shocked, so utterly and completely devastated. Even if he could never love her the way she wanted, it would be enough. She would make sure it was!

She walked straight over to the trolley, bent down and kissed him on the mouth because this wasn't the time to play games. This called for the truth, every tiny, scary bit of it. 'How *dare* you do this to me, Daniel?' she said furiously when he opened his eyes and stared at her in surprise. 'How bloody *dare you* scare me to death like this?'

There was a moment when he didn't react and then he smiled. Slowly, wolfishly, smugly. 'I was right then. It was all an act. You love me, don't you, Eleanor?'

'Yes,' she hissed, unwilling to let him off the hook after she had suffered such torments, and his smile grew bigger, bolder, even more confident before it turned into a laugh.

'Then it seems we're quits,' he murmured, his eyes holding hers as he slid his hand round the back of her neck and drew her down to him. 'Because I, Eleanor Munroe, love you too, you bloody annoying woman!'

The nurse somehow managed to find them a space in cubicles. Daniel had a sneaking suspicion it was embarrassment at the sight of people their age making out that prompted her to redouble her efforts. Granted, any privacy was illusory with only paper curtains to separate them from the patients in the adjoining cubicles but Daniel could ignore them if he couldn't see them. After all, he only had eyes and ears, and everything else, for Eleanor.

He kissed her again, slowly and deeply to make up for the torment he had suffered these past terrible weeks. After they drew apart, he waited while she pulled up a chair then took hold of her hand. 'Why?'

'Because I was afraid.' She didn't ask him what he meant—she knew. And the pain released its grip that bit more because they were so in tune that they didn't need to explain the important bits.

'That I didn't love you?' he said simply, and felt her shudder.

'Yes. I knew when I saw you with that photo that you could never love me as much as you loved Camille.'

'That isn't true.' He squeezed her fingers, only slackening his grip when he felt her wince.

'Isn't it?' she said in a lacklustre voice that cut him to the quick.

'No. I'll admit that how I feel about you is very different from how I felt about Camille. I loved her and I would have carried on loving her if she hadn't died. But she did.'

'Then how can I ever measure up to her? I can't compete with her, Daniel. I wouldn't try!'

'Good, because this isn't a contest. This is something far more important than scoring points, for me as well as for you.' He lifted her hand and kissed her knuckles, one by one, then placed their joined hands on the side of the bed. 'Camille and I were very young when we met. I was twenty-two and she was nineteen. We fell in love and grew up together, loving one another.'

'It must have been a wonderful time,' she murmured, her voice catching.

'It was. There's something magical about first love, but it doesn't mean you can't fall in love again and that it won't be just as special, maybe even more so.'

'More so?'

'Yes.' He leant over and kissed her, ignoring the throbbing in his temple. What did a bit of pain matter when he needed to sort out the rest of his life? 'The moment I met you, Eleanor, I knew you were trouble. I felt all shaken up, tense, on edge.' He laughed at her stunned expression. 'I think I have some idea how Sleeping Beauty must have felt when she was woken by her prince—totally and utterly discombobulated!'

He carried on when she didn't reply, knowing how hard she must find it to believe what he was saying. A wave of tenderness swept over him and he smiled. Heaven knew, he understood how she felt. He'd had the devil of a job getting *his* head around it and he'd had weeks, whereas he had just landed this on her without any warning. 'The trouble was that I hadn't expected to feel this way—ever. I'd settled for what I saw as my lot in life—i.e. widower, father, doctor, et cetera. I wasn't looking for more—I didn't want more, to be honest. But then you came along and there was something about you that made me start wishing for things that I wasn't sure I could or even should have.'

'You felt guilty?' she said quietly. 'About letting go of Camille and seemingly forgetting her? I would *never* expect you to do that, Daniel! I know how much she means to you and Nathan…'

'I know you do. That's why you're so special and why I can't bear to live the rest of my life without you.' He took a deep breath as all the emotions he'd held in check swirled to the surface. It felt as though they were choking him but he had to keep going, had to make sure that Eleanor understood how much he loved her.

'I fell in love with you, Eleanor, because I couldn't help myself. Yes, it scared me and, yes, I was stricken with guilt as well as fear about how Nathan would react if I had a relationship with you. But, despite all that, I couldn't not fall in love with you. You're the matching beat of my heart, you're the breath in my lungs, the heat in my blood. You're part of me and I can't live without that part because it's too hard. What I feel for you is warm and gentle and tender and sweet. It's also burning hot and all-consuming and it will continue to burn just as hotly even when we're old and grey, sitting side by side in matching bath chairs. There isn't a bit of you that I don't love, don't want, won't cherish. If you'll have me.'

Ellie could feel tears stinging her eyes even as a huge great wave of elation consumed her. Daniel loved her. He *really* loved her! She wasn't second-best but first choice, the woman he had chosen, the woman he would love for ever and always. Leaning over, she kissed him, letting her lips tell him how she felt, how overjoyed, how happy, how relieved. It was several minutes before she pulled away, although it could have been a lifetime too. It felt like it, felt as though she had been reborn as a whole new woman, the woman Daniel loved. She realised then that she had to tell him about the baby, that this was the perfect moment to layer joy on joy until it grew so huge that nothing could sweep it away. She and Daniel were going to have a child. He deserved to know just how wonderful their future was going to be!

'I've something to tell you,' she said quietly but without hesitation. 'I'm pregnant, Daniel. I'm carrying our child.'

'You…me…we…a *baby*!' The words came out in a rush, shock rippling the edges, but it was no competition for all the other emotions she could hear as well. Then all of a sudden he was standing up, drawing her into his arms, holding her close, kissing her and talking at the same time. 'I had no idea… I never suspected… Is *that* why you were leaving?'

It was easier to answer the last question first. 'Yes. I thought it was unfair to drop it on you when you didn't love me.'

'Oh, Eleanor. Darling! I can't imagine what you've been through these past weeks.' He cupped her cheek, tears pouring down his face. 'Thank you. You were mad to do such a crazy thing but I understand why you did it.'

'Because I love you too much to hurt you or cause you any pain. I also couldn't bear to think that you'd do the right thing out of a sense of…well, duty,' she admitted, not wanting to make it appear that she had been thinking solely about him and not even a little bit about herself.

'Damn! Does that mean that I can't do the right thing now, even though it's the thing I want to do more than anything else? Talk about boxing me into a corner!'

Ellie was feeling a little lost. Maybe it was the rush of emotions, Daniel's confession, and everything else, but she was finding it difficult to follow what he was saying. 'I'm sorry but I'm not sure what you mean.'

'Then I need to make myself clear.' He smiled into her eyes and she felt her heart catch when she saw the love in his. 'I should by rights be down on my knee, ring in one hand, rose in the other, with violins playing in the background, but somehow I don't think that's going to happen, so here goes. Eleanor, my love, my darling, will you marry me?'

'Marry you?' she repeated blankly.

Yes. Oh, I know it's old-fashioned in this day to get married and that a lot of people live perfectly happily without doing so, but it's not what I want.' He drew her to him and kissed her tenderly. 'I want to make a proper commitment to you and our child. I want to spend the rest of my life loving you and caring for you and knowing that we shall always be together. I always wanted another child but it simply didn't happen so this is like a double blessing. To be loved by you and to have our baby as well is more than I could have dreamed of.'

'It's more than I could have dreamt of too,' Ellie whispered, almost too moved by the admission to speak.

'So does that mean you will marry me?'

'Yes!' The word shot out of her mouth as her voice came rushing back. When Daniel bent and kissed her again, it seemed to put the seal on her happiness. She was going to marry him and they would raise their baby together, loving and caring for each other. She had everything she had ever wanted and more!

EPILOGUE

'Now, ARE YOU sure you've got everything? Passport, money, phone…?'

'Yes! I've also got a clean hanky and been to the loo and had a pee.' Nathan rolled his eyes. 'Chill out, Dad. I'm going to Australia, not the moon.'

Ellie chuckled. They were at Manchester Airport, waiting for Nathan to board his flight to Perth. He had decided to take a gap year before starting university. It was only a delay, he'd assured them. He had no intention of skipping out. But, as he had explained, he needed to find out who he was before he decided who he wanted to be.

Although most of the memory lapses had resolved themselves, there were a couple of incidents he couldn't recall and might never do so. However, he was philosophical about it and accepted that some areas might always be blank. The strange thing was that losing bits of his own memory had triggered an interest in helping others in a similar position and he was thinking about switching courses and working in that field. He'd had an interview at Liverpool and despite the fact that he would need an extra science subject, they had offered him a place studying medicine the following year. Ellie knew that he must have impressed them to have been given such an opportunity but, there again, he was turning into a very impressive young man, just like his father was.

She glanced at Daniel, feeling her heart lift as it always did whenever she looked at him. They had got married at the end of November, a simple ceremony held at Beesdale Parish Church. Her whole family had attended, even her sister. She and Gemma had had a long talk about past issues and, to Ellie's surprise, Gemma had admitted that she'd always felt jealous because their parents had *chosen* her, whereas she was just their natural child and nothing special. They had laughed about it and it had healed the rift that had existed between them since childhood. When Gemma had asked if she could be her bridesmaid, Ellie had readily agreed. Now that she was having a baby of her own, she wanted all her family around her.

'Right. Time to go. And, yes, I shall be in touch for an online video chat every single evening or I will unless I'm too busy enjoying myself to think about aged parents back home—not meaning you, obviously, Ellie,' Nathan added, winking at her.

'Obviously not,' she agreed dryly. That Nathan had accepted her relationship with Daniel and been thrilled when he had learned about the baby had doubly endeared him to her. She had no hesitation as she reached out and hugged him. 'Have a brilliant time. We're here if you need us, but I know you won't, so just enjoy yourself.'

'I will.' Nathan hugged her back, sounding ever so slightly choked. 'You've brought the fun back into my life as well as Dad's and I love you for it.' He let her go before things got too mushy, grinning broadly as he looked pointedly at her bump. 'Just make sure this little one doesn't play you up. Kids can be a trial. I'm talking from experience here, so I know!'

'Oh, I'm sure we'll cope when your sister arrives,' Daniel declared airily, getting his own back. 'Girls aren't nearly as much trouble as boys.'

'It's a girl? When did you find out?' Nathan demanded, sounding for all the world like a ten-year-old who had missed out on a treat.

'When I went for my twenty-week scan,' Ellie admitted, laughing. 'Your dad insisted that we shouldn't tell you until today. A sort of farewell gift.'

'More like an attempt to get one over on me,' Nathan declared grumpily, then suddenly laughed. 'That is *so* cool! I'm going to be a big brother to my very own baby sister. I can't wait!'

'I'm afraid you're going to have to,' Daniel declared, stepping forward to hug him. 'But don't worry, it won't be long now and we'll keep you posted—make sure you receive lots of bump photos et cetera.'

'I think I can live without them—just!' Nathan hugged Daniel back. 'Thanks, Dad, for everything. I know I've been a real pain in the backside but you never gave up on me and I won't forget it.'

'It was what I wanted to do,' Daniel told him truthfully. 'I love you too, son, and nothing will ever be too much trouble where you're concerned. I just want you to be happy. That's all I ask.'

'I shall.' Nathan picked up his bag, kissed Ellie again, then went to join Jack and a couple of others who had decided to enjoy a year of freedom before knuckling down to work. They were laughing and joking as they headed off to security.

Daniel felt his eyes prickle with tears as he watched them leave but in his heart he knew that Nathan was going to be fine. Now it was time to think about Eleanor and their new little daughter. Happiness fizzed through his veins. A world that had once seemed grey and bleak now seemed to be filled with light and colour. Sliding his arm around Eleanor's shoulders, he drew her to him, kissed her, held her, and smiled as he said softly, 'Shall we go home?'

'What a good idea.'

She snuggled against him as they left the terminal. It was still very early and although there was traffic about there seemed to be an odd sense of peace hanging over the place. But maybe the peace came from within, Daniel mused, came from his heart, from his soul, from his love for this woman who had given him her heart and taken his in return.

He breathed in deeply, not tasting the vapours of aviation fuel or the emissions from countless car exhausts. All he could taste was happiness and it had a very special flavour, one he intended to enjoy over and over again. For ever.

* * * * *

*If you enjoyed this story, check out these
other great reads from Jennifer Taylor*

*REAWAKENED BY THE SURGEON'S TOUCH
THE GREEK DOCTOR'S SECRET SON
MIRACLE UNDER THE MISTLETOE
BEST FRIEND TO PERFECT BRIDE*

All available now!

REUNITED BY THEIR PREGNANCY SURPRISE

BY
LOUISA HEATON

Published in Great Britain 2017
By Mills & Boon, an imprint of HarperCollins*Publishers*
1 London Bridge Street, London, SE1 9GF

© 2017 Louisa Heaton

ISBN: 978-0-263-92643-9

Our policy is to use papers that are natural, renewable and recyclable
products and made from wood grown in sustainable forests. The logging
and manufacturing processes conform to the legal environmental
regulations of the country of origin.

Printed and bound in Spain
by CPI, Barcelona

For my mum and dad, who had their own amnesia story.

Books by Louisa Heaton

Mills & Boon Medical Romance

The Baby That Changed Her Life
His Perfect Bride?
A Father This Christmas?
One Life-Changing Night
Seven Nights with Her Ex
Christmas with the Single Dad

Visit the Author Profile page
at millsandboon.co.uk for more titles.

**Praise for
Louisa Heaton**

'An emotional rollercoaster ride… *One Life-Changing Night* is medical drama at its best.'

—*Goodreads*

Dear Reader,

Years ago, when my dad was in the army and stationed in Singapore, he overturned a water truck in the jungle and sustained a head injury. When he woke in hospital he had no idea of who he was or what had happened. The padre in the hospital found a love letter in his uniform pocket from my mum and he wrote to her, telling her what had happened and that she would need to help my father regain his memories—and make him fall in love with her all over again!

I always told my mum that she missed a trick in not 'reprogramming' my dad into a romantic Alpha hero! But, no, she did the right thing and told him the truth instead—even though my dad had sometimes been a naughty boy!

So I *had* to write an amnesia story for myself, and I really hope you will enjoy reading about Emily and Sam as they go on their own journey to find Sam's memories and restore their love.

Happy reading!

Louisa xxx

CHAPTER ONE

HER HEELS CLICK-CLACKED down the hospital corridor, a hurried, tense staccato, as Emily headed for the familiar room that Sam had been moved to after his short stay in the ICU.

She cut a striking figure in her stylish clothes, her long honey-blonde locks held back by sunglasses on her head and her large expensive bag swinging from the crook of her elbow. Her face, beautiful without the aid of make-up, was today showing strain. Lines and dark circles framed her eyes. And those who saw her noted the way her fingers twisted and fidgeted at her wedding band.

The Beverly West Hospital was the biggest and most prestigious hospital in Beverly Hills, Los Angeles, California. Sam's care here had been amazing. From the second he'd been scooped from their crumpled, steaming vehicle and blue-lighted to its doors, Emily had not doubted for one second the level of care they had both received. Apart from that split second when she'd first received her pregnancy test results…

Outside Sam's room she could see Dr Waters and her team, standing discussing something in low voices, with the occasional glance at Sam's notes on a clipboard. They looked serious. Concerned. But why? Hadn't they just rung her with the news that he was starting to wake up? That was *good*, right?

Dr Waters looked up as she became aware of Emily's approach and, meeting her by the door to the room, pasted a polite smile onto her face. 'Mrs Saint—'

'Is he awake?' She bit her lip and again twisted the wedding ring on her finger.

This was it. *Now or never.* She would go inside her husband's room and either find a man who was happy to be alive and willing to work on any problem, or the bear of a husband she'd been used to over the last few difficult months.

'He is. He's tired, and occasionally lapses back into sleep—which is normal considering the trauma his brain has been through. Coma patients usually take a day or two to wake properly.'

'I can go in and see him? Talk to him?'

The call from Dr Waters had come in the early hours of the morning. The phone ringing had not woken her. She'd already been awake. Lying in her very empty bed, staring at the ceiling and trying—still—to decide what was best to do.

Leave Sam? Or stay and fight for their marriage?

She'd even pulled a suitcase out and laid it on the bed one day, stood staring at it in numb indecision. Her heart wavering. It had all seemed so very clear-cut before the car crash. But now…? Knowing that he was sick…knowing that she was pregnant?

She had returned the suitcase to its storage spot and closed the doors on it. Her mind ran back to the times when Sam had refused to talk to her about having children, clamming up the second she raised it. Why had he done that? Over and over again? What hadn't he been telling her? There had to be something, but his refusal even to talk to her about it had been hurtful. They'd got to a point when they had barely been speaking to one another.

Her brain had almost torn itself in two, trying to figure out his secret. Thinking of one scenario and then another. None had seemed likely, and she'd begun to believe that maybe he just didn't want to have a child with *her*.

Emily had stared at the closed closet doors, knowing that she would do what was *right*. And the right thing here was to give Sam time to recover and then let him know about the baby. Because then there was a small chance—a tiny, infinitesimal chance—that now the baby was no longer hypothetical but real and *here* he might change his mind.

She couldn't leave him without him knowing the truth. And if he heard the news about the pregnancy and *still* didn't want to be there for her and their child *then* she would go. Step out into the world on her own, even though doing so would break her heart. She didn't want to leave Sam, but he'd made life unbearable—had backed her into a corner.

Dr Waters shifted, looking at her colleagues, who all understood the implicit suggestion that perhaps they should leave, allow her to talk to Mrs Saint alone. They gave her sympathetic smiles and scurried away.

'Of course, but before you go in there's something you need to know.'

Her blood ran cold. Was there a problem? Brain injury? Dr Waters had mentioned that there might be the possibility of something like that once before. But Sam had recovered so quickly! His coma had been short, the ICP had dropped to normal levels incredibly quickly…

'What is it?'

Sam could have anything wrong. Be blind. Deaf. Find it difficult to talk or maybe swallow.

'We spoke once before about the damage that might have occurred to Sam's brain because of the injury to his head, and after a quick examination of your husband we believe that there seems to be some sort of memory deficit—mainly amnesia. It could be temporary, of course. He might remember everything after he's had another good sleep. But right now Sam seems…*confused* about his own timeline.'

Emily let out a long, slow, measured breath. Amnesia? She'd been fearing the worst! Temporary amnesia they could deal with.

'Is that all?'

Dr Waters frowned. 'Amnesia is a significant condition. I'm not sure you understand the full—'

'I'm going in to see him.' She cut off the doctor and stepped into Sam's room. She'd been waiting long enough for this moment. Ten long days. Nothing more could keep them apart.

Ten days. It had seemed like a lifetime.

Sometimes in those ten days she'd held his hand in hers, taking advantage of the fact that he was unconscious, remembering the happier times when they'd been close, pretending it was still that way. Sometimes she'd read to him from that day's newspaper, hoping that the sound of her voice would bring him back. And sometimes she'd just sat and stared at him, mulling everything over in her head, thinking of where they'd gone wrong and how she could fix it. Imagining the day he would wake—the day his eyelids would flutter open and he would see her, sitting by his bedside like a sentinel. How he would smile and say her name, reach out slowly for her hand and kiss her fingertips…

Okay, so maybe she lived in a fantasy land at times, but surely a touch of escapism had never hurt anyone.

'Sam?' So much hope, so much need was in the pitch of her voice.

Her husband lay in bed, his face pale and relaxed against pure white starched hospital pillows, his blue eyes slowly opening, wincing at the light in the room before fixing his gaze upon her.

And *smiling*!

It's been too long since you smiled at me like that...

It was like when they'd first been going out. The way he would look at her as if he was already in love with her. As if she was pure joy for him. Had no faults. Had not driven him crazy yet with endless requests to start a family. Okay, maybe not *crazy*, but she had tried to start that conversation lots of times. In the end even *she* had refused to talk. It had been too hard. Their conversations would always somehow end in arguments, and it had been easier just not to talk at all. She'd feared what would happen if they did.

Perhaps that had been a bad thing to do. Shutting down their communication. But she'd been trying to protect their relationship. She hadn't wanted it to end.

Sucking in a breath, she rushed to his side, dropping her bag on the floor, not caring as she reached for his outstretched hand, stooping down to kiss him, feeling his bristles scrape her face as his lips met hers. Nothing mattered at that moment apart from the fact that he was alive. Awake. Back with her. She never wanted to go through those ten days ever again.

It didn't matter that they'd been arguing. She was just happy that he was awake. Reacting. That he was looking at her and he was smiling and—

'How are you feeling?' She stroked his face, looking for clues, looking for any sign of discomfort that he might be trying to hide. Making sure that he wasn't in any pain. Her professional skills as a nurse-midwife were coming to the fore.

'Better for seeing you, Em,' he croaked, squeezing her fingers, and she looked down at their entwined hands and smiled.

All those days she had sat holding his hands and he had *never* squeezed back. Never shown any sign of life in his fingers. They'd just lain there, limp. Breaking her heart. It felt so good to be touching him again. Gaining strength from him.

'I've been so worried!' She sat on the bed facing him and ran her thumb over the backs of his hands.

He closed his eyes briefly, as if he couldn't stand the knowledge that she'd been so concerned for him. 'The doc says we've been in a car accident?'

The confusion in his face was heart-rending, but Emily guessed that this was the amnesia that Dr Waters had mentioned. Sam couldn't remember the crash. Sometimes people's brains would exclude certain bad experiences or memories, to help prevent itself from feeling hurt. Like a safety mechanism. If that was all that had happened to him then they'd both got away from this lightly.

'Yes.'

'Were *you* hurt?'

The concern in his voice and the way his blue eyes darkened at the thought relieved her. He *did* care for her! He *wasn't* angry at what had happened between them prior to this.

That was good, right? It took something like this to wake people up. To make them notice what was important in life. *Each other.* They were stronger together than they were apart. Even if they *had* been disagreeing. Giving each other the cold shoulder.

'Not really. Just whiplash.'

He frowned. 'Whiplash can be serious, Em. Have you been checked out by the doctors?'

He reached up to stroke her face, then his hand fell to her shoulders and neck to rub at her muscles, but he must be feeling tired because his hand dropped back to the bed, his eyes closing as he drifted in and out of sleep, before opening them again.

'Look at me. Weak as a kitten.'

'You need to rest. You've been out of it for ten days.'

'Ten days?' He looked upset.

'They had to put you in an induced coma, Sam. Your brain got shook around in that hard skull of yours.'

He sighed and closed his eyes again and she realised with a sudden pang that he had drifted back to sleep. And she hadn't had a chance to tell him their news, yet.

It can wait. It's waited this long. What's a few more hours?

Right now he was happy to see her. Relieved. All signs of their previous turmoil was gone. They were speaking to each other. Something they hadn't done properly for weeks, and she'd missed that.

But it was odd, wasn't it? That he should be so happy to see her? After the last few days of stony silences, the weeks of arguing and disagreement…

She liked it that he was being nice. Concerned about her whiplash, concerned about *her* health, but she wasn't used to it. It was throwing her slightly.

Having to wait a little longer to deliver the news that she was pregnant was just fine. Because she had no idea how he would react to that. Probably not very well, and then they would be back to being at war with each other. She didn't mind holding off on that for a while.

She liked what they had right now, thank you very much. The talking. The concern for each other's well-being. The holding hands.

Emily stared at his hand in hers, lifted it to her mouth and kissed it, inhaling the scent of him, breathing it in like vital oxygen. Then she got up off the bed and settled into her usual chair, staring long and hard at her husband.

She was getting him back. He'd smiled at her!

She felt sure there was a chance…all this just might be okay.

Sam slowly came to. He had a wicked headache, but he appeared to be still in hospital, attached to God only knew how many wires and monitors and, beside him, her head slumped to her shoulder, asleep, was his beautiful fiancée Emily.

She looked tired. Exhausted, even. Her face was a little pale beneath wave upon wave of that gorgeous hair of hers. But then he assumed she would be. Hadn't she, or someone, told him that he'd been out of it for ten days? After some accident he couldn't even recall?

Ten days. What had he missed? Probably nothing too much. That serial he'd been watching on television had been scheduled to show its last episode the other week, so probably that. There was still another month or so before Emily's birthday, so thankfully not that. He had a big surprise planned. He was hoping to take her to Las Vegas.

It was strange, though. Only ten days and he could swear that her hair seemed longer. A little more sun-bleached. Those honey tones were brighter than normal. And were those new clothes? He hadn't seen them before. But then again, Em did enjoy shopping. Perhaps she'd gone out and treated herself whilst she'd been waiting for him to recover? A little pick-me-up?

He lifted his head off the pillow to check himself out. There didn't appear to be any limbs wrapped in bandages, no plaster casts or anything like that. Had he just got a head injury? That would explain the headache, and the fact that he'd been out of it for a while. He hated it that he was laid up in hospital, because they still had so much to do. Not only did they need to tell everyone that Emily had accepted his proposal of marriage, but there was so much to do at work, too!

His idea, of building an exclusive five-star birth centre—the Monterey Birth Centre—was close to fruition. They'd toured the halls just last week and everything had looked perfect. Almost ready for their Grand Opening.

It was going to be massive. He wanted the Monterey to be the premier birthing centre in the whole of the US. He wanted people to aspire to have their babies there, to be treated as if they were royalty and enjoy the ultimate birthing experience, which he and his team would provide whilst their patients were being fed with delectable dishes provided by a team of Michelin-starred chefs in the kitchen.

It had taken a lot of planning. And sourcing funding. But he'd found people—mainly people whose babies he had already delivered safely—to sponsor and endorse the Monterey. He'd secured a great board of directors—along with himself and Emily, of course—and his excitement for this project had driven him onward like nothing he had ever experienced before. There'd been so much to think about! But he enjoyed that.

Asking Emily to marry him had been the icing on the cake. And she'd said yes. So he guessed now he'd be busy planning a wedding, too!

They hadn't been going out long. Six months? But there was something about her—something that had reached out and grabbed him. She'd seemed so...*vulnerable* when they'd first met, and he'd been cautious not to scare her with his desire to be by her side. He'd not been able to pinpoint the source of that vulnerability and, to be honest, they'd both been so busy at work, and setting up the Monterey, that it hadn't seemed all that important after a while.

Emily had blossomed by his side, driven on by their shared vision. She was everything he could have wished for and he loved her deeply. She cared for and loved delivering babies as much as he did.

But today she looked exhausted. She must have been handling any last hiccups at the birth centre, working *and* having to deal with his accident and their families all by herself. No wonder she looked shattered. Had they put off the Grand Opening whilst they'd waited for him to recover?

For a brief moment he just lay there and stared at her, his heart swelling with love for the woman at his side, but after a minute or so he couldn't stand it any more and reached out to take her hand. Needing to touch her. To connect.

She blinked herself awake in seconds. 'Sam?'

He smiled and lifted her hand to his lips, pressed a kiss upon it. 'Sleeping Beauty.'

She glanced at her watch in confusion. 'I've been asleep for three hours!' She rubbed at her eyes and then glanced at him with concern. 'How are you? Are you in any pain?'

'Just a headache.'

'Should I call a nurse?'

'No, it's fine. It's understandable, considering my head got bashed. I'm sure there's some morphine being dripped in to me somewhere…' He looked up at the various drips and then smiled at her. 'I've missed you.' He squeezed her fingers, wishing he could be holding her in his arms. Wishing he could get her to come and lie beside him upon the bed. He needed to feel her next to him.

She looked a little apprehensive. 'You've been in a coma.'

'So you keep saying. But what about *you*? How are you doing? Any problems with Monterey I need to know about?'

Emily frowned and shook her head. 'No. It's all going very well.'

He let out a sigh. 'That's great news. How did Harry get on with the window treatments? Did he make the changes we asked him to?'

His fiancée looked at him, lines furrowing her brow. 'What?'

'The curtains and sashing in The Nightingale Suite. We decided to change them to that lighter gold colour. Has he done it yet? If he hasn't we need to get on that— the Grand Opening is only a few days away.'

She continued to look at him with puzzlement. 'What are you talking about?'

'The curtains were too dark. That suite is going to be our most prestigious—we want it right for the press tour. Think of the spread of pictures…'

'Press tour? We haven't had a press tour since…' Her voice drifted away and she suddenly looked at him, her eyes searching his face as she sucked in a breath. 'Sam, what day do you think it is?'

He closed his eyes and thought about it. He'd proposed on Friday, he'd been in a coma for ten days, so today had to be... 'Monday? Tuesday, maybe?'

She shook her head, her choppy blonde locks shimmering around her shoulders. 'No. I mean the month. The *year*.'

Month and year? What was she talking about? He'd been out for ten days, they'd said! He told her the date and watched as what little colour there was leeched from her face. She turned away from him, her curtain of honey-blonde hair hiding her face from his as she pulled her hands free of his grasp.

Her recoiling from him made him feel nervous. What didn't he know? 'Why are you asking? I'm not that much out of step, am I?'

He heard her sniff. Watched as she reached into her bag and pulled out a small hankie, dabbing at her eyes before she turned back to face him, bracing herself to prepare to say something she clearly thought he wouldn't be ready to hear.

'Sam... We've been married for *eighteen months*. The Monterey has been open and running for just over a year now.'

Sam stared at her hard. He swallowed painfully and his hands scrunched up the bedding as he made fists.

Eighteen months?

No! That's ridiculous...

'Why would you say that? Why would you even play a trick like that?'

A tear dripped onto her cheek and with clear-cut pain in her voice she said, 'I'm not lying to you.'

'Emily...'

'Sam, please, listen—'

But he wasn't listening. Not any more. Em was playing some cruel trick on him, and he didn't know why, but the doctors would have to tell him the truth! The nurses would. He'd make them show him a newspaper or something. This was completely ridiculous. There was *no way* that he'd lost all that time. He'd *know*. There'd be signs!

Sam stabbed at the button that would call a nurse to his bedside and kept doing so, ignoring Emily's pleas, her cries. She was standing now, her hand covering her mouth, looking at him with those wide, tear-filled eyes...

The door opened and a nurse he hadn't seen before came in. She glanced at Emily in concern before turning to him. 'Mr Saint?'

'I need to see the doctor in charge of my care.'

The nurse kept on looking between the two of them, not sure exactly what had happened. 'Dr Waters has gone home for the evening. I can get—'

'Get *someone*! Someone who knows what they're talking about!' He glared at Emily, angry at her, and watched as she snatched up her handbag and ran from the room.

The nurse nodded and hurried out, and with both women gone he felt his anger deflate slightly.

Married eighteen months? Emily was crazy. Perhaps *she'd* had the bump on the head and not him!

He lay in the bed, fury surging through him, and waited for someone who knew what they were talking about to come and tell him the truth.

There was no way he had lost *that* amount of time.

CHAPTER TWO

EMILY RAN FROM Sam's room, throwing her bag to the floor and sagging against the wall opposite. She slid down it until she sat hunched on the floor, like a puppet without her strings.

He couldn't remember! He had no idea of how much time had passed! He thought…he thought that… She heard his words once again, spoken with such certainty, such concern. *'How did Harry get on with the window treatments? Did he make the changes we asked him to?'*

Window treatments?

I remember! It was a week before the Grand Opening. He'd proposed just the night before…

The nurse who had followed her out of Sam's room came over to her, hunched down and draped her arm softly around her shoulders. 'Are you okay, Mrs Saint?'

She could barely breathe…so, no, she wasn't okay. But she managed to suck in a deep, steadying breath and struggle back to her feet. Another breath and she nodded that she was all right.

'The doctor told me… Dr Waters…she told me that Sam had a little amnesia, but I thought that she meant that…that he'd forgotten the *accident*. Not two whole years of his *life*!'

It was so much for her to take in. And she couldn't

imagine how *he* felt! Well, she didn't have to, did she? He was furious at the idea. And she could understand why. Sam was a driven man, always pushing himself to fill every second of his life and enjoy it. The man didn't sit still for a minute.

And he'd forgotten it all. The opening of the birth centre. The massive celebrations…the parties. The first birth and all the births since. The amazing write-ups they'd received, the recommendations, the people who were attracted to the Monterey—celebrities, the rich… *Royalty* had even given birth there.

And not just everything that had happened at work. If it were true—if he really didn't remember—then he'd also forgotten their wedding. The preparations, the wedding night, the honeymoon in Paris…

The arguments… The fact that I told him I was going to leave him!

Emily bit down hard on her lip and accepted a plastic cup of water from the nurse, who had hurried to the small self-service station in the corridor. 'Thank you.'

'I'll page the on-call doctor.'

Emily nodded. 'Thank you.' She smiled weakly at the nurse, noting the relief on her face, her name badge—Melanie. 'And I think you'd better show him a webpage, or perhaps a newspaper. Prove the date to him. I'm not sure he believes me.'

Melanie looked uncertain. 'I think maybe the doctor ought to do that.'

'Maybe. Or perhaps I ought to do it? Do you have a copy of today's paper?'

Not that she *wanted* to go in there and do that to him. *Prove* to him that all that she'd said was true. That he was a man out of time with everyone else.

How did you get your head around something like that?

'I'd like whoever's on call to talk to both of us. I need to know what this means. Why it's happened. What we should be doing…' Her thoughts drifted off onto some nightmarish plane where Sam *never* regained those two years and she had to fill him in on *everything*. The long hours he'd put in, his absences from home, the arguments…

And somehow I need to tell him I'm pregnant too!

She felt sick. The weight of all this duty pressed down upon her. A thick ball of nausea sat low and curdled in her stomach and she could taste bile in the back of her throat, despite the drink of cool, refreshing water from the cup. Was there an easy way to tell a man that you were married, but that the two of you had been arguing constantly and that just under two weeks ago you'd told that same man you were going to leave him?

Because you refused to have a child with me and, oh, by the way, I'm actually pregnant! I found out after the accident. They did tests.

Yes, she really couldn't see that nugget of information going down very well with him.

It was all going wrong. Everything.

She tried to rack her brains for what she knew about amnesia, but apart from the general knowledge that it meant you couldn't remember things, she wasn't sure what else she knew about it. It wasn't something she'd specialised in. She was a certified nurse-midwife. She looked after labouring women.

She knew that there were different types of amnesia—some amnesia was permanent and some temporary. Dr Waters had said it might be so. If Sam's was temporary then he would regain his memories on his own and everything would be back to the way it was before…

But I was leaving him before.

She swallowed hard, seeing in her mind's eye that day she'd laid the suitcase upon the bed and stared at it. Then she'd lain a hand on her abdomen. This wasn't just about her and Sam any more. There was a baby to consider, and there was no way she was going to let her child be rejected by its father before it was even born. She knew what it felt like to be left behind and unwanted. It hurt. Left you bewildered. Made you question yourself. Your own value. She would not put her own child through that.

Emily swallowed the last of the water and crumpled the plastic cup. She put it into a trash can and walked back over to Sam's door, put her hand on it, waiting, taking a deep breath.

She was about to go back in when Melanie reappeared.

'I have a paper for you.'

She looked down. Saw the day's headlines. The date. 'Thank you.' Her mouth felt dry. There was a strange, tinny sort of taste in her mouth and she wondered if she were going to be sick.

'And the doctor will come down as soon as he's finished with a patient on the next floor. Ten minutes?'

Emily nodded, swallowing hard. 'Brilliant. Thanks.'

She watched as Melanie headed back to answer a ringing telephone and then with one final inhalation she pushed open Sam's door and stepped inside.

Their gazes met across the room.

If I'm going to get through this then I need to be strong.

'I've brought you something.'

'An apology?' He sounded bitter. Hurt.

'No. I don't need to give you one. But I will give you this.' She walked across the room and handed him the newspaper before stepping back. As if imagining that the second he confirmed the date for himself he would somehow explode. 'Look at the date.'

At first she didn't think he would look at it, but he finally lifted the paper and scanned the first page for the date.

She knew the exact second his gaze fell upon it. He seemed to stiffen, the muscle in his jaw flickering, the focus in his eyes intensifying before he flipped through, checking that all the other pages stated the same date, too. Then he went back to the beginning, scanned the headlines.

Sam dropped the paper as if it were contaminated, closing his eyes briefly as it all sank in.

'Two years? I've lost *two years*?'

He sounded so broken. So *hurt*. It made her heart ache. Made her feel like she needed to cross the room to him and take him in her arms and hug him better. She didn't want him to be hurting. She never had.

'I'm so sorry, Sam. But it's true. We've been married eighteen months now. We honeymooned in Paris. We were very happy.'

He instantly looked up, met her gaze, pinning her with his normally soft blue eyes. *'Were?'*

She tried not to cry. She seemed to be so emotional since finding out she was pregnant. She struggled to keep control of her voice. 'We're having one or two… problems.'

Sam bristled. 'What kind of problems?'

Emily shook her head. 'We can talk about those later. The doctor's coming to talk to you now. About the amnesia.'

'Are there problems at work? Is the Monterey *failing*?'

She could hear the fear in his voice. The concern.

'No. It's doing very well. The launch was amazing and we've had almost full capacity from day one. You haven't stopped working—working all hours to make it a success.'

At that moment the door opened and a new doctor came in, holding Sam's case notes in his hands.

Emily snapped to attention and crossed her arms, stepping back out of the doctor's way.

'Mr and Mrs Saint? I'm Dr Elijah Penn—how can I be of assistance?'

She managed a weak smile and went over to shake Dr Penn's hand. 'Hello, Doctor. My husband has just learned that he's lost two years of his memory after his head injury. We were in a car crash together ten days ago. We were wondering if you could tell us some more about what to expect, and what we can do to help him regain his memory.'

Dr Penn frowned. 'I've only had a brief read-through of your notes, Mr Saint, and without giving you a thorough examination and questioning you myself over what you remember I can't be precise here. There are many different types of amnesia caused by traumatic head injury and right now it would be hard to be specific.'

'Can you tell us what you *do* know?'

'I wouldn't like to guess, as I'm not your husband's physician and I wouldn't want to tell you anything erroneous. But if you'll give me a moment or two with your husband then I'll tell you what I can.'

Emily nodded. Okay. That sounded sensible. She left Sam's room once again and went and sat outside. From her purse she pulled out her cell phone and felt drawn to the photo album. Opening it, she began flicking through. Perhaps there was something here that might help Sam? Perhaps if he looked at their moments together that might provoke some kind of memory?

There were lots to go through. Many of the photographs were from work. Mothers-to-be whom she'd become great friends with, bouquets that she'd been sent as thanks. There were some pictures of the house after they'd had some work done on it. Other people's babies.

Why weren't there any pictures of her and Sam *together*? She had a few selfies. One or two of Sam in scrubs about to go into a Caesarean section, and then one of him relaxing at the house, reading a work journal. In neither of them was he smiling that beautiful smile she hadn't seen for such a long time. When had he last smiled at her? Apart from today? Because that didn't count any more, did it? He was of the mind-set that she'd just accepted his proposal. He thought they were *happy*.

If only...

She scrolled furiously through the rest of the photos. Nothing of them together except for one right at the beginning, when she'd first got the phone, of her and Sam, heads together, smiling at the camera.

When had that been? She checked the date stamp. It had been just after the Monterey had opened. Of course they'd been happy then. Work had been enthralling. They'd been busy. Passing like ships in the night, sometimes, but planning their wedding.

She felt the tears threaten once again and stood up abruptly, shaking them off. What on earth was she going to do? And how was Sam feeling? Thinking they were blissfully happy only to learn that he couldn't remember his own wedding and had no idea that over the last eighteen months he had slowly been distancing himself from her.

The doctor came to the door. 'Would you like to come in?'

Emily shoved the phone back in her jacket pocket and hurried through, glancing at Sam. He looked glum, but reached out his hand.

Puzzled, but hopeful, she went over to him and took his hand in hers, her heart pounding in her chest because he'd reached out to her. Needed her. He hadn't done that for such a long time.

'Bad news?'

Dr Penn held his clipboard against his chest. 'I've had a chance to chat with your husband. Ask him a few questions. See what he understands of his situation. You've both been very lucky in that you escaped the car accident with a minimum amount of injuries. But from my understanding from this limited examination I would presume to say that Sam is suffering from a retrograde amnesia.'

Emily squeezed his fingers and looked at him. 'Which is…?'

'It can be caused by various conditions including head trauma, which Sam has gone through. Retrograde amnesia means that Sam's most recent memories are less likely to be recalled, but his long-term memories are easier for him to remember.'

'Right.'

'It's usually temporary, which is the good thing—though I have to warn you, of course, that not everyone will experience it that way. Sam may be unlucky. We have no way of knowing for sure into which camp Sam will fall.'

'But if it is temporary...is there anything we can do to try and help the memories come back?'

Dr Penn nodded. 'It can help to try and provoke those memories. Show Sam familiar things—photos, videos, possessions, favourite foods, smells, clothing. Anything and everything that might help the memories come back.'

'Places? Like if I took him to where we got married or our favourite restaurant?'

'Anywhere he can be immersed for as long as possible should help. Usually it's not just one item that makes memories return but a drowning in overall sensation— place, aroma, sounds, people. All of it at once. Like déjà-vu.'

Sam spoke up. 'So if I went home...that might do it?'

'It could, but I can't promise anything. Memories can take days or even weeks to return.' He swallowed. 'Maybe longer.'

'And would they all come back straight away?'

'It's different for everyone.'

Sam squeezed her hand. 'So can I go home?'

Dr Penn shook his head. 'Not straight away. I know you didn't suffer any broken bones or organ damage, but you did have a nasty hit to the head and you had a stent fitted to drain fluid. We need to monitor you for a while yet, and if you manage to stay stable, with no spikes of temperature or complications, and physio goes well, then maybe we'll look at letting you go.' He smiled. 'Now, if you'll excuse me, I have another patient to attend to.'

They watched the doctor disappear and Emily turned to Sam, aware that they were still holding hands. It was nice. It had been a long time since he had held her like that and she hated how much she needed his touch to re-assure her. She didn't want to let him go. She never had.

'How are you feeling, Sam? After all that?'

'It's a lot to take in. But I guess I ought to look on the bright side.'

She frowned. 'Bright side?'

He nodded. 'Yes. I know who I am. I know who you are. I still have all the knowledge that lets me be an OB/GYN. I can still work—eventually.' He waited until she looked him fully in the eyes. 'I know how much I love you.'

She swallowed and smiled, trying to still the beating of her heart. It was running away with joy at his words. For how long had she yearned to hear those simple words from Sam?

But there's still so much you don't know!

Could she truly revel in those three simple words? He'd said he loved her, but he still didn't know the truth of their marriage.

He'd hurt her. She'd felt so rejected, so forgotten as Sam had stayed at work, or gone to fundraising galas without her, or disappeared to play tennis with his lawyer. All those arguments they'd had…all those harsh words they'd said to each other out of spite or desperation. How could she forget all they had gone through?

He had. Completely. Right now he was unaware of it all.

But she…? She remembered it all too well. Every argument was a scar upon her heart.

He was trying to be positive. She could see that. *Feel* that. Should she burst his bubble now? Tell him about the baby?

He needed to know. Needed to hear the truth so that

he could be in full possession of the facts. The facts he needed, anyway.

'There's something more, Sam.'

'Oh?'

'You're not going to like it.'

He smiled. 'Let me be the judge of that.'

His smile twanged her heartstrings. It was so familiar! Held so much of that gorgeous cheeky charm that she'd fallen in love with!

But she knew. Knew Sam didn't want a baby. He wasn't ready for one after being married for *eighteen months*. Why would he feel ready for one when he'd thought they weren't even married?

'They…did some tests on me after the accident. Blood tests.'

He nodded, frowning. 'Go on.'

'They found something.'

His face filled with concern and she could imagine what he was thinking. Cancer. A mass. A shadow. Some disease…

'What did they find?'

She searched his face, knowing the response he would give, knowing how his face would crumple at hearing the news, not sure if she could bear the way he would drop all contact with her, let go of the hand that he was clutching so tight. Be angry with her again just as she'd started to enjoy the way he held her hand, the way he'd smiled at her before he started to learn the truth.

She'd missed *him*. So much!

But he'd made it clear he didn't want a baby with her, so telling him this was the hardest thing she would ever have to do. It might end them. But she had no choice.

'They found…' She paused, swallowing hard, 'I'm pregnant, Sam. I'm having our baby.'

He knew he was staring at her, but he couldn't stop. She was…*pregnant*?

Images of Serena instantly flooded his brain and he blinked them away. *No.* He would not think of her. That was all too raw, still. Because even though many years had passed he'd pushed away what had happened and stamped it down low.

Pregnant. *Pregnant!* Emily. His fiancée. No. That was wrong—Emily was now apparently his wife. For almost two years. And she was having a—

He swallowed hard.

He loved this woman. He loved her so much! He should be pleased. But the way she was looking at him right now… Like she was *frightened* of his response? Like she was expecting him to start stamping around the room, or throwing things, or—

Sam knew what he ought to do. He should smile, say that it was *great news*, pretend that he was thrilled, but…

I'm going to be a father. I'm going to be…a father!

Surely she knew how he felt about this? What had happened to Serena had almost destroyed him. How had they been so careless?

Tentacles of fear wrapped themselves around him and tried to suck him down into that deep, dark well of pain he'd kept hidden for so long. Having that kind of responsibility, having to be the one to take care of a young baby every day, was just so…

His heart thudded in his chest so loudly he thought he could hear it in his ears. His skin grew hot, clammy, and he could feel the beginning of the shakes. *My body…it's surging with adrenaline...* The last time he'd felt this way had been after they'd found Serena...

Sam blinked slowly. Emily was still waiting for his reaction, and though the idea of becoming a father terrified him he loved her so much he just knew he couldn't let her see it. Couldn't let her see his inadequacies. Couldn't let her see his Achilles' heel. She would think him an absolute monster if he started on her about this, and both of them had been through too much just lately. His true reaction would have to wait. Maybe when he was out of hospital they could talk sensibly about this.

So he managed to let out a breath and grasped her fingers tightly. 'You're pregnant? Emily...that's so...' he forced the word, trying to make it sound authentic '...*amazing!*'

And he pulled her into his arms and clasped her tightly, breathing in the delicious scent of her honey hair and closing his eyes with such intense pain in his heart, hoping that she could not sense his betrayal.

He felt her relax and sink into him, gasping with relief.

'You mean it? You're happy?' Emily pulled back to search his face, her own riddled with tears, unable to believe that this was true. But true it was. Because Sam was nodding and smiling and happy. And somehow *this* Sam—this version of Sam who had believed it was two years earlier and they were newly engaged—seemed *happy* at the idea of becoming a father!

And if he's happy then...maybe we can be happy too?

She kissed his face without thinking, clutching it with hands that were trembling. She'd been about to *leave* him! She'd almost packed her things. Had written him that letter. They'd crashed their car arguing over this. It was unbelievable.

His reaction, though welcome, was startling. Now the relief of telling him about the baby had passed without bad incident she began to feel pangs of doubt.

'Of course I mean it. How could I not?' He swallowed. 'How far along are you?' he asked, with real curiosity.

She smiled, almost shyly, amazed that she was getting to talk to him about this. Normally! Without him throwing a fit and storming out! 'About nine weeks, I think.'

'Nine weeks...' He looked up at her and smiled broadly once again. 'Still in the first trimester? I guess we really ought not to tell anyone yet.'

'You could tell your family if you want to.'

Sam shook his head. 'No, I... I think it's best we wait until you're in the fourth month.'

'Okay. Whatever you think is best. I'm so glad you're happy about this. I thought—'

'Thought what?'

She shook her head, as if her answer had been too silly to contemplate. 'It doesn't matter.'

This truly was an opportunity, Emily thought, for them to save their marriage. Sam loved her. He seemed happy to be a father. Was there any need to tell him what their relationship had really been like? This might be a chance for Emily to wipe their slates clean and start again.

Although it wouldn't be a totally fresh start. Because for her the upset of the last few weeks and months was still there. Just because Sam didn't know, it didn't mean that she'd forget too. But it might be a start. A way to save them, built on who they had been in the beginning of their relationship. In love. Supporting each other's hopes and dreams. There had been no need for her to get the suitcase out of the closet.

And what harm could it do? They'd nearly separated, but now…? Now things seemed to have changed. Sam seemed happy about the baby, despite everything, and that was what she'd wanted the most. She'd been granted her wish—only a fool would throw it all away now. She'd been desperate before, when she'd been on the verge of leaving him. But now she was being presented with a second chance.

And, yes, his memories might come back to him and cause them problems later, but what if they *didn't*? And if they did—well, Sam was happy to be a dad right now. If they both worked really hard on their relationship, then surely all that was in the past…could be washed under the bridge?

This was a second chance for them, and for the sake of their unborn baby Emily was prepared to risk it.

She'd always fought for their marriage. Had tried everything to save it. What was one last secret?

The second Emily left his hospital room to head home for the night Sam slumped back against his pillows, exhausted.

A baby…

It was such a huge responsibility. For years. A lifetime. And the weight of that responsibility was not something he thought he could bear.

What had he been thinking, getting Emily pregnant? Had they not been using protection? How had he allowed himself this colossal mistake?

He couldn't be a good father. Hadn't he proved himself incapable of looking after a baby? That was why being an OB/GYN was so beautiful. He could keep babies safe at work. Get them through their nine months of gestation as safely and healthily as possible and then make sure that the mother delivered her child without problems.

At the hospital he had a team. He was supported. He had the most recent advancements, tests and medications at his fingertips. Was able to experience joy with the family as he brought new life into the world. Holding a newborn baby…there was nothing in the world like it. It was a privilege. Magical. A brand-new person and he would be the first one to hold it, before he delivered it into the hands of its parents. The elation, the thrill in the room could not be surpassed. And then, once the umbilical cord was clamped and cut, Sam's job—Sam's *responsibility*—was over. He could relax. Let go.

Sam loved delivering babies. Hadn't he wanted to do that for so long? Hadn't he delighted in the miracle of birth so much he had made it his vocation? Deciding that because he hadn't been able to save Serena he could save others?

But after the birth?

No. That was when it could all go wrong. It was why he'd interviewed and hired the best, most elite team of neonatologists and paediatricians for aftercare at his Monterey centre.

He'd vowed *never* to put himself in that position again, and when he'd first met Emily he'd thought he'd found someone just like him. Someone who loved delivering babies but who didn't want one of their own.

Wasn't that what she'd said? Early on? He felt sure that she had. He had a blurry recollection of it.

They'd met in a delivery room. Their eyes meeting

across a crowded stirrup. Em had been working as a private midwife and had brought in a couple whose home birth plan had gone awry. As the OB/GYN on call, he'd gone to the room to assist with a Ventouse delivery and had been physically struck by the sight of her beside her patient, clutching the mother's hand through each contraction, coaching her, intently focused on her.

He recalled a brief moment of wondering who this beautiful new midwife was before he'd got to work, and once the baby had arrived—safely, of course—he had left the room. Only for her to follow him outside and thank him.

I stared at her.

He smiled at the memory. He'd literally been struck dumb. Unable to speak. Her blonde hair had been messy, her cheeks rosy, and she'd been wearing these crazy dangly earrings with turquoise stones that almost matched her eyes. And she'd been wearing flats, so she'd seemed only as tall as his shoulders, and he could remember thinking that she was like an elf.

Eventually he'd managed to get his tongue and mouth to form simple words. 'You did a great job in there.'

'Me? No, it was nothing to do with me. You did all the work.'

'Well, it's my job.'

'Yes.' She'd stared back at him as if she'd been trying to work something out in her head. 'I love having babies.'

He'd frowned. 'You have children of your own?'

She'd shaken her head, as if realising she'd said something that she shouldn't. 'No! God, no! I don't want any yet.'

He'd smiled, intrigued. He'd wanted to know more about her. Wanted to see her.

His only focus had been to be with her. To soak her up. They'd had such fun together, shared so many likes and opinions.

It had been easy to get carried away in the whirlwind.

CHAPTER THREE

THE NEXT DAY a young man called Matt came to Sam's room to help him 'mobilise'. He was in the middle of trying not to feel too dizzy and light-headed after standing up for the first time when Emily came into his room.

His heart soared at seeing her, despite all his dark thoughts the previous night. She looked fresh and bright, a bohemian chic angel, as if she'd had a really good night's sleep, and she developed a huge smile on her face when she saw him standing up, holding onto a walker.

'You're up!'

'Not for long.' Sam collapsed down onto the bed and let out a heavy breath, clutching his head as if to steady it.

Matt cocked his head to one side. 'Dizzy?'

'Yeah, a little.'

'It'll pass if you take it easy. Try this: whilst you're sitting down, really push your feet into the floor and flex and release your calf muscles. It'll help pump the blood around your system and prevent a blood pressure drop next time you stand.'

Emily stood by his side and hesitantly laid a supportive hand upon his shoulder. She smelt minty fresh and was wearing a perfume he didn't recognise, but liked.

He looked up at her, expecting her to kiss him hello, but she didn't. Because of Matt's presence? It seemed unlikely. But now that she was here he wanted to show her what he could do. Show her that he was going to get stronger every day. He wanted to be back on his feet. He wanted to be up and about again. Working. Being Sam. He hated being stuck in a hospital bed.

Gripping the walker once again, Sam stood. Slower this time. He took a moment to make sure the dizziness wasn't about to make him collapse onto the floor and then pushed the walker to one side and took a step forward. Matt stood close, ready to steady him if needed.

Who knew lying on your back for ten days after a head injury would make you feel as weak as a baby bird? After just a few steps he was ready to sit down, but Sam was determined to push through. He kept going. Made it across the room, out of the door to the nurses' station and back again. By the time he got back to his bed he was exhausted, sweating as if he'd just done a full day's training in the gym, and he sank back onto the mattress with a broad grin on his face.

Matt smiled. 'So…you're one of *those* people.'

Sam raised an eyebrow in question.

'Type A. High achiever. It's good, but you also need to know when to stop.'

Emily sat beside him on the bed and passed him a towel to freshen up with. 'He's always pushed himself and strived for the best.'

'Yes, well, just keep an eye on that blood pressure. It won't always be as low as it was about five minutes ago.'

'I'm fine, Matt. Honestly. I won't stop pushing until I'm in my own home.'

Matt nodded. 'And probably not even then. I'll come back later, after your evening meal, and we'll do some more. In the meantime, rest. You're allowed to get up to use the bathroom only.' Matt saluted him and walked away.

Emily peered into his eyes. 'Do you remember home?'

Sam looked at her, tempted just to ignore the question and kiss her. Having her this close to him, smelling as good as she did, looking as beautiful as she did...

He reached up and tucked a strand of her choppy blonde hair behind her ear. 'Are we still in the apartment? The two-bedroom place with the sliding doors out onto the balcony? View across the city?'

He could picture that quite clearly. It wasn't a problem. He very much wanted to get back there.

But the slump in Emily's shoulders informed him that it wasn't the right answer. 'No. We don't live there any more.'

Sam tried to think hard. To force memories to the surface. But he couldn't. It was as if there was a thick wall in his head, blocking them, and no matter how hard he pounded against it, no matter how ferociously he yelled at it and fought to knock it down, it resolutely remained.

'Then where?'

'We have a house in Beverly Hills now. You found it for us. It's white. Very neo-classical—columns, balconies, topiaries, big doors...that sort of thing.'

He tried to imagine it, but was more concerned with the way she'd described it. 'You don't seem to like it.'

'I do. It's just...' She paused for a moment, looking down at the cover on his bed and straightening out a ripple on the surface. 'I guess we haven't made it *ours* yet.' She smiled weakly, but then stood up and tried to become more upbeat. 'But look at you! Only woke yesterday and already you're pounding the floors of the hospital!'

He could tell she wasn't telling him everything. Did she not like their home? Was it a place that *he'd* liked and pushed her into buying? There was *something*...

But he dismissed it quickly as he thought of his triumph without the walker and stood up again, pulling her into his arms, searching her gorgeous blue-green eyes for that quirky happy girl he knew so well.

'I've missed you.'

She wrapped her arms around his waist hesitantly, as if it was something she hadn't done in a long time, as if she was trying not to make it seem like she was pulling away.

But why would that be? They'd only been married a short time—surely they were still very physical?

'Kiss me.'

'*Sam!* The physio said you should be resting. You need to get back into bed!'

'And I will! But only if my wife joins me.' Sam tilted her chin up and showed her a cheeky grin before he brought his lips to hers.

The last time he'd kissed her had been... Well, just after she'd accepted his proposal. In *his* mind, anyway. And he was still full of that celebratory need to show her how much he loved her, despite all that had happened—the car crash, the pregnancy, the head injury, the amnesia. As far as he knew he'd only just slipped that ring onto her finger and he was feeling full to the brim with happiness.

However...

They were *married*. And expecting a baby. So surely they had to be getting along. And, despite his trepidation, his fears and his doubts, there was one thing clear in his mind. His love for Emily. And right now he felt that he needed her. The last few hours had been a lot to take in. To believe he had lost two whole years of his life was…mind-blowing. His pet project—his dream—the Monterey Birth Centre had opened and begun trading all without his knowledge.

Okay, so *technically* he'd been there. He'd orchestrated it, arranged it, even shown up to work there, apparently, but that was just what Emily had *told* him had happened. As far as he was concerned it still *hadn't* happened, and whilst he was stuck in this hospital life would continue to carry on without him. He needed to get home. Needed to see the Monterey in action. Needed to think about how he and Emily would tackle their new challenges.

He pulled back and looked into his wife's eyes. 'I can't wait to get home.'

She seemed breathless, her eyes glazed. 'Me too.'

It took two weeks before the hospital was even prepared to *consider* releasing Sam. In that time he received lots of welcome visitors—Emily, his parents, his siblings, some colleagues that, to him, were still relative strangers. *Those visits were weird.* He underwent a barrage of assessments—physiological, neurological, biological. He felt like every part of him had been poked and prodded or had blood drawn from it, and when that wasn't happening he had visits from occupational therapists, psychologists, neurologists and the surgical team, who'd given him the low-down on his small procedure.

Most importantly, throughout it all, he had remained *stable* and his observations had been normal. He was ready now. Anxious to leave the hospital walls and get home. Desperate to get back and see if being there would spark anything.

No memories had yet returned, despite Em's frequent visits with accompanying photos and videos of their wedding and the opening of the Monterey. She'd been so keen to show him what they had done. What they had enjoyed. But it had been like looking at photos of a stranger, even though he was in them. It had left him feeling disconcerted. As if he was in a strange bubble.

The waiting to leave hospital was more than a little infuriating, and over the last few days he'd found himself snapping at various people. The psychology team had reassured him and Emily that this was normal, as he adjusted to his new self and situation, and offered to assess him every month, for as long as he felt the need to talk about it. Mood swings, apparently, were to be expected.

He wasn't sure he did want to talk about it. Not to them, anyway. They'd already cottoned on to the fact that he didn't seem delighted at the idea of becoming a father, and he'd grown to hate his sessions with them, knowing that they would return to the questions he dreaded. He'd even tried sharing his frustration with Emily, but it seemed as if she didn't know anything about Serena.

Was that possible? That they'd been married for eighteen months and he hadn't told her? That had kept him silent on all fronts and contributed to his anger.

So he was particularly pleased that *today* the doctors had finally decided that he could return home—with the understanding that he wasn't to work for a further three months.

'But I can go in and look around? Get familiar with what's going on?' he'd asked.

'Sure. But no working. You won't be covered insurance-wise.'

And with that dire warning they'd left his bedside.

And now Emily was at his side in the car, driving them home.

She seemed really nervous. Edgy. Fidgety. But he put that down to the fact that for the last few weeks the hospital staff had been around to look after him and make sure he was recovering properly. Now that safety barrier would be gone and it would just be down to the two of them.

Well…nearly three of them.

Sam swallowed and tried not to think of the baby. Emily was nearly eleven weeks now, and apparently she was booked in for a scan in a few days. He would have to go with her. Act the dutiful husband and hold her hand if she'd let him—he'd noticed a curious reluctance and hesitation on Emily's part to be physical with him—whilst they squeezed on that cold blue gel and then smile inanely at the images on screen.

He *so wanted* to be happy about this. And a part of him was. But whenever he thought about them having a baby he pictured his baby sister Serena and what had happened to her when he'd been left in charge…

A car horn sounded, pulling him back to reality, and he flinched, looking across at his wife driving the car.

'Aren't you scared?'

'Of what?'

He wanted to know if she was afraid of becoming a parent. It had to be a big deal for anyone, right? But something stopped him from asking that particular question.

'Driving. After the accident…'

She shook her head, her honey-blonde hair shifting

around her shoulders like velvet. 'I was. Not now. But I'm being very careful. We can't just stop doing things because they make us afraid.'

Depends what worries you.

He smiled and glanced out at the streams of traffic. He knew this road. Knew this area. But he had no idea where they were headed except for the fact that Emily was taking them home.

Home. Would he recognise it? Would it spark a memory? Something—even if it was a little blurry? The doctors at the hospital had told them both that the memories *might* return, and that they might either come all at once or he'd experience the odd one or two at strange moments, in totally unexpected ways.

Brains were mysterious creatures.

Pulling off the freeway, Emily took a slip road and drove for a few more miles through beautiful streets lined with lush green trees and neat sidewalks. He saw a young woman walking a poodle that had been groomed to within an inch of its life, trotting along like a dressage horse. He saw beautiful properties, secure within their walls and at the end of long driveways, as they drove on beneath the heat of the sun in their dark saloon car, and then suddenly they were slowing and turning into a driveway.

He looked up.

A majestic house sat before him. Perfectly white, it glimmered in the midday heat against the glorious blue sky backdrop. It looked *palatial*. Like something fit for a film star or a minor member of royalty.

This is ours?

He tried to picture himself wanting to buy this and could see its perks. It was prestigious, and screamed quality, with tall oak front doors and what seemed like hundreds of windows flashing reflections of the sun into his eyes as they approached up the long, smooth driveway. It was very different from his childhood home.

As they neared, he saw grey clothed *staff* come near the car and open their car doors.

'Welcome back, Mr Saint! So good to see you up and about.'

He smiled at faces he didn't know and stepped out, looking around him. Emily appeared to be much more comfortable with her surroundings than he did, and she quickly indicated to the staff to take their bags from the trunk.

The bags were quickly hurried inside as Sam looked about him at the gardens, which were lush with green leafy trees and all-white flowers and blooms. 'It's beautiful.'

'You picked it. Don't you remember?'

He heard the trepidation in her voice. The hope that he would remember. He hated disappointing her. 'I'm sorry. I don't.'

He needed control of his life back. Something he hadn't had whilst he'd been stuck in a hospital bed as a passive observer.

'Let's go in. All your things are inside—there might be something…'

Something about the way her voice sounded made him look at her in question. Was it just the amnesia that was making him feel…? *I'm in the dark…*

It was a weird sensation, but the doctors had told him he would feel like this. That he was not to ponder on it, or worry about it, that it was normal. It was probably just him being over-sensitive right now.

Shrugging it off, he took her hand and clasped it

tightly, kissing the back of it. Then he smiled at her and nodded. 'Let's do it.'

And they walked inside.

Sam had imagined that this would be *a moment*. A moment when a flood of memories would assail him. He would spot something—a chair, a table, a painting or piece of art, perhaps—that would ignite a memory that had lain dormant and hidden behind *the wall*.

But, looking around him, he felt—and remembered—nothing. He tried not to be too disappointed. But it was hard. He'd told himself in the hospital that when he got home he would remember. That walking through the door into familiar surroundings would give his brain the nudge it needed to start releasing the information he craved.

The fact that his brain was failing him—that his memories were refusing to leap to the surface of his mind—frustrated him. He was a man who had always been perfectly in control of everything, and the fact that he couldn't even force his own brain to do something made him feel angry inside.

Emily let go of his hand and stepped away from him to lay her bag and keys down on a table. 'Anything?'

Gritting his teeth, he shook his head, trying not to be angry with himself. 'No.'

She stared at him for a while. 'Don't worry. Something will trigger it. I'll show you around.'

And she took him from room to room. Sitting room, dining room, library, study, kitchen, utility, staff quarters, the guest bedrooms, the bathrooms, shower rooms, games room… Even all the storage rooms and up into the roof space, which had been converted into yet another guest room. They were all *beautiful*. Elegantly designed. Minimalist. Expensive and sumptuous.

Remembered?

Not at all.

All the belongings, all the possessions that Emily pointed out, convinced he would remember, meant nothing. He *felt* nothing.

A simmering rage bubbled away beneath the surface of his neutral face. And for some reason he felt anger towards Emily. As if it was somehow *her* fault that he couldn't remember. He knew it wasn't. It was just because she was the closest person to him and he so desperately wanted to remember for *her* delight. *Her* joy. Plus, it would also prove to him that he could somehow conquer the two years that had been taken from him. Two years of missed birthdays and celebrations. All of it. He could somehow claim it *back*.

There had to be *something*. Something that would bring back who he was. All that he had lost and then, hopefully, somehow he would have the strength to tackle the next great challenge that awaited them both.

Awaited *him*.

Because how could he be a father when he couldn't even remember creating their child?

'And this…'

Emily swept another door open. Another opportunity for his mind to let him down. He wasn't sure he wanted to look—wasn't sure he wanted to face that part of himself again—but he did, because Emily was being so supportive.

'…is the master bedroom. Our room.'

He stepped in, his gaze instantly drawn to the large king-sized bed in the centre, a mix of blindingly white bedding with gold-accented cushions. There were so many of them! Did they have to throw them all off the bed to get—?

Emily pinned to the bed, gazing up at him, smiling wickedly, her hair spread out in wild abandon across the gold cushions, the tassels weaving into her hair, making it seem as if she had strands of pure gold in it. His lips trailing down her neck, feather-light, her laughter, her—

The sudden onslaught of memory caused Sam to reach out a hand to steady himself.

'Sam—you okay?' She caught up to him and laid a hand upon his arm, her face full of concern.

'Yeah, I'm fine, I—'

A gold cushion being thrown at his chest from across the room. Emily growling with irritation, stalking away from him, yanking the bedroom door open so hard it left a small dent in the wall. 'I hate you!'

Sam blinked and looked behind him. At the wall. There was a small dent.

'Sam? Have you remembered something?'

He met her gaze. 'You were angry with me.'

She blanched. 'What?'

'In this room—you threw a cushion at me...one of those off the bed. I was over here.' He stepped over to the part of the room that he'd seen in his memory. 'You threw it and you stormed out of the door and yelled from the corridor that you hated me.'

Emily looked awkwardly at the floor and he could see that she was biting her lip.

What had happened to make her say she *hated* him? She hadn't said he annoyed her, or irritated her, she hadn't said, *I really don't like you sometimes, Sam.* She'd said 'hate'.

What had they been arguing about? Had he done something wrong? Had she? 'What was that about?'

She grimaced. 'I'm not sure.'

He pictured the look on her face as she'd stormed away. 'You seemed pretty serious.'

Emily swallowed and sat down on the edge of the bed, fidgeting nervously. She patted the bedspread beside her and he sat down, waiting for her explanation.

'Things have been…tense sometimes.'

'Sometimes?'

'A lot.'

She seemed embarrassed to say it. As if she was letting him down by telling him this. But even though it was hurtful to hear he'd rather have the truth.

'What about?'

She sighed and her shoulders sagged. 'Family stuff. We had got to a point where we were hardly talking. When we did, we argued. Over and over again.'

'We were that bad?' He hated to ask, but Emily wasn't making it sound as if things had been good between them.

'We crashed the car arguing.'

He stared hard at the floor. 'God, Em, I'm really sorry.'

He felt the distance between them then. Even though they were next to each other on the bed she wasn't leaning into him for comfort—she wasn't seeking his support. She was stiff and straight beside him, eyes downcast.

How had things got so bad between them, so quickly? Was this why she looked startled each time he tried to hold her hand or kiss her?

'At least you remembered something…' she muttered.

He stared at the pristine white carpet on the floor. 'Yeah. I guess I did.'

* * *

Emily led Sam into his private office, hoping that *this room* above all others would mean something to her husband.

This was such a weird situation for them both. *She knew this man.* And yet because he couldn't remember the last two years it felt to her, in a way, that she was leading a stranger around their house. Seeing the way he looked at things in wonder and surprise, seeing things familiar to her but brand-new to him.

Hadn't he stood in this very doorway and kissed her? Hadn't he sat at this desk for many hours, talking on the phone, arranging galas and press nights for the Monterey? Hadn't they had one of their worst arguments in here? Leading to the first time Sam had stormed from the house, tearing down the driveway in the car so hard he'd left tyre marks?

He'd had a memory come back. A bad one. It was a scary sign. *Good* that he was remembering, but *bad* because of what it might mean for their relationship now.

It was clear that their problems weren't just going to disappear, the way his memories had. Whether he remembered their issues or not, Sam was still the same man and she needed to remember that. The issue here wasn't just the amnesia. They still had the problems of their marriage to solve, and if they were going to do that then they would have to start communicating and working together. Something they hadn't done for a long time.

She watched as he entered, noting the way his fingers trailed over the large glass-topped desk, the way he picked up the Murano glass paperweight that they'd bought in Paris, the way he stared hard at the picture of himself and Emily standing in front of the Monterey on the day of its Grand Opening. Their smiling faces, the green-garbed staff standing behind them, all with their hands in the air cheering.

She *wanted* him to remember it all. She really did. How else were they both going to recover? Right now Sam seemed happy about the pregnancy, and he was clearly wanting to be physical with her. Kissing her. Reaching out for her hand. Giving her the love that she'd craved. The *closeness* and *intimacy* that had been sadly lacking in their relationship since the arguments had started. But it was still difficult for her. Strange...

Because she *did* remember.

What would happen tonight? Would he sleep in their bed? Lately he'd been sleeping at work, and when he *had* made it home he'd either told her he'd sleep on the couch or go to a guest room. That had been embarrassing—the staff certainly knew—and also deeply hurtful.

Was it wrong to wish desperately that Sam wouldn't recall that part of their relationship? Was it wrong to be putting all her hope into this second chance they'd been given? Was it wrong to wish that Sam wouldn't regain his memories at all?

Of course it is! And I feel terrible for even giving those thoughts space in my head!

It was as if Sam were two different people right now, though she knew that it wasn't really true.

He's the same man and I need to remember that. The man who wouldn't talk to me is the same man standing next to me right now. And I'm not sure I know how we're going to sort this.

There was a baby that would need its father. Emily hadn't had one of those. Or a mother. Not really. She had been passed to an aunt by her mother so she could go rushing off after some ageing rock star and travel with him to gigs, and after that last time she'd just never come back. Even now Emily had no idea where or who she really was. Her mother had a name, but she didn't know more than that.

Staying with her Aunt Sylvia hadn't provided much insight either. Sylvia had not been a big fan of her sister, and had resented being left with a young toddler who made lots of noise and even more mess. Emily had soon stopped asking Sylvia and her Uncle Martin questions they never had answers to.

Who's my real mummy?
When is she coming back?
Does she love me?

The sound of drawers being opened and closed brought Emily back to the present. If Sam, now sitting behind his desk, was looking for something personal there he'd be disappointed. They only contained work-related paperwork and files. He looked lost in a world that should have been oh-so-familiar to him.

'It'll come back, Sam. Maybe not today. But it will.' She hated to see him hurting. It hurt her in return.

He smiled at her attempt to comfort him, but it was bitter. 'Well, a bit did come back today—only it wasn't what I expected.'

He shook his head, as if he couldn't quite believe all that she had told him. The bad memory had clearly rocked him to his core and he seemed to be thrown by that. He'd believed them to be happy. Why wouldn't they be? She wished she could explain it to him, but she didn't have any answers herself.

'We have to believe that things will get better.'

'Speaks the eternal optimist.'

Pulling deep within herself, she leaned over his desk and made him look her in the eyes. 'You're a fighter,

Sam. We would never have got the Monterey started if it hadn't been for your vision. You've got to believe that all those memories in there...the ones that make you *you*...they're still in there. They're not lost. Not really. You just don't have access yet.'

'Like membership to an exclusive club?'

She nodded. 'Exactly.'

'I'm not sure I want membership to the bad marriage club.'

Emily stood up straight. 'Me neither. But we're in it, and we both have to work together if we want to make changes.'

He looked about the room one more time, before he stood and tucked his chair under his desk. 'You're right. We do.'

The telephone call came as they were heading downstairs. Emily's cell vibrated in her pocket and she knew immediately what the call was about the second she saw the name of the caller.

'Em? It's Marc—Sophie's husband. Her waters have broken and she's having strong contractions. We're coming in to the Monterey.'

Marc and Sophie were a couple who had come to the Monterey for fertility treatment and had conceived their much wanted first child through IVF. Sophie was terrified of both hospitals and needles—something she'd had to overcome to get through her hormone treatments and appointments. Emily had *promised* from the very beginning that she would be there to help them deliver their child, and Sophie had come to rely on Emily being there as her safe harbour, her port in a storm.

Emily's heart was torn between Sophie's labour and staying with Sam, whom she'd just brought home.

'Hi, Marc. I'm at home at the moment…hang on—' She held the phone to her chest so she could privately talk to Sam. 'It's clients. Sophie and Marc? The IVF couple? Sophie's in labour—I promised I would be there.'

Sam looked blank at the names, but he nodded anyway. He knew that work was important to them both. 'You should go.'

'You've only just come home. You need someone with you.'

He smiled. 'I have *staff*, remember? Go be with Sophie.'

She loved it that this part of Sam was still here. The need to be there for their patients, putting them first, staying true to the promises they made to care for their charges.

Em lifted the phone back to her ear. 'I'll come in. How far away are you?'

'I'm already driving, but traffic is heavy. Twenty minutes?'

'I'll meet you at the entrance. See you soon.' She ended the call and smiled at Sam. 'Thank you.'

'Hey, it's not a problem. It's what we do. Go on. You don't want to miss it.'

No. She didn't. She laid a hand on his arm, smiling, and then started running down the stairs, grabbing her purse and keys from the table and hurrying out of the front door.

She hated leaving him alone. But perhaps he needed some time in their home to wander about and look at things without feeling under pressure to remember.

She told herself it was a good thing she was heading in to the Monterey. She was about to see the outcome of a long, difficult journey for Sophie and Marc. This was what their work was all about. Welcoming new life into the world. Celebrating that.

And soon it would be her and Sam's turn.

One day. Maybe.

Sophie was labouring *hard.* Her normally calm and serene face was now red and creased, and her eyes were closed tight as she tried to breathe through a contraction.

Her husband Marc stood by her, one hand clutching hers, the other rubbing hard at the small of his wife's back.

Sophie had not wanted to get into bed. She'd said it had made her too uncomfortable. She wanted to get into the large birthing tub, which was currently filling with water.

'How much longer?' Sophie asked, blowing away the last of the contraction.

Emily checked the temperature of the water, which was perfect. 'Okay. You can get into the pool now.'

Marc helped his wife strip off the last of her garments and held her arm as she gingerly stepped over the side of the pool and lowered herself, settling into the warm embrace of the water.

'Oh, my God, this is bliss!'

Marc laughed. 'That's not what you said a moment ago.'

Emily smiled at them both. It was a surprise to a lot of husbands that their partners often felt so much better between contractions. Making a note in Sophie's file, she entered the time her patient had got into the pool and then got a Sonicaid device and listened to the baby's heartbeat by pressing the probe against Sophie's abdomen. There was a little sound of interference, and then a strong, steady heartbeat sounded out in the small room.

'Sounds perfect, Sophie. You're on track. Any urge to push?'

Her patient wiped her brow. 'I'm not sure. I think so…a little with that last one.'

'Okay, let's see how you are with the next few contractions and if that feeling increases we'll check to see if you're fully dilated.'

Sophie nodded, and then braced herself against the pool as another contraction hit.

Emily watched as Marc helped his wife through it, surreptitiously timing the contraction. It was good and strong. At least a minute in length, which was what they needed. Sophie had to be close, and Emily felt a ball of excitement in the pit of her stomach, as she always did when a birth was near.

This was what she lived for. Bringing new life into the world. It was something that had fascinated her ever since she'd seen a documentary on the television one evening as a child. Sylvia and Martin had gone out to an event at their local church and Emily had turned on the television out of boredom.

She'd hardly ever seen the television switched on. Sylvia and Martin had preferred to read, or listen to a play on the radio. But Emily had known it was a source of endless fascination for her schoolfriends and so she'd switched it on that night and found a documentary about a maternity unit. There, on screen, she had watched and learned about the way babies came into the world, and she'd been captured by its raw beauty, its power. She'd been surprised to discover tears trickling down her cheeks when she'd witnessed how overwhelmed the parents were by their new child.

I want to do that.

Seeing love, in all its raw glory, was something that she'd craved.

Did my mom act like that with me?

From that day forward she'd dreamt of finding a man who would look into her eyes like that, with so much love and pride. Of carrying her own baby and experiencing that rush of love and joy as she pushed her baby into the world. Never to be alone again…never to be forgotten. Never again to be that lonely little girl, sitting in her room, wondering where her mother was.

'Emily? I need to push.'

'Okay, just breathe through it this time. I need to check you first.'

Marc glanced nervously at her. 'Shouldn't she just push?'

'If she's not fully dilated yet it could cause swelling around the cervix and make her delivery difficult.'

Marc looked confused, but nodded, because he trusted her implicitly.

With the contraction over, Emily put on some gloves and checked Sophie. She smiled. 'You're ten centimetres! You're all set.'

Sophie started to cry. 'Oh, my God! It's happening—it's really happening! Marc?' She turned to her husband and clutched his hand as if she would never let go. 'We're going to have our baby soon.'

Marc kissed his wife. 'I know, honey. I'm so proud of you.'

Sophie laid her forehead against her husband's and then started grimacing as the next contraction hit. 'What do I do, Emily?'

'I want you to take a deep breath and then bear down into your bottom until I say stop, okay?'

Sophie bore down, the strain showing in the redness of her face.

'Seven, eight, nine, ten. Okay, another breath and push again!'

Emily counted the seconds away. Sophie and Marc were so close now to seeing their miracle baby. They'd tried so hard to get pregnant, and for a long time had thought that it wouldn't happen for them. Sophie and Marc hadn't met until they were in their early forties, and after a year of trying had come to the Monterey in desperation, afraid that time was running out for both of them.

Two cycles of IVF had failed, but on their third try they'd been successful. Sophie had been a model patient—eating right, exercising, looking after herself—and Emily knew this baby was going to be cherished.

'Oh, my God, Em, how much longer?' Sophie groaned.

'Not long! I can see a head of thick dark hair! Do you want to touch?'

'Really?' Sophie reached down and felt the top of her baby's head. 'Oh!'

Emily smiled and shone a light so Marc could see, too. 'What do you think, Dad? Takes after you?'

Marc blinked away tears. 'This is…' He couldn't speak any more. He just clutched his wife's hand and kissed the back of it. 'Come on, Soph, you can do it—you're nearly there.'

It took just four more pushes and the head crowned, emerged and restituted, so that the baby faced Sophie's inner right thigh.

'Head's out, Sophie! Just one more push and you'll be a mum!'

Sophie bore down as the next contraction came.

Emily supported the baby's head and body as it came out, and looked up at Sophie. 'Are you ready to take your baby?'

Sophie looked down, gasped aloud, and then reached for her newborn. 'Oh, my God!' She pulled the baby upward and rested it against her belly, and then burst into tears as her baby let out its first beautiful cry.

'You did it, Soph! You did it!' Marc laid his hand on his newborn child and began to cry.

The dads' crying always got to Emily. She had to bite her lip to stop *herself* from crying. She didn't know what it was, but she'd seen this so many times and it never got old. It was a privilege, and one that she cherished.

'Congratulations.' She clamped the cord and handed the scissors to Marc. "Cut between the clamps.'

He did so, and laughed, laying his head against his wife's.

'Did you see what flavour you got?'

Sophie and Marc had wanted it to be a surprise.

Sophie sniffed and wiped at her eyes, before she looked down and lifted up one of her baby's legs. 'It's a girl! Marc, we have a daughter!'

Marc kissed her and put his arm around his wife.

Emily laid a towel over the baby. It soon got wet, but it helped to keep the baby warm. Sophie wanted a natural stage three, allowing the placenta to come out on its own, without the aid of drugs, and once that was done and had been checked, Emily helped Sophie get out of the bath and onto the bed.

She wrapped fresh towels around their daughter and checked Sophie for tears. All looked well. She'd done brilliantly.

'You haven't torn, Sophie. That's brilliant.'

She stared for a moment at the family picture of Sophie, Marc and their new daughter on the bed. A solid family unit.

She wanted that for her and Sam. That dream image that she'd built up in her imagination since she had first seen it on television. A mum. A dad. A baby. All wrapped together in the strong bonds of love. United.

There *had* to be a way for them to get there.

'Have you got a name for her yet?'

Marc looked up and smiled. 'Xanthe.'

Emily nodded. 'That's beautiful.'

She let the family have a few moments together, and then took Xanthe to check her over. All looked well, and she scored high on the APGAR, so she bundled Xanthe up again and handed her back to her parents. No doubt this little girl would be treasured and loved for her lifetime.

'I'll leave you guys alone for a moment. Give me a buzz if you need anything.'

Emily slipped from the room and went to write up her notes about the delivery. It was wonderful when deliveries went as smoothly as this one, and Sophie and Marc—who had been through the mill—deserved their happy-ever-after.

In her office, Emily was lost in thoughts about what would happen in the future for her and Sam. Would he regain his memories and know the whole truth about their marriage? Really, she *did* want him to, because then they could work through their issues. She just wanted them to have some time first. Time to reconnect, to fall back in love, time to strengthen their relationship.

Was that so bad? Wanting the best for them? Wanting their relationship to succeed? This time could give them what they'd never had before. The opportunity to open up to each other and work out whatever the real problem was. Because there had to be a reason Sam hadn't wanted to talk to her before.

Now, because of the accident, because of what had happened, Sam was still reeling, and he needed to anchor himself. Find himself. And if she could help him to do that then maybe, just maybe, he would see just how much she was fighting for their marriage. How much she wanted them to succeed. Surely he did, too, otherwise he wouldn't be so upset that it had gone wrong?

He'd loved her once—she just wanted to reinforce those feelings somehow. So that if everything went pear-shaped after his memories returned they would have a much better chance of staying together and having the perfect family that she wanted for them.

Her gaze fell upon the one picture she allowed herself in her office. It was of her and Sam, in front of the Eiffel Tower in Paris during their honeymoon. They'd had such a brilliant time there. It was an enchanting city, and the way she'd felt for Sam there had been overwhelming.

It was a pity they weren't there now.

But what if we could be?

The doctors had said that the best way to help Sam find his memories would be to immerse him in experience—the sights, sounds, smells of something familiar. What if they went back to Paris? Sam was signed off work for a few months. If they could get a Fit to Fly certificate from his consultant they could go back there and experience that magical place once again!

A spark of hope ignited in her chest and she stared at the photo once more. And if Sam's memories *did* come back by then it would be too late, because he would have fallen in love with her all over again!

They *needed* this.

In the past two years Sam had been working hard to get the Monterey up and running, working tirelessly behind the scenes. She'd barely seen him, and they'd argued when she had. This would be good for *her*—not just Sam.

Emily smiled and turned to her computer. Accessing the internet, she found a local travel agent and picked up the phone and dialled their number.

There was no harm in finding out.

CHAPTER FOUR

AIR FRANCE FLEW out of Los Angeles International, and after eleven hours and fifty minutes Emily and Sam touched down at Charles de Gaulle Airport, north-east of Paris.

Emily's excitement levels were high. Paris held such great memories for her and their relationship. When they'd come here before they'd been honeymooning, newly married, accomplished owners of a successful new birth centre business and blissfully happy. Everything had been going so well for them.

After making the decision to return to Paris, Emily had returned home from her successful delivery of Marc and Sophie's baby and blurted out her idea.

'Sam? We should go to Paris!'

'What?'

'We should go back to Paris. Where we honeymooned. Remember the doc said that we should immerse you in sights and sounds and aromas. Can you think of a better place than one where we were so happy?'

'I don't remember Paris.'

'Exactly! If your memory doesn't return there...well, we'll just make new memories. That both of us will remember this time.'

Sam had laughed at her enthusiasm, but then he'd seen how determined she was. He'd called his consultant to check that it was okay for him to fly. His doctor had said that he didn't think it was a problem. Sam wasn't on oxygen, he didn't have any open wounds from surgery, and air travel was only usually restricted for seven to ten days post-neurosurgery. Sam had been recovering for a month now.

A Fit to Fly certificate had been arranged and before Sam had known what was happening they'd been booked onto a flight the next day.

Emily had meant it. The last time they'd visited she had truly fallen in love with the city, and had hated having to leave after their ten days there. As they'd risen into the sky on their way home Emily had looked out of the window at the city dropping away beneath her and whispered, *'I'll come back.'*

And here they were. Strolling through the airport, through the domed concourses, dragging their bags behind them, revelling in the hustle and bustle as hundreds of different voices and languages could be heard around them.

Despite looking in a shop window and gaping at a beautiful dress that she would normally have stopped to buy, she was so keen to get them to their hotel that she quickly hurried along.

Outside they found a *station de taxi* waiting to pick up passengers. They hailed one and got inside.

'Bonjour, monsieur...madame. Où?'

Emily smiled. 'Shangri-La Hotel, *s'il vous plaît.*' She turned to her husband and smiled.

'Shangri-La? Sounds...exotic.'

'It was where we had our honeymoon—*and* I managed to get us the exact same suite we stayed in the last time.'

Sam nodded in appreciation. 'You *have* been busy.'

'I'd do anything to get you back, Sam.' She felt her cheeks flush. 'I mean…to get your memory back.'

He smiled at her. He knew what she meant. Their relationship had clearly been faltering. From that one memory it looked as if it had become a war zone. It pained him to think how bad it had got for them and, like Em, he too wanted this trip to work.

And if you wanted to get the romance back, the love, where else to go but the most romantic city in the world?

'Thanks, Em. You've been great through all of this. The accident, looking after me… It can't have been easy.' She appreciated his acknowledgement of all her hard work. 'Well, morning sickness didn't help.'

She looked out of the window as her eye caught a glimpse of some hares or rabbits darting across the grass beside the road, so she didn't notice his gaze darken at her reminder of the pregnancy.

If she were honest, she'd admit that he'd been distant from her the last couple of days. They'd still not yet made love since his return from hospital, which didn't surprise her. Not after she'd told him how much they'd been arguing. Perhaps he had felt he couldn't approach her?

But she'd not pushed for it either. She hadn't slept with her husband for a couple of months, and it would have been strange for them to have tried, knowing how bad their marriage had become.

Sam had cited headaches, which she knew were to be expected, and she'd been grateful. She needed time herself to work up to the idea of becoming intimate with her husband once again.

It hadn't taken Sam long to return to his study in their house, determined to bring himself up to speed with what had happened in the last two years. Sometimes—just as before the accident—he'd fallen asleep there. It had removed the pressure and she'd been thankful for that.

Before, there'd always been a reason why he couldn't talk, or why he couldn't come home. It had made her uneasy, and she didn't want to return to the pattern they had fallen into. So arranging this trip together had been good. They were united in the idea of working to get each other back.

Emily *needed* to get Sam back. The good Sam. The Sam who loved her and adored her. The Sam who was happy about the baby and had beamed a smile whenever he'd seen her arrive at the hospital. The husband who wanted to hold her hand. Be near her. Touch her.

She missed his touch.

It wasn't just sex with Sam—it never had been. He had always made love to her, making her feel cherished and adored. As if he worshipped her. As if he couldn't get enough of her. The way she felt…the way she tasted. And afterwards, when they'd lain in each other's arms, sated and complete, warm and loved, she'd never wished for anything more.

To lose that—to lose that precious physical connection that they'd once shared—had almost torn her apart.

As she gazed out of the taxi window, her fingers fiddling with the pendant around her neck, she hoped fervently that back here, in this place, they would be able to reclaim that part of their marriage. Not just the sex, the making love, but the closeness she'd once had with him.

They'd had it good once. They could have it again.

* * *

The drive to the hotel took about forty-five minutes. Emily felt so happy to be in Paris and she clutched Sam's hand, squeezing his fingers every time she turned to look at him and smile. She gazed at the tree-lined roads, the relaxed unhurried pedestrians and the tourists ambling along the sidewalks, gasping when there was a break in the treeline or buildings and she caught a sweeping view of the city.

This feels like home to me.

She gazed at the varied architecture, from modern glass and steel to the more aged and authentic French buildings built during the reign of Louis XIV. There was such an eclectic mix here, and it never failed to astound her.

Sam, on the other hand, was looking at the city with new eyes. She watched him to see if anything seemed familiar—a sight, a sound. But he gazed at the city as if he had never seen it before and she felt her shoulders slump.

It's still early, though. We haven't got to our suite yet. Surely he must remember that?

It would be good if some of the memories, when they returned, were *good* ones! She hated to think that all he would remember would be the bad.

Arriving outside the hotel, they paid their driver and stepped out.

The Shangri-La was beautiful to look at. Positioned in the sixteenth *arrondissement*, it was a nineteenth-century decadent-looking structure, apparently originally the private mansion of Prince Roland Bonaparte, the nephew of Napoleon. Once named the Palais Iéna, it stood in a tasteful corner of Paris, resting within the shadow of the elegant Eiffel Tower.

Sam looked up at the hotel and felt a sense of awe. History, *seeped* from this place. The entranceway with its sturdy white columns, and above the mass of ornate curlicued iron balconies, made him feel a tiny bit insignificant against this backdrop of important French history.

A uniformed porter assisted them with their bags into the hotel reception area and they stepped into a world of elegance. Even the floor was beautiful, and in the centre was a gold and glass table set with a generous, fragrant bouquet of lilies.

Sam stood back as Emily took care of all the arrangements and glanced around as he waited, studying the features, trying to see if anything would trigger a memory.

Nothing.

Maybe he needed a little more time? Perhaps if he relaxed a bit more then the memories might return? He'd had a couple. Back home. Fleeting ones, but still…it was better than nothing.

He was glad that he had agreed to this trip. Emily had seemed so sure that it was the right thing for them to do, and Sam had felt the same way after a moment or two of thought. It was what they needed—he wanted to get their marriage back on track as much as she did.

After learning that he'd lost two years of his life, and discovering that his business had become such a success, he'd felt keen to catch up on what was happening at the Monterey. But once he'd had that flashback…well, it hadn't taken him but a moment to agree to come here.

It was why he had closeted himself in his office, despite his physical need to reconnect with Em. Catching up on paperwork, accounts, reports, assessments, staff training was the only way he knew to allow her space.

He understood her distance, her reticence to kiss him, to touch him.

The birth centre had been his dream and the fact that he'd missed its launch galled him. His wedding. His honeymoon. It was all gone—hidden behind *that wall*.

He'd noticed the little looks she'd given him when she had found him in his office yet again. The looks she'd tried to hide when he had not returned to their marital bed. Had they been looks of relief or upset?

He wanted to. Of course he did. He loved her. But… Sam was a driven man, and work was important to him. Now more than ever. Emily was carrying his child, and his sense of responsibility to take care of them both lay heavy upon his shoulders. But beneath that something didn't feel right. Knowing that they'd argued, that he'd upset her… The *timing* didn't feel right. It was awkward, and because he didn't do well with *awkward* he'd focused on the one part of his life where he did do well. Work.

His thoughts drifted back to the scan. He should be pleased it had gone so well. The baby had looked good, there had been no concerns over the measurement of the nuchal fold at the back of the baby's neck, growth looked consistent with dates. The pregnancy was going well.

He should have felt joy.

But all he had been able to feel was fear.

What if he couldn't protect their baby? What if he failed their child? What if the same thing happened as before? Serena had been in *his care* and she had died. How could he possibly get things right for this baby?

Had he been mad, thinking that coming to Paris was a good idea? Their relationship was not the joyful coupling he'd thought it was back when he'd proposed.

They had been married for just over a year and already they were in trouble. But why?

Emily had mentioned his not wanting a baby, so she knew that much about his feelings. Obviously the married Sam had felt it easier to say than today's Sam. But it was becoming increasingly obvious that she knew nothing about *why* he didn't want a child. And that bothered him. He'd always assumed he would tell her at some point. Why hadn't he? Because of all their arguments?

Because you're afraid to admit what you did.

What would she think of him? An OB/GYN who delivered countless babies, head of a fabulous five-star birth centre, who had failed to realise that his baby sister had died?

The sound of the lift arriving brought Sam back to the present, and he and Emily followed the porter out of the lift and down the corridor to their suite.

'What do you think, Sam?' Emily asked as the porter swept open the door to their room.

It was tremendously beautiful. Painted in a soft cream, with original features and gold-draped windows, the room was littered with period furniture. Light from the sliding French doors that opened out onto a broad balcony welcomed them in, and just off to the right, almost within touching distance, was the tower that everyone recognised and thought of when they went to Paris.

'It's amazing.'

'It's our original suite. The one we honeymooned in.'

He turned to face her, hearing the nerves in her voice.

The honeymoon suite. A room built for seduction and intimacy. Was she nervous of being with him? Of beginning that side of their relationship again?

Sam tried to give her a reassuring smile. He couldn't blame her. She was doing so much to help him find his memories again. She was doing what she thought was right and he couldn't, *shouldn't* complain. But he was feeling the weight of her expectations and felt terrible at letting her down, because nothing about the room was sparking anything for him. And he was feeling terribly guilty about the state of their marriage. This trip *had* to work! He wanted her back. He wanted them *happy*.

Emily tipped the porter and he disappeared without notice. Then she joined her husband out on the balcony as they gazed out over the city. 'Can you feel it, Sam?'

'Feel what?'

'The city, welcoming us back.'

He smiled and reached out to curl his fingers around her own. He just wanted to touch her for a moment. To acknowledge why they were here. But he wouldn't put any pressure on her until she was ready.

'Let's go out and explore. What should we do first, do you think?'

'Well, I don't know about you, but me and the baby are starving. Can we go get something to eat? Find a little café or restaurant?'

Her reminder about the baby pierced his conscience, but he pasted a smile over his face. He couldn't let her know how concerned he was. What would she think of him if he told her the truth? That he didn't feel able to protect the baby? At least whilst it still lay within her womb it was safe, and he had no concerns about her delivering. Both of them were trained for that. It was *afterwards* that worried him. He wouldn't be looking after the baby for one night, the way he'd had to babysit Serena. This baby—their baby—he'd be looking after for the *rest of his life*.

'Food sounds good. Let's go.'

* * *

They walked through the streets hand in hand, soaking up the sights, sounds and smells of Paris. Walking past a bakery made Emily salivate with anticipation, but walking past a *poissonnerie*—a fishmongers—made her feel a little queasy.

'Maybe you should stay away from seafood, Em,' Sam joked as he wrapped a reassuring arm around her shoulders and led her towards the River Seine.

They headed down to the Jardins du Trocadero, admiring the fountain and the views of the river, before heading deep into the city, wandering down small cobbled streets, looking for something small and chic and different. Eventually they found exactly what they were looking for.

Gino's Cottage was a rooftop restaurant. All the diners got to sit out on the terrace at long banqueting tables, with views towards the Palais de Chaillot in the distance.

They were soon seated, and they ordered themselves something to drink—wine for Sam and sparkling water for Emily—before they perused the menu.

'It feels so good to be back here.'

Sam looked at her over his menu. 'We came here before?'

'No, not this place. I meant Paris. I loved it here when we came for our honeymoon.'

'Can you tell me about it? Some of the things we did?'

She blushed a little. 'Well, not all of them. Certainly not in public!'

He smiled.

'I think I'm going to have the *bruschetta des tomates* to start. What do you fancy?'

'Hmm…' His eyes scanned the options. 'I think I'll join you with that. What about your main course?'

'Hmm…lasagne, I think, for me.'

'And I'll have the carbonara.'

She laughed. 'Can you believe we've come to France and ended up choosing Italian food?'

'We'll go full-on French tomorrow.'

They placed their order with the waiter and Sam took a sip of his wine. It was perfect. Fruity. Crisp. With just a tart enough kick on the back of his throat.

'So, tell me about our first visit.'

Emily's eyes became dreamy, which he had to smile at, and as he stared at his beautiful wife he couldn't help but think just how lucky he was.

'Well, we didn't come out of our room the first day we arrived. We took full advantage of Room Service after we'd…worked up an appetite.'

He noticed her blushes and smiled slightly as his own imagination supplied him with the possibilities of what that might have been like.

She straightened her serviette on her lap. 'We did lots of walking, exploring, trying to find the *real* Paris—you know, stuff off the beaten track. We didn't just want to do the traditional touristy stuff.'

He nodded. 'Tell me one of your favourite places.'

Emily sighed happily in recollection. 'We went to the Bois de Vincennes and rowed out across the lake to the temple on the island. There's a grotto underneath and we went there quite late, at sunset. It was the most beautiful thing I ever saw.'

'We should go again, then.'

'I'd like that.' She smiled at him, and then they said nothing for a while.

* * *

Sam gazed at her from across the table and it felt good to have his full attention.

'We have been happy, Sam. I know I said we'd argued, but…there were good times, too.'

'When did it all start to change?'

She shrugged, the shift in her demeanour clear. 'I don't know. It was gradual. I can remember sitting down to dinner with you one night, like we are now, across the table from one another, and I was excited because I was going to suggest we start a family. It meant so much to me, and I honestly believed that it would to you, too. Considering what we both do for a living, it seemed the next natural step. We were married, our business was getting off the ground, financially we were solid. I couldn't see why there would be any objection. I thought that when I suggested having a baby you'd think about it briefly. Mull it over as you sipped your wine and then we'd discuss when we'd start trying.'

'But it didn't go that way?'

Her gaze was downcast, her eyes darkening. 'No. You…you became a different man. The second I mentioned it a wall seemed to come down in front of you. You closed yourself off, told me it wasn't a good idea, and suddenly said you had work to do in your office. You got up and left. That's how it was with us. We never got to talk about the important stuff like that. Work—fine. Business? No problem. Personal stuff? You backed away.'

Sam looked down at the table.

'I left the subject alone for a bit. Things returned to normal. We worked hard. You were doing a lot of fundraising, a lot of galas, a lot of promotion. I started feeling lonely. As if I didn't have a husband any more. That the one I had was married to the Monterey. I tried to ask for a bit more of your time. I wanted to get you alone, so we could talk. But there was only one subject I wanted to talk about and you just kept getting angry so I stopped asking.' She sipped her water. 'We stopped talking to one another entirely—except about business.'

Sam let out a heavy sigh and rubbed at his forehead. 'It was bad, then?'

'It wasn't great.'

The waiter arrived with their starters.

The aroma of their food was delightful, the freshness and richness of the juicy tomatoes could not be questioned, and the bread had definitely been made by hand on site and flavoured with herbs and pepper.

Sam hadn't been sure he wanted to eat after hearing all that, but the sight of the food set his mouth watering.

They ate in silence, and it probably would have continued that way, but he reminded himself that they were here to *solve* their problems.

Sam sought for a brighter topic, so they could start talking again. 'Tell me about our wedding.'

Instantly she smiled warmly at the memories. 'It was a wonderful day. The weather was perfect. Everything went so well. Though I can remember standing outside, waiting to go in, and a honeybee flew under my veil. I panicked so much I think I might have screamed! But thankfully my bridesmaids were much braver than I was and they managed to brush it off me. It set my nerves jangling, but then…when the music started and I walked down the aisle towards you…all my nerves just disappeared. I knew that what I was doing was right, and that the man waiting for me—*you*—was going to make me the happiest woman in the world.'

He smiled and raised his glass to hers, clinking them together.

'We had a huge reception—hundreds came, mostly people *you* knew. We released a pair of doves from the balcony of the hotel, and we had all these cameras on the guests' tables and they each took pictures of what was special for them. I've got all the albums in the house somewhere. I can dig them out for you, if you like?'

He nodded. 'Tell me about the Monterey.'

'What can I say? It's doing better than either of us ever imagined. It helped, I think, that one of our first guests was a Saudi princess who gave birth to twins. She arrived with all these security guards, and she had so many staff, but we were able to accommodate them by allotting them the entire third floor. After that our success rates went through the roof. Everyone wanted to come to us. Everyone wanted to have their babies in the same place that princesses had been born.'

'And the fertility clinic?'

'I'm not sure of the exact numbers, but I believe so far we've helped over a hundred couples to conceive and successfully carry their children to term. Our manager, Edward, would be able to give you exact numbers. Didn't you call him before we left?'

'Yes, I wanted numbers and cost forecasting for the next year.'

Em nodded, aware that Sam had become work-focused yet again, despite all she'd said about the state of their marriage. It was something she was familiar with.

She finished her bruschetta, sliding her knife and fork together on her plate. 'How do you think it's all looking? I try my best to keep myself informed, but the money side of things is not my forte. I prefer the hands-on work.'

'It looks like we're exceeding expectations. I'm happy about that.'

'But...?' She looked at him with concern, knowing there was something else.

'But I'm not happy that our marriage has gone downhill.'

'We were both at fault. We allowed the Monterey to be our main focus, and sadly we forgot to put just as much work into us as we did that.'

'I should never have allowed it to happen.'

'Like I said, it was both of us.'

He appreciated her trying to let him off the hook, but he still felt that it was his fault. 'I still can't believe I don't remember it.'

'You were definitely there.' She gave a slight smile.

'But I don't remember, Em! I want to recall the experience of the rush of the Monterey's opening. The worry about whether we'd succeed and the watching and the observing as everything began to get better. The tweaking of the things that weren't quite right, answering our patients' needs and serving them, making their experience the best they could ever imagine. I don't feel I was part of any of that. I've just been handed dry forecasts and accounts of where we are now and apparently, according to you, work is just fine—but *we* aren't.'

She reached for her glass of water. Sipped it. 'We can be okay again, Sam. That's why we're here. And you *did* experience it. You worked so hard. The memory is in there—you've just got to be patient.'

'I know. It's just...'

'Frustrating?'

He nodded and sat back as their waiter arrived to

clear their dishes. Once he'd disappeared, Sam sat forward again. 'I feel out of place, Em. I know the Monterey is ours, that we made it happen, but I don't *feel* like it's mine. I feel like it's something you've done. That it's been your project and you've just shown it to me. Does that make any sense?'

'A little, yes. But you have to know that it will all come back—you've already experienced one old memory. And when it does...'

He saw a shadow cross her face and knew why she looked so worried. 'Yes?'

'When it does, you'll know...everything.' She forced a smile.

'I hope so. I really do.'

'Me too.' She dabbed at her mouth with the serviette. 'I must just use the ladies' room. Excuse me.'

He watched her hurry away.

He knew why he was really so frustrated at not being there for the Monterey. It had always been *his* big project. *His* dream. He'd put so much work into it when really he should have been putting all the work into his marriage. He could vocalise his concerns about missing out on the Monterey. But he couldn't vocalise about what had gone wrong in his marriage—because Emily didn't yet know about Serena.

I've got to tell her. We won't survive otherwise.

Whilst he waited, he stared out across the darkening evening of Paris. The fairy lights had come on around the terrace, bathing them all in soft white light, but the brightest beacon of all was the lit Eiffel Tower, behind him in the distance.

It was a stunning sight—one they would no doubt be able to enjoy from their hotel window.

Sam hoped Paris would be everything they had planned it to be.

He needed his memories back.

He needed to be the man Emily had fallen in love with.

He needed to be strong.

Needed to know who he was and what he had gone through.

Why couldn't the accident have erased the memory of what happened to Serena?

Dinner was superb. The lasagne that Emily had ordered was deliciously sumptuous, and the chocolate mousse they shared for pudding was soft, rich and velvety.

As they sat drinking coffee Sam asked her an awkward question.

'Considering how things were between us, I take it the baby was a surprise?'

Hurrying to swallow her mouthful of coffee, she almost choked on it. 'Yes. It was a surprise. I didn't even know I was pregnant until after the crash, when they ran a few blood tests on me.'

'You were on the pill?'

'Yes, I was.'

He sipped his coffee carefully, not meeting her eyes. 'Did you get sick? Is that what happened?'

She shook her head. 'I don't think so. I certainly never missed any.'

'It's never been one hundred percent effective.'

'There was a lot going on, Sam. We were very busy. I was working long shifts because one of our midwives was off ill and I was covering for her. One night we'd both had a lot of wine and...'

'It happened?'

She nodded. 'Yeah. It happened.'

Emily remembered that night so clearly. She had been exhausted, tired and upset. She hadn't seen Sam for almost three days. He'd been in surgery, or in and out of meetings, and they'd barely spoken. He certainly hadn't touched her for weeks. Their arguments had grown so awful that they hadn't talked in what felt like ages.

Emily had gone back to their house and, knowing she didn't have a shift the next day, had poured herself a large glass of wine. She'd almost finished it by the time Sam had arrived home, and something about him had seemed strange. He'd been different.

He'd said he was fed up with their fighting and that he missed her. She'd not let him say another word, had gone straight into his arms, and it had been as if someone had lit a fire. Suddenly everything had been urgent. They'd craved each other's bodies intensely and they'd made love on the carpet.

Afterwards he'd scooped her up in his arms and carried her to bed, where she'd fallen asleep. But when she'd woken in the morning he'd been gone again. It had been a brief truce, a cessation in their arguments, but when she'd sought him out to talk to him about what had happened he'd been too busy, and had answered her sharply, and before she'd known it they'd been arguing again.

It had been a difficult time for her. She'd been devastated, and then hopeful as she'd lain in his arms that they might be able to work things out—only to be dropped like a hot stone afterwards. Cast aside, feeling used.

Emily didn't want to tell him any of that. How could she? Here? In this beautiful city? Sam didn't need to hear any of that. He'd hate to hear it. He'd feel so guilty, and she didn't want him feeling that. They were here to deepen their love. Not go over old, painful ground which neither of them needed to return to.

She wanted them to be happy! She wanted the fairytale that she saw being played out every day. A happy family, a *loving* family, with everyone eager and excited about their pregnancy, planning nurseries and buying tiny clothes, getting excited about the approaching labour and thinking of names and choosing godparents. All of it.

She wanted a husband who was thrilled to be a father! She wanted the love that she'd never had. To give her child the stable family home that she had never experienced. There was no way she wanted to go back to the way they'd been before.

When she'd married Sam she'd made a commitment, and Emily believed you should always honour a commitment. If you had a child, you stuck around to love it and raise it. If you got married—well, you worked with the other person to make the marriage the best it could be. You didn't just give up when things got rough. You didn't just walk out because life seemed easier chasing another dream.

She looked down at the table. Sam still didn't know just *how bad* their arguments had been. How close she had come to leaving him. If he knew what they'd really been like…the amount of times she had stood in the shower and cried…

'I just want this trip to work so badly. I can't imagine how you must feel, having lost two years of your life. To wake up to this… I've tried to imagine what it would be like if it had happened to me.'

What if she *had* been the one with amnesia? If she

thought he had just proposed and she had forgotten the wedding, the Grand Opening of their business. Their arguments? She would still feel blissfully happy after the proposal, right? Would she want to hear that she had threatened to leave him? Would she want to hear that they *weren't* the blissfully happy couple she believed them to be? Would she want to hear about some of the things they'd said to each other in the heat of the moment?

No.

'I'm okay.'

'Are you? Without memories of the opening of the birth centre, our wedding, our honeymoon…?'

'I can get all of that back.' He reached for her hand. 'Isn't that what you keep telling me? Isn't that why we're here?'

She nodded. It was. But getting his memories back was a double-edged sword. On the one hand he would have the joy of recalling all the good times they'd shared, but on the other…they could slip apart.

'Then let's work towards that. If I have any questions I'll ask you and you can answer. At least until my memories come back on their own. Okay?'

It would have to do. 'Okay.'

He smiled at her, his eyes glinting beneath the fairy lights.

The restaurant was beginning to get busy now, but they finished their coffees, paid and headed back out onto the street.

'Let's walk for a bit,' Sam suggested, draping an arm around her shoulder.

Paris at twilight was even more beautiful than it was during the day. There were still just as many people bustling about, and the roads were filled with cars and

bikes, but everything seemed just that little bit calmer.
As if everyone was more relaxed. Cafés and bistros
poured out their lights and their aromatic scents into
the streets, and they could hear conversation and muted
laughter and people *enjoying* themselves. They passed
a busker or two, food and flower stalls packing up for
the day.

Sam bought her a single rose and presented it to her.
'For *madame*.'

'Thank you, kind sir.' She lifted the bloom to her
nose and inhaled its soft sweet scent.

These were the moments that she'd yearned for. The
last time they'd been in Paris Emily had been soaking
up the atmosphere as much as Sam, but this time she
knew it all a little better and so could concentrate more
on enjoying being with Sam. Holding his hand. Being
in his arms. Being in Paris itself was an added bonus.

Sam and Emily headed back over to the Seine and
began to walk along its banks, arm in arm. It was a truce
of sorts. Both of them were keen to make this trip work.
To become close again.

They could hear accordion music in the distance,
against the soft lapping of the water against the banks.
A duck swam by, followed by a row of small ducklings,
brown and yellow.

Emily sighed and looked about her. Couples sat on
benches, hand in hand. Couples walked along the river,
just like them. Couples sat on the stone steps, staring at
the water. This really was a city meant for happiness.
Not marital woes.

Sam kissed the side of her neck, inhaling the per-
fumed scent of her hair. He looked into her eyes. 'I'm
sorry we've argued, and I'm sorry if I haven't been
spending time with you. I guess you thought the same

thing was happening again when I locked myself away in the office to catch up on things. Same old Sam, huh?'

She smiled. He was so unaware. So innocent of how bad things had actually become. She wanted to make him feel better.

'That's okay. I know you feel the need to catch up. I would do the same thing in your shoes.'

'I'm so lucky to have you, Em.'

She smiled back at him.

The music was getting closer now, and they could see an old man, sitting on top of the stone steps with a genuine accordion. It wasn't a recording, or a CD playing, but a real, actual musician. He had an ancient face, but it was filled with passion as he played an old-style Argentinian tango, his fingers moving over the buttons and shaping the accordion with ease. Around him couples were dancing against the backdrop of the river. All ages, all abilities. It didn't matter. People were just being in the moment.

Sam and Emily watched for a second or two, and then Sam took her hand and led her into the group of dancers.

'Sam! What are you doing?' She laughed.

'We're going to dance!'

She laughed out loud in disbelief! Did Sam not remember? He'd done this the last time! It didn't seem as if he knew that.

But who cared? Emily wanted to dance with him. Their honeymoon had been the only time he had danced with her. Apart from at their wedding, of course, and she loved to dance.

At least she loved to dance with *him*.

The beautiful music was at once sudden and jarring, and had Sam pulling her up tight against his body. At first she laughed, embarrassed, but then she could see Sam smiling, taking the tango seriously, staring deeply into her eyes.

The Argentine tango was a dance made for eye contact and a close embrace. They moved as one. Forward. Back. To the side. Their steps were in tune with the music, first fast, then slow. Their bodies pressed together.

Slowly Emily began to forget that there were other couples dancing with them in the same space. All she concentrated on was Sam's eyes locked with her own. *Feeling* the pace and emotion of the music.

Being close to him. Held by him.

He had such piercing blue eyes. Intense. Moving. And they bored into her own with love and adoration as he twisted her this way, then that. The music began to get a little faster. He twisted her out to the side and she swept her foot out wide, as if scraping the floor, her skirt billowing out around her, before he pulled her back in close once again.

He really was a masterful dancer.

Why don't we do this more often?

She stared once again into his eyes as he pulled her close, making her gasp. This dance represented their relationship so easily. Passionate…tempestuous. Intimate.

She slid her leg up and down his, aware of the way he was breathing with her now in the dance, enjoying their closeness to each other. Aware of the way his body felt against hers.

Oh, how I've missed this man.

As the music built to its climax Sam spun them round in tight little movements and then, at the big finish, he dipped her backwards, bending over with her. As everyone began clapping to thank the musician he brought his face towards hers and kissed her deeply.

She fell into the kiss, draping her hands around his neck, unaware that the music had begun once again and the other couples were continuing to dance.

Straightening, they simply stood in the middle of the 'dance floor' and kissed.

Emily sank into him, claiming her husband back, claiming his mouth, his tongue, his taste. She wanted him so badly. Did he want her just as much? She hoped so. It had been so long since she had felt his touch upon her like this, so long since he had stared into her eyes like this, and she craved him like a drug.

As the kiss ended they continued to stare into each other's eyes. For a moment neither of them said anything, and then she felt Sam slip his fingers into hers.

'Let's go back to the hotel.'

She nodded, understanding his intent, and together they left the dancing group.

CHAPTER FIVE

NEITHER OF THEM said anything on the way back to the hotel. They walked with purpose, through the evening light, and in their hotel room, surrounded once again by luxury, Emily suddenly realised just how much of a long day they'd had—the flight, the taxi ride, dinner, exploring Paris, and then telling Sam how bad things really were.

She felt she wanted to refresh herself. Wash away the travel. Take a few moments to prepare herself for this. They hadn't been intimate for such a long time and she wanted it to be perfect.

'I'm going to take a shower.'

Sam nodded.

Inside the shower room, Emily turned on the hot spray and removed her clothes. Stepping beneath the powerful refreshing water, she gasped at the feel of it on the back of her neck before turning around to face the water and look for soap.

That was when she became aware of the fact that Sam had joined her. She heard the glass shower door open and then sensed his presence.

Smiling to herself, she sighed in delight as she felt Sam's hands slide over the skin around her hips, before he slid them over her belly and pulled her back against him.

Emily closed her eyes with pure elation. She could feel him. Every familiar inch of him. His hands sliding over her breasts…his fingers splaying as they rubbed over her sensitive nipples. Leaning back into him, she allowed herself to enjoy the moment as his lips caressed her neck. She had not felt his touch for so long! *Too* long.

The last time Sam had joined her in the shower had been in this very shower, on their honeymoon. They'd just come back from visiting the top of the Eiffel Tower, watching the city from its viewing platforms and taking photographs. They'd hired bicycles and cycled around Paris in the midday heat, and by the end of the day they'd both been sweaty and tired. They'd fallen into the shower cubicle with giggles and laughter, holding onto each other as they kissed each other and covered each other in foam, their limbs sliding over each other.

Here they stood once again.

It gave Emily a strange sense of *déjà-vu*. Shivering, she closed her eyes as Sam's hands once again sought her peaked nipples. The heat and spray of the water, the feel of his fingers upon her, the way he kissed and nipped the skin on her neck and collarbone, his lips brushing like feathers…it was utterly delightful.

'Oh, Sam…'

He turned her to him and cupped her face, bringing her lips to his.

Oh, I've missed his touch…

A few weeks ago she could never have dreamed that they would be like this. She'd stood over a suitcase, planning to leave him! She'd felt angry at him, frustrated that he would never talk to her, or allow her to explain how she was feeling. He'd never listened—he'd ignored her, stayed away.

She'd never believed she would have *this* again.

Those days she'd spent worrying about what would happen when he woke from his coma had been swept away by the realisation that Sam couldn't remember the last two years. That, for him, their relationship was in a totally different place. And the baby! He'd not reacted badly to the news either—which she didn't want to think about. Didn't want to question.

All that mattered was the touch of his hands upon her, the feel of his arousal against her, the clear signs that he wanted *her*, wanted the baby, that he was happy despite his memory loss. And that they were reconnecting.

We can get through this. We can do it together.

A wave of tiredness swept over her, but she pushed it away. All these hours they'd spent awake—the travelling, the waiting in the airport, the long day. Her exhaustion was catching up with her, but she couldn't let it overwhelm her. She had waited for this moment with Sam. Had craved this intimacy between them. Something which had been sadly lacking for too long.

How many nights had she lain awake in bed, waiting for him to come home? Waiting for him to come to bed just so she could feel the security of him next to her on the mattress even if he did turn his back?

Too many times.

How many times had he stayed away? How many times had he left her wondering where he was actually sleeping? So she'd had to go tiptoeing through the house at night until she found the room that he was in?

Too many to count.

How did she know whether he would do it to her

again? It had to be in him, didn't it? The rejection of her. The rejection of the baby. Even if it wasn't in him now it was *part of him*. He had already done it to her. He just couldn't remember. When would it start? Was it already brewing? Was he already having secret thoughts that he was holding back? What if he used her right now and then in the morning cast her aside?

Feeling afraid and confused, Emily turned her back to him. She needed a moment. To think. To *breathe*.

Sam ran his fingers through her long wet hair and reached past her for a shampoo bottle. Squirting some into his hands, he began to stroke it into her long locks, gently massaging her scalp, making sure he touched every strand, every length, trying to make the experience pleasurable for her.

She pressed her hands against the wall of the shower cubicle and gave in to the massage. It felt so good to be loved by Sam again. Cherished. But she wasn't sure what she should be thinking. Should she just enjoy what he was initiating? Or turn and tell him the full truth? Take the bull by its very sharp, pointed horns and tell him everything?

Emily pressed her hands against the tiled wall, feeling its reassuring, very solid presence.

I can't. I'd risk everything. It's best he doesn't know I was going to leave him.

The head massage was soothing. Too soothing. She felt as if she might almost drop off to sleep, it was so nice.

Emily held her head under the shower so that the shampoo would be washed away. The hot suds ran down her body, trailed by Sam's hands, his fingertips, a feather touch down her back, over the swell of her hips and bottom and the sides of her thighs.

Then he was reaching past her for conditioner, and as he smoothed on the cold creamy hair product, smoothing it down the hair that almost fell to her waist, she let out a long sigh of pleasure.

She dipped her head under the spray once more, then turned to him. The heat within the shower was becoming too much. 'I need to get out. Cool down.'

He kissed her shoulder. 'I won't be a minute. Get into bed. I'll join you soon.'

Emily stepped out and grabbed a large fluffy bath towel, which she wrapped herself in, and then left the steamy shower room.

The hotel suite felt much cooler, and it was as if there was more air. Breathing more easily, she removed the towel and rubbed at her long hair, then padded across the suite in her bare feet towards the bed. She smiled as she slipped beneath the covers.

Tonight she would reclaim her husband.

Tonight she would get him back for good.

Sam turned off the shower and grabbed a towel to wrap around his waist and another to rub at his wet hair.

The shower had felt good. But it was even better to have shared it with Em. It was time for them to grow close—especially as he'd spent the last few days stuck in his office at the house, trying to catch up on all the paperwork that had accrued in his absence. Trying to look at business growth charts and financial losses, turnover and profit, stock ordering systems and staff training reports, and all the other reams of paper that had just seemed to grow out of nowhere and had almost brought on a headache.

Two years' worth of catching up had caused him to fall asleep there more than once! He felt sure that Em wasn't approving of that, but she hadn't complained. Not really. She'd given him a worried look or two, whenever she'd popped in with a coffee, or to say goodnight, but that was to be expected after his accident.

Now they were in Paris, and for him it felt like the first time. Sitting across from Em in that restaurant and seeing the love in her eyes for him had warmed his heart. And then later, when they'd danced together, it had been clear they hadn't touched for an age, and it had been painfully exquisite to take her in his arms once more and see the hope and elation in her eyes.

He was eager for them to improve their relationship. To find the marriage they'd had at the beginning, before the arguments had started. They'd been good together once, but hearing how he'd been with her had rung too true. He could imagine himself trying to avoid the question about having babies—could picture himself staying away, thinking that if he did that at least then they wouldn't be arguing. That somehow he'd be trying to save her from pain.

Sam threw the towel he'd been drying his hair with to the floor and stepped out of the shower room. He'd only kept her waiting for a few minutes—he felt sure she wouldn't have minded.

Em lay in the bed, her naked back to him, her still drying hair spread out over the pillow.

Smiling, he lifted the covers, removed the towel from his waist and slid in next to her, his hand roving over her naked hip and around her thigh.

'Hello again, gorgeous…'

He waited for an answer, and when he didn't get one he propped himself up in bed and peered over at her face.

Was she *asleep*?

'Em?' he whispered. *'Em?'*

She breathed steadily, her eyes closed, her face in a truly relaxed state.

She's exhausted! Must be all those hormones...

His hand resting on her belly stilled. There was a slight—ever so slight—roundness to it that hadn't been there before.

Our baby.

Sam laid his head down onto the pillow as he spooned his wife. How would he deal with what was to come? Could he do it? He'd have to, wouldn't he? The baby was already happening. Already growing within her.

He wasn't surprised that he'd not been able to find a way to tell her about Serena. He had always kept that part of him close. Tightly boxed away, never to be shown the light. But perhaps by doing that—by not telling Em—he had caused a different rift. One he could never fix. He hoped not. He hoped that there was still happiness ahead for them both. Perhaps he could find a way to tell her about his baby sister?

Sam swallowed hard. *I'm not sure I can.* He'd spoken about it to nobody. Even his own family didn't talk about it to each other. He'd learnt that from them. You take the hurt, you stamp it down and you bury it—bury it deep, where no one will ever see it. You don't mention the disturbed soil, you don't mention the empty crib, you don't say anything when you see someone crying. You stay away from all of that.

It had worked for him thus far, hadn't it?

No. Your wife was miserable!

He would have to hope this trip would give him time. Time to find a way through his concerns and fears about being a good, protective father.

Because it was real. The baby was in there, growing. He had seen it on the scan and it had taken his breath away.

Maybe a son. Maybe a daughter. Like Serena. If it was a girl, would he ever truly relax? Would he stand watch over her every night? Checking her breathing? Checking she was still okay?

Was that even possible? Not twenty-four hours a day. But how *could* he keep his baby safe? If something happened to their child Emily would be distraught! She might blame him.

And if it were a boy? Would he be any more relaxed? *No.* He supposed they could get a baby monitor that alerted you to your baby's breathing. He supposed he could get a camera for the baby's room, too. But would any of that make him feel better?

Sam wasn't sure. But what he *did* know was that they were against the clock. He had six months to get his head around this. Six months either to accept what was happening and get on with it, or…or what?

Sam cradled his wife's abdomen. The baby was safe for now.

He could only hope that it would stay that way. And they were making inroads in their marriage too. Coming here. Spending time together away from work. But there was work to do here too…on their marriage.

It took some time, but eventually he fell asleep, his eyes finally closing on the shadows crossing the room and the constant glow of light touching the ceiling, coming from the Eiffel Tower…

'Let's hire some bikes,' Sam suggested, a big smile on his face.

Indulgently, Emily smiled back, tearing a piece from her croissant as they breakfasted alfresco on their hotel suite balcony. It was a beautiful summer morning and she'd had an excellent night's sleep, waking to find herself snuggled into Sam's warm, inviting body.

'We did that the last time. And I don't want to get exhausted again.'

Em felt terrible for having fallen asleep last night. They'd both been expecting to *become more acquainted*, and yet the second she'd lain her head upon the pillow she'd gone off to the Land of Nod. Waking this morning to see the sunlight streaming through the windows, and having a distinctly empty memory of any recent lovemaking, had made her feel incredibly embarrassed and awkward. She'd slipped out of his arms and gone outside to the balcony.

'I meant those little moped things. I heard someone say yesterday that they rode around Montmartre and had an amazing time. Let's do that. No energy required.'

The buttery croissant was light and fluffy in her mouth and she swallowed it whilst smearing another piece with jam. 'Okay...sounds fun. What do you want to do in Montmartre?'

'Whatever takes our fancy. Let's just ride around and explore.'

'Okay.'

It sounded a great idea. They hadn't done *that* before, and she relished the idea of finding somewhere new to explore together. They needed to spend time like that. Who knew what might trigger his memory? Why not try something different?

'It's going to be another lovely summer's day.'

'It's always a lovely summer's day when I'm with you.'

She smiled. 'Ditto.'

'I'm going to get dressed. You enjoy breakfast. You need your strength. Don't want you flaking out on me.'

The croissant went dry in her mouth and guilt made the breakfast suddenly unpalatable. She hadn't meant to fall asleep last night, but the second she'd got into the bed she'd relaxed and closed her eyes for just a moment...

Sam must have felt so disappointed when he'd got out of the shower and found her fast asleep. Yet he was being so gentlemanly by not mentioning it.

But what could she do? It was done now, and he was obviously trying hard to not focus on it. She should do the same thing, too, and get ready for their day in Montmartre.

When she went into the bedroom she gasped to see a box upon the bed, tied with a bow. 'What's that?'

'Open it.' Sam grinned.

Puzzled, she sat on the bed and untied the bow, sliding off the ribbon before opening the box. Whatever was inside was wrapped in pale pink tissue paper, and when she opened that she gasped out loud. 'Oh, my goodness! When did you get this?'

Inside the box was the beautiful powder-blue dress that she'd spotted in the airport shop when they'd passed by at Charles de Gaulle. She'd pointed it out to him, had oohed and aahed at the dress in the window, but they'd hurried on, eager to get to their destination.

How had Sam arranged this?

'Sam...'

'I couldn't resist. I know it probably won't fit you in a few more weeks, but... I wanted you to have it.'

She stood up and draped it against her, checking herself in the mirror. 'I love it, Sam—thank you. I'm going to wear it today.'

'On a moped? Why not wear it tonight, when we get back? We could go out for a meal.'

She nodded. 'Perfect. Thank you.'

'You're worth it. I love you.'

She stroked his face, loving this side of Sam. 'I love you, too.'

He grinned. 'Okay. Get dressed and let's get ready to ride!'

At first Emily wasn't too good at riding the moped. But after a few false starts, where she kangarooed along the road, and a bit of extra tuition from a patient Sam, they finally got going and rode through the city, out towards Montmartre.

They stopped and parked on the Rue Jardieu, to get off and have a good look around the area, famed for its street painters and artists. They walked towards the Square Willette and gasped in awe at the sight of the Basilica de Sacré-Coeur—the beautiful, pure white Byzantine church that looked down the hill at them as if surveying all that it could see.

'That's just beautiful, isn't it, Sam?'

'It is. Should we go take a look around?'

She nodded.

They took their time—walking through the square, then up the terraced stairs, past a musician playing the harp, to whom they gave a few coins—and finally they stood in front of the wonderful, imposing building.

There were three arches, and above them bronze statues of a saint and a king, welcoming them in, After taking a photo or two, they stepped inside, into the cool interior.

The beautiful three-domed church was lit by dozens of stained glass windows, surrounding the building, and they walked around quietly, respecting their reverent surroundings.

Emily felt the need to slip her hand into Sam's, and she watched as Sam stopped to light a candle and stood back to stare at it, as if in contemplation.

She frowned, wondering who the candle was for. Sam still had both his parents and all five of his siblings. Was it for a grandparent? It seemed a strange thing for him to do, and she wondered about the Sam that she didn't know. There had to be something. Back in his past. And it was something he clearly hadn't forgotten about after his accident. An old memory? An old pain?

She knew Sam had secrets, and it had always pained her that he'd never chosen to share those with her. *Why* hadn't he? Was it because of the arguments, the distance between them? Why hadn't he told her about them when they *weren't* arguing? He'd had time. They talked to each other about most things back then. It hurt to think that he was keeping part of himself hidden, that he didn't trust her.

But she couldn't ask him here. Not with all these people around. She decided to wait until they were out of the church, maybe having lunch, and then she would ask him.

Watching Sam made her realise that she didn't have anyone to light a candle for. As far as she knew her mother was still alive. Her Aunt Sylvia and her Uncle Martin were too. No one had any idea who her father was. Grandparents? She had no recollection. So Emily had no need to make such a beautiful acknowledgement. It made her feel a little rootless, not knowing more about her mother and her family. As if a part of her was missing. That she was somehow incomplete. It was why she had fought so hard to save her marriage. She couldn't lose Sam, too. She would feel so lost.

They continued to look around, then eventually emerged outside, walking back around to the front steps and looking out over the city.

'It was so peaceful in there, wasn't it?' he asked.

Emily nodded. 'It was. Very.' She looked at his face for a moment, wondering whether *now* would be a good time to ask about the candle, but she saw a shadow cross his face and decided against it. Not yet. There would be a time and place soon, though.

'Where do you think we should go next?'

'I'm not sure. Should we go back and grab the mopeds? Ride around?'

She nodded. The bikes would be good. Sam's mood had changed in the basilica, and she wanted to see the joyful Sam she had witnessed that morning. This was meant to be fun, and yet they had descended into a sombre mood.

They walked back through the square, enjoying the wide expanses of grass and the flowers, the singing of the birds in the trees, until they got back to their mopeds and donned their helmets.

Their engines roared into life and they set off into the small, winding streets, looking for treasures.

It came suddenly and without warning. Sam was riding his moped, following Emily. He'd been watching the traffic, enjoying the sight of his wife's hair billowing behind her, and the memory came from nowhere.

Emily striding away from him in a hospital corridor, anger pouring from every part of her body. Stiff shoulders. Purposeful.

He called her name in exasperation. 'Emily!'

She stopped walking. Turned and her face was full of tears. Her eyes red and streaming...

Sam blinked and a car sounded its horn at him as he wavered slightly. Straightening his bike, he raised his hand in apology to the driver.

What the hell had that been?

The hospital corridor had been at the Monterey. He'd recognised it. It had been the corridor leading to Emily's office, because there'd been that picture on the wall. The watercolour of a pixie gazing at her reflection in a pool. Em had picked it out from an exhibition she'd seen.

In the memory his wife had been upset. Vastly upset. With him. *At him?*

What had happened next?

He cursed to himself, angry that the memory had been fleeting and brief. But then, strangely, his heart began to pound as he realised another memory had returned! Bad as it had been—*again*—a memory *had* returned!

Was this going to be it? Were they about to start coming back?

Should he mention it to Emily?

He pondered over that. If he told her he'd experienced another flash of memory she'd want to know what it was, and if he told her... Well, she might not want another bad memory being dragged up. Not here. Not on this holiday. She'd wanted them to enjoy this place. They were both hoping this trip to Paris would bring them closer again.

But hadn't she been the one to suggest that Paris would be the place for him to regain his memories?

This was what they were here for, after all. And, even though it was a bad memory, perhaps it seemed worse than it really was? Perhaps it was something that could be easily explained and Emily would laugh about it and tell him it was nothing?

Sam was desperate to get his memories back, and the fleeting one he'd just experienced enticed him to believe that others were there, waiting for him to claim them. If he explored this memory with Emily then it might cause others to come through.

He had to take that chance.

After they'd been driving around for a while Emily pointed over at what looked like a vast marketplace but was in fact a square, full of artists and portraitists, all sitting beneath large red umbrellas to protect themselves and their work from the sun or occasional inclement weather. The square was filled with laughter and French voices. Tourists and locals milled around, taking photographs or sitting for paintings beneath an avenue of leafy green trees.

Ahead of him, Emily removed her helmet, shaking out her hair, and slipped on her sunglasses. 'This looks great, Sam! Shall we get our picture painted?'

He loved her enthusiasm. Loved her smile. He didn't want to lose that. He decided to tell her about the memory later—perhaps when they were sitting for the picture.

'Okay.'

They locked up their mopeds, pocketing the keys, and headed into the bustling square.

There were some amazing artists there, using a vast array of techniques—acrylics, watercolour, pencil, paste, chalk. If there was a way of putting a picture onto paper or canvas, then it was here. And he knew Emily loved art.

They took their time looking about, trying to find

someone they thought might capture the two of them perfectly, and stopped when they saw a caricaturist.

'Oh, this will be fun, Sam. Let's ask this one.'

Thankfully the artist spoke English, and they negotiated a price before they sat down together and smiled at the artist who soon set to work.

'You are here on holiday?' the artist asked.

Emily smiled at him. 'Sort of a second honeymoon. It's a long story,' she explained.

'Ah, *voyage de noces. La lune de miel.*'

'That sounds beautiful.'

The artist smiled. 'It is meant to be. *C'est romantique!*'

Emily and Sam shared an odd smile. The painter obviously saw them as a couple, very much in love, and only they knew the real truth.

As the artist worked, concentrating on his drawing whilst occasionally peering around his easel at the two of them, Sam decided to let Emily know what had happened.

'You know, Em… I think whilst we were riding here I remembered something.' He glanced at her to see her reaction and noticed with alarm that she seemed to freeze, pausing for a brief millisecond as if in fear, before she let out a breath and smiled.

'You did? What?'

He shook his head. 'It was brief. Barely anything, really. We were at the Monterey, heading for your office, but…'

She looked curious. 'But?'

'You were walking away from me, and when I called your name you turned around and you were crying.'

Emily looked away from him, frowning.

Was she trying to remember the incident? Had it been a common occurrence? He knew they'd been arguing.

'I see.'

'What was that about?'

Em shook her head. 'It's not important.'

'It is,' he pressed on. 'I need to understand what was going on if we're to make this work.'

She looked down at the ground. 'If it's the argument I remember, then I'd tried to track you down at work because you hadn't been home that night. I wanted to know where you'd been.'

He stared at her, afraid of her answer. 'And?'

'You'd been out wining and dining clients, and I was annoyed because you were spending so much time wooing other people that you never had time for me.'

'I see.'

'I wasn't being selfish, Sam. I hadn't seen you for what felt like days! I'd been worried about you. Worried about *us*. I'd spent hours huddled on the couch, afraid of what might have happened, and then I learnt that you'd been out having a good time.'

He looked away. 'Oh.'

'So I was hurt and angry and I stormed away from you.'

Sam almost didn't want to believe it. But he could imagine himself doing that. Avoiding the main argument and throwing himself into something else instead, hoping that if he just never talked about the thing that bothered him then it wouldn't bother anyone else. It was what he had been taught to do.

'So your memories are starting to come back?'

He gazed at her and he could see that she was sad. But there was something else in her eyes that he couldn't

fathom. What was it? She was looking at him as if...
as if she was afraid.

No. That couldn't be true. Why would Emily be
afraid of his memories returning? She *wanted* them to.
It couldn't be fear. There was no need for it. She'd already told him how bad it had become between them.
For that he was grateful. It would have been so easy
for her to say that they'd been getting on fine. He had
to be wrong—it couldn't have been fear that he'd seen.

Shaking his head, he decided to forget about it. The
artist obviously thought they were happy, because when
he showed them the picture—the two of them beneath a
backdrop of the Eiffel Tower—he had drawn red hearts
blossoming all around them.

Sam wondered briefly how the artist might have
painted them if he'd known the truth? Would they have
had blindfolds over their eyes? Hands clamped over
their mouths?

He solemnly wished their lives were truly like the
caricature.

They decided to walk through some of the streets, snapping pictures of things they found interesting. They
found a very pretty vineyard—which seemed an odd
thing to find amongst a bustling mass of streets—then
a street of nineteenth-century villas and gardens which
were in full bloom, and in another a windmill.

Montmartre was a place of contrasts, it seemed, and
they could understand why it had once been *the* place
to be seen if you were an artist or a painter.

'We ought to get something to eat,' Emily said, rubbing at her stomach. 'I'm getting very hungry with all
this exploring.'

'What do you fancy?'

'Something quick.'

They found a small stall selling pitta pockets stuffed with a choice of chicken, beef or vegetables, served with plantains, avocado or black beans. They both chose a chicken pitta with plantain chips and two cold limeades.

'Oh, my goodness, that's delightful,' Emily said, savouring her sandwich and using her fingers to capture a piece of chicken.

'Something new for you?'

She nodded, smiling, her mouth full.

Sam smiled back. The food was indeed delicious, and he realised that he was loving today. Loving making these new memories with Em after the regret of knowing he had missed so much and that some of what he had missed had been awful. But he was determined to be positive and to look forward. He had a business that by all accounts was doing well, a gorgeous, wonderful wife whom he loved with his entire heart, and they were trying their best to tackle their problems the best they knew how.

And he was going to be a father.

That in itself was a scary thing to admit to himself, and he'd tried to put it in the 'positive' category but he couldn't. It was not something that he could escape from. He had to face it. Head-on. No matter if he had doubts.

Em took a thoughtful nibble of her pitta. 'This morning, Sam…back in the basilica…you lit a candle.'

He glanced at her, acknowledging her statement with a nod.

'Who was it for?'

So she definitely didn't know, then. He obviously hadn't told her about Serena. He supposed he knew why. He'd always kept that part of himself hidden. Had shared it with no one. And when Emily had brought up the idea of having a baby in the past he must have dug his heels in even more.

Was this the root of all their problems? His refusal to talk about his deepest, darkest secret? Had it been his fault all along? Hurting Emily by pushing her away? Causing her grief by refusing even to discuss something that was so important? It must have made her feel tiny. Belittled. She was his wife and he wouldn't even talk to her about what ailed him.

But did he want her to find out about it *here*? When they were trying to make new happy memories for themselves?

'It was for us. A candle to show the way.'

She smiled, relieved, and laid her head upon his shoulder. 'That's so sweet. For us? Thank you, Sam.'

Pressing down against the guilt he felt at lying to her, he kissed the side of her face, and he was just about to take another bite of his sandwich when something happened that seemed almost to occur in slow motion.

He looked out across the street and spotted an old man, looking for a place to cross. The road wasn't too busy, but there was a steady stream of traffic coming both ways. The side where the old man stood was clear, and he began to amble across. But halfway he spotted a motorbike, tried to hurry, then tripped—just before the motorbike collided with him.

Sam dropped his pitta pocket as the motorcyclist was thrown through the air and the old man crashed to the ground, spinning round from the impact.

His hands, frantically trying to control the steering wheel...

'Oh, my God, Sam!' Emily gripped his arm.

He was up. Dashing across the road, calling out, 'Call an ambulance! *Appelez une ambulance!*'

The rest of the traffic drew to a halt, drivers and passengers getting out to look at the crash.

The motorcyclist had been thrown clear and had rolled across the road. He was struggling to get up.

Sam ran to the old man first, who was lying motionless on the ground, with a wound on his head, bleeding profusely, his elbows and arms torn, his leg at a painful angle.

But he was breathing.

'Lie still! Don't move.' The man's eyes fluttered open as he came back to consciousness. 'Stop—*arretez*—don't move,' Sam ordered, holding the man's neck still to maintain his c-spine control. He glanced up and over at Emily. 'Check the other one!'

He watched as Emily hurried over to check the motorcyclist, who had now sat up and was trying to remove his helmet.

'No—*non*! Keep it on!' he heard her say.

The old man began to groan.

'What's your name? *Comment vous appelez-vous?*'

More groans, then, 'Alain…'

'Alain, do you speak English? *Parlez-vous Anglais?*'

Alain tried to nod, but Sam kept his head steady. 'Stay still, my friend. I'm a doctor. You must keep still—you've been hurt.'

Sam had never felt so useless in his life. He had no medical equipment with him here. He had nothing! How could he help this man and take care of him without the back-up of his team? And he wasn't an ER specialist. He dealt with labouring women. Not elderly men hurt in road traffic accidents.

Emily came running over. 'The motorcyclist is all

right. His leathers and his helmet protected him, and he wasn't going fast.'

It was a pity the same could not be said for Alain. The old man was very thin and very frail. He'd probably broken a lot of bones.

'Hold his head for me. That's it. Alain? This is my wife, Emily. Lie still for her and I'm going to check you over.'

He grabbed at his own shirt and tore off a strip, folding it and pressing it tightly against Alain's bleeding head.

Sam started checking Alain for breaks. His collarbone seemed fractured, maybe a rib or two. His right arm probably. His pelvis? To be on the safe side Sam removed his leather belt and fed it under Alain's waist, looping it over and pulling it tight to secure the pelvic basin just in case. A bleed from a break there could be disastrous. His lower leg was certainly fractured.

'Alain? Where does it hurt?'

'Partout...'

Everywhere. He wasn't surprised. He'd been hit by a motorbike. How fast had it been travelling? Forty kilometres per hour? Maybe a little less? It was hard to tell.

In the distance he could hear sirens approaching. 'Help's coming, Alain. Do you have any health conditions I should know about? Any allergies?'

'Non...'

'Okay, *c'est bon*. Anyone we can call for you? Your wife? Family?'

'Ma femme... Celine...'

'Okay, what's her number?'

Sam listened and wrote down the telephone number Alain gave. He could hand all this information over to the ambulance crew.

'You're doing well, Alain. A few broken bones and a head wound, but I think you're going to be okay. The ambulance is coming.'

'*Merci...*'

Sam looked at the motorcyclist. He did indeed appear to be okay, which was good news, but he would still need to be checked over in hospital. He stood behind them, a stream of French words falling steadily from his mouth. Sam couldn't catch it all, but he thought the man was trying to say he had not seen Alain until the last minute.

Well, that was something for the police to sort out.

He felt a moment of fear. Had this happened at *their* accident site? Had people got out of their cars and stood watching as assistance was given? Had people gazed at *his* injured head, too?

Sam needed to keep Alain stable. The main thing was that he was conscious and breathing.

An ambulance fought its way through the traffic and pulled to a halt a few yards from them. It didn't take too long for Sam to feed back to the crew what he'd seen happen and his assessment of Alain.

He stood back as they took over, fitting a proper brace to Alain's pelvis and returning Sam's belt, giving their patient oxygen, fitting a neck brace and loading him into the ambulance.

As they drove away Sam stood on the path looking after them, his arm around Emily. 'You okay, Em?'

'I'm fine. Are you? You look terrible...your poor shirt...'

'It's nothing. It's Alain I feel sorry for. Poor guy, lying on the road like that.' He turned to look at her. 'Made me think about what happened to us...'

She swallowed hard. 'We survived. So will Alain.'

'I hope so. I gave the crew my number. They promised they would ring with an update when they could.'

'You did all you could have done.'

He shook his head. 'It happened so fast…and yet I could see it about to happen, like it was in slow motion, like it triggered—' He stopped talking. Went silent.

Emily looked up at him. 'Triggered what? A memory?'

'I don't know. I need to think about it. But I think I saw…'

She looked scared. 'Saw what?'

'I think I saw *our* crash. I think I saw me spinning the wheel. I don't know…'

Emily laid a hand upon his arm. 'I think we need a strong coffee or two. Let's go find a café.'

He looked at her and nodded. That seemed sensible. He didn't want them to get onto the mopeds right after seeing that bike accident. He wouldn't feel right. And it had made him see how vulnerable Emily was, exposed like that on the bike. Anything could hit her. Could take her from him!

He couldn't have that.

'Good idea.' He resolved to get the mopeds returned as soon as possible.

CHAPTER SIX

THE COFFEE WENT some way to restoring their nerves. As did the slice of caramel *dacquoise* they shared. And once they'd returned the mopeds, and Sam had changed into a new shirt at the hotel, throwing his torn one into the wastepaper basket, they decided to head back out and reclaim the day for their own.

Em held his hand as they walked. 'So that's a couple of memories that have come back since we've been here. That's good.'

That day he'd followed her to her office at the hospital, after they'd argued about him partying, had been the day he'd accused her of being selfish, of only thinking of herself and what she wanted from their relationship.

'Selfish? You think I'm selfish because I want to start a family with you?'

'It's all you ever talk about! "I want to get pregnant..." "I want a baby..." "I want us to start trying." Do you ever ask me what I want?'

She'd shaken her head, confused.

'What do you want, Sam?'

He'd straightened, his face blanching.

'I'm not ready to be a father yet.'

'Why? Please tell me.'

'I can't...'

His voice had trailed away, and for a moment he'd looked helpless and lost. She'd feared, then, that he was unable to tell her something painful, so she'd broached the subject herself.

'Don't you love me, Sam?'

'Of course I do.'

'Then why don't you want us to have a child together? I don't understand. What's so wrong with starting a family? We help everyone else do it, day after day, why not us?'

He'd not answered her and so, frustrated, she'd stormed away from him, furious that she could never get a straight answer from him, furious with herself for allowing it to mean so much that it was tearing them apart.

She'd told him earlier today that she'd just been upset at him for staying out with those clients. Well, it had certainly been more than that. Sam hadn't come home that night but had worked straight through, and he'd only gone off shift when she'd clocked on in the morning.

It had been so humiliating! All the staff at the Monterey must have noticed. How could they not? They'd raised their voices in the hospital corridor and brought a personal matter into the workplace. Even Emily was appalled at herself for that. What must the patients have thought? A premier birthing centre set in the heart of a marital dispute!

Keen to put good memories back into Sam's head, Emily decided it was time for them to return to the Île de Reuily, otherwise known as the Temple of Love. They'd gone there on their first trip, and Emily was keen for them to go again. There was so much they needed to talk about and sort through, and now that his memories might be coming back she was keen to let him know and understand exactly where she had been coming from. Before any more came back and completely blindsided him. Damaging them for ever.

They needed to talk about the family issue. About what had been keeping them separate. It had to be confronted—probably here more than anywhere, because they were now in a place where *both of them* were trying to save their marriage.

The distance between them had been scaring her. She'd known their marriage was failing, and yet every time she'd tried to get Sam back he'd just moved farther and farther away. She'd not known who he was any more, and it had made her fear that she'd never really known him at all.

This man had made her world shine brighter once and she wanted that back again. There had to be a way for them to get there.

Sam knew a little of her background, but she'd never gone into detail. Nor had he. Their relationship had blossomed quickly and ferociously. Both of them had been swept away on an intense new love, and if they hadn't been busy planning their wedding they'd been busy planning and running their business.

They needed this trip to get to know one another properly. Away from work. On neutral ground. They needed to understand each other—who they were and what had made them that way. Maybe then, and only then, would they begin to understand where it had all gone wrong.

So when Sam had returned to their room to change his shirt Emily had picked up the full picnic basket she'd asked the hotel to provide. The temple would be the perfect spot for them to talk, to clear the air and to watch the sun set.

'Where are we going?' Sam asked.

'On a magical mystery tour. Trust me.' She smiled, making her way to the Line Eight Métro to get to their destination.

They people-watched for a while. Paris was filled with so many unique faces, both residents and visitors, but the city had a certain style, a *je ne sais quois* that oozed from every pore, every street, and the mix of cultures and voices helped provide that.

At the Michel Bizot stop they got off and began their walk up a long palm-tree-lined avenue. The weather was beautiful. Perfect for a picnic. Emily was looking forward to sitting down with him, enjoying his company with the good food that the hotel had provided.

They stopped briefly to look and take photos at the Musée National de l'Histoire de l'Immigration. It was a magnificent building that had figures and animals, trees and historic events carved into its exterior, like a stone Bayeux tapestry. Intrigued, they headed inside, and Sam asked if they could leave their picnic basket at Reception whilst they took a look around.

It was the perfect place to revive their sense of well-being after the accident they'd witnessed, and as they were looking around Sam received a call from the hospital to inform him that Alain was stable. Happy at the news, Sam draped his arm around Emily's shoulder and they walked around the numerous eclectic displays.

'I could spend all day here,' Emily said, knowing that they wouldn't. Knowing that she needed to talk to him. Confront him about the real issue. But for now she could pretend that all of that wasn't ahead of her. At least she could try to.

'Why don't we? There's a park nearby—we could eat the picnic there afterwards.'

She thought about it, but, no, she wanted them to go to the temple on the island. 'I really want to show you the lake and island I was telling you about.'

She didn't want him to know why. Yes, it was the most beautiful place she'd ever been, but it was also isolated. The perfect place for them to talk. To share. To make up some of the ground between them, to forge new bonds and strengthen themselves once again. At least that was what she hoped would happen. But it was nerve-racking. What if it all went wrong? What if he refused to talk about his past? His issues?

He nodded, seeming happy to be guided by her. Paris had been her plan, after all, and so far it was working. He'd gained a few memories that he hadn't had before.

After an hour or two spent in the museum, they headed into the park of the Bois de Vincennes.

There was an exquisite flower garden, a kaleidoscope of colour, surrounded by neat swathes of pale green lawn and dark green trees, and with the heat of the summer sun it was the ideal place for them to be after their adventure that morning.

Emily smiled as Sam looked around, bowled over by the beauty of the place. 'I told you it was worth it.'

He turned to face her. '*You're* worth it.'

She smiled back and kissed him, revelling in the taste of his lips, the sun on their faces. In the warmth of not just being with the man she loved, but the joy of knowing that she was getting back the husband she adored. That he was trying as much as she was.

But nerves were bubbling under the surface. It was nearly time. Time to say everything. Explain everything. Dig deep and find out what had truly been keeping them apart.

Where would they both be by the end of this day? A little closer? Understanding each other? Or would they be even further apart?

'Let's head for the lake. I hope you've got your arms ready to do some rowing?'

He nodded. 'I've carried this basket most of the afternoon. I'm sure my muscles are all warmed up for the oars.'

There was a long row of boats lined up by the lakeside.

'They've all got names on. I wonder if there's a rowing boat called *Emily*?'

'Or *Sam*. Not all boats are named after ladies, you know?'

The white boats were small, edged in red, with the inside of the boat painted in blue. Once they'd paid and Sam had helped Emily get in, making sure she was sitting down properly before he began, he took hold of the oars and gently pushed them out onto the lake.

It was very calm on the water. Poplars and tall grass bordered the lake, whilst weeping willows dipped their weary branches down into the water, creating little concealed areas where couples could take a boat and have a little privacy if they so wished.

But Emily knew exactly where she wanted to go.

There were hardly any other people out on the lake as she pointed across the still green water to the island in the centre. Upon the island stood a beautiful domed temple, supported by tall, slim columns of white stone. It sat on a grassy outcrop, and beneath it could be seen craggy rocks and what looked like, from a distance, numerous caves.

'Is that where we're headed?' asked Sam.

She nodded. 'It is. It's the place you first called me Mrs Saint.'

'Oh, yes? What else did I say to you there?'

She laughed. 'Lots of things! Some of them rather rude…'

'I'm intrigued!'

'Feels odd to think that we're back here and this time I'm carrying our baby.'

He glanced at her briefly, then looked behind him at the temple once more.

Sensing a shift in his mood, Emily tilted her head in question. 'Are you happy, Sam?'

He turned back to her. 'Me? Course I am. How could I not be? I'm here in Paris, with my beautiful wife, on a gorgeous day, and…' His voice trailed away.

'And…?'

'And I couldn't be any happier.'

'Really? You seem a little…sad.'

'Not sad, no. Pensive, maybe.'

'What about?'

He laughed and looked away. 'Oh, lots of little things. Nothing you need to worry about.'

But she did. This need for privacy, this *do not enter* that Sam had about him was what had caused a lot of their problems in the first place. He was *meant* to share his worries with her. *Meant* to share his concerns, his fears. She was his *wife*.

'Is it work?'

Sam shrugged. 'I am keen to get back. To me, even though logically I know the centre's open and I've worked there, I don't remember that. I want to walk the halls. I want to meet patients…'

'Of course. I have to keep reminding myself of

that fact. That you don't remember. You don't know. That what's normal to me is still the unknown to you. I mean… I've *seen* you there at the Monterey. I've watched you work.'

For a while there was silence except for the sound of the boat moving through the water, the splash and the creak of the oars in their housing either side of the boat. The water had a pleasant aroma to it—of fresh and vibrant greenery, of summer, of *life*.

Emily laid a hand upon her belly, thinking of her child's future. 'Sometimes I can't quite believe the way things have turned out myself.'

She saw him glance at her belly, and then he turned to negotiate their arrival at the island beneath the temple. He got up and jumped out, using the chain from the boat to moor them to the wooden pier. Then he reached out his hand and helped her off the boat, before going back to retrieve the picnic basket.

They headed up the steps to the temple.

The round temple was beautiful in its simplicity, with a domed roof and gorgeous views out across the lake. The setting sun reflected light off the surface, glinting as if the water was filled with jewels, and they stood appreciating it for just a moment.

Sam gazed down at his wife and noticed that her hand was still laid across her gently swelling abdomen.

He loved her so much. Was he going to ruin everything with his doubts? Would she see him for the fraud that he was? But then maybe—perhaps—he wasn't the only one with doubts? Emily had never been a mother before. Perhaps she was scared, too?

'Does the future worry you, Em?'

She gazed over the beautiful lake. 'A bit. Becoming a parent is new territory for both of us.'

He nodded. 'It is.'

'Even though I wanted this baby, I know you didn't. But it happened anyway. I always thought it would be something we would want together. That we would make it happen together.'

'We did. Despite our arguments, it seems.'

'We were drunk.'

He let out a sigh. 'Lots of babies are conceived from a drunken night.'

'I worry about whether I'll be a good mother. It's not like I was given the best example of how to do it.'

Sam frowned. He couldn't remember much about her family situation. Had she told him before? He couldn't recall.

'Tell me.'

She looked back at Sam. *Yes.* These were the things they needed to talk about. But she couldn't imagine it would be a comfortable conversation, standing here like this. This was going to be a conversation that would take time.

'Let's see if there's a blanket in that picnic basket, because this stone step is uncomfortable.'

They opened it up and, sure enough, attached to the lid of the basket was a folded, padded blanket, which they laid upon the ground. Once they were settled, and Sam had poured each of them some sparkling water, Emily continued with her story.

'You remember I don't really have any close family?'

He nodded. 'Just your aunt and uncle.'

'That's right.'

'Have you told me much about them? In the last two years, I mean?'

'I've told you the bare bones, but never the full story.'

'So tell me now.' He laid his hand on hers.

She appreciated his support and comfort. Appreciated that he was ready to listen. Open to strengthening their bonds. It was why she'd wanted to bring him to this place. What they both needed to do if they were going to move forward together. And if she shared first then maybe Sam would do so afterwards.

'My mother had always been a rebellious woman, from what Aunt Sylvia told me. If there were conventions and rules and expectations to break, then my mother did that. She got pregnant with me, without being married—which, as my aunt was fond of telling me, caused a great scandal, as if it had happened in Victorian times. The fact that my mother never knew who my father was made it worse. Apparently there were many candidates.'

Sam rubbed her hand in sympathy.

'Anyway, my mother looked after me for about six months after I was born. I don't remember her, or that time. I was too young. I do have a photograph of me on her knee. My mother was into music, big-time, and she absolutely adored this one particular band. When they came into town to play she went to see them, was invited to an after-show party and that was that. She fell madly in love and simply *had* to be with this man, *had* to travel with him when they went on tour. Only a baby didn't fit into her plans, so she turned up at my Aunt Sylvia's house one day and asked if she would look after me for the night.'

'For one night?'

Emily nodded. 'Only she lied. She never came back and I got left behind. Forgotten about.'

'I'm sure she didn't forget you.'

'I never heard from her again. I can't have been a concern to her.'

'I'm sorry.'

'Sylvia and Martin were not best pleased—no one would be, to be honest. You agree to babysit, grudgingly, for the child of a sister you never really got on with and she never comes back... They were furious. My aunt and uncle did their best, but they weren't natural parents. I was a demanding baby, just starting to learn to sit up and grab things and squeal. They had nothing for me, apart from what my mother had left, and they suddenly had to find money to buy nappies, extra food, clothing, toys... Uncle Martin didn't have the best of health either. He suffered from a really bad back. And suddenly he had to work all these extra shifts, plus overtime, to help pay for me. I hardly saw him.'

'And your aunt?'

'She'd never wanted children. Not really. She'd grown up with my mother, who had apparently stolen all the attention of their parents. My mother was "the pretty one", the "clever one". Although Sylvia never said as much, I kind of got the feeling that she felt second-best. Never appreciated as much. Never loved as much. And now here she was, having to look after her sister's child.

'They tried to make me happy, but I could feel the resentment from them both. They never said anything outright, but...it wasn't right. So as a child I dreamt of happy, loving families, all sitting around a dinner table, laughing and joking and enjoying being with each other. I pictured what it would be like if we were happy. What our family portraits might look like. But we never did anything like that. There were photos, of course. Plenty of them. Just not the kind I wanted.'

'Your aunt and uncle sound like they struggled a bit.'

'They did their best. But my aunt never really got

over her resentment of my mother, who seemed to have freedom and the world at her feet while they took care of her mistake.'

'Is that how you see yourself? As a mistake?'

'How could I not? I wanted to be loved so much. I wanted them to put their arms around me and give me a proper cuddle. I wanted someone to tell me that they loved me and that I was their whole world.'

'*I* did.'

She smiled, feeling tears at the backs of her eyes. 'Yes, you did. Meeting you was the best thing in my life—after my work. The first time we met at the hospital there was something about you that made me feel as if I couldn't even breathe.'

'How did you become a midwife? What made you go down that path? Was it something Sylvia suggested?'

'No. I saw a documentary on television. Sylvia and Martin were out at a church dinner with friends, and there was a documentary on following the journey of an embryo from single cell to living baby. It was all so fascinating to me, and when they showed the birth… The miracle of the baby being born was one thing, but all I could see was the look in the eyes of the mom and dad. Such joy…such love. Pure elation. I wanted to experience that.'

'So you started training?'

She nodded. 'I worked hard at school and got to college. So I could experience that love again and again and again. I think a small part of me wanted to believe that was how my mother had felt when she had me. It's a privilege to be in the room when a mom gives birth. I didn't realise how special it would make me feel. How honoured. I loved it. I still do. But I've always craved experiencing it myself.'

Sam let out a big sigh. 'You had it tough. With your aunt and uncle, I mean.'

'Some people have it tougher.'

Sam sipped his drink.

'What about you, Sam?'

'What do you mean?'

'Tell me more about your family. I don't really know much about them, apart from their names and what they do for a living. We hardly see them. I think the most I ever saw them was at the wedding, and then they kept themselves to themselves.'

Sam let out a big sigh. 'Where do I start?'

'At the beginning.'

He gazed at her and nodded with some reluctance. 'There really isn't much to tell.'

'I think there is. Please, Sam. I feel apart from you. I feel like I'm stuck on this tiny island and you're far out to sea with a rescue boat but you won't come in to land. We need to talk…we need to share who we are so that we can start afresh. Unburdened. Nothing hidden.' She laid a hand on his. 'I know you have a secret, Sam. I don't know what it is, but I want you to feel you can share it with me. If you don't we'll always be apart. We won't get to fix *this*.' She brushed his wedding ring.

Sam's fingers enveloped hers and his thumb stroked the back of her hand. 'I don't want to lose you, Em.'

'I don't want to lose you either. Whatever it is, you can tell me. I won't judge. I won't say anything. I'll just listen.'

He exhaled. A big, heavy sigh. 'It's hard for me.'

'I know. These things usually are. But I know from experience that they always seem massive until you unburden yourself, and then you feel a little better. A little lighter. You know what they say. A problem shared…'

'Is a problem halved?'

She smiled. 'I love you, Sam. I'm your *wife*. You need to be able to tell me.'

'I've never shared it with anyone. None of us have.'

'None of you? Your family?'

Okay, this is a start.

He nodded.

'Then maybe it's time?'

She hoped he would tell her. Whatever it was, if he and his family had kept this burden under wraps for so long then it was time it was given some air. It was like carrying a weight. No matter how small the weight, the longer you had to carry it the heavier it got—until you collapsed from under it.

'You're sure I've never told you anything?'

'I'm sure. Come on—tell me. I want to know you properly, Sam Saint, and we've only ever skimmed the surface of who you are. I've spilled my family secrets. What are yours?'

She'd told him about everything. Her runaway mother. Feeling like she was a mistake. Being left behind. Abandoned. Emily didn't want their child to feel it was a mistake, too. Conceived on a drunken night, during a truce between its parents, and then abandoned by its father. Not loved enough. Worthless.

She wouldn't accept that. She wasn't just fighting for her marriage here, but for her child. *Their* child.

She saw the agony on his face. The internal wrangling going on inside his head. The anguish. She knew his instincts were to keep it hidden still. It was what he had always done. But her words had clearly had an effect on him and she could tell that he knew what she said was true. If they didn't tell each other everything then their relationship would be doomed to fail. Already so much of who he was, was hidden by the amnesia. He didn't need to hide even more.

'You know I have five siblings and Mom and Dad...?'

She smiled and squeezed his fingers in encouragement, her heart beating faster. *He was going to share.* 'I do...'

'Well, the thing you may not know is that Dad and I don't really get on.'

'Really? You seemed okay at the wedding.'

It was true. Sam and his family had been nothing but delightful to one another. Sam had seemed incredibly warm to his mother and his younger siblings. To his dad he'd been... She saw the flash of memory. Sam standing stiff and formal, shaking his father's hand but keeping his distance. Not really talking, just a slight inclination of his head. An acknowledgement that his father had at least come to their wedding.

'Was there a free bar at the wedding? That would have kept my dad happy.'

Emily frowned. 'But he's not a drunk, is he?'

'He's a...social drinker. He has his friends that he sees every day down at the bar. I hated it that a lot of our money as a family got poured down Dad's throat when there were so many mouths to feed.'

'You're the oldest, right?'

'Yes. There's two years between me and Daniel, then a year later there was Clara then Warren, then Caleb.' He paused, looking out across the water. 'And then there was Serena.'

Emily blinked. *What?* But Sam was one of *five* siblings. Not six.

'Serena?'

Sam shook his head and got up to begin pacing, uncomfortable with this subject but knowing he had to tell her. They were married! And she was right—she had to hear this. Or they'd be torn apart because the guilt he felt over Serena's death was the one thing that was still tearing *him* apart, making him doubt his abilities to be a father.

'The only good thing my dad did was give me brothers and sisters—but all I saw growing up was my mother, heavily pregnant again, struggling to get things done. As the oldest, I had to help, and because Dad was never around, always at the bar, I sort of became a father as well as a big brother to them all.'

'That must have been hard for you.'

'Yeah, well… I don't like to focus on upsetting things.'

'I've noticed. You're a driven man. You've always wanted to be successful. Always busy.'

'It's how I was when I was a teen. There was always something to do—mow the lawn, fix a kitchen cabinet, a leaky faucet. You name it, I worked out how to do it. Because my dad couldn't.'

'Because he wasn't there?'

Sam nodded once. 'My dad was out drinking when my mom gave birth to Warren.'

'Home birth?'

'It was the same for all of us. I can remember being incredibly scared when Warren was born. Mom seemed in a lot of pain, but she was really cool about it in between contractions, you know? Like it was the most normal thing—which it was. But I was only eight. I didn't understand. The midwife asked Mom if she wanted me in the room for the birth and she said it was up to me.'

'And you said yes?'

'No. I was too scared. All the noise Mom was making was…incredible. I'd never heard anything like it.

And that was *my mom*, you know? I can remember cowering in my bedroom, listening to her in the next room, wondering why my dad wasn't there to help her. It seemed to go on for hours—it probably actually did—and then there was this second of silence before I heard a new sound. A baby. Crying. And then there was laughter and joy and I could hear my mother crying again, but this time for another reason. I went back in and there she was, propped up in bed, smiling, tears of joy running down her face… It was the most amazing thing I ever saw.'

Emily smiled.

'I remember telling my schoolfriends all about it. They all thought it was weird!' He smiled at the memory. 'And then Mom told us all she was expecting again. I couldn't wait.'

'An OB/GYN in the making?'

He laughed ruefully. 'I guess. I was eleven when Caleb was born, and yet again I got to hear this miracle from the next room. I started telling anyone who would listen that I wanted to be a doctor when I grew up, so that I could deliver babies every day and witness the joy.'

She loved the enthusiasm in his voice at the memory of his happiness. She was elated that he still had all his past memories. They were important. He might have lost all sense of who he was and *that* would have been terrible.

'And Serena?' she asked with concern.

'I was sixteen years old when Serena was born. My mom swore this was her last baby, and once again I got to hear my baby sister come into the world. She was tiny. Only six pounds. But she was beautiful. She didn't cry. She seemed quite content and calm. That was how my mom named her. Because she was so serene. That was all she kept saying. *"She's so serene."* The midwife suggested it as a name.'

'It's beautiful.'

'Things were tough. Six mouths to feed, plus their own—my parents were struggling hard. Mom would clean other people's houses for extra money, taking the little ones with her in a playpen. I already had a paper round and gave my parents most of my wages to help out. But all our money seemed to go over the bar, and I hated my dad for doing that. My mom struggled to put food on the table every day, but she did it. She made sure we were happy. And then one day I thought to myself, *Who's making Mom happy?* Dad wasn't. She wasn't. She didn't have time. So I took on extra rounds. The second I finished school I'd be out on my bike, hauling papers across yards, all around the neighbourhood. I saved the money. Kept it. When Serena was about four months old I suggested to my dad that he ought to take Mom out for a meal. Nothing expensive. Just a burger or something. I felt Mom needed it, you know?'

Emily nodded.

'I said I'd babysit.' Sam gazed out across the water and watched as a swan glided across its surface, followed by another about a metre behind. 'My mom had never left us before. She didn't want to go. I made her do it. Said she deserved a night out.'

'You wanted her to have a break?'

'Yeah. I had some tests to revise for, so I fed the kids, made sure they had their baths, and after Serena had had her bottle of milk I changed her nappy and put her in her room for the night.'

Emily could tell the bad part was coming. Sam

looked pained, with lines across his brow, and his narrowed eyes were stuck somewhere in the past. He kept rubbing at his forehead, as if the telling of the story was causing him physical pain.

'I checked on them all after an hour. They were asleep. They'd always been good sleepers. Never played up. They were all good kids.'

'What happened?'

'I thought they were okay. I made popcorn and sat down to watch a movie on the television. Mom and Dad came home and Mom, being anxious, went to check on them all.'

Emily laid a hand upon his arm to still him.

'Mom *screamed.* I can still hear it so clearly up here.' He tapped the side of his skull. 'Blood-curdling, it was. Like someone had wrenched her heart from her chest. Something *had.*'

'Serena.'

'They said it was Sudden Infant Death Syndrome. Nothing anyone could have done. Nothing anyone could have predicted. She just…died. The paramedics tried to revive her when they got to the house. I can remember sitting in the front room, hiding in the corner, hugging my legs and rocking, seeing the red-blue lights flickering through the windows and hearing footsteps above me. And all the time my mother crying. Wailing. Begging for it not to be so…'

'Sam, I'm so sorry.'

She pulled him into her arms and held him as tightly as she could. No wonder he had never told her this story. It was awful! Terrible! She couldn't imagine that happening. Not in her worst nightmares could she conceive how you would get through something like that. She knew that people *did.* They had clients at the Monterey who had lost children before, and she'd always been awed by their bravery and outlook on life.

Was this why Sam had never wanted children? Was this why they'd had so many arguments? He'd never told her before and now she could see why. And yet she'd pushed him, asking him over and over, until in the end she'd just given up and they'd stopped talking.

She felt so bad! Of course she'd wondered *why* he refused to talk to her about this, but now she knew. And she felt terrible for having pushed so hard.

'I should never have forced my parents to go out. I should have paid more attention to Serena. I should have checked on her more often. I failed her. I was meant to be looking after her and she died and—'

'Sam you were sixteen years old! You were still a child yourself. You can't shoulder that burden. They told you it was an accident. Sudden. It wasn't your fault.'

'It feels that way.'

'Is that why you never want to see your family? Why you never want them to visit?'

'I see it in their faces when they look at me. Like an unspoken accusation.'

She shook her head and grabbed his arms, making him look at her. 'They probably just miss you! Their big brother who always looked out for them suddenly doesn't want them around. They're probably hurt. They look up to you, Sam. Even I could see that. It's possible they're just wondering what they did wrong.'

He looked down at his wife's face. 'They did nothing wrong. It was me.'

'It was *not you*. You were babysitting. You did everything right. You bathed her, fed her, changed her nappy, put her to bed. That's what millions of parents do every night. They don't stand over their children's cots and count every breath. It's impossible.'

He still looked shame-faced. Still looked guilty. But he'd made a start in sharing his burden. She was glad that he had told her. And suddenly she realised. Suddenly she remembered.

'The candle was for Serena.'

He met her gaze. 'Yes.'

She let out a long, slow, steadying breath. 'Thank you for telling me, Sam. Now I understand why you—' She stopped before she could blurt out any more. He didn't need to hear that. They were here to *heal*. Paris was healing their hearts as well as their minds.

'I'm afraid, Em. Afraid that I won't be able to protect *our* baby.' He laid a hand on her belly, gently stroking it, then knelt down in front of her, laying his head against her belly as if trying to hear a heartbeat. 'What if I fail our child?'

Her heart was almost torn in two as she heard the heartbreak in his voice. He'd agonised over this. 'You won't. It's okay to be afraid, Sam. It's okay to have fears. All parents do.'

He lifted his head to look at her. 'Do *you*?' He seemed to doubt her words.

Emily rushed to reassure him. 'Of course I do! What do I know about being a great mother? Did I have a fabulous role model? Did my aunt provide me with a loving example? No. Neither of them did. I worry that I'll get this wrong all the time. What if I'm awful at being a mom? At something that I've wanted for *so long*?'

'You'll be perfect.'

'And so will you. Believe me, Sam, I know you will. You care so much. But you know what? We can be afraid together and struggle together. We're strong that way. We're determined. Driven. Remember?'

Sam stood and looked down into her face. 'What would I do without you, Mrs Saint?'

'Let's hope you never have to find out.' She smiled. 'Look, we're here—in the Temple of Love. Let's make a promise to each other to always be open and share our fears. If there's a problem, we tell each other about it. Deal?'

'Deal.'

Sam pulled her towards him for a kiss. It felt like the start of something new. An opening. An honesty between them that had never been there before. Her lips on his sealed the promise that their hearts were making.

'Thank you for telling me, Sam. It means so much to me.'

'You're right. I do feel different for having said it out loud.'

'The pain won't go. Not totally. But it can be different now—just you see.'

'Thanks, Em.'

He pulled her close once more and they stood there, in the Temple of Love, enveloped in each other's arms, and just held each other.

Em knew they'd taken a huge step forward today. She'd been right to bring him here. To ask him to share this. It shed new light on all Sam's past behaviour. Perhaps she had enlightened him, too, on why having a baby had meant so much to her?

There was still so much for them to do, but right now things were moving in a positive direction.

She could only foresee it getting better.

CHAPTER SEVEN

THEY HAD A beautiful evening picnic. The hotel had packed some delightful food in the basket—a *salade niçoise* with mixed herbs, olives, anchovies and potatoes, a sausage and potato *galette,* a *haricots verts* salad with quail eggs and tiny shrimp, goat's cheese and tomatoes. There was also raspberry *clafoutis,* pound cake and *sables* biscuits, all served with a small bottle of white wine, sparkling and still water, and a tiny bottle of alcohol-free rhubarb wine.

They sat in the temple, overlooking the water, quietly eating their evening meal and enjoying the sounds of nature in the air: the occasional duck quacking, the lapping of the water below, the wind rustling the trees.

Eventually Sam packed everything back into the basket, and on their way down the rocky stairway to the boat they paused a moment to look inside the grotto. The stony caves were a mix of dark and light, jagged rocks and stalactites.

'This place is like us, really,' Sam observed.

Emily turned to him. 'How do you mean?'

'Well, there's the beautiful Temple of Love on show for everyone to see, and it all looks wonderful. But then you dig deeper, you come down here, and there's a dark place—forbidding and scary.'

Emily stepped out of the caves' darkness, through one of the openings, to move out towards the lessening light of the day.

'But, using your analogy, we've come through it together this time and we both know it's there.'

He nodded. 'True.'

Sam still wasn't sure that he should have told Emily everything. The uselessness of his own father... Serena's brief yet painful story. He wasn't used to sharing things like that. He'd never done it and it felt strange. It made him feel naked. Exposed when he'd always had a protective wall around him.

He knew the story was safe with Emily, but did she really grasp how much his past affected him?

He'd not had a great father figure. In his eyes his father had been good for two things—making babies and drinking beer. Sam had been a better father to those kids than his own dad had—but on the other hand he had also let them down. He'd devastated them. It had been *his* plan to send his parents out for the night. *His* plan to make his mother go out. When he'd checked on Serena that time and assumed she was sleeping because she was so still, so quiet, had she really been sleeping? Or had she already passed away?

It haunted him—the idea that he might have looked down upon his baby sister with love, not realising that she lay there dead.

I should have known.

The guilt still tore him apart, and the pain was still incredibly strong. And he still felt to blame. But Emily had welcomed the load. Had asked to take it on, no matter what it was. Had said that, as his wife, she was there to help him carry it. Make it easier.

But he doubted it would ever be that. Easier.

The plain fact of the matter now was, though, that Emily knew. Perhaps from here they could have a conversation about his fears about becoming a parent. About caring for this baby to come. His son or daughter.

They would need a strong marriage. Raising a child was not easy. He knew how difficult it could be. Okay, so he and Emily did not have the financial worries his own parents had had, but it was still hard. And they would need to be united. He knew from the flashes of memory he'd had, and the admissions Em had made, that their marriage had deteriorated—and quickly.

That concerned him greatly.

He loved this woman so much, and yet they had both allowed it to crumble so quickly because neither of them had been able to talk the way they had today.

Perhaps it took nearly losing your life, being in a terrible accident, having amnesia, to turn it around? To admit the problems and vow to work through them?

He reached out to place his hand in the small of her back and guided her safely down the steps towards the boat. She turned to look at him, flashed him a smile, and—

They were walking down the aisle. Newly married. Sun gleamed through the church windows and everyone was smiling. He looked up and saw his mother's face. She was crying with happiness, her hands clutched together before her chest as if in prayer, and she was mouthing something to him. He couldn't catch her words, and then as he passed her she reached out and took his hand.

'Live, Sam. Be happy now.'

He'd smiled back. Nodded. Promised that he would. And then he'd turned back to his wife and she'd looked at him and smiled and...

He helped Emily into the boat. Made sure she was seated safely before he put the picnic basket inside and unchained the boat from the pier. With one of the wooden oars he pushed them away from the small island, and they drifted out across the water and he began to row.

His mother had wanted him to be happy. *Be happy now.* Had his own mother seen how unhappy he'd been at home after Serena died? He'd tried to make up for it. He'd tried his best to prove that he was still a good son afterwards. But nothing had made his mother smile after that.

But she smiled at the wedding. She was happy for me. She didn't resent my happiness.

Perhaps he ought to take the time actually to try and enjoy life. Was this why he was so driven? Filling his days with work and other distractions just so that he wasn't thinking about Serena? Was that why his marriage had begun to fail? Instead of looking at the faults they had created, the problems they shared, he'd done what he'd always done—pushed it to one side and filled up his time with work.

He'd thought that by ignoring the issues they would go away.

The revelation was startling.

He stopped rowing and the boat drifted quietly across the water.

Night had settled across Paris when they returned to their hotel. Emily donned the beautiful new powder-blue dress that Sam had secretly bought for her and stood in front of the mirror admiring it.

Sam came up behind her and slid his hands over her burgeoning abdomen. It was still only a slight swelling, but she smiled, looking at the reflection of his face in the mirror.

He looked content. And that was something she hadn't seen for such a long time.

'The dress is beautiful, Sam. Thank you.'

'You're more beautiful.'

Her cheeks bloomed in the mirror and she laid her hands upon his, their fingers entwining. She looked up at him, hesitant.

Was it too soon? Was it just right? If she pushed for them to make love now would it be wrong? Or just perfect?

She felt so much closer to Sam now. Before she'd described him as being on a rescue boat far out to sea, miles away from her, but since his confession—since he'd told her about his family and about Serena especially—she'd felt as if he was within arms' reach.

Should she test it and see?

She missed him. She missed the intimacy that they'd once shared. Surely now there was nothing that could keep them apart? Being together physically, emotionally, mentally, surely would just strengthen the bond that they were both trying to enforce?

She met his gaze in the reflection. 'Undo the zip.'

He looked into her eyes. 'You've just put it on.'

'Yes. And now I want you to take it off me.'

He looked hesitant. And for a brief moment she thought she'd pushed him too soon. Had asked, once again, for too much. But then—wonderfully—she watched in the mirror as his hands slid from hers, went to the zip at the nape of her neck and slowly, delicately, drew it down.

She could feel his heated breath on the back of her neck, and she closed her eyes as she felt him slip the dress from her shoulders, his hands following close after, trailing over her shoulders, arms, her hips.

The beautiful dress dropped to the floor and Emily turned to face him.

'I love you, Sam, and I want you to love me.'

'I do.' His voice was deep, emotional.

'Show me.'

Sam stared deeply into her eyes for a brief, yet agonising moment, before he finally took her in his arms and kissed her.

Emily sank into his embrace.

This was what she had craved! It had never been about the great sex, the making love. It had been about the deep intimacy they had shared when they had been together physically. The closeness, the connection. The unity.

Before, when they had been together, it had been great. Sam was a brilliant lover. But because she had never truly known her husband, never known all his secrets, there had never been that level of *trust* and *vulnerability* between them. Emily had always felt somehow, that she was being kept in the dark, and it had made her wonder if he had truly loved her.

But now she felt she *knew* him. Knew his fears. His pain. His hurt. She knew his vulnerabilities, as he did hers, and now they were equal.

She closed her eyes and gave herself up to Sam. *This* was what they needed to do. Be close like this. Intimate. They were working towards a greater good within their marriage and this was what both of them needed right now. To solidify that bond…to unite them in their vows.

As his hands and lips moved deftly over her body Emily found herself losing her train of thought. His lips upon her collarbone, her neck, were delightful. His hands had easily unclipped her bra and were now beautifully paying attention to her sensitive breasts, making her gasp and close her eyes...

Her hands were on his body...*too many clothes*...

He helped her remove them and once again she marvelled at his powerful, muscular body. The broad expanse of him, the wide shoulders, the narrow waist, the long, lean legs, his erection pressing against her stomach...

Sam scooped her up and placed her on the bed with a gentleness that belied his size. His thumbs hooked into her underwear and she lifted her bottom so that he could remove it, and then he covered her with his body as his lips began to explore even more.

Right now she just wanted to enjoy. Sam's lips. Sam's tongue. Sam's body. Moving over...*into* her.

Emily gasped, arching her body up against him as he drove in deep.

Afterwards, sated, they lay together in bed, Sam behind his wife.

It had felt good to be with her. It had felt *right*. This was where he was supposed to be. This was who he was supposed to be with. He knew it in his bones and he was feeling much better now about having shared.

It had brought them closer. Which was odd. That something so painful, so hurtful, had been the gateway for the two of them to connect.

Life was strange that way.

All this time he had kept it from her and in turn it had kept them apart. Obviously the old Sam hadn't been able to see that. Or maybe he had, but hadn't known what to do about it. How must it have felt to have seen his marriage crumbling?

He shuddered inside, glad his memories about that had not come back fully. He wasn't sure he wanted them—not now. Not now that things had changed. Now they were ready to face their future together. As one.

There was still fear about his ability as a father, but it seemed…less. How was that? All he'd done was voice it. Something he'd always believed would be the worst thing ever. He had feared that Emily would be appalled. How had he allowed himself to believe that?

But he guessed he had learned it from his parents. No one at home spoke about Serena ever. Mom was permanently depressed. Dad stayed away.

I stayed away! Was I being like my own father? A man I'd always hated for staying away and not being there?

Sam closed his eyes at the thought and pressed his lips to Emily's shoulder.

'You know, Sam, I've been thinking, and there are things that we can do.'

He frowned. 'What about?'

'When the baby arrives. Keeping it safe.'

She was so sweet. Thinking of his concerns. Knowing what he must be feeling.

'Oh?'

'We could get a monitor. Not just one of those walkie-talkie-type things, but one of those oxygen monitors—like a SATs device. We'd be able to keep an eye on it as the baby sleeps. We'd make sure it's in the *feet to foot* position in the cot, make sure no blankets cover it's head by getting a sleepsuit instead—things like that.'

He pressed the length of his body against hers. 'Thank you.'

'What for?'

'For trying to ease my worries.'

She half turned and reached for him. 'How could I not? You've already been through too much loss.'

'My whole family has.'

'I think you and your family ought to talk to someone. A counsellor, perhaps. Do you think they'd be open to that?'

'I don't know. All they've ever done is block it out.'

'And look what that did. I nearly lost you, Sam—we let it come between us. It was my fault, too. I kept pushing when I should have stopped to ask myself why.'

'You couldn't have known.'

'I could have if we'd been closer. If instead of just accepting what life had dealt us we'd fought against it. We both brought bad habits into our marriage and let them rule us, never pausing for a moment to think if it was right.'

'We worked it out in the end.'

'Yes, we did.' She smiled.

'Paris did the trick.'

'It always does.'

And as he moved to kiss her, and to make love to her once again, Emily pushed the thought of telling Sam the whole truth away.

Paris *had* helped—but not in the way they'd ever thought or hoped. They had found each other in another way, and it was better than anything she'd ever hoped for.

There was still time for Sam's memories to come back, too, and if they did she felt sure they'd be okay.

They were strong again.

They were close.

They were united.

CHAPTER EIGHT

THEY COULD NOT come to Paris without exploring the Eiffel Tower. They had deliberately left it till last, despite the way it overlooked them, like a guardian, whilst they slept in their hotel room.

'So, we have a choice. Do we want to climb the steps or use the lifts to reach each level?'

Em laughed. 'Considering my condition, I'm not sure I want to climb three hundred steps.'

'The lift it is.'

They stood at the base, craning their necks backwards to look up to the top.

It was an incredibly powerful sight. Only when you were close could you really understand its size and the work that had gone into its construction.

Emily took some photographs of them both, determined to get some pictures of them together into her phone. And then they were in the lift, travelling up with about eight others.

Opposite them was a woman, heavily pregnant, with her sprawling abdomen spilling over the top of her trousers. Emily smiled at her, imagining herself at that size in a few months. It wouldn't take long. And she couldn't wait to feel the baby kick and move around.

The woman was rubbing her hand over her abdomen.

'How many weeks are you?' asked Emily, hoping the woman spoke English.

She did. 'Thirty-five. This is our last trip before our world descends into chaos!' The woman laughed good-naturedly.

'You're British?'

'Yes. We came through the Channel Tunnel. I'm not allowed to fly now. You're American?'

Emily nodded. 'Second honeymoon.'

'Oh. Congratulations.'

'To you, too.'

The lift slowed to a stop and the doors opened. They got out on the first level of the tower.

Paris lay spread out beneath them and it looked so different. The rooftops, the buildings old and new, all basking in the afternoon sunshine.

'Look at that, Sam!'

'I see it.'

They both breathed in the view. There was something very calm and relaxing about looking at the city from here. Traffic bustled below, but up here there was a sense of peace. Of reflection.

Emily glanced around her and saw the woman from the lift. She was rubbing at the small of her back and looked uncomfortable. She nodded to Sam. 'Think she's okay?'

'I'm sure it's just backache. You'll get that big one day, and know exactly how she feels.'

Emily smiled. 'Remind me to enjoy it. I imagine I'll be quite nervous by the time I'm at thirty-five weeks.'

He draped his arm around her shoulders. 'I promise you I'll rub your feet.'

'Will you shave my legs for me?'

Sam smiled. 'I'll even paint your toenails.'

'Ooh. Can't wait, then!'

They took in the story window, showing the construction of the Eiffel Tower, and read about how the old hydraulic lifts had worked.

'Architects are amazing, when you think about it.'

'*You're* an architect, don't forget. You're building our baby. Think of all the work that goes into *that*!'

'Hmm, no wonder I get tired.' She ran her hand over her stomach. 'Should we go up to the second floor?'

Sam nodded, and back into the lift they got.

On the second floor they viewed the panoramic maps and a small red scale model of the original top of the Eiffel Tower from 1889. There was even a champagne bar.

'Hmm, not for me, though...' Emily mused.

'No. Got to look after the little one.'

She smiled at him and reached out to hold his hand. This was nice. Being able to talk about the baby easily to each other. Before it had always seemed a taboo subject. One that she shouldn't raise, knowing Sam's objections. But it was different now. And she could see them getting close to that ideal family picture she had of an excited couple preparing to welcome their new baby into the world. It was thrilling.

They got into the glass lift and ascended to the top. It was spectacular up there, but the wind riffled through her hair so much Emily had to keep tucking it behind her ears.

They were able to view Gustav Eiffel's office, which had been restored to its original layout, with wax models of the man himself and Thomas Edison, but they quickly headed back out to admire Paris.

It needed admiring. It was a truly magical place, and it had worked its magic on their relationship.

Emily felt grateful to it—so much so that her eyes

began to water and she thought she might cry. Surreptitiously she wiped her eyes and hoped Sam hadn't noticed.

Once they'd had a good look, and taken some more photographs, they decided to head back down to ground level. It felt a little sad to come back down to earth.

Emily had learnt so much this trip. Not just about Sam, but also about herself, and she'd set herself some new vows—never to let anyone push her away. And if they did to find out why. To see if there was something she could do to put things right.

People, relationships—they were important. Vital. What were any of them without those they loved? Alone. Lonely. Sad. That wasn't a life for anyone, and life was much too short to lose most of it in secrets or regret.

Sam had booked them into a restaurant for their evening meal.

It was a beautiful place. A large *conservatoire*, painted white and lit with lanterns. The wrought-iron furniture was softened by beautifully furnished cushions in bright colours, all complementing each other. Each table was adorned with a glass fishbowl, half filled with water, and in the water floated gerberas and daisies.

Emily took a seat and smiled at Sam. This was their last night in Paris. Soon they would be returning home. Back to reality. To work. The Monterey. Part of her didn't want to go back. She liked it here. She and Sam were in this nice little bubble and everything was right in their world. What if going back home changed everything?

As she pondered this she noticed the heavily pregnant woman from the Eiffel Tower entering the restaurant with her husband. They sat down at a table on the far left. Emily nodded and smiled when the woman looked up.

'I guess we've both got to return to reality when we go back,' she said.

Sam turned to see who she was looking at and nodded hello to the couple, too. 'We'll be okay.'

'I want us to be more than okay, Sam.'

'We will be.' He reached for her hand and squeezed it.

The waiter arrived and presented them with menus, and filled their glasses with water before disappearing.

Emily hid behind her menu for a moment, and then she looked over the top. 'What if we're not?' Her voice trembled on the last word and suddenly she was fighting back tears.

Claiming Sam had meant so much to her! It was her entire life. She loved him, worked with him, was married to him, was carrying his child. What if it all went wrong? She needed him to reassure her.

'Emily...' He put down his menu and leaned forward. 'I know it's scary, but we'll be all right. It's different this time. We won't return home the same people. We can't. We know the dangers now, and what to look out for. We're both fighting for this and I'm not going to let us lose what we have.'

'The Monterey takes up so much of your time, though, Sam. I'm worried it will suck you back in. You haven't seen it in operation yet—what if you're so eager to reacquaint yourself with everything that's going on that I lose you to it? It was our dream to start it, but now—'

'But now it's already up and running. It's success-ful. And as the boss and CEO I can delegate, right?'

She nodded.

'Time for us, as a couple, will take priority.'

'Okay.' Slightly reassured, she looked back down at the menu.

Everything sounded delicious, and she felt hungry enough to want to try it all. In the end she chose a French onion soup to start, a fennel and lavender lamb *noisette* for main and a *croquembouche* for dessert.

Sam ordered the same, not wanting to try the seafood, thinking it might make her feel ill.

Above them twinkling stars could be seen through the glass, and the French doors of the *conservatoire* opened up to a beautiful rose garden with a small fountain at its centre.

'It's beautiful here. I really don't think I'm ever going to forget Paris.'

'Nor me.' Sam smiled. 'Not this time.'

'Have you had any more flashbacks? Anything?'

'Not for a while.'

'It doesn't mean they've stopped.'

'I know. I'm not worried. They'll come back.' He took a sip of his water. 'You know what was great, though?'

'What?'

'For the first time today I actually pictured myself becoming a father. Wanting to be one. Holding our child in my arms. Looking down into its face.' He seemed wistful. 'I remember holding each of my siblings just after they were born, and how that felt, but to hold your *own child* must feel...incredible!'

'Oh, Sam, I'm so pleased.' She smiled back, knowing how much he'd feared becoming a father. To be thinking about it, imagining it in positive terms, was a huge leap forward for him. 'Is it scary still?'

'A bit. I was always so busy pushing the idea away, telling myself I could never be a father, that it never occurred to me to think about how much I might actually want to be one.'

'You do?'

'I do!' He laughed, incredulous. 'I'm sure you can imagine how surprised I am.'

Emily laughed with him, then sat back as their onion soup arrived, topped with herby croutons and a swirl of cream. The aroma of the onion and the richness of the soup tantalised her senses and she salivated in anticipation. 'Oh, that smells delicious!'

It was. The soup was perfect—not too thin, not too thick, rich with onion and vegetable stock. And the croutons were bite-sized crispy delights.

'It's strange. We came here to Paris to try and get my memories back, but instead I got a completely different gift.'

She smiled, pleased for him—for *them*. The last year of their marriage had been difficult, and she'd lost count of the amount of times she'd wanted Sam to want a child as much as she had. But now, since their talk on the island, they'd become closer, united, and Sam finally felt able to acknowledge that, despite his fears, he did actually want to become a father. It was more than music to her ears—it was a whole orchestra!

Everything was working out for them. And he was right. Paris had surprised them in such different ways from the ones they had expected.

Their lamb dish arrived, steaming and succulent, and the meat just melted in their mouths.

'You're going to make a great father, Sam.'

He smiled back at her with thanks. 'I hope so.'

'I know so. You care so much about getting it right.

About being there for your child. How could you be anything else?'

'Well, I appreciate your vote of confidence. You're going to make the most amazing mom, too.'

She hoped so. Becoming pregnant had made her think of so many things. Her own childhood, her marriage, what she wanted for her child... Above all she wanted her child to know without a shadow of a doubt that it was loved by both parents and that it would grow up in a stable family. Her feelings for her baby were already incredibly strong, and she couldn't imagine giving birth to a child and abandoning it six months later. Had her mother ever truly wanted her? Had there ever been that mother-baby bond?

It would be *so* different for their child. She would never make her mother's mistakes.

They were just about to start their *croquembouche*— Emily ready to tuck in with gusto, imagining those cream-filled choux pastry puffs—when there was a loud gasp from the other side of the *conservatoire* and a clanging sound as cutlery hit the floor.

The heavily pregnant woman from the Eiffel Tower had stood up, and was looking down at herself and breathing heavily. 'I think my waters just broke!'

At first Emily felt a surge of excitement for the woman. It might be a bit early, but she was about to meet her child and experience that rush of joy. But then concern filled her as the woman looked at her partner across the table and yelled, *'Something's wrong! I can feel it!'*

Waiters hurried to assist as the other diners all turned to see what was going on. The woman was gasping heavily and trying to feel through her dress.

'Oh, my God, there's something there!'

They could hear the panic in her voice—and rightly so.

Sam and Emily got up from their table and rushed over.

Sam stooped low to make eye contact. 'Remember us? From the tower? My name's Sam and I'm an OB/GYN. Do you want me to take a look?'

The woman looked terrified, and glanced to Emily for reassurance. 'And I'm a midwife. Let us help you.'

But they were in a busy restaurant, and it was almost full. There was no place for a private examination.

Emily looked at a waiter. 'Can you get some tablecloths so we can make a privacy screen?'

The waiter nodded and came back with an armful of cloths and some other members of staff. They all surrounded the frantic woman and raised the tablecloths so that she could be examined without the whole world seeing her so vulnerable.

Sam helped her lower herself to the floor and bundled up a jacket from the back of a chair to go under her head. 'I need to examine you. I won't touch, but I do need to look. Or would you prefer my wife to do it?'

The woman indicated she would prefer Emily, so they swapped places and Emily lifted the woman's skirt and adjusted her underwear. There was clearly something there that shouldn't be.

Emily turned to Sam. 'She has a prolapsed cord.'

A prolapsed cord was an emergency. The cord was what kept the baby alive, providing it with blood, nutrients and survival. If the baby's head or body compressed the prolapsed cord it might cut off all of that and the result would be foetal hypoxia, brain damage or even death.

If they'd been in a hospital they would have been able to deal with this immediately. They'd have had the equipment. They'd at least have had *gloves*. But here in the *conservatoire* they had nothing.

Sam immediately told the staff to call for an ambulance, and to bring them some hot water to clean their hands.

'What's your name?' he asked the panicking mother.

'C-C-Clare.'

'Okay, Clare, your baby's umbilical cord has prolapsed and we need to prevent compression. I want you to get onto your hands and knees and keep your butt in the air. You need to rest your chest and head against the floor. That's it. Now, my wife will have to press down against the baby, where we can see it. It's very important that she does this in order to ensure the baby is getting what it needs from the umbilical cord. Do you understand?'

Clare was crying. From fear, from embarrassment— he could only guess. But she had to do it if she wanted her baby to survive.

Sam looked at Em. 'Is the cord still pulsing?'

She nodded. It was, which was a good sign. It meant blood and nutrients were still getting to the baby. Now they just needed to keep it that way.

Normally this would never be done without gloves. With the amniotic fluid dispersed, the baby would be open to infection. But they didn't have gloves, so the hot water they'd been brought would have to do.

She found the presenting part of the baby's head pressing low. She provided pressure and felt the pulse in the cord strengthen. *Good.*

'Okay, it's working.'

Sam nodded. 'You're doing brilliantly, Clare. I know this isn't how you imagined it, but an ambulance is on its way, and before you know it you'll have this baby in your arms. Just keep thinking about that, okay? That's the important part.'

Clare nodded furiously.

They kept talking to her, trying to keep Clare's mind off what was happening to her. They even managed to make her laugh at one point. Just a small laugh. Nervous and timid. But she was looking braver.

Emily kept her eyes on Sam. He was being brilliant, lying down low on the ground, face to face with Clare, keeping her calm, keeping her positive, telling her about all the babies he'd delivered and how he'd met his wife through one such delivery. How pregnancy and birth brought different surprises, and how at the end all that mattered was a safe and healthy baby.

By the time the paramedics arrived Clare was clutching Sam's hand and staring deeply into his eyes as if he was her own personal birthing coach. Clare's husband held his wife's other hand and she was very carefully manoeuvred into the ambulance.

'There is no room for all,' the paramedic said.

'They're all coming!' insisted Clare.

But with Emily still applying pressure, and Clare still clutching Sam's hand, her husband shouted that he'd take his car. His wife's safety was clearly a priority right now.

The journey to the hospital took minutes, and Clare was rushed into the *maternité* suite, given high-flow oxygen, as she had been in the ambulance, and rushed into Theatre for an emergency Caesarean section. Her husband had not yet arrived—obviously unable to keep up with the speeding ambulance in a city he did not know.

'I want George here!' Clare insisted.

Sam shook his head. 'There's no time, Clare. I'm sorry. They've got to operate.'

Emily tried to reassure her patient as they were whisked into Theatre, with Sam left behind to wait for Clare's husband.

Once they were in the operating theatre events moved at a frightening speed for the woman on the table.

Emily did her best, trying to reassure Clare, and within seconds her baby was being lifted out of Clare's womb. Instantly it began to cry.

Emily, who had been gowned by a theatre assistant, had stepped back once the baby had been safely delivered, and she stood by the far wall as the baby was presented to the new mother. A little girl. As Clare took her new daughter in her arms the doors burst open and a frantic pair of eyes looked out over a mask, widening when they saw his wife and new baby.

Emily quietly slipped away from Theatre and found her husband. She reached for Sam's hand and they stood quietly, pondering the events of the last hour or so.

It didn't take long for their patient to come out of Theatre, and soon enough Clare and her husband George were in a postnatal room, enjoying their new daughter.

Emily and Sam wrote notes on what had happened in the restaurant to present to the hospital staff, and were about to leave when a nurse came to find them.

'Clare would like to see you.'

'Really?' Emily was delighted. She hadn't known whether they ought to say goodbye—whether they ought to intrude on Clare and George's first private moments with their baby. At the Monterey they liked to leave a family to get to know one another as quickly as possible when it was safe to do so. Those first moments together, alone as mum and dad and baby, were precious.

They knocked and went in.

Clare was sat up in bed, looking proud and happy with her baby in her arms, and beside her, his arm around his wife's shoulders, was George.

When Sam and Emily entered the room George stood up and came over to shake Sam's hand and give Emily a hug.

'Thank you so much! For all that you did.'

'It was our pleasure.'

'We were *so* lucky that you were there! If you hadn't been…' George shook his head as he tried to imagine such a terrible thing. 'We don't know what would have happened.'

'But we were and it all worked out—that's what's important. How are you feeling, Clare?'

Clare looked happy and content. Her face was a little pale, but there were two rosy spots on her cheeks from beaming at her new baby daughter. 'Fine. I'm absolutely fine!'

Emily and Sam looked down at the baby. Like all newborns she was squinting against the light in the room, snuffling, and trying to gnaw on one of her curled up hands.

'She looks hungry,' said Emily. 'And a good size for thirty-five weeks.'

'Six pounds one, they said.'

'Wow. She'd have been huge if she'd gone to term.'

They laughed.

'What are you going to call her?'

Clare looked at George and he nodded. 'We did think about calling her Emma, but we'd really like to call her Emily—if you wouldn't mind?'

Em gasped, clutching her hands together. 'Really?'

Clare nodded. 'Do you want to hold her?'

Emily took the baby carefully from her mother's arms and quickly glanced at Sam, who was smiling at her.

She'd delivered and held many babies, but this one seemed special. Perhaps because it had been such an emergency, happening away from a hospital, and they'd had to improvise with the hot water and the tablecloths and the *terror* that it could go so wrong, so quickly. She and Sam had met over a delivery and now, renewed, they had delivered another.

If that cord had become occluded, what would they have done? Performed a C-section in a restaurant without proper equipment? It would have been almost impossible, and Clare would have lost her baby.

They'd been lucky. All of them.

'She's beautiful, Clare.'

Emily passed the baby into Sam's arms. She felt her heart well up to see him standing there, holding the little girl. One day it would be their child. One day he'd be looking down at his own baby. Tears pricked her eyes and she sniffed and wiped them away as he handed the baby back to her mother.

'We'll leave you now. You need time alone.'

'Will you keep in touch? We'd love to send you a photo of baby Emily when she's older.'

They nodded, and wrote down their contact details.

It was hard to step away. But it was the right thing to do. They had merely assisted this baby to come into the world safely. It was like being back at work in a way. They'd done their part and now it was time to let the parents do theirs.

Sam sighed. 'I miss that rush.'

Emily looked at him and gave him a playful nudge. 'Well, technically you're still signed off from work for a while. You can't go back yet.'

'I know, and I'll stick to it. But it has made me wonder what I'll do when we get back. Presumably you'll be back at work?'

She sighed. 'Yes, I will. Don't forget you still don't have all your memories. You need to heal. Just because you don't have massive scars, or a plaster cast, or staples or stitches, it doesn't mean you're better. Your brain took a battering.'

'I know. But I *feel* good. Perhaps I could look to see which spare room we can make into a nursery? Start making plans?'

She turned to him, a smile on her face. 'Really?'

He nodded. 'Really. It'll be fun, I think.'

Emily laughed and reached for his hand once again. 'You make me so happy, Sam.'

'Good. Can I make you happy one more time in our hotel room? Before we have to start packing for our trip home?'

She looked at him, smiled wickedly and nodded.

They spent a rather pleasant few hours in each other's arms, leaving it until the last possible moment before they had to pack and get to the airport for their flight home.

It felt odd to Emily to be walking back through Charles de Gaulle airport. The last time she'd strode through here, through its concourses, she'd been nervous and excited. Wondering whether Paris would recover Sam's memories or not…whether it would make them or break them…whether they would rekindle their relationship and make it strong again.

Paris had exceeded her expectations. No. That wasn't right. *Sam* had exceeded her expectations. Paris had simply been a place. A setting. It was she and Sam who had done all the work. Both of them initially hiding from their feelings, being the people they had always been, but then slowly, after all their time spent together, they'd revealed their true selves.

They had eaten and danced and rowed a boat. They had biked through the artists' quarter and looked out from the Eiffel Tower. They had re-explored the city as much as they had re-explored themselves, finding places to go they had never been before and finding delight and joy and even peace in quiet, dark places.

They were returning to Beverly Hills with a united front. With their marriage a hundred times stronger than it had ever been.

Her dream had come true.

And it didn't matter now if Sam's memories came back. He'd known they'd been arguing, he'd known it had been bad, and they'd both worked out *why*. Now they had a solution and they were strong again. Sam might feel a little sad if the memories came back. Being confronted with some of the things he'd said. Some of the things *she* had said, all in the heat of the moment. But they would get over them. They would be able to reassure each other that it was all in the past.

She knew him now. All of him. Secrets and all. And she loved him more than she ever had. She was so glad, deep in her heart, that she had stayed to fight for him. Stayed to give them both the chance they deserved.

Had she ever thought she'd be discussing how to decorate a nursery with him? Whether they should have an animal or a space theme? Whether to go for soft neutrals or rich primary colours? Had she ever thought that they would discuss names? Or what type of birth she wanted?

She was so looking forward to seeing Sam become a father. Watching him learn and grow, falling in love with their child and having that happy family that she had always dreamed of.

He'd admitted that he was still scared, but who wouldn't be? She'd be worried if he wasn't. *Everyone* was worried when they had a child. Worried that they'd not be able to look after it properly. Worried that they'd mess up. Worried that it might hurt itself one day.

But that was life. No one could be wrapped in a bubble, no matter how much you might want to protect someone.

They would do their best as parents. That was all they *could* do.

As they sat on the plane, and she read the book she'd brought along in her hand luggage, she laid her hand on her abdomen. Soon she would feel her baby move. Soon she would feel kicks and flips and all those little movements mothers-to-be talked about. She would walk the halls of the Monterey pregnant. She would deliver mothers whilst heavily pregnant herself, and they would ask her if she was frightened or scared?

And she knew that she would smile and rub her belly and feel that everything was right in her world.

Sam glanced at his wife, reading her book on the plane and absently rubbing her belly, and wondered if she was as scared of returning home as he was?

They'd got everything so *right* in Paris, and though

he was keen to get back to work and restart their life together on a much better footing he still felt nervous.

He'd told Emily the truth when he'd admitted that he actually quite wanted to be a father. He'd come from a big family. He couldn't imagine it ever being just him and Em, even if he had rebelled at the idea of her getting pregnant. He'd loved having lots of siblings. Someone to play with outside, riding bikes and flying kites and making dens. And then, when it rained, playing indoors—hide and seek, cards, board games. Before Serena he remembered laughter. The way his younger siblings would look up to him for guidance.

He'd *loved* that.

To have his *own child* or even *children* do that would be the most marvellous thing he could think of.

But what if he became like his father again? It had been a revelation to him that he'd been doing the same thing. Staying away from home. Ignoring his wife. Okay, he'd not been out drinking their money away, but he'd been pretty much useless to her from all accounts.

Em must have felt so incredibly alone!

He was incredibly grateful to her, though. Because she had fought for him. Fought for their marriage. Fought for his memories. And she'd not mollycoddled him and lied about how they'd been. She'd told him the truth. Admitted they'd had problems. She'd even been scared to tell him she was pregnant!

That seemed such a long time ago. Stuck in hospital like that. Finding that out. He'd been so frightened.

He still was, really. What had happened to Serena would always haunt him, every single day, only now the pain wasn't as unbearable as it had used to be. He would worry about his own child every night. He knew he would. Perhaps he would have his fair share of sleepless nights. But he knew that every day he woke and found his child smiling up at him from its cot or bed he would feel joy and contentment on a scale he could never have imagined.

Work he would have to delegate, as he'd promised. Yes, he had a business to run. But what was more important? Work? Or his family?

He'd always put family first when he was little. He'd had to. Working to bring in money had taken up so much of his time it was probably why he'd found it so easy to let the Monterey consume him when he'd started having problems with Emily.

But he wouldn't let it do that any more. He wanted to be more hands-on with the births, not sitting in an office staring at a spreadsheet. That wasn't what he'd started the business for.

Sam laid his hand upon his wife's and leaned over to kiss her.

When they got back to America he would do everything in his power to make sure they had the life that both of them had dreamed of.

CHAPTER NINE

THEY ARRIVED HOME in good time, and the staff met them on the doorstep with huge smiles and welcomes before they hurried to the trunk of their vehicle to remove the suitcases.

Emily stepped through the door of her house and looked at it for the first time as a place she could call *home*. She'd always called it *the house*—never home. But perhaps now it could be? No longer would it be the shell that contained their failing marriage. Now it would be the *home* where she and Sam would be happy. Where they would raise their children and where they would grow old together.

Suddenly the white walls and prestigious art on the walls no longer seemed cold or ostentatious. The place looked inviting, filled with possibilities and hope.

She opened up the French doors out onto the beautiful garden and imagined children chasing each other on the manicured lawns. She could imagine a child marvelling as a butterfly perched on a bloom, or squealing loudly as it ran from a bee. They could have a swing set, a slide, a treehouse put in! They could even get a dog. As a child she'd always wanted one, but Sylvia and Martin had had cats. It was the idea of a dog that warmed her heart. Something large and fluffy with a big pink tongue, that was gentle and kind and would bounce around after her children.

'Doesn't it feel crazy to be back?' she said to Sam, who'd followed her out into the garden.

'A little.'

'We're the ones who have changed and yet it's this place that feels different.'

He looked out across the expanse of grass—at the herb garden, the large Pampas grass, the ornamental bridge. 'Or maybe just our feelings about being in it.'

She looked at him, squinting in the sun. 'What are you going to do now?'

'I'm going to get changed out of these clothes and maybe take a shower. Fancy joining me?'

She laughed and nodded. 'I'll be up in a minute. You get the water running, I just want to have a quick word with Rosie about dinner tonight.'

She wanted to continue their mood from Paris. She wanted to create a beautiful meal for them, to cook him some of his favourites, and she wanted to let the staff know they could have an evening off. Then they would be on their own, and she would arrange a nice romantic table for two, with flowers and candlelight and nice music in the background. There was no need for the romance to disappear just because they'd made it back to reality. She knew, more than anyone, the importance of making time for each other.

She watched Sam head back into the house and then went over to look at the flower garden. There were some pretty blooms there—roses, lilies, aliums. They would be perfect in a little arrangement for the table. She headed back inside to put her plan into action.

* * *

Sam trotted upstairs, keen to rid himself of his travel-worn clothes. Nearly twelve hours on a plane, and he'd spilt coffee on his trouser leg. And then, later, as he'd headed to use the bathroom, he'd had a young girl with a sticky lollipop walk into him.

He didn't mind. Accidents happened, and kids always got food on everything. Looking around at their pristine white walls, he smiled as he imagined the housekeepers shooing the children out into the garden so that they didn't get dirty handprints all over the paint.

They'd not had pristine white walls when he was a child. Their rooms had had cheap wood panelling, tough and resistant to handprints and smears. Not to mention the amount of soccer balls that had been accidentally bounced off them.

Soon this house will teem with happy life.

He was proud of himself. Of how far he'd come during their trip. When they'd left for Paris he'd never imagined he would open up the way he had. But he'd not been able to hold it back. All that wonderful time spent with Emily… He'd been so lucky that she had fought for them the way she had. All she'd gone through—the arguments, the accident, his injury, the induced coma, finding out she was pregnant and fearing his reaction—he couldn't imagine he would have been that strong!

Stepping into their bedroom, he began to unbutton his shirt, and as he undid the cuffs he stepped into the en-suite, turned on the shower and checked the water temperature. Perfect. Then he pulled off his shirt and went to put it in the hamper.

He had a small headache. It had been there since about halfway through the flight, and though he'd taken some painkillers he was due for some more. Where would they be?

He checked his bedside drawer, but there was nothing in there save for a book, a packet of gum and a phone charger. Perhaps Emily had some in her bedside drawer? He went over to her side of the bed and pulled it open. There, on top of everything, was a white envelope with his name on it—*Sam*—written in her beautiful familiar handwriting.

Intrigued, he turned it over. It was sealed. But it *was* addressed to him, so he stuck his thumb under the flap and ripped it open, and pulled out the folded piece of paper inside.

He opened it.

Sam,

I'm writing you this letter because I need to. There are things I have to say, to get off my chest, and you're not allowing me the time to sit down and talk to you properly.

You're killing me, Sam. It physically feels like you're ripping out my heart. I never, ever thought that the man who once professed to love me would be able to do this, and hurt me so effectively that I am barely able to function.

All I want is to start a family. Is that so hard? You could have said yes, and everything would have been fine. You could have said no and explained why, but you never do. You never have. Instead you just storm away. Stay away. And whenever you see me in the corridors at work you walk the other way.

Do you have any idea how that makes me feel? How small and how unimportant?

You are my husband, and I love you deeply, but I cannot stay in a relationship that is systematically destroying me.

Once you gave me hope. Now you only cause me pain. I can't live like this any more, and because you won't sit down and talk to me about it I've written this letter instead.

I'm leaving you, Sam. I'm getting out whilst I can, whilst there's still some of 'me' left. I'm not expecting you to come after me. I'm not expecting you to beg me to stay. I don't think you want that at all.

I'm doing this for both of us.

I'm sorry we didn't work out. I'm sorry we're so cut off from each other. I'm sorry to end it this way.

But you never gave me the choice.

Bye, Sam.

Emily

Sam blinked and stared at the words on the page. Was this *real*? It couldn't be! But this was Em's handwriting—he'd recognise it anywhere.

She was leaving me?

He went back to the first page and read it again. He'd not known what to expect when he'd started reading, but he'd never expected a *Dear John* letter.

She was going to leave me...

He frowned and read the words one more time, his heart thudding painfully in his chest.

And then it happened.

A flood of memories came crashing down around him, so fast and so hard he almost went dizzy.

The wedding music as he walked down the aisle with her, looking beautiful in that off-the-shoulder dress...

The honeymoon in Paris, tickling her in bed, hearing her laughter as he turned her to face him and began to kiss her frantically...

Cutting the ribbon to mark the opening of the Monterey, the camera flashes, the cheers, standing in front of the microphone and delivering a speech...

Emily curled up on the couch, her face red with tears, her hand clutching a crumpled white tissue...

Arguing in the car. 'Stop the car! I want to get out!' she'd screamed at him. He'd turned to look at her, there'd been a blare of horns, he'd looked back at the road and...

Sam crumpled the letter in his hand, as his missing years returned with full, brutal force.

Emily had left instructions for the parts of the plan she'd need help with for Rosie to pass on to the rest of the staff.

'So Paris was wonderful, Mrs Saint?'

'It was the *best,* Rosie—you have no idea.'

'I'm so pleased for you. I know it's been difficult lately.'

Emily thanked her, blushing. She'd forgotten how much the staff must have seen. Heard. Though Rosie might be staff, she was also a good friend, and had often found Emily crying in one of the rooms in the house. She'd always done what she could. Brought her a hot drink. Something sweet and indulgent. Had tried to cheer her. Rosie had stayed late many a night, just to keep Emily company.

'It's all going to be much better from now on.'

'I'm glad.' Rosie shut the fridge. 'I'd already made

rosewater pannacotta for your dessert tonight, because they needed to set. Do you still want to have those?'

Emily nodded. 'Sounds delightful. It'll save me some time. I never was any good at desserts—unless I was expected to eat them.'

Rosie laughed. 'That's fine. And I've got some lovely fillet steaks in the fridge—you could do them with a red peppercorn sauce?'

'Thanks, Rosie. Now, I'm going upstairs to wash twelve hours of aeroplane off me. Anything I should know about before I go?'

'No, I don't think so.'

'I'll pick up the correspondence from Sam's desk on my way up—he might want to take a look at that. I know how eager he is to get back to work.'

'Why don't you rest up there for a while? I can bring you up some coffee and cake about three? Would that suit?'

Emily thought that would be perfect. It would give her and Sam plenty of time to be on their own and christen the bedroom with these new versions of Sam and herself.

She left the kitchen quarters and headed up to Sam's office. There was a small pile of mail that had accrued on his desk during their few days away. And she had no doubt that their email accounts would have even more.

But all of that could wait.

She and Sam came first.

She didn't want to go into their bedroom and remind Sam that he had a pile of paperwork waiting for him, but she assumed he must be in the shower already. She could hear the water running.

I'll put it on the bureau.

Emily opened their bedroom door, and then jumped

slightly when she saw a figure standing by the bed. 'Oh! Sam! I thought you were in the shower. What are you…?'

She saw his pale face, his stunned expression. Then she saw what he was holding.

A piece of crumpled paper. Her notepaper. And on the bed behind him an envelope, torn along the top, with his name written on it.

The letter.

'Sam—'

'You were *leaving* me?'

She'd never heard him so shocked, so stunned, so hurt, so *appalled.*

Her heart began to hammer in her chest and her mouth went dry as she feverishly began to try to explain. 'Sam, I—'

'You told me countless times that we'd been arguing. I saw in my own head the memory of our arguing. But you said we were okay.'

'We were…'

'You were going to leave me. You said I was *killing you…*'

'Sam!' Emily couldn't think of what to say. His heartbreak was clear. His devastation was evident. Tears streamed from her eyes when she recalled what she'd put in that letter. She'd been *raw,* she'd been *hurting,* and she'd needed him to know that.

Why hadn't she destroyed that letter?

Because I thought I might have to use it.

She'd not known—could not have predicted—how well things were going to go. Not from the point they'd been at before his amnesia, before their trip to Paris and the strengthening of their love for one another. She hadn't meant for him even to *see* that letter. Not any more! She should have come up here the second they got home and got rid of it. Shredded it. Burnt it.

But she'd forgotten it.

And now he'd read it, and he was hurting and upset. There were even unshed tears in his eyes.

'You wrote this after the accident. You put the date.'

He showed her the letter, but she couldn't look at it. Couldn't face the evidence of her written words.

'You said that our marriage was over.'

'Sam, that was before I knew that you didn't remember. Before I knew that we would get each other back…'

'But you wrote it knowing you were pregnant? Knowing that you'd be walking out on us and leaving our child without its father?'

She heard the hurt, the accusation in his voice. 'Yes, I did. But—'

'You *know* how much I want to be a father, and how much it scares me, *terrifies* me, that I might lose a child—and yet you were willing to walk away from me with our baby?'

Emily hurried to his side, laid a hand upon his arm. 'I didn't know that *then*. All I knew was that you didn't want children! I thought that when I told you in the hospital you would go crazy! Maybe even ask me to get rid of it! I didn't know about Serena!'

'You were going to take my child from me…'

'Sam, that's not fair—'

But he wasn't listening. He dropped the letter and it fluttered to the floor as he stormed from their bedroom and began to run down the stairs.

Emily chased after him and stood at the balustrade, shouting after his disappearing form. 'Where are you going?'

'I'm getting out of here! I need to think!'

She heard the front door slam, the sound echoing through the house, and she stood there, her hands gripping the railings, knuckles gleaming white through her skin, and all she could hear was the sound of the shower running before a car roared into life and she heard the stones sizzle and spit as it roared away down the drive.

She sucked in a big breath and stared into nothing.

What have I done?

Was Sam going to come back? Should he even be driving? He might have an accident. He might get hurt. He…

Emily sank to the floor and rested her head against the stair rail, feeling numb and broken. Her gaze was fixed on the open door.

He just needed some space. Some air to breathe—air that didn't have Emily in it, complicating matters.

Sam didn't even realise the direction he was travelling. He just drove. Blindly and furiously. His mind going over and over her letter. What it meant. How bad his relationship—his *marriage*—had been.

He never would have imagined he could let it get so bad that his wife would have felt that way. *She said I was killing her…* He swallowed, his throat tight and painful. He shook his head, disbelief filling him. He'd made her feel *that* bad? That was awful. He didn't deserve a woman like that. He didn't deserve all the effort she'd put into him. All the love. Her care. Her attention. That he'd done *that* to her! Made her feel as if she was the last person on earth he'd want to have a baby with…

The baby…

Furiously he wiped at his eyes, desperate to wipe away the stinging sensation burning them. He didn't deserve a child, either.

And suddenly he was at his mom's place. On her driveway. He couldn't remember the journey at all, and as he sat there, blinking, staring at the familiar building where he had spent his childhood, he tried to recall the drive, hoping he hadn't gone through any red lights.

He'd made it here safely, anyway. That was one thing.

But it was strange to be here. He hadn't come back home for over a year. More, he figured, since he'd been married for eighteen months. He'd spoken to his parents on the phone, of course—they'd not been complete strangers—but it had been infrequent and rare. And now he could feel the weight of that guilt upon his shoulders.

Was his mom even in?

His question was answered when she opened the door and peered out to see who had arrived.

She looked the same. A little greyer, maybe, but not much. She still had on those slippers he remembered so well, with the sheepskin inlay. Still seemed to favour those 'mom jeans', with the high elasticated waist, and tucked into them was one of the simple, stripy tee shirts that had always seemed a staple item of her wardrobe.

He stepped out of the vehicle. 'Hi, Mom.'

'Samuel!'

She walked over to him, her arms outstretched, and pulled him into a hug that was as familiar, as comforting, and as painfully heart-warming as he'd remembered them to be.

'Let me look at you! Oh, you look so handsome.'

She smiled as she looked him over, but then, as she gazed carefully at his face, she must have seen, must have sensed something that concerned her.

'What's wrong?'

'Why does something have to be wrong?'

'Because you're home, Samuel, and you swore you would never come back here. Something made you come back. Don't get me wrong—I'm glad. But what is it?'

He hated it that she was so astute. He hated it that he had come here. To this place. To the house that had once held his most painful memory and the people who populated it.

It didn't hold his most painful memory now. Not any more. He had a new pain.

'I just needed to see you, that's all.'

She looked at him sideways, not quite believing him but willing to put it aside for a moment. 'Well, come on in. I'll get you a drink.'

He followed her into the house, sucking in a deep breath before he went through the front door.

It was like stepping back in time. The place looked exactly the same. The same furniture, the same paper on the walls, the same lamps, the same throw rug over the back of the couch. There was even that same old aroma of just-made coffee and freshly baked cookies.

She settled him into a seat and bustled away into the kitchen, making them both coffee and then sitting down with him in the living room.

'How are you feeling after the accident?'

He nodded. 'I'm good.'

'I did visit you. Can you remember?'

'Yeah.'

Of course he remembered. He remembered everything now. All of it. Every hurtful moment.

I can't believe I cut Emily off like that! I walked away from her when all she needed was an answer from me! I was so angry! So afraid.

He swallowed hard. 'Do you ever talk about her?'

'Emily?' His mom looked confused.

'Serena.' He hated having to ask, but he needed to. They'd never mentioned it in this house after she'd died. It was like the elephant in the room.

His mother reached for the necklace at her throat and looked back at him. 'Why do you ask?'

'I wonder about it. We never spoke about her. Not after.'

'Not in the house, no. We chose not to discuss it. You children got so upset.'

'Not in the house? So you *did* speak about her?'

'Of course! She was my baby. For a brief time there I thought I might die too, but my pastor helped to get me through.'

'I didn't know you were religious.'

'I'm not. But he met me one day in the supermarket. After the funeral. We began to talk about her and...well, we met every week after that.'

He stared at his mother. 'Every week?'

She nodded. 'I had to. If I'd kept it inside me, then who knows how I might have ended up.'

He was dumbstruck. All this time! All this time he'd thought it was a forbidden conversation, that no one dared speak her name. And yet all this time his mother had been talking her way through her grief. He was glad. Glad she'd had an outlet. But there was still a question on his mind that haunted him. A question he needed the answer to.

'Did you ever blame me?'

'*You?* Samuel, *no!* Of course not! Why would we? You were a child...you were still in school. It wasn't your fault. It was...' She leaned forward and reached out to lay her hand on his. 'What's going on?'

'I've ruined my marriage.'

She didn't gasp, didn't look shocked—just sat there calmly. 'How?'

'Because of what happened I was afraid to… Emily wanted a baby… No. That's wrong. She wanted to *talk* to me about having a baby and I wouldn't let her.'

'Oh, Samuel…'

'It never occurred to me that as I denied her a family I was hurting her. I just thought I was protecting myself. I was selfish. The way I treated her…it made her feel as if she were nothing. We kept arguing and I stayed away from home. Stayed away from Em. She was getting ready to leave me when the accident happened.'

His mother sucked in a deep breath. 'I knew she was tense when I saw her in the hospital. I thought she was just worried about you. I never knew any of that was going on.'

'She found out after the accident that she was pregnant. Of course I was in shock. I'd just learnt I'd lost nearly two years of my life and now I was going to be a father? I tried to act pleased. Tried to hide it. The fear, the guilt, eating me away inside.'

He paused.

'We went to Paris to get my memories back. Instead we got close. Closer than we'd ever been before. It was amazing. We shared things. I told her about Serena. She understood where I was coming from. And I finally, *finally* felt like everything was right between us. And then I discovered today, when we got back, that she was going to leave me. Knowing she was pregnant. She was going to walk away. Because of me. Because of how I was with her. I hurt her, Mom. Emotionally. I don't deserve to be with her. With our child…'

She gave him a sympathetic smile. 'I'm going to be a grandmother?'

He nodded. 'Congratulations.'

But he wasn't smiling.

'I don't know what to do. I got my memories back. All of them. I saw what I did. What I *said*. Quite frankly, I'm amazed she stuck around at all.'

'Oh, Samuel, it sounds like she was trying to protect you.'

'Trying to protect herself, more like.'

'I think you're being harsh.'

'I'm not. What if we've always been doomed? We couldn't tell each other basic facts about each other—even after we were married! I had to wait eighteen months before she told me about her childhood, and then I found out that she'd withheld a basic truth from me after we'd promised not to keep anything from each other ever again. We weren't just having the odd argument—we'd been drifting apart for months! We were on the verge of separating.'

He shook his head, still unable to believe how bad things had been.

'I let Paris and our hopes for the trip carry me away. The place wove some sort of magic spell because it had been our honeymoon destination, the city of romance… all of that.'

'Does she still want to leave you now?'

'Probably. After how Dad was I vowed to myself that I would be the best husband there ever could be. I would work hard, but I would be *around*. I'd be home. I'd support my wife, we'd have this great love, this mutual respect—and it turns out I was a huge disappointment. Some of the things I did…said… I was cruel.'

The more he thought about his actions, the more he hated himself. He'd become everything his dad was. Apart from the drinking part. He'd been useless! Distant. Unsupportive. Argumentative. And had he shared with her? No.

He'd let them all down—Emily, Serena, his mom. Himself.

Nobody could be more angry than he felt right now.

His marriage was in tatters.

His mom let out a heavy sigh and reached forward to take both his hands in his. 'Samuel? You deserve to be with Emily. She has *fought* for you! You can't let her down. Not now. Not now you're going to be a father. This isn't just about you any more.'

'Yeah, but—'

'Do you love her?'

He stared at her, saw the intensity in her eyes. 'Of course!'

'Then why are you still here with me?'

Rosie came up the stairs carrying coffee and fresh slices of cake and found Emily sitting on the stairwell.

'Mrs Saint?'

Emily looked up at her with tear-filled eyes.

'Are you okay?' Rosie put down the small tray and hurried over to her employer.

'I think it's all over, Rosie.'

'How? You were just saying earlier how good everything was.'

'He found this.' She pulled the letter from her pocket and passed it over, cringing inwardly as she imagined Rosie's thoughts as she read it. Would Rosie judge her, too?

'Oh...'

'I screwed up. I should have thrown it away. But I forgot it was there. I was just so excited. Sam seemed happy about the baby, we were going on a trip, and I...'

She let out a heavy sigh. 'Just as everything was working out right between us. After all those difficulties… you know what I mean. You must have seen. Heard.'

'It was hard not to hear sometimes,' Rosie replied with sadness.

'I'm sorry. You shouldn't have had to hear it at all. We should have sorted it. Been open with each other right from the beginning. We could have avoided this.'

'Mrs Saint, I don't understand everything that's happened, but there is one thing I do know. You and Mr Saint may have had your difficulties, but I have always said that you two were meant for each other. It's not my place to suggest anything, but please don't give up on him. He's a kind man. A good man. This is bound to have shocked him. It would have shocked anyone. Give him time to reflect. Sort things out.'

Emily took back the letter. 'You're very kind, Rosie, but this is what happens to me. People walk away and leave.'

'You think he's going to walk away?'

'I'm used to it, after my mother… I should have expected it.'

'I'm sure he'll come back.'

Emily looked at her sharply and Rosie quickly stood. 'I've spoken out of turn. I'm sorry. I'll leave you on your own. Call me if you need anything—I'll just be downstairs.'

Rosie hurried away and Emily instantly regretted the sharpness of her gaze. But she hadn't been able to help it. Her first thoughts had run to the fact that he was abandoning her a second time. Her mother had done it once, her husband twice. Was she going to let him do it a third time? A fourth?

It was time to draw a line in the sand.

This wasn't just about her any more. A baby was involved. She'd always vowed that when she had a child of her own it would know love from both its parents. It would grow up in a warm, loving home and would never feel the sting of rejection—certainly not before it was even born!

She was failing her child already.

CHAPTER TEN

'OKAY, SAM. I'M very happy with your progress. You may officially return to work.'

His doctor had given him the good news, expecting Sam to smile.

He hadn't.

He wasn't in a smiling mood.

Sam had spent the last few nights sleeping in his old bedroom at his mother's house, squeezing himself onto a bed that was too small and staring at the ceiling for half of the night. As each morning approached he would resign himself to the fact that he wouldn't get any sleep and then somehow he would, falling into a deep sleep literally an hour or so before he was due to wake up. Then his alarm would blare into his brain and he would jerk awake, bleary-eyed and instantly sad.

He'd not spoken to Emily. He didn't know what to say. How could he go back there? Could he ever say he was sorry enough times? He didn't deserve to be happy with her any more. Surely he'd given up all his chances?

His mother had tried to argue for Emily's side, saying that she must have done what she had to protect him.

Was that true? He tried to imagine himself in her place. Her situation. If it had been Emily in the coma with a brain injury, not him, would he have done the same thing?

Perhaps.

But there was a new equation in all this. The baby. All his life he'd pushed the idea of being a father away. It had been too scary a concept, too terrible even to imagine how that would feel. And because he'd been so busy pushing the idea away, refusing to accept it, he'd never taken a moment to think about whether he really wanted to be a dad.

Hadn't he sworn that he would never be like his own father? So he must have thought about it a little, right? Perhaps it hadn't all been about his guilt over what had happened to Serena? Perhaps his fear had come more from being given the opportunity to have what he wanted most in the world, but then failing miserably? Had it had been easier to lose his temper with Emily and refuse even to talk about having a child than to face up to the possibility that he might fail?

As he drove along the freeway, heading to work, he pondered this. Had it ever really been about Emily? About Serena? Or had it always been about *him*? He was a driven man. He'd provided for his siblings, looked after them, had sent himself to medical school, specialised, set up a thriving business... He'd been successful at everything he'd put his mind to except for what had happened to Serena. He'd failed his sister, and the weight and pain of that failure *haunted* him. Was it that same fear of failure that was driving him now? Having a baby with his wife meant an uncertain future. He couldn't possibly know if he would get it right. Was that why he'd fought against it for so long?

His memories had proved to him that he'd got his

marriage wrong once already—did that mean he would continue to get things wrong?

The painful ache in his heart was almost unbearable.

He indicated and pulled over, breathing deeply, his brain trying to sort through all the memories, putting them in order. He saw them all. The bad. The good. And he remembered their arguments—saw how he had behaved. The words that he'd said. The numerous ways that he had tried to protect himself. He'd not been thinking about Emily! He'd known he was hurting her, had seen how much she wanted a child, but he'd been so concerned about his own vulnerability that he had pushed it back on to her.

He felt sick. Nauseated. He saw over and over again how Emily had kept trying. Trying to talk to him. Trying to find a time that was good for him. Trying to understand why he kept saying no without getting a decent answer from him. He saw how she had begun to retreat from him, hurting and in pain, but how she had still tried. The times he'd come home late and found a table set for two with candles and flowers. The times he'd found her asleep on the couch because she'd been trying to wait up for him.

She fought for us. Despite what I did, she fought for us.

It must have hurt her terribly to consider walking away. To have written that letter.

Sam felt ashamed.

He'd been in the wrong and he'd allowed his fear to keep them apart.

Emily had fought for him. Always. Should he really be giving up on her? Or seeing whether she would give him one last chance? A chance to show her how much he loved *her* and how much he wanted to fight for *her*.

No one had ever fought to stay in her life.

But I'm determined to be the one who does. No matter what.

Desperate to put things right, he picked up his mobile and with trembling fingers called the Monterey.

'It's Sam. Is Emily there today?' He didn't care if the staff were wondering about why he was asking. Surely he should *know* if his wife was working?

'She's at home today, Mr Saint.'

'Thank you.'

He took a deep breath, indicated again, and pulled back out into the traffic. He knew now. He knew what he had to do to put things right.

He was not going to fail at his marriage.

Emily sucked in a deep breath and closed her eyes as she stood in the garden, the sun shining down upon her face, hoping to find the peace and calm that mindfulness—a technique she sometimes used with her labouring patients—should bring.

It had been an upsetting time since Sam had left, and she'd worried about where he'd gone until she'd received a whispered phone call from his mother to let her know he was safe and well and at her house.

She'd been grateful to his mother for letting her know. It had put her mind at rest.

The garden provided solace. Their private garden, at the back of the house, was in full bloom, populated by some of the flowers that she'd carried in her wedding bouquet—Calla lilies, baby's breath, white roses. They reminded her of that special day they'd had. The day she'd thought all her dreams were coming true.

But the worst had happened. He'd found that awful letter and reacted badly to it. But they could put it right, couldn't they? It didn't have to mean it was the end of everything. No, she hadn't told Sam the whole truth, but she'd been doing it honourably, protecting him from all the harmful things that had been said. Surely he'd be able to see that when he calmed down?

Her cell phone rang in her pocket, disturbing her thoughts.

'Em? It's Sam. I'm coming over.'

She slipped the phone back into her pocket and felt a nervousness start deep down low in her belly. She hadn't expected him to call. He'd said nothing to her for days. Why was he coming? To say goodbye?

Feeling sick, she absently rubbed at her belly.

If he was coming here to say goodbye then she would make sure she told him, one last time, that she had always fought for him, always protected him, always loved him. She would make sure that his last memory of her was one that proved she had never given up on him—even if he was going to try to give up on her.

So she quickly returned to the house, put on the powder-blue dress from Paris. When he arrived she would remind him about their wedding day and remind him of the vows they'd taken. Vows that, to her, had meant everything. She would not be meek and accept him walking away.

She returned to the garden, seeking that earlier sense of peace she was so desperate to feel again, and waited for him to arrive.

She didn't have to wait long.

She became aware that someone was looking at her, and as she turned back to the house there was Sam, standing on the stone steps leading down to the garden. He had a strange look on his face. He certainly didn't look as angry or as upset as he had the other day, when he had walked away.

Tell him now.

She stepped towards him, but he raised his hand. 'Can I speak first?'

Emily closed her mouth and nodded. She would listen to what he had to say.

'How have you been?'

It wasn't what she'd been expecting. She'd thought he'd come straight out with it. Keep it short. *I'm leaving you for good.*

She refused to cry, but already she could feel tears pressing against her eyes. 'How do you *think* I've been?'

He nodded, his gaze dropping to her belly and then moving up again, to her face. 'I should have told you where I was.'

'You were at your mother's house. She told me.'

'She did?' He seemed surprised, but then he nodded, smiling. 'I should have known.'

'You should have done it yourself.'

He looked right at her, then. 'You're right. I'm sorry.'

Seeing him like this was painful. This man was someone she'd thought she would get to love for ever. Now he was standing across from her like a stranger, and all she could think about was how it felt to be in his loving arms!

'You don't deserve someone like me, Em. Someone who's hurt you like I did. I'm sorry I made you feel that way.'

She sucked in some air. He was building up to it, wasn't he? Why didn't he just say it? Get it out in the open so that she could weep and wail and cry when he was gone?

'Well...'

'Can you give me another chance?'

She stopped breathing. What? What had he just said? She looked up into his face. 'I'm sorry?'

Sam walked up to her. 'I remember.'

Emily frowned. What? He remembered? 'Have you had another memory come back?'

He nodded. 'I've had them *all* come back. I remember it all. The good, the bad. The ugly.'

A small divot formed between her eyebrows.

'I've come here to say I'm sorry. I should never have walked away from you the other day. It was...an old habit. You see, I've learned one or two things since I left. I've realised that most of this—our problems, our disagreements—they were all my fault.'

Really? He was actually saying all these words? Words that meant so much—words that were on the way to healing them. Mending them. Bringing them back together. Was it possible?

Her heart began to pound. But she couldn't let him shoulder all the responsibility.

'No, Sam. It was me. I kept pushing you. Pushing you to commit to a family because I thought if I didn't push you would drift away from me—like everyone else. And you weren't ready.'

'I *was* ready, though. I was just terrified of failing at it.'

She shook her head, not understanding.

'I've always succeeded at everything, but when I lost my baby sister I experienced feelings I didn't know how to deal with. I was sixteen, and no one at home talked about it, so I had to process it myself. Something in me must have decided that I was *never* going to feel that way again. Like I was losing myself. Like I'd lost control. When you asked for a baby that wasn't unreasonable, but I saw it as something I could fail at. I had no certainties, no assurances that everything would be fine and so I pushed it away. Pushed you away. And then I began to fail at my marriage. And though I saw that it was crumbling I tried to pretend that it wasn't happening. I'm sorry.'

'Oh, Sam! I should never have pushed you so hard. There were so many things I'd never been given answers to, and there you were doing it too! I couldn't stand that, when I loved you so much. I still don't know why I was so easy for my mother to leave me behind, but when *you* left me too? I feared there might be something wrong with me. That there was something inherently unloveable about me that made people leave.'

He reached for her hand.

'Or perhaps I pushed them away? I pushed you.'

'No Em. You were never in the wrong. You were—are—incredibly loving and loveable. You didn't push your mother—or me. To me, you said what needed to be said. And I'm glad you did, because it forced me to confront myself. I needed to do that, to see why I behaved like I did, and I'm sorry if I hurt you with anything I have said. I never meant it. I just lashed out verbally because it was easier than dealing with my own issues. I'm sorry, Em. I truly am.'

Emily sank into his arms, her head against his chest. 'Don't be. I trust you, Sam. With my whole heart. I would give it up to you right now.'

They held each other for a moment—a beautiful moment in which the birds sang in the trees around them and the gentle breeze played with the hem of her dress.

'I love you, Sam.'

'I love you, Em.'

They looked at each other, seeing the love they needed, thrived on, lived on. Emily pulled him to her so that her lips could meet his.

The kiss was gentle, solemn, heartfelt. Emily was thrilled that his memories had returned at last, and that he appeared to have worked through his issues. Obviously his time away had helped heal him. If he and his mother had talked about Serena, then hopefully she was healing, too.

When the kiss ended Emily looked up into his eyes and smiled. 'I'd marry you again right now if I could. To prove to you how I feel.'

Sam looked at her and laughed. 'Me too. But, you know, I remember the first lot of vows, and they were pretty damn good.'

'They certainly were.'

He stooped and scooped her up into his arms, and she laughed, surprised.

'Allow me, though, to carry you over the threshold.'

He started heading back towards the house and Emily laid her head against his chest.

This was the dashing Sam she remembered. The man who'd used to be full of romantic overtures. The gentleman.

The man she loved.

She knew they would be okay now. There was nothing left to break them. No secrets that Sam didn't know. No memories left unremembered.

He knew everything. The good, the bad and the ugly.

Now they could focus on creating more of the good and more of the amazing. She and Sam were united. Husband and wife. Soon to be a family.

The baby would start kicking soon.

And then they would both enjoy their new adventure as parents.

Together.

EPILOGUE

Sam had seen many babies come into the world, and each of those births had put a smile upon his face. But nothing could have prepared him for the way he felt when his own daughter made it into the world.

Emily had been great. She'd not written a birth plan. She'd just told everyone that she would do what her body told her to do. And when the contractions had got stronger and longer she had chosen to get into the tub.

Her labour had been very relaxed and soothing. Even during the most intense of contractions she had breathed carefully through it, her eyes closed, intent on what was happening within her.

He'd held her hands as she'd got onto her knees in the water. He'd coached her.

'One…two…three…four… And breathe…'

When she'd begun to push the strain on her face had been incredible, but she had borne the pains well and worked with them, using them to help deliver the baby slowly and safely.

As Mia Saint had slithered into the water Emily had gasped and reached down between her legs and brought their daughter to the surface for her first breath.

I'm a father!

She was so beautiful! So perfect!

He hadn't known he could cry so much. He wasn't even aware that tears were pouring down his face until Emily looked up at him with so much love and reached up to wipe them away. He pressed her hand to his face and then kissed her palm, before he laid his hand upon his daughter's head.

No matter what was to come he would protect them both. He would love them to the end of his days. And if there were challenges or difficulties then he knew they would face them together.

These last few months he and Emily had just got stronger and stronger.

He'd delegated, as promised. He'd never worked more than sixty hours a week. And when he was home, he was *present*. Sometimes things didn't get done, but that was okay—because the most important thing was his family.

And now, as he held Mia in his arms, he realised that he was still scared of the responsibility, but he knew in his heart that every father felt the same way. It was natural. Normal.

And, as a father, he knew his daughter would rule his heart.

He would grant her every wish.

If he failed at something, then he would learn from it, and if he needed to lean on Emily then he knew she would be there for him.

He didn't have to do anything alone any more.

He kissed Mia's squashed little nose, then leaned forward and kissed Emily. 'I love you. I'm so proud of you.'

She smiled back and stroked his face. 'And I love you. Don't forget—we're a great team, you and me.'

He kissed her. Slowly. Softly. 'I never forget.'

* * * * *

If you enjoyed this story, check out these other great reads from Louisa Heaton

CHRISTMAS WITH THE SINGLE DAD
SEVEN NIGHTS WITH HER EX
ONE LIFE-CHANGING NIGHT
A FATHER THIS CHRISTMAS?

All available now!

MILLS & BOON®

MEDICAL ROMANCE™

THE ULTIMATE IN ROMANTIC MEDICAL DRAMA

A sneak peek at next month's titles...

In stores from 4th May 2017:

Mummy, Nurse...Duchess? – Kate Hardy
and **Falling for the Foster Mum** – Karin Baine

The Doctor and the Princess – Scarlet Wilson
and **Miracle for the Neurosurgeon** – Lynne Marshall

English Rose for the Sicilian Doc – Annie Claydon
and **Engaged to the Doctor Sheikh** – Meredith Webber

Just can't wait?
Buy our books online before they hit the shops!
www.millsandboon.co.uk

Also available as eBooks.

MILLS & BOON®

EXCLUSIVE EXTRACT

Their chemistry is undeniable!
But will Sullivan Darcy follow his heart
when doctor princess Gabrielle Cartier
must return home to rule?

Read on for a sneak preview of
THE DOCTOR AND THE PRINCESS

He turned the palm of his hand, extending it out towards her. 'Give me Gabrielle back, please.'

She frowned with confusion. 'What do you mean?'

He was giving her a knowing kind of smile. 'I had her. I had her right there with me, then you just flipped back into princess mode.'

A little chill spread over her skin. He was right. She had. One second she'd been enjoying dinner with Sullivan, contemplating some fun, and the next? She'd been sucked back into the wave of responsibility that felt as if it could suffocate her.

Tears prickled in her eyes. But Sullivan kept his voice light, almost teasing. 'When Gabrielle hears this tune, there's only one thing she can do.'

'I thought you didn't dance?' She smirked as the heat of his body pressed up against hers. Apart from the night she'd lain in his arms, this was the first time since Paris she'd really been in a place she wanted to be.

'I thought you needed to let your hair down a little,' he said huskily. 'Remember what it is to have some fun.'

She swung her head. 'But my hair is down,' she argued, as her curls bounced around her shoulders.

'Is it?' he asked as he swung her round and dipped her.

She squealed, laughing, her arms slipping up and fastening around his neck. He held her there for a second, his mouth just inches from hers. She glanced up at his dark hair, running a finger along the edges. 'This is the longest I've seen your hair. Is that a little kink? Does your normal buzz cut hide curls?' She was teasing. She couldn't help it.

This was the kind of life she wanted to live. She wanted to be free to work hard during the day and laugh, joke and flirt her way with a man who made her heart sing through the nights.

He swung her back up, so close her breasts pressed against his chest. 'Now, that, my lovely lady, would be telling.'

Don't miss
THE DOCTOR AND THE PRINCESS
By Scarlet Wilson

Available May 2017
www.millsandboon.co.uk

Join Britain's BIGGEST Romance Book Club

- **EXCLUSIVE** offers every month
- **FREE** delivery direc to your door
- **NEVER MISS** a title
- **EARN** Bonus Book points

Call Customer Services
0844 844 1358*

or visit
millsandboon.co.uk/subscription